The Princess Sister Swap

JESSICA GILMORE

MILLS & BOON

CINDERELLA AND THE VICOMTE
© 2022 by Jessica Gilmore
Australian Copyright 2022
New Zealand Copyright 2022
First Published 2022
First Australian Paperback Edition 2022
ISBN 978 1 867 26528 3

THE PRINCESS AND THE SINGLE DAD
© 2022 by Jessica Gilmore
Australian Copyright 2022
New Zealand Copyright 2022
First Published 2022
Third Australian Paperback Edition 2022
ISBN 978 1 867 26528 3

MIX
Paper | Supporting responsible forestry
FSC® C001695
www.fsc.org

Published by
Mills & Boon
An imprint of Harlequin Enterprises (Australia) Pty Limited (ABN 47 001 180 918), a subsidiary of HarperCollins Publishers Australia Pty Limited (ABN 36 009 913 517)
Level 13, 201 Elizabeth Street
SYDNEY NSW 2000
AUSTRALIA

Printed and bound in Australia by McPherson's Printing Group

CONTENTS

Incorrigible lover of a happy-ever-after, **Jessica Gilmore** is lucky enough to work for one of London's best-known theaters. Married with one daughter, one fluffy dog and two dog-loathing cats, she can usually be found with her nose in a book. Jessica writes emotional romance with a hint of humor, a splash of sunshine, delicious food—and equally delicious heroes!

Books by Jessica Gilmore

Harlequin Forever

Billion-Dollar Matches

Indonesian Date with the Single Dad

Fairytale Brides

Cinderella's Secret Royal Fling
Reawakened by His Christmas Kiss
Bound by the Prince's Baby

Wedding Island

Baby Surprise for the Spanish Billionaire

Summer Romance with the Italian Tycoon
Mediterranean Fling to Wedding Ring
Winning Back His Runaway Bride
Christmas with His Cinderella

Visit the Author Profile page
at millsandboon.com.au for more titles.

Clem

Praise for
Jessica Gilmore

"Totally loved every page. I was hooked right into the story, reading every single word. This book has to be my new favourite. Honestly this book is most entertaining."

—*Goodreads* on *Honeymooning with Her Brazilian Boss*

Dear Reader,

I love a life-swap story, the opportunity for a character to step into someone else's shoes and see if the grass really is greener. And what if the shoes belonged to a princess, to your very own half sister? That's the opportunity that awaits Clem in the first story in my The Princess Sister Swap duet. When she sees that her sister needs some time away from royal duties, she jumps at the chance to explore the life that might have been hers.

Up-and-coming politician Akil is facing a huge decision, one that will change the rest of his life, and the last thing he needs is an instant connection with state-secret, scandal-in-waiting Clem. But after their first encounter, he finds he can't stop thinking about her and soon has to decide which matters more—his career and the vow he made to his father or his growing feelings for Clem.

I loved writing about these two lonely people brought together by fate. I hope you love it, too.

Love,

Jessica

For Jess

See you in SF x

CHAPTER ONE

'"FOR NEVER WAS a story of more woe, than this of Juliet and her Romeo."'

For one breathless moment the silence seemed overwhelming and then, like one of the waves crashing onto the shore behind her, loud applause rang out. Clemence Beaumont lay perfectly still for one last second as the still-real emotion swirled through her and then, as reality started to return, she raised her head and allowed Ed, her co-star, to pull her to her feet, letting the dagger fall to the floor. Taking his hand, she walked to the front of the curved stage, the rest of the cast falling in behind them, and bowed. Straightening with a grin, she took in the audience for the first time since she'd stepped onto the stage in answer to the nurse's call.

Semicircular seating rose up away from the stage, the outdoor theatre more amphitheatre than traditional auditorium, respectably full for an amateur fundraising performance. Clem bowed again as the whoops and cheers rang out, the welcome and much-missed post-performance adrenaline flooding her veins. Blinking, she started to make out individuals in the crowd: her best friend, Sally, who must have found a babysitter after all; Mrs Atkins, her favourite primary school teacher, beaming away; Mr Reynolds, her English teacher, nodding at her in approval, he adored Shakespeare and tried to make sure all his pupils did too; her neighbour Trinny, dressed to the nines as always; her sister…

Hang on. Her gaze skittered back. Her *sister*? Arrosa was *here*, in Cornwall? How had she managed to get away—not just get away but also seemingly alone? Clem couldn't see her bodyguard anywhere although she knew Henri couldn't be far behind. Arrosa hadn't gone out in public without the special-service-trained protection officer in the last decade.

Her seatmates didn't seem to have recognised her although her face regularly adorned front pages and gossip sites, probably thanks to the hat pulled low over her sleek, dark curls and the thick-rimmed glasses shading her face, but Clem would have recognised her in twice the disguise. After all, a similar face looked out at her from the mirror every morning. The sisters shared the same cheekbones and nose, the same dimples and long-lashed hazel eyes. But whereas Arrosa was a princess, legitimate daughter of King Zorien of Asturia, Clem was the unplanned result of a gap-year romance, her existence hidden away from half her family and the country her father ruled. A country she had never even visited.

She continued to bow and smile mechanically, but her mind was no longer on the performance and applause. What on *earth* was her sister doing here? Clem had sent her an invite of course, but she hadn't actually expected her to come. She never had before. It was hard for Arrosa to get away.

Finally, the applause came to an end and the cast filed backstage, chattering loudly as the post-production euphoria spread through all the crew and actors.

'Everyone back to ours,' Ed proclaimed, his arm around Tybalt, normally known as Tom and Ed's other half. 'Clem? Ready to party?'

'It's not that I don't want to…' she started, and his face softened.

'You were sensational tonight, Clem, and you should celebrate. I know it's not the same, but she'd want you to.'

Not the same without her mother, he meant. Simone Beaumont had produced and directed many of the village plays, been at the forefront of the restoration campaign that had transformed the neglected open-air theatre. If she were still alive she would be spearheading the Save Our Theatre battle against a local developer who wanted to change the beloved community asset into yet another commercial venture catering to tourists. Her mother had loved a cause. Clem had lost count of all her campaigns and passions long ago. It had used to infuriate her, feeling that her own feelings and needs came second to whatever—or whoever—her mother was championing at the time, but now she would give anything to walk into the kitchen and see her mother furiously making a placard—*Save the Seals, Save the Birds, Clean up the Sewage, Save our Post Office*. Simone Beaumont. Champion of the underdog.

'We'll give you a lift,' Tom added, but Clem shook her head.

'I'll try and make it, but I think I saw my cousin in the audience.'

'Bring them along.'

'I'll see what she says. We don't see each other often so she may want to catch up at home. Enjoy the party. You were both brilliant tonight, thank you.' She kissed both men on the cheek and headed off to change. She'd been looking forward to the post-show celebration but knew her promise to try and make it wouldn't be fulfilled. It had been a long time since Arrosa had dared to be seen publicly with her, or even attend a party without prior clearance; her half-sister might have the title, a luxurious lifestyle, more money than Clem could imagine, and a real relationship with their father, but Clem knew she had a freedom Arrosa could never have.

She changed quickly and removed her stage make-up and within fifteen minutes she made her way out of the theatre to walk the short distance home. She'd been born and brought up in the pretty coastal village her mother had moved to after she'd found out that her lover wasn't just a fellow student at the Sorbonne, but a prince with an arranged marriage due to take place imminently. Three months after moving to Cornwall Simone gave birth alone in a strange town—and six months later the birth of a new princess was celebrated in Asturia. Clem couldn't imagine how alone her mother must have felt, an orphan, single mother and betrayed lover. But she knew that Simone had loved the curve of the harbour, the pretty fishermen's cottages that clustered up the cliff, the wide sweep of beach, and Clem did too; she wouldn't swap her home for any palace. Which was a good thing because here she was, recalled home by her mother's long, lingering illness.

In the six months since her mother had died Clem had toyed with the idea of returning to London, to keep trying to make it as a professional actress, but making any decision seemed too hard, her grief still paralyzingly raw. In a world where she had no one, leaving the familiarity of home was more than she could manage.

She turned in at the small path that led to the cottage Zorien had bought them all those years ago. Clem hadn't been able to bring herself to change a thing. Her mother's clothes still hung in her wardrobe; her wax jacket swung from her peg in the hallway.

Arrosa had her own key and when Clem walked into the sitting room, her sister was curled up on the sofa. She'd discarded the hat and glasses, her long dark curls tumbling free, her expression thoughtful and more than a little wistful as she stared into the unlit fireplace. She looked up as Clem opened the door, jumping to her feet and rushing over to give Clem a warm hug.

'It's not that I'm not happy to see you, Rosy, but what on earth are you doing here?' Clem asked as she accepted a glass of the excellent wine Arrosa had brought with her and inspected the delicious array of goodies spread out on the coffee table, more crammed inside the Fortnum & Mason's hamper by her feet. She selected a piece of cheese and sat back.

'Apart from watching my sister play Juliet? Clem, you were brilliant.' Arrosa's English was perfect thanks to a British nanny and five years in an English boarding school, with no trace of an accent unless she was emotional or excited. Which was a shame. Clem loved her sister's accent, a reminder of the country she had never known. The small and much contested independent kingdom was positioned between France and Spain and the dialect was close to French, but the accent owed more to their Spanish neighbour.

'You've never come to see me act before.'

Arrosa curled back up on the sofa. 'I wish I had. Clem, I'm so sorry I didn't come to Simone's funeral. I loved her so much, but…'

'That's okay, she would have understood. And you sent such beautiful flowers.'

'But you're my sister, I should have been there for you.'

'It's hard for you to get away. I know that.' But Clem had looked for her that long, sad day and her absence had hurt. Clem wasn't lying, she *did* understand the restrictions on their relationship, but there were times she was tired of being the skeleton in the family cupboard. Of shouldering life's burdens alone.

'It was easier when we were children. Especially when I was at school and could spend my exeat weekends here as well as some of the holidays.'

Some people might have found it strange that Simone had agreed to Zorien's request that Arrosa spend time with them anonymously, posing as Clem's cousin so that she could get to know her sister, but Simone, with her trick of embracing lost causes, had taken one look at Arrosa and enfolded her into the family. 'A palace is no place to raise a child,' she would say. 'She needs some fun, to be allowed to run wild.' And run wild they had, long halcyon beach days drenched in sun and sea.

Halcyon days that had ended as they'd left their teens and Arrosa had had to take on state duties. Now they barely got the chance to meet, their long weekly phone calls their sole communication.

And Arrosa hadn't mentioned anything about a visit the last time they spoke just a few days ago.

'Fess up, why are you here apart from coming to see me as Juliet? Don't think I'm not pleased to see you, but I know you and impulsive isn't in your schedule. Is everything okay?'

Arrosa took a swig of wine, a shadow passing over her face. 'I'm not sure. I think I just asked someone to marry me.'

'You think or you did? Are congratulations in order?' Clem tried to keep the surprise off her face. She was sure there was no one special in Arrosa's life. No one *not* special either. Asturia was a small patriarchal society with old-fashioned values and their Crown Princess was supposed to embody those values. 'Who is the lucky man?'

'Akil. He's the Vicomte d'Ortiz, a rising star of the opposition. His father, the Duc d'Ortiz, was one of Papa's most vocal critics. Our families have been enemies for generations, you know how Asturians can be, but Akil and I are friends of a sort. We have a lot in common. Family honour and expectations and that kind of thing.'

'Friends? You're not even dating? Is this a friends-to-lovers thing? Rosy, marriage is a big first step. Why not start off with dinner and a film? Besides…' Clem topped up their wine glasses before turning to face her sister '…what do you mean you *think* you asked him to marry you?'

Arrosa reddened. 'Akil has been instrumental into getting the opposition parties to agree to the change in law that will allow me to inherit the throne. You know, it's really important that there's consensus, it's such a change. Asturia is so traditional that any hint of controversy, even a politician voting against the change, could make it harder for the people to accept me.'

Arrosa had told Clem more than once how relieved she was that the Asturian primogeniture laws meant she would never have to become Queen, but when it had become clear that no son would succeed him, her father—their father—had thrown himself into changing the law. Now, eight years later they were just weeks away from the law being ratified and Arrosa becoming the official heir to the throne. Whatever Arrosa's personal feelings about her new destiny, she had shouldered the change with her usual, intelligent grace.

'Oh, now I get it, in return for his help he gets half the kingdom and the Princess's hand in marriage. That still is the going rate?'

But Arrosa didn't answer her teasing smile, taking another sip of her wine as she stared pensively into the empty fireplace. 'Clem, everyone—my parents, my advisers, the newspapers—has been pushing me to marry. To start thinking about an heir of my own. And the country will see me as more settled, more mature, if I am married. I don't like being rushed, but I see the sense in it. The problem is, not only am I single, but I don't see that changing. On the rare occasion I meet someone I like the whole princess thing scares them off. Queen-to-be is going to make that a hundred times worse. I like Akil, and he understands the court and my world, and we have similar ambitions for Asturia… We were talking about what I wanted to achieve as the heir and realised how aligned our goals were, and I suddenly thought, well, he's the right age, single, understands my world. I could do a lot worse.'

'So you asked him if he'd do you the honour?' She

knew the situation wasn't funny, but humour was all that Clem had right now. Pity wouldn't help anyone, least of all her sister.

'Not exactly. I just said maybe he'd achieve more as Prince Consort and then fled the scene in mortification. What if he says yes?'

'Do you *want* him to say yes?'

'It's not what I dreamed of as a little girl. But it *would* make things easier.'

'The last of the true romantics. What's he like? Is he good-looking?' Other words hovered unsaid—is he kind, will he respect you, can you fall in love with him?

'I think so. He's pleasant enough to look at.'

Arrosa handed over her phone to Clem, who sucked in a breath. *Pleasant enough to look at?* Understatement of the century. With cheekbones sharp enough to slice through ice, a determined chin, sensuous mouth and a knowing glint in dark eyes, the Vicomte was film-star handsome. And if Arrosa couldn't see that then she really shouldn't marry him.

'Yes, pleasant enough,' she said wryly.

'He's a good man.' Was Arrosa trying to convince Clem—or herself?

'But?'

Arrosa rubbed her eyes. 'Queens make sacrifices for the common good. I know that. But I'm giving up any last hope of privacy, of choosing my own path. Is marrying someone I don't love one sacrifice too many? Being the monarch is lonely enough. It would be easier with a real partner by my side. Someone who wants to marry me because of me, not my title. But I'm not sure that person is out there. Akil is a sensible choice. Maybe that should be enough.'

'Rosy, I think this is something you need to take some time and think about. Really think about.' In fact, she shouldn't be making any decisions while she was clearly overwhelmed. Clem had never seen her sister so pale, never seen such huge shadows under her eyes or her usually laughter-filled face so solemn. 'You need a break.'

Arrosa sighed. 'I know. It's been intense. But don't worry, I'm slowing down for the summer, I've cleared my diary for the next few weeks leading up to the ratification as things will get really busy once I'm confirmed. Papa wants me to take on some decision-making duties straight away. There's a lot to learn. He's still young, but of course he inherited the throne long before he thought he would. He wants me to be ready.'

'A break? So you'll go on holiday?'

Her smile was wan. 'I wouldn't go that far. There's a lot to do, to organise, but at least I've got no engagements or formal meetings.'

'Then organise it from here.' Clem turned to her sister eagerly. 'Stay here for a few weeks, Rosy. You know the Cornish air does you good.' And then they could spend some real time together. Maybe for the last time.

'I'd love to,' Arrosa said wistfully. 'But I'm heading back tonight.'

'Tonight? Oh, Rosy.' Disappointment hit Clem hard. She hadn't realised how lonely she was until she had seen her sister sitting high up in the amphitheatre. She had friends, lots of them, but nobody who was hers alone.

How she wished she and Arrosa could actually *be* sisters properly. Have more than a weekly phone call and a few snatched hours here and there.

'I know, but I'll be missed if I'm gone too long.'

'You said yourself that you have no meetings.'

'I don't, but the speculation if I'm not seen even from the distance could be damaging this close to the ratification. I didn't go anywhere for a couple of weeks when I had flu last year and according to the tabloids I was having a facelift, had joined a cult and eloped with a soldier. I know it's silly and I shouldn't care but it's not just that I don't want any rumours circulating at home—eventually the press would find me and then they'd start wondering who *you* are and that's the last thing you need. It's safest for you if we're not seen together, Clem.'

'*If* they find you. After all, why would they look for you here?' But Clem knew all too well that Arrosa was always tracked down eventually. Once Arrosa had turned eighteen the press had turned their lenses on her and she had become a front-page staple. There weren't many beautiful, young single princesses around and what she wore and ate, who she spoke to and where she went were all put under intense scrutiny.

But no one in Cornwall had ever realised that the child and teenager who spent so many holidays with the Beaumonts was the Asturian Princess. In fact, some of Clem's friends and neighbours still asked after her cousin. People saw what they expected to see, and nobody expected to see a European princess eating ice cream on a Cornish beach. And look at her! Worryingly pale and thin. She obviously needed a proper holiday. One here in the Cornish air. Time away from politics and diplomacy and Court. Time to decide if marrying someone because he had done her a good turn and understood her world was really what she wanted.

Maybe there was a way to make it happen.

'I could go back to Asturia in your place,' Clem said slowly, trying the words on for size.

Arrosa started to laugh but the sound died away as her eyes grew big with shock. 'You're serious? Clem, no one would ever think you were me.'

'Up close, no, but in the back of a car, hair all neat like you, in your clothes, with those big sunglasses you wear... Why wouldn't they? People see what they expect to see.' She repeated the words she'd just thought, the truth of them becoming clearer with every second. 'We're the same build and height, the same colouring. And I'm an actress, I can walk like you, hold myself like you. You could have the summer here and I'll spend it in Asturia making sure the press get enough glimpses to think you're busy preparing for the ratification, leaving you free to get some serious relaxation. I talk about my cousin all the time. No one here will think anything of it if we say I've got a job and you're cat-sitting. The only unbelievable part will be that I've been cast in anything. I'll have to claim I ended up on the cutting-room floor.'

'That's the craziest thing I've ever heard. We'd never get away with it.'

A tendril of hope in Arrosa's voice made Clem push away her own doubts.

'If you lived in the main castle or had dozens of servants then I agree, it would be impossible…'

'But I have my own cottage in the grounds of the Palais d'Artega,' Arrosa said slowly. 'I make my own meals when I'm there, people do come in to clean but not when I'm around. Only Marie is there regularly, but of course she and Henri would need to know if there was any chance of this succeeding… But it would be lonely, Clem. You'd have to be careful that no maids, no gardeners, no staff at all saw you. Some are new but some have been at the palais since I was a baby. What would you do with yourself?'

Lonely. That was a state Clem had got all too used to over the last year and a half. 'I'll make sure the press see Henri drive me around, dressed as you, of course, but in between I'll wear my own clothes, let my hair go back to natural wildness and explore Asturia incognito. I've always wanted to go but somehow I never have.' She'd always hoped that Zorien would find a way to invite her over, but of course he had always said it was too risky. 'It would be a chance for me to see our father too. It'd be easier for him to spend time with me if I'm living at yours. No one would question him visiting you.' She tried to keep the bitterness from her voice. She knew Zorien was a distant father to Arrosa in many ways too, but at least they had a real relationship, not just an awkward meeting every few years. She was grateful for the cottage and for the money he'd settled on her but would gladly swap both for a real father.

'But what's the point of me being here if you aren't?'

'Well, Gus needs feeding, for a start.' Clem pointed at the slim black cat occupying the window seat. 'The sea needs swimming in, scones need eating, beaches need walking on and you need time to be you, not the Crown Princess and future Queen. This gives you that time. And I need a change of scene too. I've been putting off making plans for my future, just existing for too long. Maybe some time away will give me some much-needed perspective. You'd be doing me a favour.'

'Sure, *I'd* be doing *you* the favour.' Arrosa shook her head affectionately at Clem.

'We'll do each other a favour. We both need some time away from our lives, so why not swap for a while? Your mother's not at home, is she?' She knew that Iara Artega rarely spent much time in the Artega country estate, preferring to spend her time socialising in the small capital or journeying abroad.

'No, she's spending the summer on Ischia on a retreat.'

'Then we're safe.' Arrosa's mother knew about Clem, but the two had never met and Clem sensed the Queen would prefer to keep it that way. 'We could do this. Your call, Rosy. What will it be? Six weeks of avoiding Akil, ducking away from the press and worrying yourself into a shadow or all the cream teas you can eat and a summer lazing on the beach?'

'We must be mad to even consider this would work.' But there was a hint of the old fire in Arrosa's eyes and Clem knew she was close to agreeing.

'It's easy enough to swap back if we need to,' she pointed out and Arrosa nodded then laughed.

'You're right. Let's give it a week and see where we are. Thank you, Clem. Cornwall is just what I need, and I think maybe Asturia is where you need to be as well. To a change of scenery.' She held up her glass and Clem clinked it with hers.

'To the princess swap.'

CHAPTER TWO

AKIL STRODE ACROSS the ornate hallway and into the formal receiving room. His own taste ran to simple but the decor in his ancestral home had clearly not got the memo. Gilt and marble prevailed, every piece of furniture was priceless, old and incredibly uncomfortable and portraits of bewigged disapproving ancestors glared down from every wall.

Every one of them no doubt had an opinion on the dilemma he'd not been able to stop turning over and over since his last conversation with Arrosa had taken an unexpected turn.

It was an enticing prospect, an effortless climb to the very top of Asturia but, then again, he was doing pretty fine as he was. More than fine: Shadow Minister of the Interior at thirty with the possibility of making it to party leader before forty, a decade before his father had achieved the title. And as leader of the opposition, maybe even First Minister one day if the swing away from the traditionalists continued,

Akil would wield a lot of power, the kind of power he had been born and bred to wield. But in Asturia the throne still held a lot of influence and nothing happened without the court's approval.

And that was the heart of his dilemma. Because he couldn't deny that if he were right next to the throne, married to a woman he knew shared many of his ideals, then together they could enact real change. The change so desperately needed if Asturia was ever to move forward, to be more than a curious little country sandwiched between France and Spain, a pub quiz answer and a quirky holiday destination. More, it would ensure that Ortiz blood would run in the veins of future kings and queens. He knew what his father would say. He would tell him to stop hesitating and act. Propose formally and marry her before she had a chance to change her mind.

But it wasn't that simple. He liked Arrosa, admired her grace and intelligence, appreciated her beauty, but he didn't *know* her, not in the way he should know a woman he was considering marrying. Akil knew that he needed to marry carefully, strategically; after all, as his mother knew to her cost, being married to a politician meant sacrifices. But he did want compatibility. Companionship. Not the chilly battleground he'd grown up in.

Blinking, his eyes readjusted as the door swung shut behind him. The heavy velvet drapes were pulled against the midday sun, the large, dark room dimly lit by lamps. His mother lay on a chaise, barely mustering a smile as Akil walked over and bowed over her outstretched hand.

'You look more like your father every day.' It wasn't a compliment.

'Mama.' He suppressed a grimace and sat down on the low stool beside her. 'You look well.'

'That's very kind of you, *cheri*.' Her tone made it clear that she didn't find him kind at all. His mother made a study of ill health and excelled, but Akil found it hard to indulge her when, thanks to his volunteering work, he saw real ill people in the overstretched public hospitals. 'But my head has been bad recently. I thought you knew, but of course you are so busy, how could you remember such an insignificant detail?' Her sigh was perfectly calculated to sit midway between heartbroken and plaintive.

It should be perfectly calculated. She'd worked on it long enough.

Nerea Ortiz was still nearer fifty than sixty, her dark hair owing more to nature than her hairdresser's art, her figure still slim and toned, her face unlined. But she reclined as if she were a Victorian great-aunt, a small, fat lapdog snoring at her feet, a shawl around her shoulders and a selection of herbal remedies cluttering up a small table that also held a china cup half filled with weak tea and a matching plate holding two wafer-thin biscuits. A water bottle sat on another table—that was if it was water. Early as it was, it could easily be gin.

Not for the first time, Akil thought that his mother lived in entirely the wrong era.

'I'm sorry to hear that,' he said with the patience born of long practice. 'But I'm here now and I can assure you that you have my full attention.'

Akil managed a dutiful hour by his mother's side before pleading work duties and taking his leave. As he left the room his eye was caught by a photo. His mother at twenty, beautiful and glowing, full of life. It was easy to forget that when Akil had been young, very young, she had been that vibrant young woman. But years of his father's disapproval and dislike had worn away all her *joie de vivre* until ill health became her only defence against her husband's scathing tongue. His weapons were anger and contempt, sarcasm and noise, hers tears and shrinking, martyrdom and illness.

And drink. Never spoken about, never acknowledged, all too often present.

No wonder Akil had spent as much of his childhood and now adulthood elsewhere, only coming back to the Ortiz ancestral home when duty commanded. Now he was the head of the family he had to visit more often but had resisted moving back to the place where he had been so unhappy, his father's disappointment still reverberating in every room. Although, since recovering from the heart attack that had felled him eight years ago, his father now spent most of his time in the family's Swiss villa.

Apparently not alone.

Akil sighed. Thoughts of his father were always complicated: guilt, dislike and yet, still, that frustrating, inexplicable and yet ever-present need to make him proud—and to beat him. To show that Akil had everything it took to be the Duc, the head of the family, to bear the Ortiz name. His father had always urged Akil to marry tactically. 'Don't let your head get turned by some pretty lightweight like I did,' he'd told Akil more than once. 'Marry a woman who brings influence and power. Who can further the family cause.' Who better than the Crown Princess?

The beep of his phone recalled him to his surroundings and Akil paused on the top of the wide stone steps that led from the grand double-height entrance way down to the curved driveway. He pulled his phone out of his pocket and glared at the screen, the tension leaving his body when he saw the name on it.

Elixane.

'Hey, what's up?' He walked slowly down the steps, an invisible load lifting more with every inch he moved away from the house. His car was right in front of him but he carried on, turning onto a gravelled path that ran across the front of the house and into the walled garden, which had been Akil's favourite hiding place as a small boy.

'I meant to return your call before now but things have been crazy,' his sister said. 'Everything okay?'

Akil hesitated. He'd called Elixane right after Arrosa had—possibly, maybe—suggested he consider becoming her Prince Consort, desperate to talk the conversation over with someone, but the more time passed, the less he felt able to articulate what had been said. 'Everything's fine.' He paused. 'I've just visited Mama.'

'How is she?'

'Much the same.'

She sighed. 'That's not good. I did try and suggest she drank less last time I saw her, but she pretended she didn't know what I was talking about. It isn't even the quantity I worry about, it's the drinking alone. How about Papa?'

'Last I heard he was much the same too.'

'You mean he's also drinking too much and eating too much and probably spending too much time with the mistresses we're not supposed to know the old hypocrite has, while you fulfil his dreams for him?'

She had a point. 'He nearly died.'

'Of bad temper. Eight years ago.'

'Early retirement was the best option.'

'For who? Not for you, that's for sure. I still can't believe he guilted you into dropping your studies to take over from him.'

'Elixane,' Akil said warningly. 'I made my own decisions then and I make my own decisions now.'

'Which is why I'm the one doing a surgical residency in New York?'

'And I couldn't be happier for you.' He stepped through the small, hidden archway that led into the garden and the last of the tension left him as he entered. Old, twisted fruit trees covered with fresh green leaves, blossom petals carpeting the grass, little winding paths darting between them, wildflowers populating the grass.

'Now what can I say to that?' Elixane complained. 'Maybe you are better off as a politician. You always know what to say.'

'Not always. I had an interesting conversation with the Princess the other day and I had no idea how to respond,' he said, his eyes fixed on a bee busily divesting a flower of nectar. 'She's being pressured to marry.'

'Poor Arrosa, I can just imagine.' Elixane was the same age as the Princess and despite the family rivalry the girls had been friends of a sort growing up. 'You're in the Senate, you know what that bunch of dinosaurs are like. They still think a woman needs a man's steadying hand. I don't envy her. She's got an uphill battle with that lot.'

'She recognises that. She's not afraid, but I think she feels it would be easier if she wasn't facing them alone. She...' He coughed, the words feeling as ridiculous as he knew they would sound. 'She asked how I felt about being the Prince Consort.'

'She *what*? She *proposed*?' Elixane's voice rose to shrill frequency and Akil winced. 'To *you*? I didn't know you two were that close.'

'We're not, and no.' Akil wasn't sure exactly what had happened in that conversation, but he was sure about that. 'She didn't propose exactly. It was more of a sounding me out, I think.'

'And you said how flattering but no thank you.'

'I didn't say anything.' He hadn't had a chance to formulate any kind of response before Arrosa had blushed furiously, made an excuse and left.

'My brother a prince. That would bring Papa hot-footing it home from Switzerland. But it's ridiculous, of course. Please let me be there when you tell him you had the chance to marry into the royal family and turned it down.'

Akil didn't answer and Elixane's voice tightened. 'You are turning it down, aren't you?'

'I don't know. Not yet. I'd be a fool not to at least consider it, Elixane.'

'But, Akil, you don't love her. You barely know her!'

'I've spent some time with her recently and I like her. Respect her. Besides, love isn't necessary for a happy marriage.'

'Love doesn't guarantee a happy marriage but it sure as hell helps. You can't base your decisions on the disaster that's our parents' marriage. They didn't love each other. They were infatuated and that's a whole different ball game.'

'Love or infatuation, it's undeniable that everything they wanted and needed in a marriage was incompatible and I will never make that mistake.' Never raise children amongst the hostility and unhappiness of a toxic marriage. 'If I marry, then I need a politician's wife, someone diplomatic, intelligent, with shared goals. Why not Arrosa? Being part of the court rather than parliament would be a different kind of politics but together we could achieve great things.'

'At what cost?'

'There's always a cost to power, Elixane. You just need to decide what you're willing to pay.'

'I haven't seen Arrosa for years,' his sister said after a long pause. 'We were friendly but not close. She's not close to anyone as far as I know, but I liked her. Like her. She's nice.'

'Yes,' Akil agreed. 'She's nice.'

'And that's enough?'

Akil leaned against a tree. 'It's a hell of a lot better than not nice,' he pointed out. 'Look, we both want this country to move beyond ancient feuds, we want a modern democracy.'

'And marriage is the only way to achieve that?' Akil could hear the scepticism in his sister's voice. 'It's the twenty-first century.'

Akil couldn't help his wry smile. 'In the rest of Europe maybe, but you know as well as I do that for over half this country it might as well be the seventeenth century.'

'You know what I think you should do?'

'Do I want to know what you think?'

'I think you're insane and you shouldn't give this any more thought, but if this is something you are really considering then you should get to really know her. Don't make any decisions either way until you've spent some time with the woman, not the Princess.

Make sure this marriage is something that you both can live with.'

Another fat bee buzzed past Akil's ear before landing on a climbing rose. Akil watched it move from flower to flower as he considered his sister's words. He didn't know what he felt about Arrosa's surprising proposition or if she had even meant it. Spending some time with her when they weren't working on bills and treatises might be the way to find out if they were compatible. 'You may be right.'

'I *know* I'm right. You might think that you don't have to fall in love with her, but you have to admit that you need to know that you can live with her.'

Elixane's words hung in the air until a beep reminded Akil that he had a meeting to get to. 'Look, I've got to go. Thank you.'

'Call me if you need me. Any time.'

And with that she was gone. Akil pocketed his phone, frowning. His little sister was annoyingly right. If Arrosa had meant those softly spoken words—and if he was truly considering agreeing—then they needed to see if they could live in harmony. His parents' marriage was an example of everything he didn't want: thwarted passion, disappointment, anger and resentment. He wanted civilised, compatible and mutual respect. Maybe it was time to stop thinking and talk to Arrosa, discover if she had been serious and then decide what, if anything, that meant for him.

Before Akil left the Palais d'Ortiz he cancelled his morning meetings, and instead of heading back to the city drove further out into the countryside towards the huge Artega estate. He'd hesitated over whether he should ask his assistant to forewarn Arrosa that he was on his way; after all, even a rising politician working closely with the Princess shouldn't just rock up uninvited at a royal residence. But if he and Arrosa were to discuss something as important as marriage then surely they should be able to discuss it without formality and pomp—and a possible fiancé shouldn't need to make an appointment to see his intended.

Akil had visited Arrosa at home enough times to be waved through by the guards at the gate and he drove up the long, tree-lined drive, past the imposing chateau with its fairy-tale turrets and intricate stone-work and headed towards the villa half a kilometre away where Arrosa resided. As he pulled up in front of the pretty white one-storey building he felt a momentary pang of unaccustomed doubt. Whatever they discussed here would set the tone for the rest of his life and he still didn't know what the outcome would be—or what he wanted it to be.

The nineteenth-century villa had an idyllic setting with its lakeside location and flower-filled gardens, a small orchard to one side. But despite the peaceful pastoral feeling, Akil knew that at least one secret service agent would be concealed somewhere close by, and that CCTV cameras meant that his every move would be fed back to the soldiers at the gate. It was a sobering thought; he was used to living with a certain degree of high security, thanks to his father's position and now his own, and he had spent time himself in the special forces during his national service, but he had never been watched twenty-four-seven.

Unexpected pity for the Princess flooded through him; never alone, never private and now asking a man she surely didn't love to be her husband.

Akil strode down the paved garden path to the front door and knocked on it. The last couple of times he been here either Arrosa herself had opened it or her maid, Marie, would usher him in. Arrosa had no live-in staff at the villa. In fact she lived a surprisingly self-sufficient life; apart from the staff who ran her office from the court in the capital city her only permanent staff were Marie and her bodyguard.

He waited but nobody answered the door, although he could see several open windows and hear the sound of music from within the house. He rapped on the door once again and when there was still no answer headed around to the back of the villa. The long, terraced garden led down to the lake, where he could see a small boathouse and changing hut positioned by a short wooden jetty. Arrosa sat on the jetty, her back to him, her hair cascading down, wilder than he'd ever seen it before.

She didn't turn as he made his way down the garden towards her and Akil hesitated before he called out, not wanting to startle her.

'Arrosa,' he said softly and saw her whole body stiffen. 'I did knock but nobody answered. I'm sorry to show up without notice.' Every sense told him that something wasn't quite right; he felt wrong-footed with no idea why. 'But what I have to say is too important to wait, and under the circumstances I felt some informality was warranted. I hope it goes without saying that I very much enjoy working with you, and I hope whatever happens that we will continue to work together over the years ahead. I have also come to value your companionship, friendship almost.'

Arrosa didn't speak, nor did she turn to face him. He couldn't read her body language at all. She was still rigid, like a deer scenting a predator, unsure whether to run or try to fade into the background.

'But marriage is a big commitment and not something either of us should enter into lightly,' he continued. 'If you didn't mean what you said the other day, if I misread your intention, or if you changed your mind, then I'll leave right now with no hard feelings and a promise never to mention it again. But if you did mean it then I think we need to spend some time together without titles between us, without work as a commonality, to see how compatible we are when all that is stripped away.'

Something about her stillness made it hard for him to let the silence fall but he made himself stop, wait for her to respond as the silence lengthened, the tension thickening with every long second until finally she spoke.

'Thank you.'

Akil frowned, that sense of wrongness intensifying.

Just two words but they sounded off, her voice lower, her accent subtly different.

'But now isn't a good time…' she continued slowly. 'Could we do this later?' She hesitated. It was as if she was measuring every word. 'I know this is important.'

Was she ill? Upset? Hurt? Akil couldn't just walk away without knowing Arrosa was all right. Princess or no princess, possible fiancée or not, she was a human being without many people to confide in. Whatever the future held, he could at least be her friend. Akil stepped onto the narrow wooden jetty and in a few decisive strides reached the still seated figure.

'Arrosa? What's wrong?' He squatted next to her and touched her shoulder, turning her gently towards him. But her face was at once familiar and yet strange. There was the same dark waving hair, the same hazel eyes, although these were subtly lighter, more gold than brown, the same olive skin, even that same tilt to the nose adding personality to a face that otherwise could have been blandly beautiful, and the same full mouth.

But this was not the Princess. This was not Arrosa.

His hand dropped and he straightened, taking an instinctive step back. 'Where's the Princess—and who on earth are you?'

CHAPTER THREE

CLEM STAYED COMPLETELY still for another long moment, unsure how to play this. She had no script, no director's notes. It was a good thing she had done so many improvisations but unfortunately this time she had no idea what her part should be.

After all, less than twenty-four hours ago she had been readying herself to play Juliet with no plans beyond the play and the party. But in the end she'd barely had time to remind Arrosa to water the plants and feed the cat, before finding herself hustled into the car that had brought Arrosa to Cornwall and whisked off to the private jet her sister had commandeered. It had been long past midnight when she'd arrived at the Palais d'Artega and Henri had shown her to the pretty lakeside villa Arrosa had moved into on her twenty-first birthday where, despite all her excitement and trepidation, she had fallen asleep straight away. No opportunity to have second thoughts or wonder how this madcap scheme might work in practice.

No opportunity until now. Unfortunately she had still been trying to get her thoughts in order when Akil Ortiz had inconsiderately shown up and complicated an already difficult situation. Who just showed up without calling first? Especially when calling on a princess?

However, she did know one thing. She wasn't having this conversation sitting down. Slowly she clambered to her feet and brushed the dust off her skirt before tilting her chin and turning to face Akil, meeting his suspicious gaze squarely, only to falter as she took him in.

If her first thought was, *Wow, that photo really didn't do him justice*, then her second was *Lucky, lucky Arrosa.*

Clem had been to one of the UK's most prestigious drama schools and as a result some of her classmates were now global heart-throbs. But not one of the attractive charismatic men she'd studied with, acted with, and sometimes dated had anything near the sheer magnetism of the Asturian Vicomte.

He was tall and broad, with his almost black hair ruthlessly swept back, but Clem could see hints of a rebellious wave in the strands that fell over his brow, strong brows framing keen dark brown eyes, a straight Roman nose turning his good looks characterful. His powerful body was showcased by a navy suit that had clearly been made to fit him, his olive skin set off by the crisp white of his linen open-collared shirt.

To her horror Clem felt a jolt of attraction pulsing low in her stomach, tingling through her whole body.

No, down, bad girl, she told herself fiercely as she summoned up her most regal smile, the one she'd used when playing Olivia in *Twelfth Night* during their third-year showcase.

'You must be the Vicomte d'Ortiz. I'm sorry, but Arrosa isn't here right now.'

'I see.' Suspicion lurked in his dark eyes as he surveyed her. 'When will she be back?'

'Not for a while. I'm house-sitting for her.' Did princesses who lived on their family estate surrounded by servants need house-sitters? Judging by the way Akil's eyes narrowed, he didn't think so. 'I needed a place for a while,' she added hurriedly. 'Really she's the one doing me the favour.'

'And you are?'

'Clem, Clemence Beaumont.' Surely knowing her name wouldn't do any harm? She wasn't linked anywhere with her father and sister. If he searched for her online all Akil would find would be some reviews of plays, her profile on her agent's website and her mother's obituary where Clem was buried beneath all the causes Simone had supported. 'I can let Arrosa know you dropped by, or you could tell her yourself, of course.'

'She didn't tell me she was going away.'

'It was all very sudden. And she doesn't want it to be common knowledge so please don't tell anyone.' She took a step forward but he didn't move. The only way past meant either brushing past him or going into the water and neither appealed. 'I'm sorry you had a wasted journey, but it was really nice to meet you,' she said pointedly. 'I'd offer you a coffee, but I really have to get on.'

If only that were true. Now she was here, Clem had no idea what to do next. Arrosa had promised to contact their father straight away to let him know what they were doing and she was anxiously hoping to hear from him. In the meantime her plans to explore had been thwarted by the realisation that Arrosa didn't have her own car and that she was driven everywhere by Henri. That was fine for the times she planned to dress as the Princess and be driven somewhere in order to make it seem as if Arrosa were here in Asturia, but the bulletproof limousine was far too conspicuous for her to use to be a tourist. Lovely as the villa was and inviting as the lake was, she didn't want to spend six weeks alone with nothing to do. She could do that back in Cornwall.

'You didn't say how you know Arrosa.' He clearly wasn't shifting. Maybe it was a good sign, this protectiveness. Although Arrosa already had a bodyguard watching her every move.

'No,' she said lightly. 'I didn't. Now if you'll excuse me.' He moved then, slowly and clearly reluctantly, and she slipped past him. 'I'm sure you can see your own way out. After all, you found your own way in.' She didn't look back as she headed up the path but she could feel his gaze boring into her as if he were trying to strip her secrets from her.

The garden was split onto three terraces. Lawn abutted the lake, then steps led up to a colourful flower-filled area, alive with bees and butterflies. The third terrace was paved with pots of plants providing shade and colour, an outdoor sofa and chairs on one side and a dining table and chairs on the other. It seemed to take an age to get to the French doors that led into the house and safety, and it wasn't until her hand was finally on the handle when he spoke.

'Wait.'

Reluctantly Clem turned. Akil had followed her onto the top terrace and he stood by the table, hands clenched.

'Just tell me, is Arrosa all right?'

Clem paused, trying to read him. Did he care about her sister as a person, or was he thinking about the power and influence she could give him?

But Arrosa had said that he was a good man and she was a shrewd judge of character. She'd had to be. And Clem had overheard words never meant for her ears after all. Words which, although she still wanted a lot more for her sister than a diplomatic convenient marriage, had gone a long way towards reassuring her that Akil wouldn't take advantage of her sister.

'She's fine.'

'Is there anything I can do to help? I got the impression the other day that she needed a friend. I hope she knows she can come to me if she's in trouble.'

It clearly cost him to ask the question, to look that vulnerable in front of a stranger, a stranger who he had already inadvertently spilled secrets to. The situation needed rebalancing. He deserved some truth from her. And this was a good chance for her to evaluate the man her sister definitely didn't love but thought of highly enough to consider entrusting her future happiness to.

'Maybe I do have time for a coffee after all,' she said. 'Do you?'

Clem still didn't know her way around her sister's well-appointed kitchen and it took some time to locate everything she needed and to load it onto a tray and carry it to the outside table where Akil awaited her. Despite her invitation, Akil hadn't sat; instead he stood at the edge of the terrace gazing out towards the lake. As Clem exited the house, he turned and quickly strode towards her, relieving her of the tray despite her protestations and setting it onto the wooden table. Clem followed him and took a seat, reaching for the cafetière gratefully. She was definitely in need of caffeine.

There was something peculiarly intimate about sitting opposite someone, asking them how they took their coffee, pouring it and adding the milk. Intimate and yet distancing, the lack of knowledge a sign that they were strangers. Although here at least she had the advantage. She knew who Akil was; he had no idea she even existed.

He accepted the coffee but made no move to drink it, instead setting the cup onto the table and looking at her with a frown. 'I spoke to Arrosa just two days ago and she made no mention of going away. The ratification is in just a couple of months' time. This is no time for her to disappear. What's going on?'

Clem sat back and regarded him steadily. 'Once the law has been ratified and Arrosa is officially the Crown Princess, how much time will she have to go away? How much privacy? She's already constrained in so many ways, guarded at all times, and it's only going to get worse. This is a perfect time for her to have some space. Maybe the last chance she has.'

He inclined his head briefly as if acknowledging her point. 'But that doesn't explain what you're doing here or who you are, Clemence Beaumont. I don't believe I've heard Arrosa mention you before.'

'Does Arrosa know all your friends?' Clem asked sweetly and only the slightest narrowing of his eyes showed his displeasure with her answer.

'Your resemblance to her is quite startling, too startling for it to be a coincidence although Beaumont is not an Asturian name. You must be related, but I know all her relatives around your age and you're not one of them.'

'You've done quite the study on her genealogy.'

To her surprise Akil laughed, transforming his face from an austere, remote handsomeness to something warmer—and dangerously attractive. 'Asturia is a small country and everybody knows everybody. And *I* know that I've never seen you before and I've not heard your name and so I'm wondering why someone who looks so like the Crown Princess is living in her house when the Crown Princess has unexpectedly disappeared.'

'You have a vivid imagination. You should write crime books.' Clem took a sip of coffee and smiled. 'But there's no mystery here. Text Arrosa, she will tell you that she is fine.'

'It just seems a strange coincidence that just a couple of days after our conversation she disappears.' He stopped then, his mouth tightening as if he'd realised that he'd said too much. But it was a little bit too late to pretend ignorance about the possible match between her sister and this disturbing man when she'd heard his opening speech.

'Look,' she said, setting her cup onto the table. 'I can't pretend I didn't hear what you said earlier, and I can't pretend that I don't know what you're talking about. I also can't comment on where Arrosa is or why she's there. That's her personal business and if you need to know more than that you should ask her. She has her phone. I spoke to her this morning. As for me, I'm here partly because, like Arrosa, I could do with some time away from my life, but mainly to give her this time. You know how hard it is for her to have any peace. As you said, we look alike, and from a distance, with the right hair and make-up, through the windows of her car most people would mistake me for her. If I make sure I'm seen dressed as her two or three times a week from a distance, then nobody will think to go looking for her. I'm giving her the space she needs. Nothing more sinister than that.'

Without taking his eyes off her Akil pulled out his phone and dictated a quick message.

Arrosa, I'm at your house with Clem, let me know everything's all right.

He put his phone down. 'Okay, that's why you're here. But I still don't know who you are, or that I can trust you.'

'Arrosa trusts me, shouldn't that be enough?'

'It would be if you didn't know more about my personal business than I'm comfortable with.' He sat back and folded his arms. 'I'll tell you what I do know. Number one, you resemble Arrosa so closely you have to be a near relative, number two, she's never mentioned you but you clearly know a lot about her life, number three, you're not Asturian, you speak the language well but there's a hint of an accent. Not French, not Spanish. If I had to bet I'd say English. So why is an English girl in Asturia pretending to be the Crown Princess?'

'I'm an actress.'

'So this is a job? All above board? Signed off by the King?'

'It's more of a private arrangement.'

'Give me one good reason why I shouldn't alert the guards to your presence here.' He didn't take his eyes off her and she knew he wasn't bluffing.

'Because I'm her half-sister,' she said. 'The family secret. And no one in Asturia is supposed to know I exist. Happy now?'

* * *

What had she just said? It took more than a few seconds for Akil's brain to process the words he'd just heard.

'You're Arrosa's half-*sister*?' He knew that the King and Queen lived largely separate lives, but he'd never heard rumours of any affairs—and certainly none of any other children. But Clem's resemblance to Arrosa was startling, sisters made perfect sense. How had this scandal been hushed up for so long in this small country? Who else knew?

Clem nodded. 'I'm six months older than Rosy. Look, my existence is only known to a very, very few people.' She looked across at him pleadingly. 'Please don't tell anyone. If the truth got out it would hurt Rosy more than me. Any family scandal might rebound on her even though she's obviously not responsible for anything apart from treating me as much like a sister as possible. The next few months are key, you know that. Maybe I shouldn't have come to Asturia, maybe it was too risky, but Rosy lives such a quiet life outside her duties I didn't think anyone would find out if I stuck to her villa and slipped out to explore incognito. Shows how much I know. I managed less than twenty-four hours here before you found me.'

Akil sat back and sipped his coffee, his mind racing. Clem had a point—more than one. If news of her very existence got out then the ensuing scandal would overshadow the new hereditary law, and possibly disrupt the ratification. Change came slowly to

Asturia and a consensus was still very much in the balance, as was public opinion, especially amongst the older generations. But Clem was also right about Arrosa's need for time away. She'd looked increasingly pale and thin over the last few months and Akil knew her offer to him came from a need for companionship and help, not from any deeper feelings. Some time away was exactly what she needed—and if he hadn't turned up unexpectedly then who was to say that the ruse wouldn't have worked the way the sisters had planned it?

'I won't say a word,' he promised. 'But how is this even possible? You're six months older than Arrosa, you say, which must mean Zorien is your father? Who's your mother?' It was unlike Akil to be so overtly curious but he was intrigued beyond politeness by this secret at the very heart of the court.

Clem flushed, her eyes fixed on her cup. 'One thing you need to know is that this isn't easy for me. I have never told anyone who I am, not even my old boyfriends, or my best friend. Anyone from home who has met Rosy thinks she's my cousin. Just saying the truth aloud feels like I've broken some law.'

'You don't have to tell me anything you don't want to,' Akil assured her and her answering smile was grateful.

'I know. But in a strange way, I do want to tell you. It's probably better that you know the whole truth rather than leaving you with just bits of it. I would hate for you to think badly of my mother, or even my father. He's not exactly been there for me, but I do understand how difficult things were for him and he has ensured that Rosy and I know each other. I will always be grateful to him for that.'

Akil did some rapid mental calculations. 'Arrosa was born a year after Zorien and Iara married—so you would have been conceived three months before?'

Clem nodded. 'What you have to remember is that Zorien's marriage was brought forward after his father's illness meant he decided to abdicate in favour of his son. There had been an informal agreement between the families that Zorien and Iara would marry but they weren't technically engaged when Zorien dated my mother. It's a bit of a technicality because the marriage was very much in the pipeline, but my father wasn't a total cad. A bit of one but not a *total* cad.' Her voice rang with sincerity. It was obviously important to her that Akil believed this—that she believed it.

Akil had never really thought about the King's marriage before, or how it had come to be. But this was Asturian politics, nothing happened without planning for the long game, his own parents' disastrous marriage aside. 'Queen Iara comes from an old and wealthy aristocratic family with links to European royalty on both sides. I believe it was a popular marriage among the people and politically sound,' he remembered. 'And for the most part it seems to have worked well; apart from her propensity to take long retreats abroad, she's a good queen. Not loved, exactly, but respected.'

'From what I've gleaned they live mostly separate lives but put on a united front. Neither had any romantic fantasies about the marriage. Iara's family wanted her to be Queen and she liked the idea. Zorien knew his position as a young king would be stabilised by a good marriage. After the plans were agreed, but before they got engaged, Zorien was allowed to go to the Sorbonne for a year's MBA as reward. He enrolled anonymously and that's where he met my mother. They fell in love. At least, my mother told me it was love.' Her voice softened, became wistful. 'He told her the truth when his father's declining health meant the court decided to bring the engagement forward, followed by a wedding just six weeks later. What neither of them knew when they parted was that she was pregnant with me. By the time she found out the wedding was less than a month away and the abdication planned. A different man might have broken off the engagement and married my mother despite the court's objections and weathered the scandal, or even walked away from the throne altogether, but Zorien decided to put Asturia first, go ahead with the wedding and make sure no one knew about my mother or about me.'

'That must have been difficult for your mother.' And for the daughter, which made her presence here today rather remarkable. Made *her* rather remarkable. Strong, forgiving, compassionate.

Beautiful.

Desirable.

The realisation made him catch his breath. Yes, she resembled her sister, but she was very much her own person; there was a piquancy to her features that differentiated her, made her unique. Made her desirable in a way Arrosa wasn't. Not that Akil had any right to dwell on either her beauty or her desirability.

Clem's mouth twisted into a wry smile. 'My mother was a doer not a dweller.' Akil noted the *was* and the way she blinked sudden tears away at the word. 'She moved to England where I was born, fell in love with Cornwall and retrained as a teacher, although Zorien was very generous, money-wise at least. She never married, never really dated seriously as far as I know although she had plenty of suitors. Instead she threw herself into campaigns and causes, never happier than when she was directing the village play or organising a march or painting a placard. To be honest I'm not sure being a queen would have agreed with her. She liked to say exactly what was on her mind, to take action. Diplomacy wasn't really her thing.'

'How did you and Arrosa get to know each other?'

'Apparently Zorien told Iara about my mother and the pregnancy before they married. When it started to seem likely that Arrosa was going to be their only child she agreed that we should be allowed to meet. In the end Rosy used to come to us, incognito of course, for most holidays and nearly all of the summer. She loved the chance to do normal things. To go surfing or bowling, to eat chips on the beach. To get dirty and have tangled hair and old clothes. We had amazing summers. We don't get to spend time together now but we speak weekly. She's my sister, my closest friend. I love her and her happiness matters.' Her gaze was direct. 'So I am glad you and I got the chance to meet. To talk.'

Her meaning was clear. 'She told you about her proposition?'

'Yes, and that's why I urged her to stay in Cornwall. What the two of you decide is your business, but she was too tired, too run-down to make any life-altering decisions right now. I hope you will respect that she needs time and space. Her parents married for an alliance, because it made political sense, and nothing she has ever told me has persuaded me that it was a good match. I want more for her than that.'

'Understood.' He did—and he admired the way Clem had her sister's interests at heart. He'd thought Arrosa alone but how could she be with her sister on her side? He pushed his chair back. 'It was nice meeting you, Clem. Thank you for entrusting me with your secret. I promise it's safe with me. What are your plans for the next six weeks?'

She winced. 'That's a good question. I'd hoped to get to know Asturia. I've never been here before and I have always wanted to explore it. But we're miles from anywhere, Rosy doesn't own a car and the limousine isn't exactly inconspicuous. I'm not really sure how to get out and about. I can't just call a taxi when as far as anyone knows the person living here is Arrosa and never goes anywhere unaccompanied and without clearance. I'll figure out a way, but it's more complicated than I realised.'

He sympathised with her, but her predicament was none of his business. His life was complicated enough without embroiling himself in the affairs of the King's illegitimate daughter. But there was something about the wistful look in Clem's eyes and the way she tried to cover it with her cheery matter-of-fact tone that spoke to him. It *was* a shame that she couldn't get to know the country her father ruled over and her sister would one day inherit.

'I cleared my diary for the rest of the day so I could take you out this afternoon if you wanted,' he said, surprising himself with the offer. 'If you put your hair up and sunglasses on, the guards at the gate will assume you're Arrosa—I've driven her to the city before and I trained with the secret service during my national service, which means clearance has never been an issue before. The guards will assume we're working. And once we're away from here you should be fine. You don't look so like your sister that anyone would mistake you for her close up, especially if you don't dress formally.'

Hope sparked in the hazel eyes but almost immediately dimmed. 'That's very kind but I can't ask you to give up your afternoon for me.'

'You didn't ask, I offered. Your choice, Clem. A chance to explore or an afternoon staring at the lake.

What will it be?' Akil didn't want to analyse why he really wanted her to say yes.

She laughed at that, the sound unexpectedly rich and melodic. 'It's not really a choice when you put it that way. Thank you, I really appreciate it and I would love to accept. Let's explore. Just give me five minutes to get ready.'

'Take as long as you need.' Akil ignored the sense of anticipation creeping through him at the prospect of an afternoon spent with the English girl, the pleasure that she had accepted his offer. He was doing a favour for his friend's sister. Nothing more, nothing less.

CHAPTER FOUR

ANTICIPATION FIZZED THROUGH Clem as she pulled on a pair of Arrosa's oversized sunglasses and added one of her sister's bright scarves and a large, low-brimmed hat. The perfect disguise as all three could be discarded as soon as she had safely left the estate grounds. She tipped her own sunglasses, phone and purse into one of Arrosa's bags and practically ran back outside.

'Ready!'

Akil was frowning at his phone but as he looked up a slow, approving smile curved his mouth and a jolt of attraction hit her low in her stomach, the heat spreading through her. 'You really were just five minutes.'

'I'm an actress, remember? Quick changes are my trade.'

'When my sister says five minutes I usually know I need to settle in for half an hour at least.'

'You have a sister?'

He nodded. 'Elixane. She's in New York at the moment, doing a surgical residency.' A shadow, so fleeting she wasn't sure if she'd imagined it, crossed his face. 'She plans to be Surgeon General here one day.'

'A woman with ambition. I approve.'

Clem quickly sent a message to Marie and Henri to let them know her plans and then followed Akil round to the front of the villa. She let out a low whistle as she took in his car. A sporty two-seater, so far so playboy but the classy silvery blue colour he'd chosen suggested a car bought to drive and enjoy as opposed to a mere status symbol. 'What a beauty! Can we have the top down?'

'If you want.'

'I do, although maybe when we're away from here and I can shed the hat. It would be a bit inconvenient if it got blown off by the wind just as we got waved through!'

Akil unlocked the car and Clem slid in, luxuriating in the comfortable leather seats. The car might seem a cliché in a less skilled driver's hands, but he handled her beautifully, the car purring under his guidance. Clem sneaked a look at Akil as he accelerated down the drive, sunglasses shading his eyes, his face intent on the road ahead, muscles taut on his bare arms, and her pulse accelerated. He really was a ridiculously attractive man.

His arrival at the villa could so easily have been a disaster but it was looking as if it was a blessing in disguise. Not only was she finally getting an opportunity to explore Asturia, but this was an unexpected opportunity to find out who Akil really was behind the hot body and the political career, her chance to make sure he was worthy of her sister, to find out what he really thought of Arrosa's proposition.

She tensed up as they reached the gate and Akil gave her another of those slow smiles, her stomach flipping in response. 'Relax,' he said. 'You're doing fine.' Sure enough, the soldiers saluted as they opened the gates and within seconds they were accelerating away, Clem discarding the hat and sunglasses, replacing Arrosa's designer dark sunglasses with her own quirkier vintage ones and wriggling back in her seat.

'Where are we going?'

'I can tell you,' Akil said. 'Or it could be a surprise. Your call.'

Everywhere was new to her and she wanted to see it all. 'I trust you. Surprise me. I'm sure anywhere you choose will be fine.'

Akil nodded as he pressed the button to lower the roof and the whistle of the wind combined with the purr of the engine. Clem stared around at the countryside, taking it all in with avid eyes. She'd seen so many pictures, read so many books, watched any programme or film set here and now she was actually here, breathing Asturian air.

Asturia was as beautiful as she had hoped, green and unspoilt with verges filled with wild flowers. Her very soul felt repleted as she inhaled the tartly fresh air as if something in her had always craved it. As if she were home. Asturia might be backward in many ways but that meant its countryside was relatively undeveloped and the country was now getting a reputation for biodiversity and attracting eco-conscious tourists. Rolling hills and fields gave way to mountains at the further end of the horizon, the sun beating down from a cloudless sky. She sighed in appreciation. 'It's so beautiful.'

'It really is,' Akil agreed. 'There's nowhere else like it.'

'And so quiet. As if there's no one else here.'

'Hmm.' He glanced in the mirror. 'Apart from the car that's been tailing us since we left the castle. Is Henri not with Arrosa? I thought he never left her side?'

She looked round at the sleek black car hanging a discreet distance behind. 'Poor Henri. He was torn between returning with me and staying with Rosy. As people are meant to think I'm her he knew he needed to be here for business as usual, but he takes protecting her very seriously. It took some persuading for him to agree that she'd look too conspicuous if he stayed. No one expects my cousin to have a bodyguard! Although I expect Zorien has dispatched someone to keep an eye on her.'

'Your father knows you've swapped?'

'Rosy messaged him last night. I was hoping to hear from him today but of course he's very busy. This would be such a good opportunity for us to spend some time together.' She could hear the self-pity in her voice and winced, relieved when Akil didn't pursue the subject.

They crested a hill and as they reached the top and

the sea came into view Clem gasped. There it was, laid out before them, turquoise and silver and so dazzling she was glad of her sunglasses. She took in a wondering breath as Akil began to navigate his way down the curving road.

'It's like something out of a fairy tale,' she said softly, transfixed as the flower-covered cliffs came into view, the sea tumbling against them. Asturia wasn't the most famous of tourist resorts, but there was no coastline to rival it, not even her beloved Cornwall. 'Just like I imagined,' she almost whispered.

They carried on heading along the coast road until Akil turned off down a narrow lane, heading towards the sea and a tiny cluster of houses dotted around a wooden, slightly tatty harbour. Clem knew that there were plenty of glamorous beaches along the coast, home to exclusive beach clubs and harbours filled with fancy boats, but this seemed like the kind of place she loved, small and known only to a few locals.

Akil pulled into a car park and killed the engine. Clem looked around eagerly. Fishing boats bobbed by the wooden pier, bigger boats moored further out, a mix of working and leisure craft. In front of them a small hut overlooked the sea flanked by a few plastic tables and chairs.

'Okay, then,' he said. 'Here we are. I hope you're hungry.'

It was as if Akil had seen inside her soul and knew exactly what she craved. She followed him to the hut and took a seat on a battered but clean and comfortable plastic chair perched on the edge of a tiny stone harbour, fine white sand inviting her on the beach to their right.

'What do you fancy?' Akil asked. 'I can recommend the fried clams.'

'Clams and fries? Perfect.'

'The local beer is good, or they make their own lemonade.'

'A beer sounds good. In a way I am on holiday, I suppose.' Not that she'd been gainfully employed for longer than she cared to remember. Money wasn't an issue, thanks to the money Zorien had set aside for her, but she needed an occupation. She needed a purpose, a reason to exist. She pushed the thought away for another day and tilted her chin. 'Besides, this is my first outing in Asturia. I should celebrate.'

Akil held her gaze for one charged second, the corner of his mouth turned up in amusement—and approval. Clem's pulse thudded under his studied gaze and she turned to exclaim at the view, breaking the spell with a stream of meaningless words.

The food was as wonderful as promised, the clams fat and salty, tasting like the sea, the fries crispy on the outside, meltingly soft inside, tart with vinegar. The salad wasn't the token collection of browned limp leaves Clem was expecting, but sweet crunchy leaves, tiny, delicious tomatoes and tart red peppers, another reminder that she was in the Mediterranean, not on the English coast.

Even better was the view. On one side the sea, calm

and bright and endlessly beautiful, and on the other Akil. Six feet of broad-shouldered, olive-skinned, dark-eyed deliciousness. And she *really* needed to stop thinking about Akil that way. She wasn't here on a date. She didn't know him, nor he her. He was just being kind to a lonely girl. And no doubt it suited him to do it. He must know that Clem would tell Arrosa all about the afternoon.

But she couldn't deny that this really was her idea of a dream date. And that spelt trouble in all kinds of ways she wasn't going to allow herself to think about.

Instead, she was going to keep busy and push the words *dream* and *date* right out of her mind.

'That was amazing,' she said, jumping to her feet and collecting up the plates and beer bottles and returning them to the hut with a smile. 'Thank you for bringing me here.' She didn't return to her seat, leaning over the railing and looking out to sea, her pulse hammering with nerves. *Keep talking, Clem.* She glanced back at Akil. 'So this is a favourite place of yours?'

'Since I was a boy,' he confirmed, lounging back in his chair. 'My aunt has a holiday home near here, me, my sister and our cousins spent our summers sailing on these waters and spending all our money on snacks here at this very shack. Not that it spoiled our appetites.' His grin was reminiscently boyish and her stomach tumbled. She could cope with him being handsome. She wasn't sure she could manage charming as well.

'I was brought up by the sea. I love sailing. Surfing, paddle-boarding, kayaking, I did it all. I just love being out on the water.'

'It can be arranged, just say the word. My boat is moored here.'

He had a boat? Could he tick any more boxes? Regretfully she shook her head. 'I can't let poor Henri follow us in a dinghy.' She grimaced. 'I'd never realised how limiting it is being followed all the time. I know that Henri is kind, careful not to impose, but he's always there. I don't know how Rosy manages it.'

'What she has now is freedom compared to how her life will be once she's the heir to the throne.'

It was a sobering thought. No wonder her sister wanted companionship. Two sisters equally lonely but for very different reasons. Maybe Rosy should marry Akil. He was kind, intelligent and understood her world.

But then again she didn't love him and, of all people, didn't her sister deserve love?

'Maybe I should stick around and be her body double for good and then she could escape whenever she needed,' she half joked and Akil grinned.

'Maybe you should. Although poor Henri would definitely want to clone himself if you two made a habit of this.' He nodded towards the beach. 'Fancy walking some of that off?'

'Absolutely. I'm dying to explore.'

The beach was a long straight strip of white sand, the sea lapping at the edges. In the distance Clem could see a gentle curve and a high tumble of rocks against the high cliff that marked the end of the bay. They started to walk, first slowly and then faster as they took the measure of each other's stride, and Clem enjoyed the pace, the stretch in her muscles as she matched Akil step for step. She could hear the occasional hum of a car, the screech of gulls out at sea, but otherwise it was as if it were just the two of them—and Henri, several hundred yards behind.

Neither spoke, their strides perfectly matched. Clem was totally aware of Akil's every movement, the swing of his arms, the flex of his hands. She swallowed, trying to ignore the all-encompassing awareness of him that seemed to grow with every passing minute. *Behave*, she scolded herself, aware that she needed to stop staring at his wrists, stop finding herself transfixed by the pulse at his throat, stop dwelling on the lines of his mouth, stop allowing herself to trace the outlines of his strong, broad body.

It was just attraction, but it was inconvenient and misjudged.

'Are you seriously considering it?' she asked abruptly. 'Rosy's idea?'

Akil's brows drew together in surprise, a haughty expression crossing his face, and she winced at her gaucheness, scrambling to explain. 'I meant what I said earlier, it's your decision and not really my business. But in some ways it *is*. I've spent just a few hours in my sister's shoes and I can see why she feels she needs someone permanent on her side, in her team.

It's pretty lonely being a princess. But I still think rushing into an engagement, into a marriage, is just a temporary fix. Because if you're not right for each other she'll end up lonelier than before. I love her,' she said awkwardly. 'And I hate that I can't support her the way a sister should. So maybe I'm interfering but I can't just pretend that this situation isn't worrying me.'

Akil's face softened as she spoke. 'My parents are the perfect example of a hasty ill-thought-out marriage so please be assured I would never rush into any kind of decision. My father was an ambitious man, my mother a country girl. Theirs was a summer romance which should have stayed a lovely memory but instead became an unhappy marriage.'

'That sounds tough. They're still together?'

'Legally, but in reality they see very little of each other. My mother resides at the family home, my father retired after a heart attack eight years ago and now lives mainly in Switzerland.' A heart attack Akil had been responsible for. He could never forget that.

'What happened?'

He didn't answer for a while, instead he paused and turned, his gaze far away on the horizon. 'My mother understood little of politics and hated my father's absences,' he said at last. 'She didn't want a husband who spent most of his time away from home, whereas he wanted a hostess to work the room, someone to charm allies and rivals and know all the gossip, not a shy, paranoid wife who drank too much to work up the courage to have a conversation. They were very different, too different. They made each other unhappy, everyone around them unhappy. With different partners, in another life, they might have been better people, happier people, but we'll never know. If I marry, then I know to look for shared goals, compatibility, not momentary attraction.'

'And love? Do you want love?'

'Love can complicate things. It's not essential for me. Liking and respect mean more to me than love.'

She nodded. 'Thank you for your honesty.'

'And?'

'And what?'

'Did I pass?'

It was her turn to pause and think, to search for the right words. 'I like your honesty and self-awareness and I like the fact that you understand my sister's world and aren't intimidated by it. But I still think she should wait for someone who loves her, not her job, someone who would marry her if she ran the shack on the beach or cleaned her office. And we both know that's not you. But,' she added hurriedly, aware she was interfering in a way she had promised herself not to, 'this isn't about what I think. You two have to decide what's best for you. But can I ask you something?'

'Anything. It doesn't mean I'll answer but you can ask.'

'What's in it for you? You don't strike me as the kind of man who likes to play second fiddle, and I know what a macho culture Asturia has. Do you really see yourself as a consort?'

Akil was floored by Clem's directness, by her honesty. Floored—and intrigued and more than a little impressed. It was so far from the kind of language used in the Senate and at Court, no dancing around, no double-speak. Instead she aimed straight for the heart of the matter and hit it.

'Power,' he said simply. 'If I marry your sister, if I became Prince Consort, then I will always be at the very heart of policy, of government, a decision maker, and influencer.'

Her brow furrowed. 'And that matters to you?'

He laughed shortly. 'I'm a politician. Power is all that matters, Clem.'

'Power for power's sake?'

He hated the uncertainty in her voice. 'No, but without power nothing can be achieved. My family has been at the heart of government for generations, carrying on their work is my destiny whether I like it or not. I haven't always agreed, but when my father had his heart attack and had to take early retirement I promised him that I would fulfil his dreams. That promise means a lot to me. But, as I said, I know the pitfalls of marrying rashly and wrongly. I could achieve great things in my current role too. I just need to weigh it all up.'

'You're close to your father?' He could hear the

wistfulness in her voice as she asked the question and winced.

'I wouldn't say close,' he said wryly. 'I don't think anyone is. My father is...very single-minded. He sees no views but his own, brooks no opinion but his own. He's not an easy man.'

'But he must be proud of you,' she argued. 'Rosy said that you are the youngest, most influential politician in Asturia. And look at your sister, a surgeon in New York. Surely that success means a lot to him?'

'The only thing that would make my father proud is if my sister marries someone he approves of and if I keep climbing the political ladder. Would he approve of me marrying your sister? Without a doubt. Does that influence me? It shouldn't, but...' he shrugged '... I can't deny that his approval is something I seek. Maybe it's a weakness.' He strode on, appalled at how much he'd said, how much he'd revealed, how much he'd exposed. It wasn't like him to speak about his family, about his own insecurities and complicated feelings around his father's push for Akil to do more, to be more. What was it about this woman that made him speak without fear or thought?

He sensed Clem catch up beside him and they walked along in silence for a little longer. 'I understand better than you know,' she said at last, her voice quiet. 'I've only met my father a handful of times, he's never seen me act, never said well done after an exam result, he wasn't there the day I buried my mother. I should hate him, sometimes I do, but more than anything I want him to notice me, want him to be proud of me. I want him to acknowledge I exist.'

Akil didn't know what to say, so instead of words he reached out and took her hand. It was warm in his, fitted him as if made for him to hold. 'I'm sure he knows. He's like my father, not a man to show his emotions.' Akil reluctantly dropped her hand, his own instantly cold.

'True, but knowing it's not personal doesn't make it any easier. I hate that I care. I'm twenty-seven, a grown woman. I shouldn't let the way I feel about him affect my life. But it does. Sometimes I think the only reason I became an actress was to be seen. For the moment the applause rings out for me and I relish the validation that gives me. Pathetic, isn't it?' She shook her head, her mouth compressed tight.

'Not at all,' he said softly. 'We all need validation. What about your mother? Did you have a good relationship with her?'

Clem stared down at the sand, digging into it with her trainer toes. 'I did, we were very close, and I miss her every day. But my mother, she was a force of nature. Not many women would take in their ex-lover's daughter every summer, but my mother loved every waif and stray. Every cat we owned was a runaway she ended up feeding. She was a woman who embraced causes, was at the heart of every campaign, her life was big and filled and sometimes it felt like there was little room for me. Everything was open to anyone who needed it, from Christmases to time together. She just had this endless capacity to scoop people up and look after them, but it meant I always had to share her.' She gave a little laugh. 'I know that I sound so selfish, so spoiled. But sometimes I just wanted to be first with one of my parents just once. If I ever marry, if I ever have kids, it will be different. Maybe it's boring, but I want the house and garden and the kids playing on the trampoline and a husband who loves me. Who sees me. And I want that for Rosy too, because she needs it just as much, more in some ways.'

Akil turned to face her. 'Are you warning me off?'

'No.' She shook her head. 'Not at all. And I'll tell Rosy all about this conversation. I just want you to know that there's more to her than the practical Princess and I bet there's more to you than the ambitious politician and you both need to take that into consideration.'

'I will,' he vowed, and he meant it. 'Come on, I'd better get you back.'

'Have I frightened you off?'

He laughed at that. 'No. In fact you've intrigued me. I'm glad I met you today, Clem. I can't help thinking that in another time, another place, we might have been friends.'

That was only partly true, because in another time and another place he would have liked to have known her a lot better, to have explored the attraction he could feel building between them.

'Friends?' she echoed. 'Yes, I would have liked that. Thank you for today, Akil. Not just for the trip and the food, but for listening.'

'Any time.' And he meant it. It was just a shame their paths were unlikely to cross again.

CHAPTER FIVE

HEART POUNDING, LEGS ACHING, Akil reached his apartment door, opened it and staggered in to collapse on the sofa, his water bottle within reach. Ten miles in the heat of the early afternoon at that pace had been foolish but he'd needed the exercise.

Needed to get Clem out of his mind.

It had been *one* meeting. One afternoon. Just a few hours spent together. But somehow in those hours he'd been more honest with her than he had been with any other human being for years—including himself. He couldn't hide from the question she'd asked him. Instead it swirled throughout his mind relentlessly.

What was in it for him if he married Arrosa?

The answers came quickly and glibly. The same answers he'd given her: power, the ability to get things done, a place at the heart of all decision-making, marriage to someone compatible without any of the emotions or passions that could so easily turn dark and disrupt the equilibrium he craved. And most importantly of all, a chance to show his father that he was not only a true Ortiz, but he was better than him, had achieved more, to not just keep his promise, but to surpass it. Surpass him.

To show himself that giving up his own dreams had been worth it. Arrosa would never have made the suggestion if he'd become a doctor, no matter how skilled or successful he might have been.

Akil sank onto the sofa. They were all compelling reasons, but no matter how often he repeated them he couldn't make them ring true. He liked Arrosa, respected her, but he couldn't imagine spending a lifetime with her. Couldn't imagine treading someone else's path, not again. He'd already compromised his life's purpose once and had vowed never again.

And there were other reasons to refuse, as compelling as those in favour. The Ortizes were an old family but not known outside Asturia. Whoever married Arrosa would be instantly targeted by the world's press. Look what that meant for the royal family, even the unacknowledged daughter: Clem never having the opportunity to build a real relationship with her father, Arrosa resorting to subterfuge to get time alone, bodyguards always around. It wouldn't take much digging to uncover the truth about his family, about his mother's drinking and his father's affairs. There was no way Akil wanted their dirty laundry spread all over the Internet.

At that moment his phone rang and Akil reached for it, only mildly surprised when he saw the Princess's name flash up. She'd messaged him yesterday in reply to his question checking in on her, but of course she'd have had the opportunity to speak to Clem since then. The question was, what had Clem said about their time together? Would the Princess want to pursue her idea or was this call to let him down?

Either way his mind was made up.

'Your Highness, you're alive,' he said as he answered it. 'I have to say it comes as some relief. I've been hoping that I wasn't taken in by a very clever con artist.'

Arrosa laughed, sounding far more relaxed than he'd ever heard her sound before. 'Clem is definitely good enough an actress to be a con artist, but she's far too straight talking.'

Akil smiled wryly. 'I noticed that myself.'

'Yes, I bet you did. She gave me a very interesting account of your conversation. I'm not going to apologise, it's nice to know that someone is looking out for me, but I hope it wasn't too bruising.'

'Bracing maybe, but not bruising. She certainly made me think.'

A trace of caution entered Arrosa's voice. 'She's good at that. That's why she insisted that I take some time away, to give *me* time to look at what I really want for my future. And I have. I know I've only been gone a couple of days but being away from Asturia, away from the court, away from all the pressure and hysteria around the ratification, has been exactly what I needed.'

She paused and he heard her inhale. 'Look, Akil, I think I owe you an apology...'

And there it was, his get-out-of-becoming-royalty card. The relief that filled him was surprisingly overwhelming. 'You don't need to say anything,' he said. 'Let's just pretend that the end of that last conversation never happened.'

'I shouldn't have said anything. I was tired and honestly a little scared of what's happening this year...'

'Listen, I'm flattered, but Clem's right. You deserve more.'

'She said that?'

'And the rest. Arrosa, I hope it goes without saying that I will continue to do all I can to support you, and I hope we can work together for many years. More than that, I hope that we can become friends, real friends.'

'I'd like that. Friends sounds good.'

'In that case, Arrosa, as your friend, can I ask if you're okay?'

She paused again and when she spoke her voice broke a little. 'Yes, in some ways I'm more okay than I have been for a long time. And with Clem covering for me I'm perfectly safe. Life in Asturia can be very suffocating. I am appreciating having the chance to breathe.'

'That's good.'

'It really is. Although I feel guilty that Clem must now be feeling hemmed in, especially as she can't really go out and meet people. So thank you for taking her out, for giving her a chance to see something of the country. I really appreciate it.'

It seemed wrong to be thanked for one of the most enjoyable afternoons he'd had in a long time. 'You don't need to thank me. Your sister's an interesting woman. I enjoyed her company very much—and it strikes me that she knows exactly what she signed up for and is determined to see it through.'

'I offered to swap back, but she won't hear of it.' The relief in Arrosa's voice was palpable; no wonder Clem had insisted on maintaining the charade a little bit longer. Admiration for the Englishwoman filled him. He knew it wasn't easy for her trapped alone in the villa, no matter how beautiful the outlook and luxurious the furnishings.

'I think she's made up her mind to make sure you get a good long break. It's an honourable thing she's doing. She has integrity.'

'She's the best sister I could have. I just wish I could tell the whole world who she is, that she could be part of my life openly. I hope she's not too bored. I know she won't tell me if she is. Life at the estate can be confining, even though I insisted on moving out of the palais into the lake house, and of course she doesn't have work to keep her occupied. She says she's fine and it's a change of scene, but six weeks is a long time to be stuck in one place and alone.'

'I could pop in and check on her, if you want.' Akil's tone was nonchalant but he could feel his pulse speed up at the thought.

'That would be really kind. I would really appreciate it.' Was that amusement in Arrosa's voice?

'I'll see if I can spare the time.'

'Thank you, Akil. For everything.'

'Enjoy your break.' As Akil ended the call he couldn't shake the feeling that he'd been set up in some way.

Maybe checking on Clem wasn't such a good idea. He couldn't deny that he was attracted to her, was intrigued by her, but she was only here for a short while and he had too much going on to invite the kind of complications she posed further into his life. Better to leave her as a memorable momentary encounter.

It was definitely safer and wiser that way.

But he couldn't help wishing that she had been someone else.

For the next few days Akil kept himself too busy to dwell on might-have-beens and if-onlys. It was the parliamentary summer recess and, although there were always briefing notes to read and events to react to, it gave him more time to do the things he truly loved. His dream of being a doctor might have died the day his father had collapsed with a heart attack, but his desire to help, be part of and reform the creaky, unequal health system in Asturia hadn't and he had undertaken mountain rescue training and now volunteered whenever he could. It wasn't what he'd once hoped for, but it was better than nothing and the insight the volunteering gave him helped him push for the reforms the country needed. Even his father approved—a politician who got involved with mountain rescue played well in the polls. Now it was early summer there were plenty of inexperienced hikers walking Asturia's famous mountain trails spraining ankles and getting lost and Akil could easily spend twelve hours a day either coordinating searches or out himself. By the time he got in most evenings he was no good for anything but feeding his cat, grabbing a beer and a sandwich and collapsing on the sofa.

One night he had ended up being called out late to help locate a missing couple who had gone out to look at the stars and not returned and it was the early hours before he got back in. Too wired to sleep, he didn't get to bed until it was almost dawn, sleeping in until noon, almost unheard of with his busy schedule. Looking around, he realised the toll the last few days had taken: he had little food in and his usually neat apartment felt both untidy and unlived in, his cat grumpy and aloof as if indignant at being left alone for so long.

After toasting the end of the loaf and whisking up his last two eggs, he sank onto the sofa and switched on the TV to catch the news. His counterpart had made an announcement about a new security law, and although Akil had read some of the online reactions he was interested to see what the state TV news would say. It was the lead item, and once it was finished he fumbled for the remote to switch over to the sports channel when the sight of a familiar profile made him pause.

To any casual onlooker the profile through the tinted window looked enough like Arrosa for there to be no doubt that this was the Princess being driven back to her home from the capital city. Huge sunglasses shielded most of her face, but the features were familiar, her hair was up in the kind of complicated knot Arrosa favoured and her posture and half-smile were so like Arrosa's own he'd have been fooled himself if he hadn't known better. Warmth filled him as he watched the brief clip of Clem doing what she'd come here to do: fool the press into thinking Arrosa was safe in Asturia.

Warmth that soon faded as he remembered his unfulfilled promise. What had she been doing for the last four days? Had her father come to see her? He doubted it. She was probably all alone.

But she shouldn't be because he'd promised Arrosa he'd look in on her and, unlike many other politicians, he prided himself on keeping his promises. It was wrong of him to stay away just because he was attracted to her—after all, he'd been attracted to lots of women in his life and been perfectly capable of spending time with them.

Before he could think better of it, he quickly texted Arrosa and asked for Clem's number. The reply came back lightning quick, as if Arrosa had been waiting for the question. Akil saved the number and sent a quick exploratory message. There, it was up to her now. He didn't mind either way.

So why was he checking his phone to see the message had been read?

'I'm a fool, Tiger,' he said to his cat, who as usual ignored him. But just as he put his phone out of reach, determined to concentrate on the game, his phone pinged.

His pulse sped as he reached for the phone and checked the name of the sender. Clem. She'd replied. His finger hovered over her name; it shouldn't matter if she gave him a polite brush off or an acceptance, but Akil couldn't deny the thrill of anticipation as he contemplated the message.

Nor could he deny how much he hoped her answer was a yes.

Clem was doing her best to put a Pollyanna spin on her experience. Number one: the weather was beautiful and her tan was coming along nicely. Number two: Arrosa's villa was luxuriously and comfortably furnished with everything she could need and more besides, including some seriously luxurious toiletries, which turned every day into a spa day. Number three: she had the lake at her disposal. The small rowing boat in the boathouse was perfect for spending a couple of hours sculling up and down the lake in, and the water, although cold, was clean and clear enough for some serious swimming. She had got into the habit of taking both a morning dip and sunset swim and on a hot day could be found spending most of the afternoon in the water as well. She just hoped this behaviour wasn't so out of character that it was raising eyebrows amongst bodyguards and staff who saw her from afar. Number four: there was a castle kitchen at her disposal. All she had to do was order her food and it turned up, like magic in her kitchen although she'd never seen anyone bring it over or put it out for her. Even when she didn't order anything the kitchen was mysteriously stocked in her absence, freshly made bread, cream butter, sharp cheese, olives and delicious little cakes replenishing themselves or so it seemed. Her sister might live independently, but she definitely had all the perks of living at home. Her laundry disappeared too, only to return clean and pressed.

And, last but not least, she had the time she needed to think about her future. Time away from Cornwall and the memories of her mother. Time to ready herself to move on to whatever the next stage of her life entailed.

But even Clem at her most determined couldn't be Pollyanna all the time, and when she stopped the reality of her situation came crashing down on her. She had been here nearly a week and her father still hadn't found time to come and see her. She wasn't so naive as to expect him to drop everything and rush over straight away, although that would have been nice, but she had hoped that now she was just a half-hour drive away he might have been able to carve out a little bit of time to see her. *Idiot*, she scolded herself. She should have known better than to expect anything from him.

He'd made sure she was materially provided for and that was all she realistically could and should expect.

Plus, although she'd told herself that what she needed was time away, it turned out you really could have too much of a good thing. Her days seemed endless and her mind was whirling with possibilities and fears. It seemed impossible that less than two years ago she had been sharing a flat with friends in Battersea, filling her days with classes and auditions and sometimes even work, her evenings with bars and restaurants and plays. She'd never doubted that she would make it, that her talent and drive weren't enough. It was just a matter of when her break would be, not if.

But then she'd received the call from her mother and all that fell away, her life became a worried regime of hospital appointments and waiting rooms, too brief moments of hope and long days of bitter grief, watching her home turn slowly into a hospice for those last long, painful months.

For the three months after the packed-out funeral she had been numb with grief, wandering along the beach, curling up in her mother's bed, until the opportunity to play Juliet and the possibility of the theatre's privatisation had galvanised her back into some kind of action and routine. She'd joined the Save Our Theatre campaign, aware of just how proud her mother would have been, attending planning meetings and organising petitions, turning the cottage into a campaign headquarters just as it had been throughout her life. But although both had filled her thoughts and hours, neither were a solution to the question of what came next. In the end she'd followed her sister's advice and written a list of possibilities along with pros and cons and scores out of ten for how each one inspired her. It was time to revisit it.

Almost reluctantly she brought up the file on her tablet and set it before her on the outside table. She had a fresh coffee and a bowl of mixed fruit so she couldn't distract herself with a trip to the kitchen. Taking a deep breath, Clem read through the short list.

First and most obvious: acting. Not only had she trained for it, but she still had an agent somehow, despite her long break. Plus, she'd loved playing Juliet and was enjoying impersonating her sister and getting into character as the Crown Princess, even if it was for just an hour sitting in a car. But she knew that at some point in the last eighteen months she'd lost the resilience she needed to face the constant rejection that awaited every aspiring actor. Did she really want the high point of her month to be a recall for a toothpaste ad? Did she want to spend another three months as an understudy, sitting in the dressing room every night trying not to wish a broken ankle on the star? At twenty-five that had just been part and parcel of the process, but at twenty-seven she needed more than constant knock-backs and waiting around for her break.

Secondly, and maybe even more obviously, she could follow so many of her drama school friends into teaching. Clem sighed. It was a worthy career and her mother, with her zeal and passion for change, had been a wonderful teacher. But she didn't feel a vocation and surely that was important?

Or she could carry on putting off making a decision and go travelling, hoping she would find her vocation as she did so. After all, her mother had backpacked around the world more than once before enrolling at the Sorbonne. She had been full of stories of the time she had worked in a school in Ecuador or had crewed on a Greenpeace ship. Simone Beaumont, trying to save the world even as a backpacker. She'd always encouraged Clem to follow her example and why not? It wasn't as if she didn't have the money and the time. But she didn't want to do it alone.

She didn't want to do any of it alone, not any more. She wanted people of her own to live and laugh and love with. That was what mattered to her. That was what she needed.

But that wasn't something she could just make happen.

Clem sat back and rubbed her eyes. 'Get over yourself, Beaumont,' she muttered. 'You are luckier than so many other people. You have a home and you don't need to worry about money, you have qualifications and prospects even if you're not sure what they are yet. Stop feeling sorry for yourself. What would Maman say?'

Simone Beaumont had had no time for self-pity.

Her phone pinged and, glad of the distraction, she

picked up her phone to look at the notification—an unknown number.

'Ooh, what kind of spam will it be? An uncollected parcel or a tax rebate? Or maybe it's not spam but a producer hearing about how devastating I was as Juliet and wanting me in the West End.'

She missed her mother's cat. Talking out loud didn't feel as foolish when she was addressing Gus, who always seemed on the verge of saying something wise.

She clicked it open, unprepared for the thrill of anticipation that ran through her when she saw who it was from.

Akil.

It had been five days since their lunch. After their parting she'd not expected to hear from him again, although a tiny part of her had hoped to be proved wrong, especially once Arrosa had told her that they had decided to remain just friends and colleagues after all. But after a couple of days had passed with no word from him, she'd done her best to put him out of her mind. Now here he was. What did he want?

The message was short and to the point.

If you're still finding it hard to play tourist, I have a spare afternoon tomorrow. Shall I pick you up? Let me know. Akil

Clem sat back, unable to stop a small smile playing on her mouth. The part of her that had stopped knowing how to enjoy life over the last eighteen months, the part of her that knew that sometimes the worst did happen, advised caution. But the part of her that had propelled her here, that acknowledged how very attractive she found Akil—and was all too aware that Akil was now unattached—urged her towards acceptance. Without stopping to think she pressed reply and quickly typed.

That sounds great. I'm due another trip out as Arrosa, so why don't I get Henri to take me somewhere where I can do a quick change afterwards and then meet you at your apartment? Send me your address and let me know what time. Thanks so much. Clem

She read it over quickly, and then before she lost her nerve she pressed send. Excitement and nerves warred but she pushed both back. It was an afternoon out, nothing more, nothing less. She deserved some fun.

Clem did her best to return her attention to the list, but right now the future seemed far away. Tomorrow she was going sightseeing with an attractive man. That was good enough for now.

CHAPTER SIX

AKIL STRODE ACROSS his apartment to pick out a different shirt and realised that he was whistling. Again.

Actually, he'd been whistling all morning. He'd even sung in the shower and it was a long time since he'd done that. Not since he'd accepted his role as a politician in fact. Yet here he was. Whistling and deliberating over his outfit. As if he were fifteen again and arranging to meet a girl on a beach.

At least his hands weren't clammy, and he'd learned not to gel his hair in the last fifteen years. But maybe he should channel that boy and lose the suit. It was a little over the top for an afternoon sightseeing. He checked his watch. Clem would be here soon so if he was going to change he'd better do it now. He didn't want to greet her half naked.

He'd just finished changing when his buzzer sounded and he strolled across to the videocam and pressed the button but, instead of Clem, Henri, suited and stern, filled the small screen.

'Subject ready. All clear?' Henri barked and Akil resisted the urge to salute.

'Everything's fine, send her up,' he said easily and pressed the button, opening the front door.

Akil waited by the open door, trying to ignore his heart hammering with anticipation. Light footsteps tripped up the stairs and there she was at his door, dressed like the tourist she was rather than the Crown Princess she'd pretended to be earlier that day, in a pretty vintage-style green sundress teamed with a denim jacket and trainers, and white sunglasses, her hair cascading loose and wild.

She looked utterly beautiful.

'Hi,' he said, mouth dry.

'Hi.' She hovered on the other side of the door, and he stood back.

'You found it okay? No problem getting here without anyone thinking you were your sister?'

'All good thanks to Henri,' she said. 'I did a quick change in a secret underground car park he knows and then he brought me here in a different car. I feel like a glamorous spy!'

'Where is he?'

'Lurking outside in case anyone followed us. Obviously a high level of paranoia is part of all bodyguard training.'

'A prerequisite,' he agreed. 'Ah, do you want to come in?'

'I thought you'd never ask.' Her hazel eyes gleamed, more green than brown today, thanks to the vibrancy of her dress. She stepped inside and glanced around. 'So this is where Asturia's most promising young politician lives?'

'It's where *I* live.' Akil tried to see his home through her eyes. His apartment was in a medieval building, all thick stone walls and tall arched windows. The floor gleamed honey brown, the old wood polished to a shine and covered by antique faded rugs. The walls were exposed stone, bookcases lining one wall, filled with books picked up over the years. Faded brown leather sofas grouped around the fireplace, one occupied by a fat ginger cat. Arrosa gave a little cry of delight and went straight over to rub its head.

'You have a *cat*?' She couldn't have sounded more incredulous if he'd had a panther in his apartment.

'You're not allergic?'

'No, I love cats. What's his name?'

'How do you know it's a he?'

'Ginger cats usually are.' She smiled as the cat rolled over to expose a fluffy white tummy. 'Oh, aren't you handsome? Name?'

'Tiger.' Akil tried not to grimace as she unsuccessfully tried to hide a smile.

'Oh, very original.'

'I didn't name him.'

'Really.' She gave him a disbelieving look. 'Who did?'

'A neighbour's kid. Tiger belongs to them really but they had to move abroad and couldn't take him so I said I would look after him.'

'So a cat man not a dog man. Interesting!'

'I wouldn't say that. But I live in an apartment, I work a lot. It wouldn't be fair on a dog. You?'

'I like both.'

'Very diplomatic.'

'And true. We always had cats growing up. Maman said we were too busy for a dog, it wouldn't be fair. But one day I will have one—and several cats too.' She scratched the top of Tiger's head again and the feline tilted his head up, eyes half closed, purring under the caresses. Akil felt a stab of something that felt remarkably and absurdly like jealousy.

'Come on, I'll show you the rest.'

It didn't take long to show her the open-plan kitchen and dining room and the small second bedroom he used as an office. They didn't go into his bedroom; it felt too intimate. Instead he swung the door open to show her the neat room, and he just indicated the bathroom. Clem noted every detail, asking about the photographs and paintings he'd chosen, lingering over his books and greeting them like old friends.

'I like your apartment,' she said, leafing through a poetry anthology. 'But it's not what I expected.'

'What did you expect?'

'Something to match your car, all modern and sleek and styled. This…' She waved a hand. 'This feels like a home.'

'Thank you.' He tried for light, but he was surprisingly touched by her words. 'I think so too.'

'So what's the plan?'

'We're going to be tourists in the city. I hope you're wearing sturdy shoes. We have a lot of ground to cover.'

She didn't answer for a long moment, anxiety creasing her forehead, and he looked enquiringly at her.

'The city?' she said at last. 'That's pretty busy. Is it safe?'

'Asturia's one of the safest countries in the world.'

'I mean for me, for you, for us to be seen together? Won't people wonder who you're with? You're not exactly unknown and in my experience young, single, prominent men attract attention, especially when accompanied by women.'

'The Asturian press is a lot more respectful of private lives than most of the European press and most people aren't interested in what politicians do in their own time as long as they're not obviously corrupt. If I took you to an official event or we were seen together at the races or a regatta or some other society occasion, then we would expect to be photographed and questions asked, but not if we're just walking around the city. And although you look a lot like your sister, you're not so alike that anyone would seriously mistake you for her, especially when you dress so casually. We're safe.'

She exhaled and he saw her visibly relax. 'Okay, that's reassuring. In that case what are we waiting for?'

'You to stop reading poetry.'

She closed the book and carefully reshelved it. 'Done! Come on, then, let's go.'

'After you.' He held the door open for her to precede him out and closed it behind him, realising how much he was looking forward to the afternoon. To spending time with Clem, to showing her the city he loved. This might only be their second meeting but he was already comfortable with her in a way that was unusual for Akil. His family, his position, his own natural reserve created barriers between him and most people, but somehow Clem had effortlessly battered them aside without him even noticing. This afternoon was supposed to be a favour for Arrosa, a day out for Clem, but it was turning into an unexpected treat for him too.

Clem broke into a skip as she walked through the busy streets at Akil's side, relieved to be out and about, surrounded by people like a normal person once again. Akil was right, nobody gave them a second look, even though Akil still cut an imposing figure dressed down in jeans and a T-shirt.

Although maybe he was *especially* imposing dressed down in jeans and a T-shirt. The grey T-shirt was faded, clearly well worn, but it looked as if it had been expensive, well cut and fitted, clinging to toned arms and showing off the breadth of his chest and shoulders, the flatness of his stomach. His jeans were perfectly cut, riding low on narrow hips and showcasing what she couldn't help but notice was a very nice butt—she was only human after all—and clinging to muscled thighs.

The sun shone, a perfect Mediterranean mid June day, and she was glad of her sunglasses as it bounced and sparkled off the paved streets, marble pavements and shop windows as she eagerly looked around, drinking in every sight, sound and smell.

The Asturian capital city, Asturia Valle, was a medieval city set in a large valley and ringed by the mountains that made up the bulk of the small country. Beautiful as the coastline was, it was the mountains that lured the tourists in, skiers in winter, walkers in summer, the blue lakes that dotted the valleys and mountain shelfs a magnet for skaters, swimmers and water sports enthusiasts.

Clem wanted to explore every inch of her country. And this was the perfect start. Akil knew exactly where he was going, steering her to one of the tourist booths dotted around the city, where he left her for a couple of minutes, reappearing with a map and a couple of tickets.

'I've got us these,' he said, handing her one of the tickets.

Clem squinted at it as she made out the small printed words. 'A one-day city pass?'

'This gets us in everywhere.'

'Everywhere?'

'The castle, the city museum, the zoo, the cable car, the funicular railway, the steam railway, the cathedral, the walking tours, all five of them, discounts at the theatre and the opera house and several restaurants and cafes. Pretty much everywhere.' His smile was smug, but she had to allow he deserved it. This was a great idea.

'That *does* seem to cover pretty much everywhere. What time is it?'

'Just after one.'

'And they are one-day passes?'

'Yep.'

'Then we have no time to waste.' She whirled around to look at a nearby sign with a city map displayed on it. 'Okay. We need to approach this strategically. What is the nearest attraction?'

Akil stared at her, clearly bemused. 'You want to do it *all*?'

'Well,' she conceded. 'Maybe not *both* the theatre and the opera house, and obviously trying all the restaurants and all five of the walking tours would be a stretch, but let's try and do as much as we can before midnight when the tickets run out.'

'Is this a challenge?'

'Are you up to it?' She removed her sunglasses and met that cool amused gaze, her mouth responding automatically to the smile in his eyes.

'I'm an Ortiz. I never turn down a challenge.'

'Good to know. Okay, where shall we start? Where's nearest?'

'The castle.' He paused. 'Are you comfortable with that? Your father doesn't make a habit of crossing over into the public areas, but you never know. This might be the day he makes an exception. It could be awkward if you bumped into him in public.'

Clem bit her lip as she considered it. The castle was a much rebuilt and redesigned fortress perched on the edge of the valley overlooking the mountain pass that had once been the only way into the city. Most of it was now open to the public, who could tour the old staterooms, the rooms occupied by long-dead royalty, the courtyards and gardens, as well as the dungeons and defensive walls showcasing the country's often violent history.

But well away from the public areas were the royal apartments and the offices of the court, with a private entrance to parliament, whose equally impressive medieval building was right next door.

The royal apartments comprised living quarters for the King and his family as well as rooms for courtiers and staff and reception rooms for ambassadors and other dignitaries, plus rooms of varying sizes for official events.

As it was the parliamentary recess most parliamentarians and the aristocrats who made up the upper chamber were at home in their country estates or their seaside retreats. But the King, as Clem knew too well, rarely returned to the Palais d'Artega, staying at Court year-round. Which meant he might well be in the castle right now and she would be in the same building as him for the first time in almost a decade. But as a tourist she'd be as removed from him as she was when she was at home in Cornwall.

'He knows I'm here,' she said, trying to keep the bitterness from her voice. 'But to be honest he hasn't seen me for so long he'd be more likely to recognise you than me. Let's do it. I've always wanted to visit.'

She shook the lingering sadness off and consulted the map in front of them, tracing the routes with her finger. 'Okay, I propose we spend an hour in the castle, half an hour each in the cathedral and the city museum, get the cable car up the mountain and the funicular down and then take the railway to the zoo for the hour before closing time. If we leave promptly we should make the evening walking tour, which possibly gives us time for tonight's concert at the opera house. We'll need refreshments so a snack after we've gone up the cable car and dinner after the concert. What do you think?'

Akil pretended to sag against the post, holding the map. 'I'm exhausted just listening to all that.'

'Too much for you?' She turned to face him, hands on her hips, allowing a flirtatious challenge to enter her voice, even as she acknowledged to herself that she was skating on very thin ice. This wasn't a date. But that didn't mean she couldn't enjoy it.

He held her gaze, suddenly serious, and Clem felt the air suck out of her lungs.

'Too much for me? Not at all. But I'm worried about you, my lady. Can you handle it?'

'It's my suggestion, remember. Come on, we're wasting precious time.' Clem rammed her sunglasses back onto her face, glad to break the disturbingly intense connection, and marched away, knowing he was right behind her, laughing as she strode as fast as she could as he effortlessly matched her stride. It was companionable. Nice.

She just needed to dial the flirting down to zero.

The castle was as fascinating and informative as Clem had hoped, and far more macabre than she'd expected, especially the dank underground rooms full of terrifying-looking devices.

'Nice types, my ancestors,' she muttered as she took in the rusted manacles stained with what she fervently hoped wasn't blood.

Akil nodded. 'Mine too. Before they dominated parliament they were generals and military leaders. I bet they condemned a lot of people to these rooms.'

'What does that do?' She wandered over to a tall, beamed contraption hung with ropes to read the horribly visual interpretation board and shuddered. 'I could have quite happily lived without ever knowing that.'

'What kind of mind even invents something like that?' Akil was standing right behind her. At least two inches separated them, but she was acutely aware of every part of him, the proximity between them lighting up every nerve.

'No wonder they put this bit before the Crown jewels. We'll need all the glitter and pomp to wipe this out of our minds. If I never come down here again it's too soon.'

The tour led them through a bewildering array of corridors and courtyards and Akil kept her entertained with what Clem was pretty sure were completely made-up facts about every part. She couldn't remember the last time she'd laughed, really laughed, the last time it had been this easy to be with someone.

The last time it had been this easy to just be.

Finally they reached a dark, heavily guarded building where they followed the path around display cases filled with fur-trimmed cloaks and padded surcoats, jewelled scabbards and wicked-looking swords until they reached a big display case set into a thick wall. Sightseers were kept well back by a rope, and, more effectively, guards at either end holding serious-looking rifles, in case anyone decided to try and steal the valuable items.

Clem stared at the state jewels in a mixture of awe and a painful melancholy, a sense of loss she couldn't quite explain. This was her family history but she had to see it as a paying tourist, always on the outside, held back by ropes and shatterproof glass and guards. She tried to hide her feelings, her voice unnaturally bright. 'The crown is huge! It must be really heavy. Like wearing a concrete hat.'

'It's very bling,' he said, blinking. 'I've seen it plenty of times but I'd never really noticed how many jewels it has before. And just how *gold* it is.'

'Maybe because the chain of office is equally bling.' Clem stared at the heavy gold chain studded with rubies. 'The sceptre is pretty big too. The whole lot together is very dazzling. I wouldn't say it's particularly tasteful though. All that velvet and gold and those huge rubies. It's a bit try hard.'

'The King makes it look so effortless,' Akil said.

'He makes the crown look like it weighs nothing. Whether you agree with him or not politically, he is good at what he does. He works well with the Assembly and controls the Senate. It needs a strong person to wear that crown.'

'Rosy is strong, one of the strongest people I know,' Clem said, still transfixed by the crown. 'But no one should have to bear that weight alone. If only I could be by her side, support her the way a sister should, make sure she wasn't alone. Seeing this makes it all much more understandable.'

'It all?'

'What she asked you. I almost wish...' She paused and he looked down at her, his expression inscrutable.

'What do you almost wish?'

'That things were different and you could have said yes...been what, who she needed.'

His expression didn't change, his eyes dark pools she was losing herself in. 'I could never have been who or what she needed. I knew it straight away, I think. I just had to work through it. And I am glad I realised in time.'

'In time?'

Clem couldn't breathe, couldn't move, all she could do was look up at him, so close she could see his dilated pupils, the rise and fall of his chest. It would be so easy to close the small distance between them and press herself against him but she was paralysed by the blood surging through her, the roaring in her ears.

'It's one thing to marry out of respect and friendship and support. They can be good bedrocks of a successful union, I believe that. But it would be unfair to marry one woman while attracted to her sister. Don't you think?'

Thinking was beyond her. She was caught in his mesmerising gaze, dark and hot, stirring desire throughout her. 'I...' She stared at him a moment longer, trying to find something to say—*I think you're attractive too. What does this mean? Kiss me*—when the sound of a family approaching, children arguing noisily, broke the spell and Akil stepped back, a rueful smile on his lips.

'Come on,' he said. 'We've got a long itinerary and I think we're at least five minutes behind.'

Yet as they walked away she couldn't help but look back at the case and the glittering crown that represented her sister's future. Akil might find her attractive—and she might reciprocate his feelings—but she had no place, no future here. She couldn't let herself forget it.

CHAPTER SEVEN

Akil couldn't remember the last time he'd enjoyed an afternoon so much nor the last time he'd had the leisure—or inclination—to dedicate a day to nothing but fun. It had been a genius plan to explore his city with fresh eyes, joining the tourists on the well-trodden trails around the sights. They'd done a mad dash around the cathedral and the city museum and made up the lost time as they did so because—as Clem said a little guiltily—there were only so many religious paintings a person could admire before they all merged into one.

'Do you think they'd ever actually seen a baby before?' she asked as they checked out their twentieth old master rendition of a Madonna and Child, this one with a baby Jesus almost the same size as his mother. The one before the baby had been the approximate size of an orange. 'They remind me of my attempts of art at school and I always got a *Could do better.* Who knew I was actually painting in the style of the fourteenth century? My teachers should have given me more credit.'

After the museum they enjoyed the breathtaking views from the cable car that ascended up to the mountain shelf overlooking the city, a popular day-trip destination, where they stopped for a snack before taking the funicular back down and catching the small steam train to the zoo.

'I have very conflicted feelings about zoos,' Clem said as they wandered around the world-renowned attraction, known for its ground-breaking breeding programmes and successful conservation work. 'I know that if this tiger wasn't here it wouldn't be roaming free in the jungle, it wouldn't exist at all. And I know that if it wasn't for places like this there might be no tigers at all in a few years' time, but it seems wrong to see such beautiful creatures caged up, for us to be able to stand and stare while they have nowhere to hide.'

Her face softened as she watched the tiger prowl, its tail swishing irritably. 'I wish I could set you free.'

'Now that would make an interesting headline. *Fake Princess Sets Tiger on Horrified Population.*' He gave her a keen glance. 'Do you think you might be over identifying?'

'Hmm?'

'Beautiful creature locked away?'

She laughed a little nervously. 'I'm not…'

'Beautiful? I hope you know that's not true.'

Their glances caught and held and Akil could feel his blood thundering around his body as her cheeks pinked, her pupils dilated. He'd felt in his very bones that this attraction was not one-sided, but her reaction gave him all the proof he needed. Primal jubilation filled him as he ran one finger slowly down her cheek. She stood acquiescent, quivering under his touch, her gaze still fixed on his.

'Akil…' Her voice was husky, half protest half entreaty, and he dropped his hand, fighting the urge to pull her close, to taste those full lips. 'I…' She cleared her throat, adorably flustered, still flushed a rosy pink. 'I was going to say locked away. I can get out, you know, it's just not easy. Besides, it's only temporary. Come on, we need to get on or we'll miss the walking tour.'

'Yes, ma'am.' He saluted. 'Begging your pardon for forgetting the itinerary, ma'am.'

She threw him a mock stern look. 'I'll let you off this once.'

Despite Clem's protestation that they would be late, Akil insisted on stopping at the food cart at the zoo exit to buy them tart chilled lemonade and toasted cheese sandwiches, hot and oozing with melted cheese. 'We've walked miles already and your schedule doesn't allow for dinner until after the opera,' he said as he handed her the sandwich. 'A man's got to eat. Especially this man.'

'That's good to know about you. Hangry unless fed, noted. Mmm, that's delicious.' She took another, bigger bite, laughing as she tried not to spill any cheese on her dress, and Akil couldn't help but join in as he watched her inelegantly scoop up a glop of cheese with her tongue.

It had been a long time since he'd laughed this much, talked this much, about nothing and everything. Clem was easy company—apart from the way his body reacted to her every move, the way he wanted to pull her close and kiss her until they were both breathless.

But she was here for such a short while and her life was complicated enough. It wasn't for him to complicate it further than he already had and it would be too easy to do so, considering how thrown she'd been when he'd told her how attractive he found her.

'You are very good at saluting,' Clem said as they walked along the pretty pedestrianised street that led back to the centre, flowers in planters on either side and leafy trees protecting them from the worst of the sun.

'You can thank national service for that.'

'Of course. It seems so strange to me that you have to give up two years of your life! Even Rosy had to enlist before she went to university.'

'Every Asturian does, even royalty. Your sister and mine worked in the medical corps together. But it wasn't two years for me, it was four. Two in the infantry, like all good Ortiz men, then two in the secret service. I came out at twenty-two to go to university.'

'What did you study?'

'Economics and politics of course.'

'Of course. Was that what you wanted to do?'

And that was the million-dollar question. Usually Akil went along with the fiction that studying politics in readiness for taking the Ortiz seat in the upper house was his own ambition. It was easier that way.

But he didn't want to dissimulate with Clem. It was nice having someone he could be himself with. 'Truthfully no. I had a place at medical school.'

'Really? Like your sister?'

'Only I'm older and got my place first, so really she was copying me.' He couldn't help grinning as he said it. 'The sibling rivalry between us is real. Elixane hates that she's both four years younger than me and a girl in a country which still favours male heirs.'

'You should be flattered that she wanted to follow in your footsteps. It's nice that you inspire her.'

'I don't think she'd put it that way, but I'll be sure to mention it to her.' His grin widened as he imagined his sister's indignant response if he referred to himself as her inspiration. 'Honestly, I'm not sure why we both chose that path. There are no medics in the family.'

'So what happened? Why didn't you take up your place?'

Akil carried on walking, deliberating how much to say. He rarely allowed himself to think about that time. 'I don't know if you know this, but the seats in the Senate, our upper chamber, are hereditary—and the line of inheritance is on the male side. Even when things change next month those seats which belong to the old aristocratic titles, like mine, will only go to males—it's the same in the UK.'

'I am beginning to sympathise with your sister,' Clem murmured.

'We're making some headway in reforming this, but we have a long way to go.'

'Of course,' she said consideringly. 'Inheritance really should go through the matriarchal line. Before DNA testing, it was obvious who the mother was but the father was taken on trust.'

'You would get on far too well with my sister, she often makes the same point, although, as I tell her, I am still older and that makes me the head of the family and future Duc no matter if the law changed.'

'I'll bet she loves that.'

'She really does, although occasionally she will admit that she is much happier as a younger sibling—there's a lot more freedom for her than for me. But what you need to understand is that the Duc d'Ortiz has always been an important person in Asturia, for centuries we were in charge of the military. Sometimes the Duc was the Crown's right hand, even Regent on two occasions, sometimes its most implacable opposition. Since the Second World War, as Asturia's military need has waned, my family have turned to politics to build power and influence, with the Duc using his hereditary seat to make sure they are right at the centre. My father made it clear that I was shirking the responsibility inherent in my future title by not pursuing politics.'

Clem frowned. 'But your father is still alive, right?

So why couldn't you do both? Be a doctor now and then a politician later?'

Exactly what he had pointed out eight years ago. 'My father is not a man to do things by half, not work, not food, not drink.' Not women. 'Nor is he a man to take his doctor's advice. He has little time for the medical profession. He sees it as a job for the bourgeoisie, not his heir. His health was not good eight years ago so when we disagreed and it got far too heated he collapsed. He nearly died of a heart attack.'

A heart attack Akil had known was a risk, and yet he still hadn't walked away when the argument had started to get out of hand, had still allowed all his anger at his father, at his selfishness and implacability, to pour out. Had enjoyed reducing his father to incoherent rage, out-arguing him. What kind of man did that make him? No better than his father for all his self-righteousness.

Clem stopped, her hand flying to her mouth as she turned to him. 'Oh, Akil, I am so sorry. It must have been terrifying.'

'It was. Worse was the knowledge that I was responsible.'

Her forehead creased. 'How? You said yourself that he didn't take his doctor's advice. Surely that's on him.'

'True,' he acknowledged. 'But I was young and implacable as only the young can be, convinced I alone knew the right path. I wanted to be a doctor and yet I allowed a man I knew to be at risk to get agitated to lose control. Worse, I goaded him. Pushed him beyond what was safe. What kind of son, what kind of aspiring doctor, does that?'

'Families make everything complicated. We're not always our best selves with them,' she said, laying a comforting hand on his arm. 'So you gave up your dream? As what? Atonement?'

In part. 'I promised him that if he just held on I would do my duty as the Vicomte d'Ortiz. So when he recovered he stepped down on grounds of ill health and the Senate voted to allow me to take the Ortiz seat early. My father now spends most of his time in Switzerland still not looking after his health and I am as you see me. Fulfilling my promise.'

'Do you ever regret it?'

'I don't allow myself to regret it.' Suddenly he regretted saying so much. 'Come, there's still a lot to fit in.' Without looking back, he marched on. Because that was what he did, eyes fixed on the future, no dwelling on the past. It was easier that way. It was safer. It was what he knew.

Clem stole a glance at Akil as they walked towards the medieval square where the walking tour was due to meet. He'd been silent over the last few minutes, seemingly lost in thought.

Not that it was surprising. It must be hard, living one life when you had once had a vocation for something else. But then again wasn't that the future she was facing? It would be some consolation if she was as successful in her second-choice career as Akil was in his.

But she still ached with sympathy for him. Maybe it was better having a father as hands off as hers rather than one who raged and manipulated and used a promise extracted on a possible deathbed to push his son down a path he didn't want. And it wasn't as if Akil wanted to give it all up to become a pop star or something equally ridiculous! He wanted to be a doctor—every parent she knew would throw a party if their child expressed such a wish.

Her mother would have. She'd supported Clem, it hadn't been in her nature not to, but she'd have preferred Clem to have chosen something more worthy than acting.

She peeked at Akil again; his expression was still far away. 'What's the tour?' she asked, wanting to break the silence.

He blinked as if he had forgotten where they were going. 'Hmm? Oh, the twilight tour. Apparently it's ghosts, ghouls and gore. Ready?'

She pulled a face. 'I'm not sure I can face ghouls and gore after the dungeons earlier. I'm already dreading the nightmares.'

'This is our heritage. We should embrace it.'

'Not too enthusiastically, I hope.'

'We don't have to go on the tour,' he reminded her. 'We could always skip it and do something else.'

'Skip it? And lose the challenge? Absolutely not.'

'Of course.' She was relieved to hear laughter in his voice. 'The schedule. How could I forget?'

'So this finishes at seven, conveniently right by the opera house, which gives us time to get our tickets. I hope they're not sold out. What is it?'

Akil pulled out his phone and checked. 'There are tickets and it's *Tosca*—oh, good, there's a warning. Contains depictions of torture, murder and suicide. There's a definite theme to the day so far.'

'In that case I want to eat at the cheesiest, most kitsch restaurant as possible afterwards,' Clem warned him. 'I'll need it after all the horror and death.'

'I'll see what I can do,' he promised.

They lapsed into another silence, but this one was more companionable, their stride perfectly in time, arms swinging together, so close their fingers almost touched. Almost.

As they entered the square she saw a small group of people waiting by the meeting point. A couple of families, several older couples and a young couple who smiled as Akil and Clem approached. They probably saw a mirror of themselves, a couple enjoying a romantic break in the picturesque ancient city, and Clem allowed herself to bask in the fantasy that she and Akil were here properly together. Before she thought better of it she reached out and took his hand, slipping her fingers through his. She felt him momentarily freeze before his fingers clasped hers, warm and strong, his thumb circling the back of her hand, a minute gesture that shuddered through her.

'Okay, gather round.' A tour guide dressed in the colourful Asturian national costume called out in English and then again in French. 'Does everyone have their tickets ready? Great. Okay, let's begin right here, with the great siege of 1412.'

Despite the theme the tour was a lot of fun, the guide engaging as well as knowledgeable, and Clem found herself laughing uncontrollably as he took them on a whistle-stop tour of the least palatable parts of Asturian history, pitching his spiel perfectly between scaring the children just enough and amusing the adults. Throughout the tour she was aware of Akil's hand in hers, the breadth of him, height of him, the sheer handsomeness of him taking her breath away, the wonder that he wanted to be here with her—the wonder that he wanted her—dizzying her. Possibility hung thick between them, the possibility that this adventure wouldn't end when the tickets expired at midnight, but this Cinderella might keep her bewitched existence a little longer.

Just a few hours ago she had been reminding herself that she had no future here, warning herself to be careful, but now those sensible thoughts belonged to someone else. What did the future matter when there was now?

The group clustered around a cannon that pointed out towards the mountain pass and was, they were informed, haunted by a young soldier who had refused to abandon his post when the city was under attack and stayed there still to protect Asturia. The guide's voice had dropped to a carrying whisper as he told the tale and the children on the tour pressed forward, eyes wide in the deepening dusk, only to jump back in exaggerated fright when he boomed out the end. As they jumped, one tripped and before anyone could catch her fell into the road—and straight into the path of a car. Time seemed to slow as the small body was scooped up onto the low bonnet as the car screeched to a desperate but too late halt.

Everyone was paralysed with shock and fear—everyone but Akil. He dropped Clem's hand and sprang into the road even as the car finally braked, shouting instructions to call an ambulance. He bent over the girl, his finger on her neck, and then ran his hands carefully over her.

'Stay back, she needs space,' he called out. 'Where are her parents?' An American couple were at his side in seconds, one holding a smaller girl, faces pale and shocked. 'She's breathing,' he reassured them. 'That's a good thing. Her leg is certainly broken, and I can't rule out internal bleeding or concussion, but the hospital isn't far.'

'Are you a doctor?' the woman asked, and Clem was proud to see he didn't wince as he shook his head.

'No, but I volunteer with the mountain rescue and I am paramedic trained. She'll be in good hands, I promise.'

It took the ambulance less than ten minutes to arrive and Clem stayed back as Akil assisted the paramedics as they moved the still unconscious girl onto the trolley and checked her over. The rest of the group were still huddled together, silent, and as she was loaded into the ambulance Akil came over.

'I am going to accompany her to the hospital,' he told Clem quietly. 'Her parents don't speak Asturian or French and it will be helpful for them to have a translator.'

'Of course,' she said hurriedly. 'I told Henri I'd call him as soon as we were done, so he can collect me and I can transform back on the way back to the palais. It's dark now so I only need to get through the gates and the guards never check Henri anyway.'

'I'm sorry we didn't make the opera.'

'Another time.' But even as she said it she could feel the possibility slipping away. In the cold light of day would this live-for-the-moment promise she had made to herself last? Or would she remember all the reasons getting close to Akil—to anyone in Asturia—was such a bad idea?

Akil drew her close, his arm an anchor. 'Of course. We'll rearrange and we can pick up our schedule. Carry on as we planned.'

'That would be lovely.' She could hear the lack of conviction in her words and she knew he heard it too. Before she could back away he bent his head and brushed her mouth with his. It was the briefest of caresses, almost chaste, but the touch lit her up, flames swooshing through her from the tips of her fingers to the ends of her toes. All she could do was look up dazed as Akil smiled ruefully and stepped away. 'I'll see you soon.'

Clem stared after him, drinking in his tall figure, allowing herself one last look at the way his jeans encased him so perfectly, the fit of his T-shirt, the strength and grace in the fully muscled body. She swallowed, fighting the need to run after him, to call his name, to kiss him once again. Instead she watched him step into the ambulance and exchange a few words with the paramedic before the doors shut and he was driven away.

'Goodbye,' she said at last. But whether she meant for tonight or for keeps, she didn't know.

CHAPTER EIGHT

It was late by the time Clem returned to the villa but despite her exhaustion she found it hard to sleep, replaying the events of the day over and over, lingering on the brief kiss until she had no idea what was memory and what was fantasy. When she finally got up the next day she was convinced she hadn't slept at all, and her activity watch confirmed her suspicions. With a groan she took her coffee and a book onto the comfortable terrace sofa and curled up, promising herself a lazy day.

She'd messaged Akil last night to check on the injured girl and he'd promised to send her an update. To her relief when she checked her phone, she found a message from Akil sent some time early that morning letting her know that although the girl's leg was broken and she'd severely bruised her ribs, there was no internal bleeding and she'd somehow managed to avoid concussion. The hospital were going to keep her in for several days for observation but she'd been very lucky.

Clem pressed the reply arrow and then sat there for some time staring at the blank screen before typing a simple thank-you. After another couple of minutes' thought she added:

You were brilliant yesterday.

Before she could think better of it she sent the message and then lay back on the sofa and stared up at the cloudless sky, mind an exhausted whirl.

What would have happened if there had been no accident? Would they have gone to the opera? For dinner? Would possibility have hung in the air throughout? Would she have gone back to Akil's apartment? And if so, then what?

She'd never know…

At that moment her phone vibrated and when she picked it up her sister's name filled the screen. Clem took a deep breath and then answered it, injecting as much vibrancy into her voice as she possibly could.

'Hi, you, what are you up to?'

'Just checking in,' her sister said, and Clem felt some of the tension leave her as she took in just how relaxed Arrosa sounded. 'Is everything okay with you? Have you heard from our father yet?'

'Not yet.' Clem tried to sound breezy, as if the continued silence didn't bother her at all, but of course her sister knew better and she didn't try and hide her sigh of exasperation.

'Honestly, what's he playing at? Do you want me to say something?'

'No, no, it's fine.' Clem *did* want to see him, but more, she wanted *him* to want to see *her*, not for him to pay her a duty visit because his other, legitimate daughter had scolded him into doing it. 'There's plenty of time yet. I'm sure we'll catch up sooner rather than later.'

'You're sure? And you're fine to stay? It's been a week now and I feel a lot better so if you're bored of being driven around like a ceremonial doll, just say.'

'I'm fine. It's very relaxing sitting in the back of a limousine in designer clothing, so let me enjoy it a little longer. What have you been up to anyway? Did you and Sally have that cinema trip? And did the theatre action group find somewhere else to meet?'

Clem sat back and sipped her coffee as Arrosa filled her in on all the local news and told her all about meeting Sally for a couple of drinks at the local pub. Not exactly the most rock and roll evening for a single twenty-six-year-old, but probably the most freedom her sister had had in years.

'Clem?' A diffident note had entered her sister's voice and Clem put her coffee down, all senses on alert. 'What do you know about Jack Treloar?'

'Jack Treloar? As in our "local bad boy done good, trying to take over the town theatre and commercialise it" Jack Treloar?'

'That's the one.'

Clem's first instinct was to demand an explanation

why Arrosa was interested in *Jack Treloar* of all people but, knowing what it must have cost Rosy to ask the question and provoke the inevitable reaction, she made herself hold back.

'Not much,' she said, sifting through her scant knowledge and trying to exclude gossip and hearsay. 'He's about four years older than me so we were never in the same school year and didn't hang around with the same group, although from what I remember he was always quite solitary. His dad was absent a lot, drifted in and out of his life, his mother did her best but he had a real reputation. If there was ever any trouble it was attributed to him. Then he took up with the local bigwig's daughter, next thing she was pregnant and they got married. I don't think they were more than eighteen, it was quite the scandal. They disappeared off to London where somehow he made money hand over fist. I think she died tragically a couple of years back, then six months ago he returned with his daughters and bought the most expensive house in the village. No one knows why he came back. Goodness knows he can't have many happy memories of living in Cornwall. He left the town under the shadow of a scandal and has returned the same, especially now he's trying to strong-arm the council into selling or leasing the theatre to him.'

She paused before giving in and asking the burning question. 'Why? How have you come across him? He usually doesn't descend from his clifftop mansion to mix with us mere mortals.'

'He was at your play, so sometimes he does. Anyway, I've found myself babysitting for his daughters,' Arrosa said, an evasive tone in her voice, and Clem nearly choked on her coffee.

'You are *what*? How on earth did that come about?'

'It's a long story. I'll fill you in some other time.'

'I've got time now,' Clem offered, but her sister was clearly not going to be drawn.

'Honestly, it's not very interesting. But what *is* interesting is what's going on with you. Has the gorgeous Akil contacted you yet?'

'I didn't think that you thought he was that good-looking,' Clem countered, and her sister laughed.

'Objectively I can see that he is, but more importantly I know that you think so. Come on, spill the beans, what's going on? He asked for your number a couple of days ago. Has he been in contact?'

'We met up yesterday but nothing is going on, he's just being kind.' It was Clem's turn to prevaricate as her sister let out a disbelieving—and most un-princess-like—snort.

'If you say so. I've known Akil a long time and he has a real sense of honour and justice, but I wouldn't have called him kind, not in the "give up a second afternoon to entertain a stranger" way.'

'I don't know, it seems completely in character to me. Did you know that he works for the mountain rescue?'

'I've seen it mentioned in interviews, but he's usually pretty quiet about it. Not really one for sharing at all. So he's mentioned it to you, has he?'

'I saw him in action. There was an accident and I just froze, it was horrid, but he knew exactly what to do. It was impressive.'

'Handsome and heroic. He's quite the catch.'

'Rosy. Tell me honestly, are you having second thoughts?'

Clem held her breath while she waited for her sister's answer. Arrosa and Akil belonged in the same world, the same social circles, the higher echelons of the same country, had shared goals. It would make perfect sense for her sister to have reconsidered, and if she did then it would be Clem's duty to step aside and hide her own feelings. She might not be a princess, but she was a princess's sister and she knew what that entailed. She'd seen the weight of that crown yesterday.

'Not a second or a third or a fourth thought,' Arrosa said emphatically. 'And I can tell you something, nor is he.'

'How do you know?' Clem hoped her sister couldn't hear how desperately she wanted that to be true.

'Because he's attracted to *you*, Clem. It was so obvious when I spoke to him. And it's obvious that you like him so what kind of sister would I be if I came between you, even if that's what I wanted? Which for the record I don't.'

'He kissed me,' Clem confessed and winced as her sister let out a whoop.

'I knew it!'

'It was only a brief kiss goodbye as he was heading for the ambulance.'

'But you wanted more?'

Clem closed her eyes and relived the feeling of his mouth brushing hers again. 'Yes,' she confessed.

'This is *marvellous*. I'm so excited for you. What's the next step? When are you going to see him again?'

'I don't know, Rosy.' Clem tried to gather her racing thoughts. 'Akil lives such a different life from me. For a start he lives in a different country. And he knows what he wants while I'm floundering. He has his life all planned out. Plus, he wants a well-connected wife who knows his world and understands politics and diplomacy. I'm a walking national scandal. That's the last thing he needs.'

'I hate that you see yourself that way,' Arrosa said softly.

'It's not how I see myself, it's how others see me. It's how our father sees me, how the very few people in the court who know I even exist see me. The truth is that although Akil can squire me around he couldn't be seen with me anywhere that matters. We both know that's true. So what future could we possibly have?'

There was a startled pause. 'You feel that strongly about him? Are you falling in love with him, Clem?'

'Am I *what*?' Clem winced as she realised just how ridiculous she was being. 'I've only met him twice, of course I'm not. In lust, yes, and I like him a lot. But it's way too early to even think about love.'

'In that case,' Arrosa said, 'what's the harm in spending some time with him? What's the worst that could happen, Clem?'

He might reject me because of who I am. He might realise I'm not good enough.

But of course she couldn't say that aloud, not even to the sister she loved.

'You're right,' she said instead. 'I'm being a drama queen. It comes with the job, you know that. But if I see Akil again will you promise me something? Be careful with Jack Treloar.'

'Only if you promise *not* to be careful.' And, laughing, her sister hung up, leaving Clem staring at her phone. She hadn't lied to Rosy; it *was* far too early to think about love. But she was in far deeper than two meetings should warrant and that left heartbreak as an inevitable outcome.

She would allow herself to see what, if anything, happened next, but she would guard her heart and her soul. It was the only way to keep herself safe.

It had been another long night. By the time Lucy, the injured American girl, had been settled in and checked, and all her family's questions answered and concerns addressed, it had been after three a.m. Akil had stumbled back to his apartment, luckily less than half a mile away, and collapsed on the sofa, where he'd fallen into a deep sleep only to awaken three hours later when Tiger had jumped on him and insistently demanded some breakfast. Akil had drunk some water and eaten the very last of the bread before sending the promised text to Clem to fill her in on Lucy's progress, and falling back asleep. He'd woken a couple of hours later, neck stiff but feeling refreshed. Coffee, a quick shower and change of clothes and he was ready for the day ahead.

But for once, for the first time in longer than he could remember, he had no plans. There was of course work, recess or no recess his inbox was overflowing, but his assistants were filtering it for him and there was nothing urgent to address. He wasn't rostered in to be on call with the mountain rescue and wouldn't be again until next week after all the shifts he'd recently pulled.

He strode around the apartment restlessly, his gaze falling on the poetry book Clem had looked at just the day before, and smiled wryly. Maybe he'd unconsciously kept the time free in case he and Clem wanted to spend another day together. After all, if things had gone the way they'd been heading last night, she might have been here with him now. They might have been planning another day of exploring and getting to know each other. Or they might still have been in bed.

It was an intoxicating thought. He wasn't sure why the Englishwoman had got under his skin like this. She was beautiful, yes, but he knew plenty of beautiful women. It went beyond a physical attraction. She was both funny and straight talking, a combination he appreciated, and there was a hidden vulnerability that made him want to take care of her, to make her smile, to make her feel appreciated.

Goodness knew, someone should. It might be none of his business but one day Akil would tell Zorien exactly what he thought of his parenting style.

He picked up his phone and reread the message she'd sent in reply to his update.

Are you free? If so come over. Let's go out.

He should reply, but he just wasn't sure what to say. Or was it actually better that last night had been cut short? Was it safer for them both not to take this attraction between them further? There was no future after all.

But did he always need to plan for the long term? Couldn't he occasionally just enjoy life as it was. It was summer; she was here for a finite time. Why was he overcomplicating this?

One thing he did know: he wasn't going to make any sensible decisions on an empty stomach.

Akil headed out of the apartment, popping into one of the many local cafes for a quick savoury pastry and a small cup of the potent espresso Asturians loved. It took him less than a minute to finish his breakfast and he decided to go back to the hospital and check in on Lucy and her family before making any further plans. Clem would want to know how they were, after all.

Lucy had been placed in a small private room, and Akil made his way there, stopping to chat with a couple of the nurses and a doctor he knew and catching up with one of his fellow volunteers who had just finished a shift. It was nearly lunch time by the time he reached the children's ward to be buzzed in by a nurse who recognised him. Lucy's door was ajar and to his surprise he could hear a familiar voice within. What was Clem doing here?

He stood there for a moment, pleasure and apprehension warring inside him. Whatever happened next between them would be decided soon whether he was ready or not. As he waited, he began to make sense of the words within and he realised that Clem was reading to the small girl. He stepped a little closer and leaned against the door frame listening.

She was good, very good, her rich voice bringing the text to life, giving each character a distinct voice. Lucy was still pale, her leg extended before her, lines of pain on her small face, but she was smiling, looking eagerly at Clem as Clem continued to read, clearly transported to the magical world Clem was bringing vividly to life. Akil waited until the end of the chapter before pushing the door further open and entering the room, not wanting to break the spell Clem cast.

'How's the patient?' he asked in English and Lucy smiled at him.

'Clem came to read to me. She's really good.'

Clem met his eye although her expression was adorably flustered and she'd reddened. 'I wanted to see how Lucy was doing so got Henri to drop me near here. I didn't expect to be allowed in but I saw her mother outside getting some air. Her family seemed exhausted so I insisted that they went back to the hotel to get some food and a change of clothes and promised I'd keep an eye on her.'

Akil eyed the small girl keenly. 'She seems to be doing pretty well, but she looks like she needs a bit of a rest. Do you want to try to get some sleep, Lucy? We will wait just outside until your parents get back so if you need anything or you get lonely just press that button.'

'I am a little sleepy,' the little girl admitted. 'But can we read another chapter later, Clem?'

'Of course.' Clem brushed her fringe back and smiled down at the wan face. 'I'd love to. Are you comfy? Those pillows okay?' Akil watched as she expertly settled the child with soothing hands. Of course, she'd helped care for her mother and recently too. Being here must bring back some difficult memories. His admiration for her deepened.

Once Lucy was settled, Akil steered Clem out to the comfortable chairs in the adjacent waiting room. 'You want a coffee or anything?'

'No, I'm fine. How about you? What time did you get to bed?'

Akil grimaced. 'Not so much bed, more the sofa, but I've had some sleep. It was kind of you to come and check on Lucy. Even kinder to offer to watch her.'

Clem brushed the compliment aside. 'Not at all. I've spent a lot of time waiting in hospitals, I know how time takes a different element here. And her parents have another child who was definitely at the exhausted and fractious stage. I wasn't sure how they'd feel about leaving Lucy with me, but I managed to persuade them that they would be much more use to her if they were rested, fed and changed. I don't think her mother will be gone long, but a shower and time away from here will do her good.'

'It was a clever idea to read to her. You definitely put her at her ease.'

'It was no big deal. I actually really enjoyed doing it.' She sounded surprised and he quirked an eyebrow at her.

'You're an actress, don't you grab at any opportunity to perform?'

'After my mum died, I didn't think I'd ever want to set foot in a hospital again. But now I'm here, I'm remembering all the things that helped. All the volunteers as well as the nurses who made such unbearable times surprisingly bearable. The value of having people who would sit with Maman just to listen, to be there, allowing her to say all the things she couldn't say to me. The same for me, people who would listen when I was angry or selfish or frustrated. That was invaluable, priceless. Reading to one small girl is a very, very small way of giving back.'

She looked so small, almost defenceless, and yet there was an indomitable spirit about her that he was drawn to. In two steps he was next to her, drawing her up into his arms. Akil looked down into the heart-shaped face, at the gold-flecked eyes shadowed with exhaustion, and knew that for once he didn't care what the future held, he wanted her, he needed her, and by some miracle she wanted him too.

'It wasn't small to Lucy or her family. It was everything.'

'Being here is helping me too. It might be a different hospital in a different country but the smell, the look, is pretty much universal. It's making me realise how my life pretty much just stopped eighteen months ago. No wonder I don't know what to do next, I've forgotten how to move forward. But I'm ready, Akil. I'm ready to live, not just exist at last.'

She cupped his face with her hands. They were warm against his skin, the gentle touch setting him on fire, and he closed his eyes briefly to allow the sensation to soak in.

'Help me live again, Akil,' she whispered, and he was helpless against her soft entreaty, against her touch.

Slowly, deliberately, not wanting to rush a single moment, he dipped his head and captured her full inviting mouth with his for a second time. But this was no mere brush, no promise, but an intent and she responded in kind, opening up to him, her hands moving to the nape of his neck as he moulded her body to his. He pulled back slightly to look down at her, eyes glazed, mouth parted.

'Anything,' he promised her. 'Whatever you want, whatever you need, anything.' And he kissed her again, the sounds of the hospital fading away, the feel of her, the taste of her all he wanted, all he knew.

CHAPTER NINE

CLEM TURNED IN to the pretty medieval square where Akil lived, aware of Henri standing watching her, making sure she was okay. It was funny how used to his discreet presence she'd got, no longer troubled by the knowledge that even when she couldn't see him he was only a few seconds away. The only time he wasn't close by was when she was with Akil. His secret service training meant that Henri usually didn't accompany them, although he was always on call and, she suspected, never that far away.

They'd fallen into a routine over the last couple of weeks. Every morning Henri drove her out, ostensibly to the court but in reality facilitating the discreet change that allowed her to explore the country with Akil or head to the hospital, often both, then reversing the process late each evening. Her life couldn't be more different from that first lonely week. Now her days were packed. She spent a lot of time at the hospital; Lucy had been discharged over a week ago to fly home, but news of Clem's reading had spread throughout the children's ward and she now did a group session for those in the big general ward. She enjoyed it far more than she had expected to. It wasn't acting exactly, but she was transporting them into other worlds, creating magic, and that, for Clem, was as fulfilling as a big production, although if she had more time she would have liked to look into doing something bigger, maybe trying to stage some kind of small production. The volunteering was certainly opening up some possibilities and, although she was deliberately not worrying about the future just yet, ideas were percolating away.

And when she wasn't at the hospital she was with Akil. He still volunteered two days a week, and spent most mornings buried in his inbox, but the afternoons and evenings were hers. They had finally made it to the opera and to the theatre—this time a comedy, much to her relief—and to several friendly neighbourhood restaurants, the kind where a prominent politician wouldn't expect to be photographed. Any high-profile venues were out, any events where society people mingled too dangerous, but Akil was sure that if they stuck to the tourist trail no one would give them a second glance. So far that had been true, and it was getting easier and easier to forget that she was here under false pretences and not a tourist at all.

They'd hiked some of the mountain trails, pausing for cold beers and well-stuffed sandwiches at the cafes at the summit, and explored some of the picture-perfect villages and towns dotted throughout valleys and mountain shelves, cliff tops and riversides. One day they kayaked along a river, racing each other, another day they abseiled down a mountainside. She felt fitter and more resilient than she had for a long, long time.

And then there was Akil himself, his slow smile and intent gaze, his sure touch and sweet, sweet kisses. They were still at the courting phase, and although their kisses and caresses were getting increasingly heated—and increasingly intimate—neither had been in any rush to move to the next stage. It was as if they had all the time in the world.

Only of course they didn't.

Checking her watch, Clem realised she was a little early so rather than head straight to Akil's apartment she decided to have a little explore around the neighbourhood. He lived in a charming part of the old quarter, filled with cafes and local artisan shops. Just the kind of place she liked.

Fixing her sunglasses firmly on her nose, Clem headed along the nearest alley, emerging into a narrow cobbled street. Cafes and shops nestled next to each other, the old buildings four storeys high, their upper levels lurching drunkenly over the street. This part of the city was centuries old, the country's history in every cobble, every plastered and timbered front, the butchers and tanners giving way to tourist-friendly jewellers and art galleries. Clem moved slowly along, enjoying examining all the enticing wares laid out in the shop windows, the sun warming her arms, the sounds of the city a lively soundtrack.

She paused in front of a jeweller and examined the tree-inspired bracelets in silver and gold. Her mother would have loved them. Everything she'd worn had had some kind of link to nature whether it was the floral prints she'd preferred or the delicate swallow earring she'd always worn. Maybe she should buy one. Not that she needed jewellery to remember her mother, but she couldn't resist the impulse and headed in, emerging a few moments later clutching a bag, having bought a bracelet for herself and one for her sister, and a pair of cufflinks for Akil. They weren't really at the present stage, but she wanted him to have something to remember her by when this was all over.

Finally she stopped to look at some delicious pastries, her mouth watering at the sight of the nut and honey confections; she'd developed a taste for the local delicacies over the last couple of weeks. She couldn't resist popping in to buy some and they were still warm when she returned to the square and rang the buzzer to Akil's apartment. She took the now familiar stairs up to his first-floor apartment two at a time and as she reached Akil's front door he opened it.

'Hi,' she said a little stupidly as he leaned against the door frame, his dark eyes glowing in admiration as he looked her up and down. Clem resisted the urge to smooth her shirt down, glad she'd picked the floaty sunshine-yellow silk skirt and teamed it with a short delicate lace white blouse. It wasn't the most practical of outfits, but she liked how feminine she felt, liked the way the skirt swirled around her calves, the flattering fit of the shirt, deceptively demure with its high neck, yet cut to flatter her every curve—and Akil's not too subtle once-over proved it did.

'Hi. You're looking beautiful today.' His voice was a low rumble and she felt it vibrate through her.

'Thank you. You're not looking too bad yourself.' Now that was an understatement. He was delectably handsome in a white linen shirt and jeans, off duty and perfectly masculine. 'I've bought pastries.' She handed him the bag and he unleashed one of his devastating smiles.

'Now you're doubly welcome.' He bent his head to drop a lingering kiss on her mouth and her body responded enthusiastically. This kind of passion was so different from anything she'd experienced she'd never actually gone weak at the knees before.

Clem entered the apartment and headed straight over to Tiger, who uttered a miaow as she reached him, stretching out so that she could reach his cream and ginger tummy.

'Hello, gorgeous,' she crooned, and Tiger stretched even further demanding worship. 'How are you?'

'Is it wrong I'm jealous of my cat?' Akil asked and she threw him a mischievous grin.

'Cats need to be paid their dues first, you know that.'

She continued to croon at Tiger while Akil put the pastries onto a plate and poured fresh coffee, bringing them over to her and sitting next to her on the big leather sofa. She loved the domesticity of it, cuddling up to him, ignoring the world outside.

'How was the hospital this morning?'

'Good. There's a couple of new kids in, but they came to the reading. I still can't believe that this is something I do! I keep waiting for someone to ask who I am and why I'm there. To throw me out.'

'They're always looking for ways to make it an easier experience for the children. And don't worry, I vouched for you.'

'And it's that easy? No background check, no references?'

'You're not alone with the children at any time, are you?'

'No, of course not. But I didn't mean for it to get to be a regular thing. What happens when I leave in three weeks' time?'

'I'm on the hospital board...'

She turned to face him. 'You never said.'

He shrugged. 'It didn't come up.' No wonder no one had challenged her presence. 'But you've shown that we have a need for this kind of entertainment, maybe in more than the children's ward. It's being looked at.'

'Look at me influencing hospital policy.'

'You have good instincts and a good heart. It would never have occurred to me if you hadn't shown me the way.'

An unexpected pride washed over her. She might

not be the Crown Princess, but she might have achieved some good in the time she was in her sister's country.

'So what's the plan for today?' she asked as she finished the pastry.

Akil flashed a grin at her. 'I was thinking that it's time I introduced you to the most important woman in my life.'

Clem stiffened. His *what*? Surely he didn't mean his mother? She had never got the impression that they were that close and it was way too early—and too temporary—for that, and wasn't his sister abroad? He must have seen her alarm because he hastily added, 'My boat.'

That was more like it. 'I love boats. Did you know I grew up by the sea?'

'You may have mentioned it a hundred times or more, which is why I hoped you would like this idea. Then it's a date?'

'Absolutely!'

'Let's pick up some provisions, then…'

'Look at you with the nautical terms.'

'I'll have no insubordination on my ship, thank you. Tell Henri I'll drive you back. It may be late.'

She saluted, her smile cheeky. 'Yes, Captain. Anything you say, Captain.' With a roar he pinned her to the sofa, strong body moulding round hers, kissing her until she was breathless, tickling her until she begged for mercy and promised that she would be properly respectful once on the boat.

Just the two of them, out on the sea. Anticipation quivered through every nerve. She was loving this slow sensual discovery but maybe it was time to take things to the next level. She pulled Akil down to her again, luxuriating in the weight of him, the strength of him, the sureness of his kiss. Today was going to be a very good day.

Akil knew that this thing with Clem couldn't last, and he was also all too aware that the closer they got, the harder their inevitable parting would be, but paradoxically he didn't care because every day they spent together he fell for her more and more.

He liked her frank, no-nonsense sense of humour. Enjoyed the conversation that flowed so easily between them. And he had never been so physically aware of a woman in his life.

Neither of them had discussed taking it slow, but somehow it felt right, learning each other bit by bit. It was tantalising in all the right ways. Especially as they were building up to something more; they both knew it. Awareness simmered between them as they got ready for their trip, every touch searing, every glance full of promise.

Before heading to the coast they stocked up on enough provisions to last them a week at sea. Shopping together should have been a mundane task, but it was a glimpse at a future that seemed infinitely desirable, if impossible, standing in a shop debating which cheese to select and what bread would go best with their choices, deciding if they wanted cakes or biscuits or both and how many raspberries were too many. They ended up laden with bags and baskets as they loaded up the car and set off to the harbour where he kept his boat.

'Oh, I like it here,' Clem exclaimed as Akil drove into the small car park at the harbour and parked up. 'This is where you brought me that first time—only this time we're Henri free.'

Akil slid out of the car and walked round to open the door. 'It must be a relief to have some time away from him. Lucky for you that I have secret service training.'

'Don't forget my black belt in karate.' Clem jumped out of the car and joined him at the back of the vehicle as he opened the catch and let the boot spring up. 'I have skills too.'

'That you do.' He swung the first of the picnic hampers out of the car, then more cautiously lifted out the second basket containing the drinks, setting it gently on the ground.

'I'll get these.' Clem reached in and pulled out the paper bags containing the fruit they'd chosen and the box of cakes. He kept crockery, cutlery, towels and cushions on board so all they'd needed to get was the food.

'You sure?'

'Well, fun as it would be for me to skip ahead while you stumble laden behind me, I can carry my share.

You're meant to be advocating dismantling the patriarchy, remember?'

'It's chivalry, not patriarchy,' he protested, and she laughed.

'Tell you what. I'll let you help me aboard.'

'It's my boat. I need to formally invite you anyway.'

'Like a vampire? Will I burst into flame if I put a foot aboard without a formal invitation? That must be an Asturian thing. I'm pretty sure we're not so formal in Cornwall.'

She gathered up the food and set off towards the harbour, Akil falling in beside her.

'I don't think poor Henri knows what to do with himself,' she said as they navigated the narrow path. 'He doesn't really do free time. I did point out to him that I look a lot more suspicious being shadowed by a six-foot-five rock of a man, but actually he does have this amazing ability to blend into the scenery. But he would literally give his life for Rosy so I guess that's a good thing. One less thing to worry about.'

'You worry about her?'

'She's going to be a queen one day. That's a tough gig. Of course I worry. I'm glad she has you as a friend though.'

They reached the small curve of the harbour and Akil exhaled as they stepped onto the jetty. It was a perfect sailing day. The sky was cloudless, the sea calm, the scent of salt and lemon permeating the air. He loved this moment of anticipation, the gorse-covered cliffs green behind him, the mountains rising majestically beyond, while turquoise seas stretched endlessly ahead. Here he wasn't the Vicomte d'Ortiz, carrier of his family's hopes and his father's thwarted ambitions. Here he wasn't a politician, a man who had put his own dreams aside. Here he was simply Akil. It was a rare pleasure.

Even rarer were the times he got to share this with someone. *Wanted* to share this with someone. And he had never brought a woman out to his boat before. Never wanted to share this most personal of pleasures. Never until now.

'Which is it?' Clem asked as they neared the end of the jetty. Most boats were moored further out, their dinghies bobbing off the jetty and harbour wall ready to ferry owners out. Akil reached his own dinghy and put the hampers at one end, before pointing out his boat.

'She's there.' He tried to keep the pride out of his voice but knew he'd failed as Clem laughed.

'You sound like a proud father. Or husband.'

'She is the love of my life,' he admitted. He was only half joking. There were so few times when Akil felt really comfortable being himself, even when he was with his sister or with his fellow volunteers at the mountain rescue. He was always conscious of the image he projected, the weight of responsibility and expectation he carried. It was only out on the water where he could drop all his barriers. It was just a shame he rarely got to enjoy it.

'I can see why you're so proud, she is a beauty. Small but perfectly formed.'

'I didn't want the kind of superyacht I needed a crew for. Something small enough for me to manage myself, but big enough to take out to sea, to spend a week exploring the coast if I wanted.'

'Sounds idyllic.' The yearning in her voice was palpable. 'I've always wanted my own boat—but I could never justify the cost for the use I'd get from one. Not that I ever had the money even if I could justify it. Jobbing actress is not a lucrative profession and although I do have a trust fund it doesn't run to luxuries like keeping a boat. Do you get away often?'

'Not nearly enough. To be honest, I *can't* justify her really. She deserves more than the few days every now and then I can give her.'

'But you're here today.'

'We're here today. So let's make the most of it. Hop in.'

Clem stepped gracefully into the small inflatable tender and sat herself at the bow as Akil untied the rope and started the engine, steering the dinghy out towards where his boat was moored. She knew what she was doing, taking the rudder as he pulled alongside and secured the dinghy to the dock at the back and climbed aboard, extending a hand to help her up the ladder. She then helped him winch the dinghy up and secure it before turning around to survey his prized possession.

'Nice,' she said. 'Very nice.'

Akil wasn't being modest, the boat was compact with just one cabin although it had a comfortable double bed and plenty of storage. But the boat was perfect for him, combining swift, comfortable handling, with plenty of space on deck including seating, a built-in grill and bar and swimming platform while its size meant he could moor up in any port or cove he wished. With the sea literally within a second's access he had no need for the hot tubs or fancy fittings many of his peers enjoyed on their larger, more ostentatious vessels.

It didn't take long to give Clem the tour, and she was suitably appreciative, helping him stow away the provisions as she admired all the gadgets and clever use of space.

'Some of my friends' families have boats, small fishing boats or glorified dinghies, but nothing like this. She's in a class of her own. But I do know my way around a rope so set me to work.'

'In that case...' Akil motioned her towards the tiller. 'Do you want to take her out?'

'Really?' Her smile was all the reward he needed.

'Absolutely. Here, you turn this to get her started and the gears are here. Let me know if you need any help. I'll get the anchor.'

Akil's faith in Clem was justified as she expertly steered them towards the open sea. He leaned against the side and watched her as she confidently found a path through the buoys marking the way out. Her hair blew in the slight breeze, her eyes crinkling as she concentrated on the horizon, her poise strong and true.

She looked utterly beautiful, a sea naiad in her natural world. Akil's mouth dried. He'd never dared dream of being fully in sync with someone. Had never imagined it could be so easy spending time with another human, being himself. The irony of knowing it was temporary was not lost on him. But he pushed the thought aside. Akil knew how to make the best of things. How to snatch at moments of happiness while steadfastly doing his duty. This time wasn't any different.

'Which way shall I go?' Clem roused him from his thoughts and he straightened, joining her at the tiller.

'Up to you. Left will take us to the glitzy resorts just along the coast so head that way if you want cocktails and sophistication. It's quite a sight.'

'I'll bet. And what happens if I turn right?'

'Then you'll see tiny coves that can only be accessed by boat, isolation, stunning views, some of the best swimming you'll ever experience and an idyllic picnic spot.'

'Hmm, difficult decision.' She angled the boat towards the right. 'How will I choose? The only thing...'

'Is?'

'I didn't come dressed for sailing, as you can see.' She flashed him a smile. 'Silk and lace are not really picnic attire but I can manage. But more crucially, I should have realised earlier when we were shopping, I don't have a bathing suit.'

Akil dropped a kiss onto her neck, his hand resting on the curve of her hip. 'Who said anything about costumes?'

Clem stilled. He could see her chest rise and fall as her breathing quickened, her cheeks and neck turned pink, her pupils dilated. He was so attuned to her every response, his own breathing sped up along with hers, heat rising throughout his body. When she finally spoke her voice was husky.

'I bet you say that to all the girls. Is this your routine? Invite a girl out for a sail and then suggest a dip but, oops, no costumes?'

'Not so far.' He paused, then said deliberately, 'You're the only woman I've ever invited abroad.'

She didn't respond, not at first, but he could see her work through the implications of that statement, before she turned and twined her arms around his neck, reaching up to press her mouth against his.

'What are we doing, Akil?' she half whispered, and he smoothed her hair back from her face.

'I don't know,' he said honestly. 'But we don't have to do anything, be anything. We can just sail or I can take us back. Just say the word.'

She shook her head emphatically. 'I don't want to go back,' she said, and he knew instinctively that she was talking about more than this trip.

'Then let's see where the wind takes us.'

She stared up at him, her eyes solemn and almost fearful until she seemed to shake her thoughts away, managing a smile as she turned back to the tiller. Akil leaned against her as she steered, his arm around her waist, holding her steady, wishing that she were someone less complicated, that he were someone without a predetermined path, that this could be the start of a longer voyage, the start of something real.

CHAPTER TEN

'THAT WAS A ridiculously delicious picnic.' Clem took another longing look at the leftovers before pushing her plate away with a groan. 'No. Don't let me eat any more. You might need to lose some ballast to get us back at the rate I've been consuming.'

She repressed a sigh at the thought of *back*. How she wished they could just sail on for ever. No worries about tomorrow, no family expectations—or in her case lack of family expectations—just the sea, a fair wind and each other. Because with Akil she was completely herself. Her hair was windblown, her skirt watermarked and her make-up non-existent and he didn't notice, didn't care. It was intoxicating.

'No more food. Got it. But we're now respectably heading towards evening so I could open the champagne and we can toast the view?'

It was a view worth toasting. Clem had kept hold of the tiller and taken them twenty miles up the rocky, dramatic coast where they'd moored up just inside a wide, deserted bay. They'd deliberated taking the tender in to picnic on the sandy beach but in the end elected to stay here on deck, the boat rocking gently with the tide.

'Champagne? Sounds good but should we drink and boat? I guess we could get Henri to pick us up at the other end.'

Akil leaned back in his seat and stretched and she did her best not to look at the tantalising glimpse of bared, muscled stomach. 'Of course, the best thing about a boat is that you don't have to worry about sailing under the influence, you can just stay where you are.'

Her whole body tingled at the thought. 'You mean just stay here? Overnight?'

'Here or further up the coast.' His eyes gleamed. 'There are many possibilities.'

'I see, so was this trip just a ruse, a plan to spirit me away like a pirate and sail away on the seven seas?' She was a very modern woman but she couldn't help but thrill at the thought. There *was* something piratical about Akil. He was usually so well put together, but here on the boat, the top few buttons of his shirt undone showcasing a tanned, muscular vee of chest, shirt sleeves rolled up to expose strong corded wrists, hair ruffled by the breeze, she could see traces of his warrior ancestors. Ancestors who might whisk an enemy princess away on their boat.

'Tempting.' His voice was husky, and it trembled

through her, setting every nerve vibrating. 'But nothing so uncivilised.'

She held his gaze. 'Pity,' she said, and her stomach tumbled at his wolfish smile.

'You see,' he said, and it was as if he were undressing her with his eyes, 'I wouldn't want any woman who didn't want me with every part of her. Who I didn't want with every atom in me. And I do want you, Clem. So, what shall we do? It's up to you, it's always been up to you. Maybe you're the pirate…the pirate princess seducing the warrior into doing her bidding.'

His voice was hypnotic, low and mesmerising and she couldn't have moved if she'd tried. And she wasn't trying. Not when Akil was so close, the scent of him wrapping around her senses, making her dizzy with that intoxicating mix of salt and sandalwood. Not when her whole body buzzed with his proximity, her nerves alight, her legs weak and her breasts full, aching for a release so tantalisingly close.

She couldn't even speak, just quivered as he drew one finger along her cheek, brushing the tender outline of her mouth. 'Your move, Clem.'

No, she wanted to cry out. It wasn't fair, he couldn't leave this decision solely up to her, not when she instinctively knew that making love with Akil would make her more vulnerable than she had ever been before. Not when she needed reassurances and promises that this was right, that she was right. That *they* were right. That they had a future, even if that reassurance could only be a lie.

For a moment she desperately thought about changing the subject, backing away, even as her body cried out for her to just get on with it already. She was so close, so close to getting in too deep. Surely making love with Akil would tip her over the edge. If she wasn't there already and, oh, how she feared she might be.

But if she didn't she knew she would regret this moment of cowardice for the rest of her life. She wanted to know him fully, for him to know her. And besides, wasn't this where they had been heading since the day of the tour? More, since that very first meeting? Wasn't this what she craved, what she wanted more than air or water? If so, then how could she not?

More importantly, how could she not when he was allowing her to set the parameters, when he was putting her first? For a woman so often left in the shadows, that power was the most seductive thing of all.

'I have decided.' She stood up and faced him. No more thought. No more fears or doubts. Suddenly it was all very clear. She wanted Akil and he wanted her and that was all that mattered. 'I do want you. Here, tonight.'

It was his turn to stand, one hand on the boat rail, his gaze locked on her, his mouth curved into a wicked smile, one that sent shivers trembling through her. 'In that case, come here.'

He was now supremely arrogant, no longer the suave suitor or the sweet-tongued seducer. He was a man who knew what he wanted—*her*—and knew his goal was within reach. But she could match him, in desire, in need and in confidence that she was desired and needed in turn. The ultimate aphrodisiac. And, chin tilted, a sway in her step, fire consuming her, she stepped forward. Just one step.

'Now you.'

He raised an eyebrow, laughter lighting the darkness of his gaze as he casually stepped forward. But she wasn't fooled; for all his amusement there was a predatory air as he moved that showed his blood was up and he was fully focused on moving in for the finish. There was still space between them and he stared at her, daring her to complete it. Instead, Clem reached for her top button and, eyes fixed on him, flicked it open. She watched him swallow and allowed herself a feline grin.

'It's a little hot, don't you think?' Another button and then a third. 'Maybe we should cool off.' Another two and she slipped the blouse off her shoulders, her hands moving to the zip on her skirt. 'You did say this was a good swimming spot?' She stepped out of the skirt, leaving it pooled on the floor and, without looking away, undid the snap of her bra and let it fall away, feeling as much as hearing Akil's intake of breath as she did so. 'So, let's swim.' She kept her pants on, not quite ready to lose that last layer of protection as she stepped onto the swimming platform and pushed her hair back, looking back at him challengingly. 'Race you to the beach.'

* * *

It took Akil all of two seconds to react. He'd frozen in place while Clem discarded her clothes, unable to move a muscle as inch after delicious inch was bared, brown and lithe and delectable and—so it seemed—his. And then, just as he managed to wake up enough to reach for her she was gone, diving with clean precision into the sea and striking out for the beach. He allowed himself one lingering moment to take in the lines of her body forging through the water before tearing off his shirt and trousers and following her in.

The water was perfect, cool and refreshing, calm enough to make swimming a pleasure as Akil followed Clem, his blood up, closing in on his prey. Clem was a good swimmer, but he was better and he caught up with her with ease, then keeping pace alongside her until the water reached his chest at which point he stopped, reaching out to hook her and pull her close. Her hair, sleek with water, fell heavily around her shoulders, her chest rising and falling with exertion, water drying on her shoulders. She was all sea nymph, salt and water and flesh in a package he wanted to consume, like Poseidon claiming his prize. The water was deep enough to hide the rest of her body, but he knew just what was concealed, the high round breasts, a lighter shade than the rest of her olive body, the planes of her stomach and long, long legs, the triangle of silk that revealed as much as it concealed, now wet and translucent. Heat flooded him despite the chill of the water as he finally, finally, crushed her to him and took her mouth with his, not gently or sweetly but with a fierce possessiveness. A possessiveness she reciprocated. This was no coy naiad, rather a fierce and wild goddess as she wound her hands in his hair to pull him closer, her tongue entwined in his, hot and sweet, her breasts soft against his chest as he pulled her closer still.

Akil couldn't have said how long they stood, chest high in the waves, all he knew was that at some point he wanted, needed more, needed to touch as well as taste, needed to explore every inch of bared flesh. Slowly, unable to break the embrace, as if by doing so he might break the spell, he inched her back, back until the water receded, the sand soft under his feet, the early evening sun hot on his shoulders. But not as hot as the trail her hands blazed across his neck and down his back, not as hot as the flesh he skimmed as he finally, finally palmed one perfect breast, her damp skin silk under his touch. She inhaled sharply as his thumb reached her nipple, and he circled the tight bud slowly and with intent as he kissed his way down her jaw, down the proud slim column of her neck until he could replace his thumb with his mouth, cupping her other breast as he did so.

Blood surged triumphantly through his whole body, pooling at his groin, the urge to take her there and then almost overwhelming. *Steady*, he told himself. *Not yet.* He sank to his knees, pulling her with him, until she was supine on the sand beneath him, her beautiful body laid out like an offering, returning to her mouth as he straddled her.

Impatient, Clem pulled at him but Akil resisted with a low laugh, refusing to rush now that he had her here beneath him. Instead he concentrated on discovering every previously hidden inch, the places that made her gasp and buck and reach for him, holding onto his control with everything he had as his body clamoured for release.

'Now,' she whispered first softly and then impatiently but he resisted with painful restraint, pulling back to cup her face and kiss her with a melting slowness that almost undid him.

'Clem,' he murmured against her mouth. 'We need to return to the boat. I didn't get a chance to bring any protection.'

For one millisecond, Clem didn't care. For one moment she understood for the first time how desire and sensation could overwhelm common sense, but before she had time to act upon her instincts reality reasserted itself and she sat up, reluctantly, almost embarrassed by the abandon she'd displayed just moments before. 'Oh.'

'Oh, indeed. But I've seen you swim. I think we can be back on board in less than five minutes and carry on where we left off. What do you think?'

Again he was giving her the control, even though the evidence of his desire was all too visible, and that control only solidified her need. 'I think the quicker we get back, the better.' She allowed herself the luxury of running her eyes over him slowly and with intent, taking in every plane and hollow, every piece of hard sculpted flesh, and she could see him visibly shake with the effort of standing still as she caressed him with her gaze.

This time it was no mad dash, instead they kept pace with each other, knowing what awaited them at the return to the boat. Clem reached the ladder first and climbed, Akil right behind her. As soon as she was on the boat she turned, needing to kiss him, to hold him, to be held in turn. The water hadn't quenched her desire, instead the wait, the anticipation, had only stoked it and she pulled him close, entwining herself around him, until, with a muttered curse, he swept her up, laying her on the double sun lounger. She stayed still, drinking him in as he loomed above her.

'Don't move,' he ordered, and she obeyed, unable to do anything but wait, every nerve quivering, every sense greedily needy until he returned, tall and powerful and gloriously nude, a packet in his hands. He paused despite her whimpering protest and she felt his gaze wander over her as if he were touching her, her flesh goosepimpling under his study. 'You are beautiful,' he breathed. 'A sea goddess.'

'No more talking,' she managed and he laughed softly, sitting beside her.

'No? But I could write a poem to your eyes…' his finger brushed over them '…a sonnet to your mouth…' it moved lower still '…and a haiku about your neck. Your breasts deserve an ode.' She sucked in a breath as he lazily circled a nipple, replacing his finger with a tongue. 'Your stomach an elegy. And as for the soft skin here.' He moved his hand down to the tenderness of her inner thigh. 'Oh, I could write an epic poem about the way you feel here.'

She was panting now, her breasts rising and falling as need built inside her higher and higher, hotter and hotter. She'd never felt so wanted before, so desirable, so tempting. But then again no man had ever looked at her as if she were the answer to all his prayers.

And she had never wanted a man so fiercely either. The play of his muscles under her eager hands, the strength in his arms and chest, the tautness of his stomach. The way he hissed as her hand moved lower as he fought fire with fire, moving lower until he was kissing her stomach, her hips, her thighs, her inner thighs, his hand moving further up, knowing and sure.

'And here,' he whispered. 'Only a ballad would do for here.' Clem cried out, she couldn't fight back now, all thought disappearing under almost unbearable sensation until at last she broke, riding the wave again and again, exultant as he joined her, as if he were made for her, as if she were made for him.

Time ceased to have any meaning until she came to, wrapped around him, limp and sated, the stars shining down on them. Clem lay there, not knowing what to say or do. It had never felt like that before, never been as intense, as overwhelming. Part of her wanted to shout out in happiness, some part of her wanted to cry and, as if he understood, Akil rolled over to pull her closer, to envelop her in his arms.

'Are you okay?'

'Better than okay,' she reassured him, then, worried, 'You?'

His laugh rumbled through her. 'Better than okay.'

'Good, that's good.'

'It is.'

They lay there breathing in time until Akil sat up. 'I promised you champagne.'

'It's fine,' she reassured him, just wanting him back next to her but he was already on his feet.

'No, you should have champagne. We have the sound of the sea, we have the stars, we shouldn't waste it.'

'Well, if you insist.'

It took him less than two minutes to return with the chilled champagne and a bowl of the raspberries they'd bought earlier and, completely unselfconsciously, they stayed on deck, sipping and nibbling on the raspberries and talking nonsense as they gazed up at the stars. At some point, most of the champagne drunk, Akil kissed her once again and desire sprang back up as if they hadn't made love earlier, Clem responding with an ardency and urgency that would have surprised her if she'd had any room to think.

Later, much later, still under the stars but under a blanket Akil had brought up from the cabin, she began to fall asleep, safe in Akil's arms.

'I love you,' she murmured, so almost asleep she

wasn't sure if she was imagining saying the words or not. Nor did she know if she imagined the pause that followed or the almost breathed response.

'*Je t'aime*, Clemence Beaumont. *Je t'aime*.'

CHAPTER ELEVEN

CLEM LAY BACK on the sunbed and breathed in. It was another hot, sunny day, the kind where she was glad to have little to do but swim and sleep. And she knew she needed to make the most of it, she wouldn't be able to stay in this idyll for much longer, nor enjoy almost guaranteed sun once she was back in the uncertainty of a UK summer.

Not that there was much summer left. She couldn't believe how quickly time had flown, but here she was facing the end of her stay. In less than a week she'd be returning to Cornwall and Arrosa would come home and start preparing for the ratification. She hadn't spoken to her sister for a couple of weeks, they'd just hurriedly exchanged a few messages, and she had no idea how she felt about returning to her normal life. Clem wasn't sure how she felt about her return to normality either.

On one hand, fun as being a tourist and enjoying the benefits of living in Arrosa's house were, she didn't think she was suited for a life without purpose. Sunbathing and swimming were fun, but she got just as much enjoyment out of the sessions at the hospital, more in fact, looking forward to the moment she sat down and transported the children away. After discussing it with Akil she'd started to do some research into what she'd need to do to qualify in occupational therapy and dramatherapy and had contacted a friend who worked in a theatre company that specialised in working with children in hospital and other non-home settings. She still had no concrete plans, but just having an idea of a path was a huge step forward.

But, of course, returning to Cornwall meant leaving Akil. And if that thought had been difficult *before* the trip out on the boat, it was almost unbearable now. She continued to see him nearly every day, although as summer drew to the end so his responsibilities grew, like a warning sign their time was nearly up. The need for discretion was as high as ever; the last thing either of them wanted was speculation about who Clem was or, worse, for people to start gossiping about how much time he spent at the palais with Arrosa. So she continued leaving the estate in one outfit and changing in a discreet location, and when they did venture out they mingled with tourists and sightseers far away from anywhere where Akil might meet friends or colleagues.

Clem wriggled again, trying to get comfortable. What had been fun at the beginning, an amusing subterfuge, was beginning to lose its charm. A reminder of why their relationship had to be secret, and that an end date was in sight. Fun as it was for them to lie in bed building castles in the air about a life sailing around Cornwall, she knew that leaving Asturia was not an option for him, just as staying was not an option for her. All she had ever wanted was someone to love her, to see her, to put her first. Ironic really that she had found someone who fitted the first two but couldn't fulfil the third.

At least neither of them had been foolish enough to mention love again. It didn't stop her thinking it though. Feeling it.

She closed her eyes, resolutely pushing the thoughts away although she knew that their reckoning was coming. They still had nearly a week. Maybe they would think of a solution before then. Maybe he'd ask her to stay, or she could suggest it. No one knew who she was: What did Clem Beaumont from England have to do with the royal family? Did he want more than a holiday romance? Did she? They had never discussed it.

She did her best to concentrate on the sensuous warmth of the sun across her body, the sound of the birds singing overhead and the distant drone of an aeroplane. Occasionally she heard voices from outside the villa gardens as the palais gardeners moved around, a burst of radio from one of the guards and his reply, footsteps coming down her path.

Hang on? *Footsteps.* Clem peeled her eyes open, suddenly alert. She wasn't expecting anybody. Akil was working this morning and nobody else ever came to see her. Feeling a little vulnerable in just her bikini, she sat up and grabbed her wrap, turning towards the path and the figure striding down it.

'There you are, Clemence.'

She blinked, myriad emotions whirlpooling through her, the way they always did on the rare occasions she saw her father, the less rare occasions she thought about him.

Sitting back, she peered over her sunglasses, deliberately cool and collected. 'Hello, Zorien. I wasn't expecting you. I must have missed your message.'

It was a long time since she'd called him *Daddy*; it had been made very clear to her that the word was not for her to use, not even in private, in case they were ever overheard. Safety trumped reality every time.

'You look well,' she added. 'Would you like to sit down? I'm sure I can manage some coffee.'

It had been several years since she'd last seen him, but he looked exactly the same, tall, slim and straight-backed, his hair not yet silvering. The hazel eyes so similar to hers and Arrosa's were cool and assessing, his expression inscrutable.

'Your sister stands when I first enter a room, curtseys, says *Your Majesty* and waits for me to speak.'

It was like that, was it? Clem smiled, affecting an insouciance she didn't feel. 'I missed the day my local comprehensive taught court manners. But on the other hand, we're outside so this isn't actually a room and you're not *My* Majesty. I'm not an Asturian citizen, remember?'

One of many points of contention. Zorien wasn't named on her birth certificate so she had no claim to citizenship although thanks to her mother she held French as well as British citizenship.

'But any guard or member of staff could see you not adhering to protocol. You should know better than to let your guard down, Clemence.'

'No one's looking. Besides, what will they do? Arrest me for lack of courtesy and take me to the tower?'

'You are always so argumentative, Clemence.' The first time they'd met in years and already they were at odds, the same old pattern. It was like the time he'd come to see her on her eighteenth birthday, and they had managed about fifteen minutes before she'd crashed out of the house in a rage, angry that he wouldn't be there for her last school play, one she had helped direct as well as starred in, a labour of love she had wanted to share with both her parents. Angry that he wouldn't even come for a walk with her in case they were seen. Angry that he'd refused her request to spend the summer in Asturia. She'd said bitter words, a lifetime of resentment and hurt spilling out, and in the end he had simply walked away. Soon after he'd made it clear it was no longer safe for Arrosa to spend her summers in Cornwall.

Their relationship had never really recovered; it had never had the opportunity. It wasn't as if they ever spent time together to repair it, his calls infrequent, his visits even more so.

Zorien Artega had done his duty materially. Her trust fund had been set up before she was born, more money was deposited in her account every birthday and Christmas and upon her mother's death she'd found out the house had been held in trust for her. There were times when she'd wanted to throw her trust fund back at him, to tell him that she needed nothing from him. But without it she had nothing. No family, no security net, no proof of who she was and that anyone had ever cared about her.

But he was here now, and this was what she had wanted, had hoped for. She couldn't allow her temper and age-old hurt to get in the way. 'I'm going to make coffee,' she said in as conciliatory a manner as she could manage. 'Sure you don't want some?'

He continued to survey her for another long moment, then nodded. 'Coffee would be nice.'

They didn't speak again until Clem had set the coffee pot onto the table, quickly ducking into the bedroom and throwing a dress over her bikini and pulling a comb through her hair. After a moment's hesitation she added a wrap, a dash of lipstick and some mascara. It wasn't that she wanted to impress her father, but she did want the protection of respectability. She returned to the kitchen, pouring the milk into a jug and tipping some biscuits onto a plate, carrying the lot outside. She took a seat opposite him and handed him a cup.

'It's beautiful here. I always thought the house in Cornwall the most perfect setting, and I do like to be beside the sea, but if I can't have the sea then a lake is certainly a good substitute.'

'Your sister seems happy here,' Zorien said. 'I had my doubts when she wanted to move out of her apartments in the palais, but this seemed like a good compromise. She is still protected by the palais guards, still looked after by the staff but she has some independence.'

Some was the relevant word here; Clem knew her sister's comings and goings were recorded and scrutinised but it was a compromise Arrosa had made and it wasn't for her to comment.

Zorien sipped his coffee then set his cup down. 'How are you, Clem? It can't have been easy for you the last few months.'

'I'm fine,' she said as brightly as she could. 'Aren't I always? Stay out of trouble and need nothing, that's my role.'

But he didn't rise to the bait, looking her over with eyes that were suddenly kind, and she blinked; kindness was almost more than she could bear. 'You shouldn't have had to deal with your mother's illness alone,' he said. 'I'm more sorry about that than you can know.'

'The nurses you paid for were more than helpful.' The least she could do was give credit where credit was due. 'And Maman loved the gifts you sent. You always seemed to know what would cheer her up.'

Every day something new would arrive, her mother's favourite flowers, gloriously soft cashmere socks and wraps, fresh baskets of fruit, luxury creams and lotions, delicate cakes to tempt a disappearing appetite.

'I should have been there, come to see her before the end. I think…' For a brief second, he looked vulnerable. 'I think I was in denial; your mother was so full of life it seemed impossible that life could be cut short. If anyone could beat a diagnosis like hers, I thought she would.'

There were so many things Clem could respond with. She could point out that if he had been there, if he'd seen her mother, he'd have known how ill she was, that those who cared for her day to day didn't have the luxury of dreaming that everything was going to be okay. But what was the point? 'I think we all hoped that,' she said instead.

Silence fell once again, thoughts of her mother permeating the air around them. She was the link, their common ground, the woman they both had loved. Now she was gone, was anything left in their relationship to salvage? Did her father even want to salvage it? Would it be far more convenient for him if Clem disappeared never to be seen again?

'You seem to have been very busy while you have been here,' he said at last.

Clem looked at him warily, but he seemed to be genuine. 'I've heard good reports about the impact your reading is having at the hospital. It's kind of you to give up your time. It's the sort of thing I could imagine your mother doing.'

'I kind of fell into it really, but I am enjoying it.'

'Will you continue when you go back?'

When you go back: there was clearly no doubt in her father's mind that her stay here was temporary. 'Possibly,' she conceded. 'I've been wondering what to do with my life. Taking eighteen months out has changed everything. Acting doesn't seem like the be-all and end-all any more. Doesn't seem as important as it once did. I've been thinking about maybe retraining, looking at something like occupational therapy. It's early days, I don't want to rush into anything, but it might be a rewarding thing to do.' She paused, hating how much she wanted his opinion, his approbation, but she could feel his approval warming her through as he slowly nodded.

'That sounds like a good plan. You'd be good at that.'

'Thank you.'

'I've also heard,' he continued, and something in the way he shifted told Clem that this was the purpose of the meeting. He wasn't here to catch up with her, nor to compliment her on her work at the hospital, he was here to deliver a message. She straightened and met his gaze coolly, glad of the lipstick and combed hair. 'That you've been spending a great deal of time with the Ortiz heir.'

'Akil? Yes, he's been very kind.'

'The pair of you have been very discreet and I appreciate that, but he's a young man on the rise and the press will start to take notice sooner rather than later. Will want to know who you are.'

'All they would find out is that I'm an English actress here on holiday.' She knew she sounded defensive and tried to rein it in. 'There is nothing to link me to you. That's what you're worried about, isn't it?'

'You are staying in my home, accompanied by your sister's bodyguard, there's a link. It would take one enterprising journalist to work that out. But there's more, Clem. Your behaviour is rousing suspicion. People are wondering where Arrosa is every day. She sets off for Court but no one sees her. I have put off any queries, as far as anyone knows she's with me, but people won't really believe she's shut up in my private apartments all day every day. It's stretching credulity. The gate logs from here come to me, but they also go to the Army General. They show Arrosa as coming back late or not coming back at all. Sooner or later, this will leak, people will wonder where she is, what she's doing.'

Heat flooded her cheeks; to think she'd been congratulating herself how discreet she and Akil had been. Of course her behaviour would be noticed and reported on, no matter what she, Akil and Henri did to mitigate it. And now her father was having to cover for her and Akil.

'I'll be more careful. I'm leaving soon anyway.' But she knew that wasn't the right answer. He wasn't here to ask her to be more discreet, he was telling her to stop seeing Akil.

Zorien leaned forward and although his eyes were kind, they were also implacable. 'You've done a good thing, Clem. Your sister needed time away and you made that happen. But when she returns, things are going to get more and more intense. Her life was difficult as my only child.'

Clem did her best not to wince at his words. *Only child.* That put her very firmly in her place.

'It's been very difficult as we have worked to change the law, especially as I know she has no real desire to be Queen and part of her would have been happy leaving things as they were. But nothing can really prepare her for what life will be like in just a few weeks when she officially becomes my heir. Everything she says, everything she does, will be under intense scrutiny, at home and internationally. She has to show that she is fit to rule, that she has what it takes to manage this country. Everything we do needs to support that. Do you understand what I'm saying?'

'Yes. I understand, I've never done anything but understand. Asturia comes first, I come second. That's how it's always been, isn't it, Zorien?'

He shook his head. 'Not you, Clem. *Us.* We Artegas. Asturia comes first, the family second. We are the servants of this country, and we can never forget it.'

'But it's *not* my country. That's been made very clear to me.'

'But you're here, and you love it, don't you? You've

explored the mountains, the villages, and the seas. You've spent time in hospitals, eating our food, walking our streets, exploring our heritage—your heritage. Don't think that I don't know that the sacrifice you make is greater in some ways than the sacrifices your sister and I have to make.'

'But you have each other.' She hated the tears filling her eyes, the wobble in her voice. 'I have no one.' No one but Akil—and she had known she would need to say goodbye, she had just hoped for more time.

'Please don't think that I don't want to be more involved in your life, and I know Arrosa wishes she could be a proper sister to you. But this is what we do, all of us, and you have your part to play as well. The last thing we need right now is the publicity that would surround us if there was any suspicion of who you really are. I'm glad you had a chance to be here, to get to know the country, but it's time for you and Arrosa to resume your normal lives. Your life is in England, Clem. That's what your mother chose for you.'

'But what if that's not what I want?'

'What we want is secondary to what we need to do. Look at you, Clem, you're an Artega through and through. Our blood into your veins and I know I can trust you to do what's right. You've given your sister the space she needed to prepare for her future, to grow into her role. Your plans for your future sound exciting, and I will help in any way I can.'

'As long as I pursue them away from here?'

Her father nodded. 'The last year and a half have

been difficult for you, and you deserved some fun, but it's time for the fun to stop. I'm sorry, Clem. I wish it could be different, but it's time you went home.'

It wasn't like Clem not to reply to his messages, but a couple of hours after letting her know he was free, Akil had still not heard from her, nor was she at the hospital. He had tried to be discreet about visiting her at the Palais d'Artega, not wanting his presence there too often to be noted, but when his third call went to voicemail his worry intensified and he headed out towards the country estate, discretion the last thing on his mind.

It wasn't just that it was unlike her to go AWOL. He needed to see her. It had been hard to settle to work that morning; every hour that passed was a reminder that summer was nearly over, and Clem would be returning to England soon. It had been easy to ignore that realisation; when they had started to get close, summer had seemed endless. Besides, they had both known the score. Theirs was just a holiday fling, some fun while Clem was in Asturia.

But what they had was stronger, deeper, than a fling. And now, as every day got dark a little earlier and the noonday sun sank a little lower, reality was setting in. He loved her.

The irony didn't escape him; he was a man who didn't really believe in love and certainly didn't believe in love at first sight, but he couldn't deny that something in him had shifted the very first time they'd met. He'd grown up to think of love as weakness, as destructive, but being with Clem just made him stronger. Talking to her, listening to her, finding out her perspective made him a better politician, a more strategic thinker—look at his plans for the hospital inspired by her. Was she the politician's wife of his dreams? No, but he was very glad he hadn't met the well-connected and diplomatic hostess he'd thought he wanted to marry. He needed someone to challenge him, someone to complement him. Love wasn't weakness, as he had feared, but strength, allowing himself vulnerability in front of another human being.

And he was sure that she needed him, too. For all her strength she needed to be loved, to be needed; she'd been alone too long. Which was why Akil was going to ask her to stay in Asturia. To stay with him. A smile curved his mouth at the thought of evenings curled up and days out exploring, of long nights loving and laughing. It was more than he'd ever thought he'd have and now it was within his grasp. How could one person change everything so completely?

He'd known since the first night on the boat that he couldn't just let her leave, but now time was running out and he still hadn't found the right time or words. He'd even considered proposing, but his natural caution urged him against making such an irrevocable move just yet. After all, his parents' marriage stemmed from a summer romance gone wrong, and he didn't want to repeat that mistake. He and Clem needed to spend every season together before making such a commitment. But he was looking forward to every one of those seasons.

He knew it wouldn't be easy. Even if she were just an English tourist here for the summer then there would still be some obstacles to overcome. Her life was overseas, she had no job here, and his work and the obligations of his title were both demanding. But she wasn't just an English tourist, she was the illegitimate daughter of the King, and from everything she'd told him he knew Zorien and those court officials who knew of her existence would not welcome her presence in Asturia full-time. But they couldn't let that stop them. If she wanted to stay, they would find a way to make it work.

By the time he reached the Palais d'Artega he'd still not heard from her, and tension gripped him as he turned in through the gates. As usual he was waved through but, this time, he was aware of some curious glances from the usually inscrutable guards and knew that he wouldn't be able to visit her here again. If his presence here was being noted, it had to stop.

As he drove along the formal driveway another car was coming the other way and Akil slowed and pulled in to allow it to pass. As it drew close, Akil saw Zorien at the wheel, his expression dark and filled with pain. His gaze met Akil's and he nodded curtly. Akil's pulse began to hammer as he noted what looked like pity in the King's eyes and the feeling of tension increased as he sped a little faster than usual past the palais and out towards the villa.

He pulled up outside and jumped out of his car, making his way around to the back of the house, instinctively knowing that Clem would be standing by the lake. He knew at times of stress she gravitated towards water and sure enough she was standing on the platform where he had first seen her, wearing a long green sundress that fell around her ankles. Her head was bent but she looked up as he approached, and he saw her eyes were red. Her father had made her cry.

He clenched his fists; he knew better than anyone that family relationships were complicated, but Clem had nobody. Surely Zorien understood that? Would it have cost him to be kind?

'Hi,' she said, her voice a little husky.

'I'm glad you're okay. I got a little worried when I didn't hear from you.'

'Sorry, my father was here. I haven't had a chance to check my phone.'

'I saw him on the way out. I'm glad he managed to visit you. How was it?'

Her smile was tremulous. 'As expected. He's given me my marching orders.'

Anger and possessiveness rose in him, almost overwhelming as he strode forward to take her hands. 'He can't do that.'

'He's the King. I'm pretty sure he can do anything he likes.'

'We're a democracy and you're of age. You can do anything you want, Clem.'

She pulled her hands away and tried another smile.

'What does it matter, Akil? We knew this day was coming, it's just a little earlier than expected. This was only a summer fling.'

He took her shoulders and looked down at her defiant face. 'Is that really true, Clem? Because it isn't for me. I love you—and I think that you love me.'

CHAPTER TWELVE

CLEM STARED UP at Akil, her eyes filling with unwanted tears. She tried to blink them back, not wanting to show any sign of weakness. 'Love is a big word, Akil.'

'It's not one I use lightly.' His voice was teasing, warm, but his face was full of concern—for her.

She twisted away, not sure she'd be able to do what had to be done if he was touching her. 'Say I was falling in love with you, what difference would it make? My life is far away from here, and there's nothing for you in Cornwall.'

'Apart from you.'

She closed her eyes, trying to regain control of her voice. 'But I wouldn't be enough. We both know that. You have your role here, your title, the promise you made to your father. You couldn't give that up for me.' Although a selfish part of her wished he could.

'No, maybe not long term, although I'd love to visit your home,' he conceded. 'But, Clem, you could stay.

You could extend your role at the hospital; we could look into funding to make it a real job if that's what you wanted.'

'And what? Live with you?'

'Why not?'

'Because I don't belong here. I'm not wanted here.'

'I want you, and I bet your sister does too.'

She knew he was trying to help but how she wished he wouldn't; every word just made it worse, showing her a future she could never inhabit. 'My mother left France because it was considered too close to Asturia, too risky. At one point my father tried to persuade her that she should move to New Zealand in order to protect the secret of my existence, but she didn't want to go so far alone so they compromised on Cornwall. I don't think, judging on the conversation we've just had, that he's changed his mind.'

'This isn't about him.'

'No, it's about me. He reminded me that if word got out about who I was then life will be even more difficult for Rosy—and it's going to be hard enough for her from now on, we both know that. I love my sister, Akil, she is the one constant I have. I couldn't live knowing my existence was like some time bomb waiting to explode.'

'Have you asked her? Because I bet you anything she would tell you that she doesn't care about any possible scandal, that she would give anything to have you close by. She loves you too, Clem. She would want you to be happy.'

'But how could I be happy living so close to a father and sister who can't acknowledge me? If you and I were together then wouldn't there be times we were in the same place and at the same events? And we would have to be strangers! I can't live like that, I can't. I can't be here unacknowledged, unwanted. It would break me, Akil.' The words were torn from her, and the tears she so desperately tried to keep back made it through the barriers. 'How could I live as a stranger to my family?'

He enfolded her in his arms, and she allowed herself the luxury of leaning in against him. 'You're not unwanted, Clem. Never that. I'd be by your side throughout.'

How she wished she could believe him. 'And if we didn't work out? We barely know each other after all, it's just been a few weeks. You're the one who said that mutual goals were a better basis for a relationship than love. That love complicates things, that your parents married as a result of a summer romance and made each other miserable. What if that is us? What if we realised in a week, or a month or a year that it wasn't working? Where would I be then? Surely it's better to make a clean break before we're in too deep?' She allowed herself another second of absorbing his strength, memorising every muscle, before she stepped back, trying to keep her expression neutral, to hide how much every word hurt.

'I did say that.' His smile was rueful. 'And I meant it. But that was because I didn't know what love was.

I'd never been in love before, you see. I do know now, though, thanks to you, Clem, and my feelings aren't going to change. You just need to trust me.'

'I can't. I can't, Akil. I wish I could. It's a nice idea, extending whatever this is between us, but it's not practical. Better to realise that what we have here is a summer romance, a lovely, memorable time out from reality. I'll always cherish it.'

'Or maybe it's more, maybe we have the chance of something extraordinary.'

'Maybe in another life.'

'We only get this one chance, Clem.'

'I'm sorry,' she whispered, not able to prolong the torture for another moment. 'But you have to go. I need to pack.'

Akil stood stock-still, dark eyes blazing. 'Don't just give up on us, Clem. Don't give in without a fight.' He stared at her for a moment longer and, unable to bear the weight of his gaze, she looked away. By the time she looked back, he was gone.

Clem stood frozen to the spot for one moment and then sank to her knees, letting out a howl of such grief it shocked her, and then another one wracking her body. She crouched there, allowing the tears to flow and the sobs to pour out until she was spent with emotion, and then clambered to her feet. Her chest and throat ached, but the pain in her chest, which had tightened the whole time Akil had been here, was gone. Now she could move.

Her father had arranged for the plane to fly her back

that evening, so she headed back up the garden to the villa mechanically. She'd brought very little with her, so as not to arouse suspicion, and it didn't take long to put her scant few belongings in her bag. A paper bag on the dressing table held the bracelets and cufflinks she'd bought a few weeks ago and she slipped one bangle onto her wrist, leaving the other for her sister. She held the cufflinks tight in her hand for one long moment then slipped them into her pocket—she'd ask Henri to deliver them. Her bag packed, she took it through to the hallway and then began to tidy up the coffee she'd made earlier.

She needed to keep busy. She couldn't allow herself to think, to feel, to understand that this was her last day in Asturia, that she'd never see Akil again, had no idea when she'd see her sister again.

Finally, there was nothing else to do and Clem wandered back out into the garden and down to the bathing platform staring out at the lake, at the magnificent palais in the distance. She'd never wanted to grow up here; beautiful as it was, she preferred the Cornish cottage, and was immensely grateful she'd not had to deal with all the rigmarole and ceremonial nonsense Arrosa had had to navigate. But she'd like to have been able to visit here, to share this house with her sister, for them to be sitting here by the lake together gossiping, a chilled bottle of wine awaiting them on the terrace.

If she'd said yes to Akil, if she'd been braver, stronger, would that have been a possibility? How could it have been? She and Rosy could have no public relationship; that was why she had to go home, for her sister.

Clem sat down and trailed her hand in the cold water, closing her eyes and remembering the moment Akil had kissed her in the sea, the overwhelming sensations. It had all been overwhelming. Yes, she wanted to protect her sister, but she also needed to protect herself. She was frightened of being hurt, frightened of being left behind, frightened of not being enough.

But it was too late. She had let Akil into her heart and now she was hurting, more than she'd ever imagined possible. But it wasn't Akil's fault; she was doing it to herself. He wanted her to stay; he wanted her to be with him. She was the one turning away.

She knelt down and stared at her reflection in the water, pale and big eyed. What if she did stay? What was the worst that could happen? She couldn't control what her father did or said, and she'd have to be respectful of Arrosa's wishes around any kind of public relationship, but really who would connect Clemence Beaumont with the royal family? Her similarity to her sister was striking, but wild dark curls and hazel eyes were common enough in Asturia.

Akil loved her. She rocked back as the truth of the words hit her. What must it have cost him to have said that? To have made himself so vulnerable, he who lived a life led by duty and responsibility? But he loved her and wanted her no matter the consequences. It was what she'd always wanted and yet she was willing to throw it away.

How could she when she loved him? Could she really return home and carry on living without him? Carry on as if all this had never happened? Of course she couldn't. She was no longer that grieving girl with no idea who she was and what she wanted, who had arrived here just a few weeks before. Akil had helped her find the way. And her way was with him.

She just had to find a way to tell him.

Akil didn't know where he was going to go or what he was going to do as he drove away from the Palais d'Artega, but one thing he did know for sure. This was *not* the end of the conversation. He was not going to just give up.

It would be one thing if Clem had decided to go back to Cornwall of her own volition; if she didn't care enough about him to stay. He wasn't going to pretend that it wouldn't hurt, but he'd have to accept her decision. But he was pretty sure that was not what was going on here. He had no idea exactly what Zorien had said to her but whatever it was had clearly persuaded her that she had no place in Asturia, that her very presence was a danger to her sister.

But the real danger was the secret itself. Secrets had power, a power that only existed as long as the secret did, a power that disappeared once freed. Clem was in her twenties now, and Zorien had technically been a free man when she'd been conceived. The news of her existence would undoubtably cause some scandal, but it would be a short-lived one, especially if both the Artega and the Ortiz families rallied around her.

But what could Akil do? It wasn't his secret to spill, his call to make.

Before he could think better of it, he tapped the call button on his dashboard and commanded his phone to call Arrosa. It rang several times before she picked up.

'Akil, is everything okay?'

'Not exactly. Have you spoken to your father?'

'Funny you should ask that. He's left me a voice-mail and a couple of messages, telling me it's time to come home.' He couldn't quite tell what the Princess thought of her father's command.

'He's told Clem the same thing, that her time here is up,' he said grimly.

'I guess we always knew it wasn't for ever,' Arrosa said, a shadow of unhappiness in her voice.

'You certainly couldn't keep this pretence up for ever. At some point people will want to see the Princess's face,' Akil said dryly. 'Clem needs to be able to leave the palais without disguises and subterfuge. But that doesn't mean that things should have to go back to the way they were. Don't you agree?'

There was a startled silence at the end of the phone. 'What do you mean?' she asked at last.

'We're about to begin a new era here in Asturia, spearheaded by you, Arrosa. Don't you think it's time for a new start in every way?'

'Is this about Clem?'

'I love her,' he said deliberately. 'And I think that she loves me, but she won't stay here with me, she won't put her happiness first, because your father has told her that if anyone finds out who she is the scandal would be too much for you and she loves you too much to be a burden to you.'

'But that's not it at all, Akil. I would love everyone to know who she is, I am so proud of her, but how could I do that to her? Clem has never been the target of the press. She's never been followed anywhere, she's never been commented on, she's never had her outfits dissected, her love life speculated on, her every expression misinterpreted until she had to learn to show no expression at all. She has a freedom that I can never have, and that freedom is the greatest gift I can give her. If anyone knew who she was, she'd lose that.'

'I think that should be her decision, don't you? Arrosa, don't you see, you're protecting her and she's protecting you and the only people losing out are the two of you?'

'And this is all altruistic on your part?'

'I don't deny that I would like her to stay in Asturia, that I would like to carry on seeing her, but this is beyond us, whatever we are. She is all alone, Arrosa. She is going back to Cornwall with no family, no one who really cares about her apart from you and me.'

There was another long silence before she asked, 'What do you want me to do?'

'I'm going to go see your father to tell him that I

think he should come out and acknowledge her if that's what she wants. And then I am going to see if I can persuade your stubborn sister to give us a chance. I just need to know; will you back me up or not?'

'If that's what Clem wants, then yes. I will.'

'Thank you, that's all I needed.'

Akil said goodbye then hung up, and headed towards the castle, parking in his usual spot just outside parliament, and striding into the building, flashing his pass at every barrier and guard post until he'd reached the doorway that separated the royal apartments from the parliamentary building. There he was forced to halt and give his name to a footman and request a meeting with Zorien.

'He'll see me,' he said with a certainty that made the footman look taken aback. Sure enough, the man was back within minutes.

'He said to bring you straight in,' he said in obvious surprise. 'Follow me.' He led Akil through several corridors until they finally reached the heavy oak door that barred the way to Zorien's private office. The footman knocked and opened it, gesturing for Akil to go in.

The King stood at the window gazing out, turning as Akil walked towards him and made a swift bow. 'I was wondering if I'd see you today,' he said.

'Your Majesty.' He straightened. 'I think you know why I'm here.'

Zorien gestured towards a chair. 'Sit down, d'Ortiz. Brandy? No? You're sure?' He sat opposite Akil and sighed. 'It's for her own good, you know,' he said. 'For both their good.'

Akil made himself consider every word, use his politician's diplomacy, not the righteous anger that rumbled through him. 'Isn't that their decision to make now? They're not children any more, Your Majesty. They are women, strong women who have been through a great deal in different ways. They need each other, want to support each other as the sisters they are. It should be their choice where Clem lives and whether they see each other, not yours.'

'So this is an intervention on their behalf? I think both my daughters are capable of speaking for themselves.'

'So do I. But thanks to you they both think silence benefits the other. I don't know if that is deliberate manipulation or an unfortunate misunderstanding, but while they both think they are doing what's best for the other they are not going to challenge you. I, on the other hand, have no such scruples. Instead, I wanted to give you fair warning.' Akil held the King's gaze. 'I love Clem, I want to make a life with her, and I don't care whether you are happy for her to stay in Asturia or not. But *she* cares and that matters to me.'

'So you're here for my blessing.'

'I don't need anyone's blessing. But Clem does. She needs to know that you love her, that you care about her, that you want her in your life. And you should want her. She's an amazing woman, kind and intelligent—and she tells it how it is, which is a really rare quality. She could be a real asset to you, and a real asset to Arrosa. But that's not why you should acknowledge her. You should do it because it's the right thing to do. Because she has nobody else, and you are her father.'

'And you think it's as easy as that, do you?'

Akil smiled at that. 'You and I both know that in politics the easiest decision is rarely the right one. Of course it won't be easy. There will be a lot of talk and a lot of speculation, and it will be unpleasant for a while.'

'I have a wife who is innocent in all this.'

'And a daughter who is also innocent. Clem deserves to hear you stand up for her, for you to say publicly that you're proud of her. Whether you do so is up to you. It's not up to me to spill your secrets. But it's not for me to hide them either. I am going to do everything in my power to persuade Clem to make a life with me here whether you like it or not. And if I do then you will have to find a way to live with that that makes her happy—because if I see you snub her even once, if I ever see her look the way she looked after your visit today again, then this won't be such a civilised conversation.'

'You've made yourself very clear, d'Ortiz.'

'Good.'

The King sighed. 'Are you sure you don't want a drink? I think I need one.' He stood up and poured two generous measures of brandy, setting one before Akil. 'I have to say, I am half hoping she turns you down. You would be an exhausting son-in-law. But maybe it would be better to have you close. You could also be an asset as Arrosa starts to take the reins. A brother-in-law like you on her side would be a formidable weapon.'

'As would Clem, if she has a place here. You'll consider it?'

'I need to talk to Arrosa and I need to talk to my wife, but if Clem wants me to publicly recognise her, then maybe it's time. Tell her I will think about it.'

Akil stood up, his brandy untouched. 'Thank you, sir.'

'Good luck, d'Ortiz.'

Akil grinned then. 'I'll need it. Your daughter can be very stubborn, sir.'

'Don't I know it. She's very like her mother.' The rather austere face softened. 'I did what I thought was right at the time, what I thought was right for Asturia, and I don't do regrets. Iara has been a good queen, maybe better than I deserve, and I love my daughter more than she'll ever know. But I wish I could have been a father to Clem, shown her how proud I am of her.'

'It's not too late, sir.' Akil just hoped it wasn't too late for him as well. But he came from a long line of warriors. It was time to fight.

CHAPTER THIRTEEN

CLEM TURNED AWAY from the lake and marched back up to the villa full of purpose. As she reached the terrace she saw a tall figure waiting for her. Her heart leapt, only to sink again when she realised it was Henri; his usually impassive face was full of sympathy.

'The plane is waiting for you, Your Highness.'

'Henri, you really don't have to *Your Highness* me. You never did. I'm just Clem,' she said, and a smile crinkled the usually austere face.

'No matter what, you're the King's daughter, and you deserve the title.'

'Thank you. I'm glad Rosy has you to look out for her. Just let me get my things.'

Clem collected her bag and jacket then stood in the hallway looking around for a moment, picturing her sister working at the desk in the study, stirring something on the stovetop, relaxing in front of the TV. If things went the way Clem hoped, would she be here with her sometimes?

'This isn't goodbye,' she said. 'But *au revoir*, I hope.'

She cast one look around and then followed Henri out to the car, waiting until he opened the door and ushered her inside. As he settled himself inside the driver's seat she leaned forward.

'Henri, will you do me a favour?'

'You look just like your sister when you ask that,' he said suspiciously. She smiled.

'Can we go via the beach? You remember the beach I went to with Akil that first week? I just want to walk on the beach one last time, see the sea so I can remember it.'

She crossed her fingers, hoping that Henri wouldn't point out that she lived by the beach and could see the sea any time she wanted, but simply nodded as he turned on the engine. Clem sat back and pulled her phone out of her bag, typing a brief message.

I'm on the beach. Can we talk?

It wasn't a long drive, but Clem looked out and learnt every piece of it by heart as she pondered the conversation that awaited her—if Akil showed up. She knew one thing: she couldn't allow her future to be decided by Akil. If for whatever reason he changed his mind, if he decided that he'd been right all along and that love was too messy and unpredictable, if he decided he wanted that diplomatic polite marriage after all, she couldn't blame him, nor could she use that as an excuse to run home and hide from the consequences of her decisions.

She had to decide whether Asturia was part of her future or not, not Akil. She had to set the boundaries for any future relationship with her family, not him. She'd been passive long enough. It was time she came out of the shadows. Of course she wanted Akil by her side when she did, but thanks to him she was strong enough to do it alone if she had to.

She just hoped she didn't.

It was mid-afternoon by the time they reached the beach and the car park was busier than she'd seen it, families unloading picnics and groups of teens with surfboards. Many stopped to stare curiously at the limousine.

'Don't open the door for me, Henri,' Clem asked as he pulled the handbrake. 'I don't think anybody will mistake me for my sister, but if they see you acting all chauffeurish someone might put two and two together and make six.'

Sure enough, although a few people stared at her as she opened the door and slid out, no eyes widened with recognition and no one showed any sign of being interested in taking her photo or speaking to her. How different it must be for her sister, not able to even have a simple walk on the beach without Henri's presence to keep onlookers away. If Akil was right, if her sister was prepared to risk scandal and have Clem close by, then was Clem prepared to be the scandal? To be stared at and whispered about and photographed?

With her sister and Akil by her side, she could weather anything.

Clem slipped off her shoes and walked barefoot onto the beach, heading towards the shoreline where gentle waves lapped the sand, holding up her skirt so she could wade in up to her ankles, tipping her head up to look at the sky, the same deep blue as the sea. How she loved the smell of sea air, the salt and water and air combining into something more than the sum of its parts. It smelt like home. She could live anywhere as long as she could feel sand beneath her toes and submerge herself in the sea.

She checked her phone, there was no message, no answer from Akil, but there was a brief message from her sister.

I just want to say that whatever you do decide I have your back, always. I'm proud of you and I'm proud to have you in my life and I am happy to shout it from the rooftops to anyone and everyone if that's what you want. I love you, big sis.

Clem swallowed. She'd cried more than enough today, but it was hard to read the message through blurry tears. She quickly sent a reply.

Right back atcha!

Casting a hopeful look back towards the harbour, Clem continued her slow wade through the soft surf feeling freer than she had done for longer than she could remember. Free of worries, free of insecurities, free to be herself whoever and whatever that meant.

Without allowing herself to think what she was doing, she headed back to the beach and pulled her dress over her head, wrapping her phone in it and laying them on her shoes, and then she turned to wade right back in, heading out until she was waist deep and then diving into the waves, submerging herself, letting the water wash away the last of the doubt and the insecurity. Not the grief; that would never quite go, but with time she would learn to manage it.

As Akil left the castle his phone buzzed and his heart rate sped up, only to decrease when he realised it was from Arrosa.

Whatever Clem wants, whatever Clem decides, I will always back her.

He inhaled, relief filling him. He didn't necessarily need the Princess on his side, but he did need her on Clem's. He replied quickly.

Thank you. I've just had an interesting conversation with your father, I think we've reached a similar consensus.

He sent the message and jammed the phone back into his pocket as he reached the car, unlocking it and sitting behind the wheel trying to decide where he should go, what he should do. In one way nothing had changed since he had left Clem and yet at the same time everything had changed. He understood her position a little bit better, thanks to his conversations with Arrosa and with the King, and he knew that he could promise with truth that if Clem decided to stay she wouldn't be reliant on him, but that her sister would also have space for her, that there was the possibility of a more open relationship with her father, but they were just words. How could he make her see his truth when through fear for herself and love for her sister she'd erected barriers so tall and so thick it would take more than words for Akil to battle through them?

Think, he told himself fiercely. *Think*.

Finally Akil jumped out of the car and half jogged through the streets until he reached his home, letting himself into the apartment where, after quickly feeding Tiger, he rooted around looking for his spare key. Pocketing it, he checked his watch, still not sure if Clem was meant to be heading back to the UK that night, and wended his way through the maze of alleyways behind his apartment until he reached the small jeweller's shop where he and Clem had browsed just a few days before.

The shop specialised in sea glass, and Clem had exclaimed at the beautiful turquoise and greens of the polished jewels. Akil stepped inside and selected a keyring and a matching necklace, quickly paying before jogging back to his car. He slid inside and took the key from his pocket, carefully fastening it onto the keyring, and put the keyring and necklace onto the passenger seat. Right, he had a plan, he just needed the girl.

He pulled out his phone to check it again, his heart speeding up when he saw her name. She was on the beach. That had to be a good sign. He didn't need to ask which beach, quickly starting the car and driving as quickly as he legally could out of the city and across the hilly terrain until he reached the harbour. To his relief he saw her limousine parked up at one end of the car park, Henri leaning against it, the usual inscrutable expression on his face. Akil parked next to it and got out, palming the key and necklace and putting them in his back pocket.

'Is she still here?' he asked, and Henri nodded.

'She went for a walk.'

'How strict are your instructions? Is it a case of getting her to the airfield no matter what, or is there some flexibility?'

'I think they were open to interpretation,' Henri said. 'She'll be safe with you?'

'Always.'

Henri nodded. 'Her bag is in the car.'

It was almost heartbreaking to see how little she had with her, just one small duffel bag that fitted even in Akil's tiny boot. He locked the car and nodded one more time at Henri.

'Thanks for looking after her.'

Akil set off for the beach, standing on the edge and looking out across the sands. It was busy, families gathered for picnics and groups of teens sunbathing and splashing in the waves. He scanned the scene carefully, looking for a single figure walking alone, but couldn't see Clem anywhere. He was going to have to play this one by instinct. He navigated his way through the crowds, until he reached the quieter section a little further away from the harbour. There was still no sign of her.

'Where are you, Clem?' he muttered, looking around, his attention snagged by a piece of material waving in the wind, the same green as the dress Clem had been wearing earlier. He walked over to see the dress neatly folded on a rock, her shoes underneath and, turning, he looked out at the sea. There she was, swimming strong and sure like the naiad he called her, complete in her own natural habitat.

Akil didn't stop to think, unfastening his shirt, kicking off his trainers and discarding his trousers, leaving his clothes in a heap on the sand beside her dress. He walked quickly into the surf and struck out to join her.

The sea was coolly refreshing, filling him with hope and anticipation as he recalled the last time they'd swum together and the time before that—swimming usually ended up with them in bed, salty damp limbs curled around each other. It didn't take him long to reach her; she'd stopped to tread water, her face tilted up to the sky, and he swam up to face her.

'Nice day for a swim,' he said, and she started, submerging for a second then resurfacing with a gasp. His heart pounded at the sight. She was in her underwear, a pale lemon lace, that clung to her wet curves, her hair sleeked back.

'You scared me,' she said through her splutters.

'I scared you? You're not the one who found a small pile of clothes on the beach with no sight of you to be had,' he pointed out and she smiled up at him.

'I was bored waiting for you and the water looked so refreshing. I feel more like me when I'm in the sea, like a different person, a better person.'

'I'm sure you were a mermaid in a different life.'

'I'm sorry,' she said suddenly, the smile dimmed. 'I am so sorry for what I said earlier today. It's not that I didn't love you, that I don't love you. I do, Akil.'

'I know,' he said—and he did know. Knew with every fibre in him.

'But I was scared. Scared of what my life might be like here if my father decides he doesn't want me here, scared of what my life would be like if you tired of me, if you found me too complicated. Your life is so different from mine, Akil, what you need in a partner is so different from who I am. It's not as if you're unaffected by Court decisions. If my family don't want me around then that will affect you. Affect things that are important to you. I don't want that to happen to you, but, more than that, I don't want to see the look on your face when you realise I'm hampering your career, that I'm in the way. I've seen the look before, you see, on my father's face. I couldn't bear to see it on yours.'

Akil fought to find the right words. 'Clem, you will never see that look on my face, because I will always be proud of you, always want you by my side. I don't know what the future holds for you and your family, although I hope it will be better than what you anticipate, but even if they wanted to banish you completely, never recognise you, I'd still be proud to call you mine. I'll always be proud that you're mine. And you are mine,' he said possessively fiercely, exultant as she nodded.

'I said that all I wanted was someone to love me, and put me first, then here you were offering me just that and I was too terrified to reach out and take it. I'm still scared, Akil,' she admitted. 'I like to project this image of myself as fearless, and in some ways I am, I can go on stage in front of thousands without a single nerve, but when it comes to my heart I'm the biggest coward of all.'

'I meant what I said, Clem. I love you and you will always have a home with me if you want one. I don't want some dull and respectable marriage of convenience to further my career, I want a straight-talking, big-hearted English girl who is happiest in the sea, and thinks nothing of trying to cram twenty activities into one day. I want you and I love you, and I think you and I can do great things here in Asturia; you're already *doing* great things.' He swam closer and touched her cheek, willing his truth into her. 'The work you have started in the hospital is inspiring, Clem. I meant what I said earlier. I'm sure we can find ways to expand it if that's what you want. But if your family make it too difficult for you to be here and that really hurts you, then I'm open to other possibilities. I'm not saying it would be easy, politics isn't really the kind of career that translates well to other countries, but I've had invitations to lecture before and offers of fellowships. I could make it work.'

Clem gazed at Akil wonderingly. 'You would do that for me?'

He smiled into her eyes. 'I hoped you might know by now that I would do anything for you.'

It wasn't just the words, it was the sincerity in his voice and Clem knew that he meant every word, that Akil would walk away from the promise he'd made his father, from the title, from his life here if she asked him to, not because it would be easy or he wanted to, but because her happiness mattered to him. But that kind of strength had to run both ways.

'I don't want to run away. I love it here. I love it here because of you, because of the Asturia that *you* show me, the country that *you* love. The country you dedicate yourself to with your job, with the volunteering you do, with everything you are. How could I not love it? You inspire me with everything you do. I hope that if I stay I can be the kind of asset you need. I'm not really sure how to work a room, but I can learn. It's just another form of acting after all.'

Akil laughed at that, pulling her closer, and she moved in to meet him, her hands on his shoulders, legs entwined as his lips met hers in a brief kiss that sent them both back under the surface. She held onto him as she kicked her way back up, kissing him again as soon as they hit the air.

'My naiad,' he said, smoothing her hair off her face, and she leaned into the caress. 'Could you bear to come back to shore?'

'Maybe this once,' she said, holding his hand as they made their way through the waves back to where they'd abandoned their clothes. It was still so warm that the water began to dry on her skin as soon as they left the sea, and she pulled her dress over her underwear while Akil shrugged his shirt back on, leaving it open. She reached out to run her hand down his chest, enjoying the play of muscles and his intake of breath.

'I've got something for you,' he said, looking uncharacteristically nervous as he picked up his jeans and slid his hand into the pocket. 'I don't want you to feel like you never have a home, Clem. This is yours, for always, to use every day, I hope, but if not whenever you want to.' Clem blinked as she looked at the key, attached to a beautiful turquoise oval of sea glass.

'What's this?'

'It's a key to my apartment,' Akil said, smiling down at her. 'You said the first time you visited that it felt home like. I'm glad you think so because I'd like it to be your home for a while at least. Maybe at some time we could look for a place together, somewhere by the sea, with direct access so you can swim to your heart's content.'

She turned it over, letting the sea glass catch the sun and watching the metal glinting, the symbolism almost more than she could take in. 'You've given me a key?'

'Maybe it's not the most romantic of gifts…'

'It is, it's the most romantic thing I've ever received.' She stepped over the sand and cupped his face in her hands, kissing him fiercely, putting all her love and longing into the embrace. 'It's perfect, Akil, it's absolutely perfect. Thank you, and yes, I would love to have a key to your apartment and yes, I would love to stay there with you and one day move to a house by the sea. I need to go back to Cornwall first. I need to pack up my mother's things and decide what I need and move Gus across. I hope Tiger won't mind a roommate.'

'I know parliament is due back, but I would love to come with you, to see the place you grew up and meet your friends.'

'That would be perfect. I don't believe in ghosts, but the cottage still feels like my mother. I would love her to meet you. I know that sounds silly…'

He slipped an arm around her shoulders. 'It doesn't sound silly at all. I'd be honoured.'

'Oh,' she remembered. 'I have something for you too. I was going to ask Henri to give it to you.' She felt in her pocket and brought out the paper bag. 'I bought it the day we first went on the boat, with matching bracelets for Rosy and me. My mother loved trees the way I love the sea. She always wore nature-inspired things but trees were extra special to her. The very first campaign I remember was her trying to save an old oak from demolition and she got involved with at least two bypass protests—chained herself onto branches and everything. At the time I thought it was totally embarrassing and wished she could just be normal, now I'd give anything to chain myself up next to her. Anyway, I saw these and thought of her.' She handed him the bag and said shyly, 'If you don't like them…'

'I love them.' He held up the delicate cufflinks. 'I'll wear them to the Senate and let myself be inspired by your mother.'

'Be careful, who knows what she'll make you vote for?'

'She raised you, didn't she? I trust her instincts.'

'I think she would like you, Akil Ortiz.' Clem pressed herself close and kissed him, luxuriating in the feel and taste and solidity of him. This wasn't just a fling, this was real, as real as she wanted it to be. She was no fool. She knew relationships needed work and compromise, but she also knew this man was worth it.

'I know it's too early,' he said at last. 'But I want you to know that at some point this year I am going to ask you to marry me. There's a lot to work out, where we'll live, what path we'll take, but as long as we're together we can do it.'

'And I want you to know that I will say yes,' she told him, blinking back happy tears. 'That my home is where you are. I do have one condition…'

'Anything.'

'That once a month we sail away and for at least one night.'

'I'll build it into our marriage vows,' he promised, and she laughed.

'I love you, Akil. Thank you for giving me the space to figure out who I am and what I want, thank you for believing in me. Thank you for loving me.'

'That's the easy part,' he told her and then he kissed her again until she was lost in him. She didn't need a stage or an audience to feel validated any more; she wasn't lost. Thanks to Akil she knew exactly who she was and what she wanted.

'I love you,' she whispered against his mouth and felt him smile.

'And I love you, and I am more than ready to demonstrate how much. Let's go and let your father know that, thank you, but you won't be returning to Cornwall just yet, and then I suggest a few nights at sea, while we get used to this for ever thing.'

'That sounds perfect.' She kissed him again and then, his hand clasping hers, turned towards the harbour. Akil was by her side and had vowed to stay there; she wasn't alone any more. She had a family: a sister and this man. She had a place. She looked up at the late afternoon sky, the sun still beating down, and raised her face to the warmth, sending a moment of love towards her mother, wherever she was, before allowing Akil to tug her towards the harbour. Towards their life together. Their future. She couldn't wait.

★ ★ ★ ★ ★

Princess Arrosa

Dear Reader,

Welcome to part two of The Princess Sister Swap.

One of my favorite films is *Roman Holiday*, not just because Gregory Peck is gorgeous and Audrey Hepburn utterly beautiful, but because it's so bittersweet. Much as Audrey Hepburn's princess adores every moment of her escape into Rome, she knows that duty calls in the end. And that's how it is for Arrosa, the heroine of the second book in this series. She is loving her time in Cornwall masquerading as Clem's cousin Rosy, and she's enjoying getting to spend time with handsome tycoon Jack Treloar and his two adorable daughters, but she knows that eventually she has to go back to Asturia and take up her role as the Crown Princess.

I loved revisiting Clem, Arrosa and Asturia, exploring what happened when Arrosa was in Cornwall, and peeking into Clem and Akil's future, and it's always a joy to spend time in Cornwall, even if it is in my imagination. I hope you enjoy Arrosa and Jack's story as much as I enjoyed writing it.

Love,

Jessica

This book is for everyone who has been able to escape from the trials of the last couple of years through reading romance. Here's to escapism and brighter days.

CHAPTER ONE

Jack Treloar sat back in the rather uncomfortable stone seat and surveyed his fellow audience members. No surprises here. The audience was exactly what he had expected, people from the village and the surrounding towns, mostly friends and family of the cast, together with a smattering of tourists. An easily pleased, uncritical, warm audience predisposed to be supportive of the amateur production.

Everything he wanted to change.

Although he had to admit to being pleasantly surprised by the performance itself. Yes, it was amateurish, yes, the costumes were clearly home-made, and the backdrops and props owed more to enthusiasm than skill, but some of the acting was really good, good enough to transport him—momentarily—from noticing the chill of the stone seat and the laboured scene changes. Juliet was especially good, although that was no real surprise. After all, Clem Beaumont was a professional, one who, in Jack's opinion, should go back to finding proper paid work and spend less time poking her nose into his business.

At least what he *hoped* would be his business if he could just win round the very community sitting here to his vision. He allowed his gaze to wander around the auditorium once again. This place was a gem, an open-air amphitheatre, stone seats rising up from a semi-circular stage, the sea visible beyond creating a truly atmospheric backdrop as the early June sky began to tinge pink, the sun sinking at last.

At least, it should be a gem. But right now it was more unpolished diamond than jewel in the village crown. Ticket-buyers for the pitifully few shows put on here headed in through a plain reception area where, instead of a bar and restaurant, volunteers sold lukewarm white wine and cans of beer from a trestle table. There was nowhere to mingle, to enjoy an interval drink, to soak up the atmosphere. But the potential was here for anyone with half an eye—and Jack had that eye. He could turn this theatre and Polhallow into a *destination.* A place people flocked to not just for the sea, beautiful as it was, or for the scenery or any of the other reasons that made the Cornish village such an attractive place to holiday, but for the theatre, just as people visited St Ives for art or Padstow for food. Jack had done his research; the stage was big enough to tempt the major touring companies, and the venue could host bands as well as musicals and plays. He could put Polhallow on the map.

But to say that the local community didn't share

his vision would be putting it mildly; you'd think he was planning on tearing the whole thing down and replacing it with some kind of concrete monstrosity rather than trying to bring jobs and prosperity to the village outside the crucial summer season. He'd even guaranteed that the local schools, dance troupes and amateur companies could still use the theatre—so why couldn't the village see that everyone would benefit? Probably because he was the one behind the scheme. Clearly it didn't matter how rich and successful he was, the people of Polhallow would only ever see him as the town tearaway.

Well, they would learn to look again. Polhallow was the right place to raise his daughters—fresh air, outdoor pursuits and less of the monied hedonism that characterised their affluent London neighbourhood. If he had to win the townsfolk round to smooth his daughters' path then that was what he would do. Not that he would mind seeing respect, no matter how grudging, in the eyes of everyone who had doubted or judged him in the past.

Jack had intended to leave at the interval but, despite himself, he found himself getting caught up in the tragedy unfolding on the stage, even though he knew all too well where teen melodrama could lead. The play was brought to life by Clem's charisma and skill and the rest of the cast rose to meet her, some of them achieving what Jack suspected were hitherto unexpected heights. By the time Juliet collapsed on her lover's tomb and the final epilogue was spoken,

Jack was shocked to feel the prickling of tears in his eyes. He looked around hurriedly, hoping nobody had seen the weakness. He needn't have worried, because although his presence had attracted a few stares and pointed comments when he'd arrived, most people were too absorbed in the play to give him more than a second glance and were now applauding the cast with gusto.

The woman sitting next to Jack was no exception. She was on her feet clapping and whooping as if she had been watching the Royal Shakespeare Company, tears trickling down her cheeks, visible despite her huge sunglasses, her shouts of 'Bravo! Bravo!' ringing out. She sat back down, removing her sunglasses to quickly wipe away the tears, and caught Jack's amused gaze with a slightly self-deprecating shrug.

'Wasn't that amazing?' She spoke English fluently and with no real discernible accent but there was a trace of something he couldn't place, almost Spanish, or southern French.

'It wasn't what I expected,' Jack said diplomatically. Amazing was maybe pushing it, but he couldn't deny the play hadn't been the car crash he had been expecting.

'Clem is so talented, I had no idea.' The woman continued clapping again enthusiastically and bouncing to her feet as the lead actress came forward. There was a definite similarity between the smiling actress and his neighbour, both had long dark curls and a similar slant to their high cheek-boned oval faces with long-lashed hazel eyes above full mouths. A sense of recognition tugged at him.

'Have we met?' Jack asked.

She shook her head, replacing the sunglasses firmly. 'I don't think so, I'm not from around here. I'm a cousin of Clem's.'

'That explains the resemblance,' he said, and she smiled but with a hint of nervousness that surely his innocuous comment couldn't have provoked.

'Are you staying here long?'

'No.' She slumped very slightly, her tone dejected. 'I have to get back; you know how it is. Duty calls, but I wish I could stay. There is something so special about Polhallow, don't you think? I would love to spend more time here.'

'I know what you mean. I just moved back from London, and I can't believe it's taken me so long.' It was definitely the right idea to move his family back to Cornwall. London felt too big, too dirty, too dangerous for his girls. He wanted them to grow up with beaches to play on and with sea air filling their lungs.

Of course, their childhood was very different to his, thanks to the big clifftop house, the swimming pool and treehouse, the playroom filled with everything their hearts desired. Jack knew the dangers of spoiling his girls, but he also knew what it was like to go without, and it was hard not to be indulgent when they'd lost their mother at such a tender age. He wanted to give them everything he had never had—including a name that was respected. His fortune and success impressed some people, but to far too many he was still that wild Treloar boy.

The cast had taken their final bow and moved off the stage and the audience around them began to move. 'It was nice meeting you.' He held out a hand. 'I'm Jack Treloar. Have a good rest of your visit and do pass my congratulations on to Clem. She's quite something.'

The woman hesitated before taking his hand. As his hand closed round her soft, cool fingers a tingle shot up his arm, unexpected and potent, and it was all he could do not to drop her hand; it had been a long time since he'd had such a powerful physical reaction to a woman, not since Lily. Sometimes he thought that part of him had been buried with his wife.

'Rosy,' she said after a brief pause. 'My friends call me Rosy.' A flower name. His chest squeezed. His wife had insisted on flower names for their daughters, to mirror hers.

'Nice to meet you, Rosy. If you find yourself making a longer stay than expected, look me up. I'd love to buy you a drink.'

Rosy looked as astonished by his offer as he felt having made it. He had been a married man since he was just eighteen thanks to an unplanned pregnancy, widowed for just two years. Jack couldn't remember the last time he'd asked a woman out. Dimples flashed in her cheeks, adding an elfin charm to her undeniable beauty.

'That's a very kind offer, Jack. Maybe one day I'll

be able to take you up on it.' She nodded towards the exit. 'I need to go. Enjoy the rest of your evening.'

Jack watched the slim, graceful woman make her way out and a wry smile twisted his mouth. The first time in years he'd been tempted to make a move on a woman, and she couldn't get out of there fast enough.

Nice job, Treloar.

He watched her for another couple of seconds before making his own way out of the theatre, acknowledging the few who acknowledged him but not stopping to join any of the chattering groups. He wouldn't be welcome anyway. Besides, he was keen to get home and check in on his sleeping girls, to drop a kiss on their foreheads and whisper his daily affirmation that he was here, and they were safe.

Glancing towards the exit Rosy had disappeared through, he headed in the opposite direction towards home. He was unlikely to see her again and that was a good thing. He didn't have time to date. His family came first, his business second and restoring his name third. That was his choice and he stood by it.

But part of him was still disappointed that they wouldn't have time for that drink before Clem's mysterious cousin disappeared again.

Arrosa Artega, soon to be the Crown Princess of Asturia, made it back to the little clifftop cottage where Clem lived before her half-sister and let herself in with the key she valued far more than any of her heirloom jewels. Henri, her ever-present driver and bodyguard, manoeuvred the bulky hamper she'd brought with her into the house before returning to guard the outside while Arrosa poured herself a glass of wine and curled up on the sofa in the sitting room waiting for Clem to return.

Maybe it was foolishness to risk exposing Clem's identity for such a fleeting visit, but Arrosa hadn't seen her sister in so long. She'd wanted to see her sister act, true, but she was also in a real tangle and Clem was the person who always helped her see straight.

As she sipped the wine she looked around the cosy room with its filled bookshelves and colourful paintings, Gus, the latest in a string of rescue cats, asleep on the window seat. This cottage always felt like home to her, far more than the luxurious château in which she had been raised, and she would always be grateful to Clem's mother for letting her be part of the family, even if Arrosa's—and Clem's—father, Zorien, had deceived the French woman about who he was, and then paid her off to keep Clem's existence a secret. The room was filled with Simone Beaumont's eclectic taste, reflecting her larger-than-life personality, and Arrosa's heart ached with grief for the woman who had been a second mother to her, remembering the summers she had spent here and Simone's warm wisdom and affection.

She was still lost in memory when she heard the sounds of Clem's return and jumped up to embrace her before standing back to examine her closely, drinking in the sister she barely saw.

'It's not that I'm not happy to see you, Rosy, but what on earth are you doing here?' Clem asked as Arrosa handed her a glass of wine.

'Apart from watching my sister play Juliet? Clem, you were brilliant.'

'You've never come to see me act before.'

Guilt hit her hard as she curled back up on the sofa. 'I wish I had. Clem, I'm so sorry I didn't come to Simone's funeral. I loved her so much, but…'

'That's okay, she would have understood. And you sent such beautiful flowers.'

'But you're my sister, I should have been there for you.'

'It's hard for you to get away. I know that.'

It was, but that was no real excuse, not when Clem needed her. 'It was easier when we were children,' she said wistfully. 'Especially when I was at school and could spend my exeat weekends here as well as some of the holidays.' It had been eight long years since she had last spent time here in Polhallow as plain Rosy, Clem's French cousin. In her memory every day had been sunny and filled with laughter and happiness. The joy of being just Rosy, not a princess.

Clem came and sat next to her, squeezing her hand. 'Fess up, why are you here, apart from coming to see me as Juliet? Don't think I'm not pleased to see you, but I know you and impulsive isn't in your schedule. Is everything okay?'

Arrosa took a swig of wine and summoned up the courage to say the words she had barely dared to think, memories of her conversation with Akil Ortiz echoing through her mind. 'I'm not sure.' She paused and glanced at her sister. 'I think I just asked someone to marry me.'

'You *think* or you did? Are congratulations in order? Who is the lucky man?' She could hear the worry in Clem's voice and tried not to wince.

'Akil. He's the Vicomte d'Ortiz, a rising star of the opposition. His father, the Duc d'Ortiz, was one of Papa's most vocal critics. Our families have been enemies for generations, you know how Asturians can be, but Akil and I are friends of a sort. We have a lot in common. Family honour and expectations and that kind of thing.'

'Friends of a sort? You're not even dating? Besides, what do you mean, you *think* you asked him to marry you?'

Feeling suddenly overwhelmingly weary, Arrosa tried to find the words to explain how helpful Akil had been in unifying the opposition parties behind the new inheritance law that was due to be ratified at the end of the summer. A law that would change the course of her already restricted life, undoing the primogeniture laws and making her the official heir to the throne.

'Clem, everyone—my parents, my advisers, the newspapers—have been pushing me to marry,' she went on, taking another sip of her wine as her stomach knotted with apprehension about the weeks and months and years ahead. 'To start thinking about an heir of my own. And the country will see me as more settled, more mature if I am married. I don't like being rushed, but I see the sense in it. The problem is, not only am I single but I don't see that changing. On the rare occasion I meet someone I like, the whole princess thing scares them off. Queen-to-be is going to make that a hundred times worse.' She sighed. 'I like Akil and he understands the court and my world and we have similar ambitions for Asturia… We were talking about what I wanted to achieve as the heir and realised how aligned our goals were, and I suddenly thought, well, he's the right age, single, understands my world. I could do a lot worse.' But even as she said the words, she could hear how hollow they were, how defeatist. She wasn't quite twenty-seven yet. Did she really want to settle, no matter how sensible her choice? Looking at Clem's expression, she knew her sister was thinking the same thing.

'Rosy, I think this is something you need to take some time and think about.' Clem was obviously picking her words with care. 'Really think about. You need a break. Stay here for a few weeks, Rosy. You know the Cornish air does you good.'

Closing her eyes, Arrosa imagined waking up to the Cornish sun, long walks on the beach and carefree days. 'I'd love to, but I'm heading back tonight.' It had been hard enough concealing her movements for this one evening, any longer would be too dangerous.

'Tonight? Oh, Rosy. You said yourself that you have no meetings.'

'I don't, but the speculation if I'm not seen, even from a distance, could be damaging this close to the ratification. I didn't go anywhere for a couple of weeks when I had flu last year and, according to the tabloids, I was having a facelift, had joined a cult and eloped with a soldier.' She tried for a laugh, but she knew it was unconvincing and could see Clem's face crease with concern. 'I know it's silly and I shouldn't care, but it's not just that I don't want any rumours circulating at home—eventually the press would find me and then they'd start wondering who *you* are and that's the last thing you need. It's safest for you if we're not seen together, Clem.'

How she hated the subterfuge and lies, wished she and Clem could be sisters openly, but she had spent eight years being the target of press interest and speculation. There was no way she was subjecting her sister to that intrusion.

'*If* they find you. After all, why would they look for you here?' Clem paused, a thoughtful expression crossing her face. 'I could go back to Asturia in your place.'

What had she just said? Arrosa couldn't have heard her sister correctly. But Clem had a determined air that Arrosa recognised all too well, one that usually preceded a piece of mischief.

'You're serious? Clem, no one would *ever* think you were me.'

'Up close, no. But in the back of a car, hair all neat like yours, in your clothes, with those big sunglasses you wear? Why wouldn't they? People see what they expect to see. We're the same build and height, the same colouring. And I'm an actress, I can walk like you, hold myself like you. You could have the summer here and I'll spend it in Asturia making sure the press gets enough glimpses to think you're busy preparing for the ratification and leaving you free to get some serious relaxation. I talk about my cousin all the time. No one here will think anything of it if we say I've got a job and you're cat-sitting. The only unbelievable part will be that I've been cast in anything. I'll have to claim I ended up on the cutting room floor.'

'That's the craziest thing I've ever heard. We'd never get away with it.' But how she wished they could.

'If you lived in the main castle or had dozens of servants then I agree, it would be impossible…'

'But I have my own cottage in the grounds of the Palais d'Artega,' Arrosa said slowly, the idea beginning to take shape. It was crazy and impossible, but she couldn't help imagining how it might work. 'People do come in to clean, but not when I'm around. Only Marie is there regularly, but of course she and Henri would need to know if there was any chance of this succeeding…'

Was there a chance? Clem was right, she had no appointments, no duties, no meetings for the next six weeks. No one was expecting to see her so who would know she wasn't actually there if Clem posed as her a couple of times a week in the back of a car? For a moment she allowed herself to visualise it, waking up to freedom, walks in public with no one taking any notice of her. But then reality inserted itself into her dreams. 'But it would be lonely, Clem. You'd have to be careful that no maids, no gardeners, no staff at all saw you. Some are new but some have been at the Palais since I was a baby. What would you do with yourself?'

'I'll make sure the press see Henri drive me around dressed as you, of course, but in between I'll wear my own clothes, let my hair go back to natural wildness and explore Asturia incognito. I've always wanted to go but somehow I never have. It would be a chance for me to see our father too. It'd be easier for him to spend time with me if I'm living at yours. No one would question him visiting you.'

Arrosa took another sip of wine and sat back. Clem no longer sounded speculative or concerned—she sounded hopeful. Arrosa knew how much her sister longed for a real relationship with their father, more so since she'd lost her mother. Zorien was a politician and diplomat first, a family man second and Arrosa wasn't sure he would ever be what Clem wanted him to be, but her sister deserved the chance to find that out for herself. A few weeks living in Asturia, able to visit Zorien openly, might give her that opportunity.

Another objection occurred to her. 'But what's the point of me being here if you aren't?' Most of the joy of being in Cornwall was being with Clem.

'Well, Gus needs feeding for a start. The sea needs

swimming in, scones need eating, beaches need walking on, and you need time to be you, not the Crown Princess and future Queen. This gives you that time. And I need a change of scene too. I've been putting off making plans for my future, just existing for too long. Maybe some time away will give me some much-needed perspective. You'd be doing me a favour.'

'Sure, *I'd* be doing *you* the favour.' Arrosa shook her head affectionately at Clem.

'We'll do each other a favour. We both need some time away from our lives, so why not swap for a while? Your mother's not at home, is she?'

'No, she's spending the summer on Ischia on a retreat.'

'Then we're safe. We could do this. Your call, Rosy. What will it be? Six weeks of avoiding Akil, ducking away from the press and worrying yourself into a shadow, or all the cream teas you can eat and a summer lazing on the beach?'

'We must be mad to even consider this would work.' But she couldn't deny she was tempted.

'It's easy enough to swap back if we need to,' Clem pointed out. Arrosa stared at her for another minute, unable to deny how sorely tempted she was. Not just tempted, she needed this, more than she wanted to admit. Why not agree and see what happened?

'You're right. Let's give it a week and see where we are. Thank you, Clem. Cornwall is just what I need, and I think maybe Asturia is where you need to be as well. To a change of scenery.' She held up her glass and Clem clinked it with hers.

'To the princess swap.'

CHAPTER TWO

IT TOOK ARROSA several moments to realise where she was the next morning. So many nights she'd dreamt she was back in the Cornish cottage, it was almost a shock to find herself there in actuality and not just in her imagination. The cosy bedroom was exactly the same as it had been the last time she had slept here. It never failed to touch her that Simone and Clem had kept a room just for her. The imposing château in which she had been raised had never felt like home the way the cottage did, and even though at twenty-one she'd moved out to a villa in the estate grounds, when she thought of home she thought of here.

The walls were the same sea green she'd picked at fifteen, the curtains and bedspread the ones she'd chosen at the same time. The dressing table still held some out-of-date cosmetics and the hairbrush she'd left here eight years ago and the small built-in wardrobe was filled with her clothes, most of which still fitted despite being bought for a teen. She'd rifled through it nostalgically the night before, searching for pyjamas. Some of the clothes were a little out of date and some not suitable for a woman in her mid-twenties, but nobody would be photographing her here; there was no need to be the fashionable designer Princess who graced countless magazine covers. Here she could just be Rosy in a pair of shorts and bikini top. Besides, there was always Clem's room to raid if she needed anything more.

It wasn't just her room that had been preserved in time. Clem had left home at eighteen to go to drama school and her room, which had been redecorated the same time as Arrosa's, was still decorated in the grey and white with orange accents theme she'd chosen back then. As for Simone's room… A lump filled Arrosa's throat as she stood at the doorway. There was no trace of the sickroom it had become. Rather it was as if Simone would walk in at any time to pick up one of the chic scarves with which she would transform her deceptively simple clothes. Her jewellery hung from pegs on the wall, her bed heaped high with cushions, the window seat overlooking the sea dressed with her favourite cashmere throw. It was impossible to believe that she wouldn't be coming back.

It took Arrosa a couple of hours to get herself together and dressed, padding around the cottage as she reacquainted herself with every nook and cranny. She took coffee, fruit and yogurt outside to breakfast in the pretty cottage garden before donning some of her old denim shorts, teaming them with a bright pink vest top, tucking her curls into a ponytail and adding some sunglasses as she readied herself to leave the house.

Walking down the road, weaving in and out of crowds of tourists, browsing shop windows felt like a five-star luxury experience. Nobody was watching her, nobody was judging her, she didn't need to watch her facial expressions or ensure that every hair was in place. Almost unconsciously her stride lengthened, her pace got jauntier as she breathed in the fresh sea air and drank in the scenery. She was almost lost to her surroundings as she stepped into the road, only to stop with a shock as a car screeched to a halt, a heavy hand on the horn alerting her to the fact she had nearly got herself run over. Of course, they drove on the left here. Holding up her hands in apology, Arrosa stepped back, only to halt in surprise as she recognised the irate driver at the wheel. It was the man who'd spoken to her yesterday, Jack something. The one she'd told she wouldn't be sticking around, the one who had asked her out for a drink. Recognition mingled with interest and a pull deep down she barely recognised, a flare of attraction as she took in the broad shoulders, sensual mouth and hooded eyes.

Arrosa sensed the moment he recognised her in return, his expression changing from annoyed to momentary surprise to inscrutable. She flushed, realising that he must think that she'd lied to him to get out of the offered drink. To her surprise she felt a need to explain, to tell him that she had been tempted, surprisingly tempted, to accept, that she really hadn't expected to be here this morning. But as she stood there, hands outstretched in both apology and almost a plea to be heard, he nodded curtly before accelerating away.

'Dammit,' she muttered. But then again, what did it matter? It wasn't as if she'd see him again. But some of the jauntiness left her step as she continued her walk, looking out for traffic a little more carefully.

Attraction was almost a foreign feeling to her. She'd spent so long schooling her emotions to be the perfect princess, the perfect diplomat, that her own personal preferences were almost indiscernible even to her. It had been a long time since she'd had such an instinctive reaction to someone. It was nice in a way to know that she still could feel an instant attraction.

Remembering Clem's instructions to swim and eat, Arrosa popped into the bakery to buy some fresh scones, and then into the delicatessen to add jam, cream and strawberries to her bag, promising herself a jog, swim or both before she tucked in to the delicacies. As she left the deli she bumped into Clem's friend Sally who she'd known as a teen and, after explaining Clem's sudden absence and her own appearance, was delighted to be asked to come along to the pub on Saturday and invited to see the latest in a superhero series at the cinema with Sally and her daughter in a few days' time. The cinema usually meant formal premieres complete with red carpets and receptions and uncomfortable corseted ballgowns. The prospect of a normal seat with popcorn and company she'd chosen was enticing and she accepted with alacrity, promising to let Sally know about the evening drink as well.

Returning to the cottage with her bag bulging with local delicacies, Arrosa started to put them away, pausing to look at remembered plates and mugs, blinking back tears as she saw the jars of jams and chutneys labelled in Simone's exuberant script. She'd just started to chop up some salad for lunch when her phone pinged with a message and she picked it up, expecting to see Clem's name, only for embarrassment to surge through her when she saw Akil's name on the screen. Embarrassment and guilt; she couldn't believe she'd just run away from the awkward situation she'd put them both in. With no little trepidation she opened the message.

Arrosa, I'm at your house with Clem. Let me know everything is all right.

Biting her lip, she reread it. So much for her confidence that nobody would come seeking her and discover their subterfuge. Here they were, less than twenty-four hours after Clem had suggested swapping, and they'd already been found out. Did this mean that she would need to return home? With a heavy heart she tapped out a returning message.

Everything is absolutely fine. I just needed some space. You can trust Clem with anything.

Reading one of Simone's adored vintage crime books with lunch cleared her head somewhat, as did a run followed by a refreshing swim, and by the time she sat back down in the garden to catch the late afternoon sun, Gus at her feet, with a fresh cup of tea and her book some of the anxiety had faded. There was no need for Akil to tell anybody that Clem was in Asturia instead of Arrosa and she knew he was no gossip, that was one of the reasons she trusted him. But she couldn't help but be relieved when her phone rang and Clem's name lit up the screen.

'How's it going?' her sister asked.

'I've had a run, a swim and I've got a week's worth of calories waiting for me in the form of cream and buttered scones so I'm absolutely fine. I'm more worried about you. What happened with Akil?'

'He came to see you. It was all slightly mortifying. I couldn't pretend that I didn't know about your not-quite-a-proposal as he mistook me for you at a distance and by the time he realised I wasn't you he'd already mentioned it. In the end I didn't really have a choice, I had to tell him who I am. But don't worry, our secret's safe.'

Arrosa sat back, trying to decipher Clem's tone. There was a suppressed emotion she couldn't quite identify, a strange kind of self-consciousness, almost excitement, in her sister's voice. What *exactly* had she and Akil talked about?

'What did you think of him?'

'I liked him. I liked him a lot. Obviously, he's handsome, and he's clearly successful, but there's a lot more to him than that. You could do a lot worse, Arrosa.' Clem paused. 'But that's by the by. Being able to do worse is not enough. I still think you need more, you of all people, with the path you have to tread. You need a real partner, someone who loves you and will always put you first. And I told him so.'

Arrosa could just imagine it. Her sister was always forthright. 'What did he say?'

'He agreed that you both had a lot of thinking to do. But I'm going to say to you what I said to him: I can see why on paper you're a good match. You can trust him; he knows your world. But I think that if you focus on that rather than what's in your hearts then there'll be trouble down the line. You both deserve more than something second-best.'

Arrosa's eyebrows shot up. *Both* deserve more? It sounded as if Clem and Akil had had quite the chat. It also sounded as if Akil had made quite the impact on Clem. Interesting. But it was also reassuring to know that someone cared enough about her to be so blunt, to put her interests first. She might feel alone far too often, but she always had her sister.

'Look, Clem,' she said reluctantly. 'My assumption that nobody would come and visit me, that we could pull this off with no one the wiser, was obviously completely wrong. It's been one day and already you've had to explain who you are to someone. I feel better already, just having the chance to walk down the road without anybody knowing who I was is the tonic I needed. It gave me the space to untangle my head a little.' She blew out a deep breath and stared out at the sea in the distance, trying to crystallise her thoughts, rationalise her relief at being away, that odd jolt of attraction that reminded her that she was a woman as well as a princess.

'I think you're probably right,' she said slowly, feeling her way through her tangled thoughts. 'I suggested marriage to Akil out of fear and panic and they're not the right reasons for marriage. Who knows what the future holds? It'd be silly of me to close down any chance of a meaningful relationship just because I'm a little bit scared. So, job done, I feel better and I'm ready to call Akil and apologise for putting him in such an awkward situation. With all that in mind, maybe we should swap back.' She closed her eyes as she made the offer. It was the last thing she wanted, this tantalising hint of freedom to be lost before she'd really had a chance to enjoy it.

'You must be crazy,' Clem said emphatically. 'Unless you've gone around proposing marriage to several other suitable men, I can't see anyone else just turning up at a guarded palace without an invitation. Akil was clearly a special case. And no way is twenty-four hours enough time for you to be completely rested. And *I'm* not ready yet either. I've not seen our father and I've hardly started exploring. One trip to one beach and one lunch of clams, delicious as they were, isn't exactly the exploring I'd intended.'

'Which beach did you go to?'

'I'm not sure.' Self-consciousness entered Clem's voice. 'Akil took me out for lunch and for a walk.'

'That was nice of him.' The two had clearly hit it off. Arrosa wasn't sure what that meant but she resolved to clear the air—and clear up the situation—with Akil as soon as possible.

'Yes, it was. Look, Rosy, let's carry on for a little bit longer and see where we are. But I'm glad you're feeling better and I'm glad you've decided not to marry Akil. I really liked him and if you were in love with him would welcome him as a brother-in-law…' There was a tinge of reservation in her voice that Arrosa noted. Yup, Akil clearly had made *quite* the impression on Clem. 'But as you're not I really think it's for the best. And it's also for the best that you get a good long rest.'

'You're sure?' Relief flooded through Arrosa as she double-checked. It had been the right thing to offer to switch back but she didn't want to, not yet. If possible, she wanted the full six weeks. She wanted more scones, several trips to the cinema, to walk down the street every single day relishing her anonymity.

'I'm sure. Now, go eat that scone and don't forget to send me a picture of Gus so I know you're remembering to feed him. Love you.'

'I love you too.' Arrosa ended the call and placed her phone back on the table, thinking about the next call she needed to make, and sooner rather than later. She might have more time but, before she could really enjoy it, she needed to clear things up with Akil. Not just for her own sake but for her sister's. The things Clem hadn't said were more telling than the things she had, and that self-consciousness in her voice was new.

Maybe she should suggest that Akil take Clem out for more sightseeing?

As for herself, if she saw Jack again she would apologise and offer to buy him a drink. It was the least she could do after misleading him, after all.

'Daddy, please come bodyboarding with us.' Clover tugged at Jack's hand and his phone nearly fell from his grasp, his email half drafted.

'Careful,' he said as he returned his attention to it. 'I need to finish this first. Why don't you carry on with your sandcastle?' He reread the carefully crafted words and added another line. It was time to pull in the big guns, get an external agency to advise on the comms strategy before his theatre plans were washed away by public disapproval.

'I finished my castle. Look, Daddy.'

The plaintive note in her voice tugged at his heart and Jack looked up to see Clover's disappointed expression, the familiar heavy feeling of guilt pressing down on him. He'd never really appreciated it before it had happened to him, the ever-present feeling of not being enough, not doing enough, that accompanied being a single parent. Not for the first time, and he knew not for the last, Jack wished he could go back in time and change all the careless things he'd said to his mother, the times he'd shown his own disappointment when he'd known full well that she was doing her best.

And that was all that anybody could ask, that he did his best. Which meant in this case heading into a crowded sea on a hot June weekend. 'Go on then,' he said, and Clover's bright smile was all the reward he needed. That was the thing about being six, tears turned to smiles in an instant. 'What about you, Tansy?' But he wasn't surprised when his eldest daughter shook her head, the long silky blonde hair and pointed chin so reminiscent of her mother it sometimes hurt to look at her, a reminder of his failures.

'I'll keep an eye on our things,' she said. 'Besides, I've got my reading list to finish.'

Jack touched her hair. 'You've been reading all morning. Come with us, your sister would love it.' But Tansy shook her head and returned to her book with a martyred air that was as worrying as it was irritating.

She'd always been a serious child, too serious her mother had said, with a sense of responsibility that seemed to negate her ability to just let go and have fun. But since Lily's death those traits had become more pronounced, a line of worry too often on her brow, a line wrong on an eleven-year-old girl. He caressed her hair again, telling himself not to mind as she shrugged him off with an exaggerated sigh.

'I'm *working*, Dad.'

'Okay, but you know where we are if you change your mind.' Jack looked back at the small erect figure, still worrying, as Clover pulled him into the cold waves. That was the thing about Cornwall. No matter how hot the outside temperature—and today was practically Mediterranean—the sea was always bracing. Clover didn't seem to notice as she hopped over waves, chattering on about her recent surfing lesson and how close she'd been to standing up. Some of the worry lifted as he listened. This was what he had brought them back here for, this kind of outdoor life, and the pink in her cheeks and happiness babbling through Clover's voice was all the affirmation he needed. Tansy would settle in soon enough.

As Jack and Clover waded in, waiting for the right wave to bodyboard into, he became aware of a slight figure standing further along, waist deep in the water. There was something about her that snagged his attention, the poised, graceful way she stood, almost regally, despite the surf pushing and pulling her. Jack noted dark wavy hair piled high, tendrils curling around a long neck, sunglasses shading high cheekbones. It was the woman from the theatre, the one he'd almost run into the other day. Rosy.

She wasn't moving, just standing still and letting the waves crash over her, but there was something about the way she looked up at the sky, the way she held her hands out that symbolised freedom. She looked as if she had been relieved of a huge burden and was taking this moment to celebrate with the elements. His mouth twisted wryly at the thought. It wasn't like him to be so fanciful, let alone weave stories around complete strangers—besides, she had told him that she wasn't staying around, she'd clearly wanted to let him down gently. He'd obviously imagined the strange instant connection that had seemed to sizzle between them.

As he stood and stared, Rosy turned slowly and her eyes locked on his for a breathless moment, a half-smile lingering on her full mouth before she held up one hand in a half wave. Jack nodded in return and then returned his attention to his daughter, trying his best to put the woman—Rosy—out of his mind.

The rest of the afternoon wasn't the success he'd hoped for when he'd suggested a beach day. It was hot, very hot, and the beach was crowded with the tourists who flocked to Polhallow during the summer months. As the day went on the noise on the beach grew, the sea crammed with swimmers and surfers, and Clover got first sand and then saltwater in her eyes. No sooner was that resolved than she started to cry because she was too hot, and then because she was hungry. Tansy read steadfastly on, pausing only to tend to her sister as if she were her mother, pulling first wet wipes and then suntan cream out of her bag.

'You can trust me to pack for us,' Jack said, half amused, half put out as his eldest daughter raised disbelieving eyebrows.

'Remember last time?' she said. 'You didn't remember Clover's juice.'

'That was different, I didn't expect it to be so hot last time.' And there it was again, that insidious feeling of guilt. He'd been back in Cornwall for over two months and this was only the second time he'd brought his girls to the beach—and the truth was he wouldn't be here now if the nanny hadn't broken her foot and returned to her parents for a few weeks. His daughters only had one parent. Providing for them wasn't enough, he had to make sure he met their emotional needs as well. He needed to play with them more—and somehow get Tansy to relax and trust him to have things under control.

Finally, he packed up their things, promising Clover an ice cream as they wended their way through the families, couples and groups of friends picnicking and lazing on the beach until they reached the beach café. A queue was snaking its way along the path and after a quick look at Clover's mutinous face Jack knew he would be there for some time. There was no way she was going any further without the promised ice cream and no amount of money or infamy would help him jump the queue. Forget the theatre, maybe he should buy an ice cream shop instead. He tried not to huff, jiggle impatiently or check his phone as they waited. Instead, he scanned the queue and, with that same feeling of almost inevitable recognition, clocked Rosy near the front.

Her hair was still tied up and she wore a long pink sundress over her bikini, a bag thrown over her shoulder, and yet she looked as cool and elegant as if she were in the middle of Paris, not on a hot sandy beach. As if aware of his gaze, she turned and looked at him, at Clover hopping from foot to foot and Tansy, who was sighing again as if Jack had conjured up the queue to annoy her, and waved, saying loudly and deliberately, 'Jack. *Jack*, I'm here!'

Both girls looked up at him in surprise. 'Who's that, Daddy?' Clover asked.

Jack squeezed her hand. 'Possibly the answer to our prayers. Just play along girls.'

Tansy said nothing but gave him a suspicious glance as Jack waved back and said extra heartily, 'There you are! I didn't see you, Rosy. Come on, girls. Let's tell Rosy what we want.' Nobody seemed to question the ruse as they joined Rosy at the front of the queue.

'Thank you,' Jack muttered with heartfelt gratitude and Rosy smiled radiantly, filling him with a warmth the situation hardly warranted. 'You've saved me from a long wait, which is no fun with overtired children.'

'It's no bother at all,' she said. 'Least I can do after stepping out in front of you the other day. I've been wanting to apologise. What can I get you—and, more importantly, what do the girls want?'

After some discussion, Clover decided on chocolate and Tansy vanilla with sprinkles.

'And you?' Rosy asked Jack.

He shrugged. 'I wasn't going to…'

'Daddy likes cherry,' Clover said, and Rosy's smile widened.

'Got it,' she said as she stepped up to the counter. She wouldn't take any money from him for the ice creams, insisting that it was her treat, and it seemed only polite that they fell into step with her as they walked away from the café.

'That was really kind of you,' Jack said. 'I think Clover was on the verge of a meltdown. I probably kept her out too long. Tansy was right, as usual.'

'That happens a lot?'

'More and more since her mother died.'

'I'm sorry,' Rosy said, compassion in her eyes. 'That must be really hard for all of you.'

'It's been a couple of years, but there are still challenges. Right now, the nanny has broken her foot, so she's gone home to her family for a few weeks. The timing is difficult. We only moved back here recently so the girls haven't started school here yet and I have a lot to do. But I know how lucky I am to afford a nanny at all. I'll figure something out.'

'At least they have you. They're beautiful girls.'

'They take after their mother.'

Tansy and Clover had walked ahead and now they sat down on the sea wall to finish their ice creams and as Jack reached them and stopped, Rosy did too.

'Thank you for my ice cream,' Tansy said, and Clover echoed the thanks.

'You're very welcome. Actually, you did me a favour. Ice cream tastes better with company.' Rosy said.

'You decided to stay in Polhallow after all?' Jack asked, and she shot him a slightly embarrassed grin.

'I wasn't lying,' she assured him. 'I had every intention of returning home after the play, but Clem got an unexpected job offer and needed someone to watch the house and feed the cat. I realised I could actually work from here for a few weeks, so here I am.' She shrugged a little self-consciously.

'That worked well for us. We'd still be in the queue now if it wasn't for you.'

'Where do you live?' Clover asked. 'We used to live in London, but Daddy moved here. Are you from London?'

Rosy shook her head. 'No, I come from a small country called Asturia, have you heard of it? Not many people have. But I came to school here in England, so I know London well.'

'I miss school,' Clover said.

'Ah, yes, your daddy said you haven't started school here yet. Are you looking forward to it?'

'Not really, mine is miles away.' Tansy glared at Jack.

It was an old argument, and not one Jack wanted to have in front of a stranger. 'It's a great school. You'll be fine. As we moved here just after Easter, I thought they might enjoy a long summer, especially as Tansy is starting secondary school. It didn't make sense sending her somewhere new for just one term,' he explained to Rosy. 'Tansy's school is about ten miles from here, and Clover is going to one the next town over.'

'Which means that not only do we not know anyone in Polhallow now, we won't know anyone here once we're at school either,' Tansy said.

'That's not true,' Jack said. 'There are children from Polhallow who go to both your new schools. You'll be fine.' He had the money to send the girls to the best schools possible and that was exactly what he was going to do.

'It can be tough to meet people when you move,' Rosy said sympathetically. 'But I know a little girl about your age,' she said to Clover. 'I'm going to the cinema with her and her mummy tomorrow in fact, to see that new superhero film. Do you want to come along and meet her?'

Clover's eyes widened as she turned to Jack imploringly. 'Can I, Daddy?'

'I don't know, honey.' He didn't know this woman beyond a jolt of attraction and a couple of random meetings. 'We wouldn't want to impose.'

'I'm sorry,' Rosy said, flushing. 'That was really clumsy of me. You don't even know me and here I am inviting your children out. I promise I'd take care of them. I can give you Sally's details—she's lived here all her life. Her little girl, Alice, goes to the local primary school and is Clover's age. I'm going to the cinema anyway; it really wouldn't be any trouble to take Clover as well—and Tansy if she would like to come.'

Jack hesitated. 'Sally Fletcher?'

'That's right, do you know her?'

'Only by sight. She was a few years younger than me at school, as was your cousin.' He must have seen Rosy around as a teen—but four years was a big gap at that age, and he'd left Polhallow when Sally and Clem had still been in their early teens. Still, the distant connection rooted Rosy, made her less a stranger.

He looked at the girls and realised that not only was Clover looking hopeful but so was Tansy and his chest squeezed. She so seldom asked for anything. 'Are you sure it wouldn't be an imposition?'

'Not at all. In fact I haven't seen the first in the series so if the girls can bring me up to speed before the film starts, they'll be the ones doing me a favour.'

'Well, if you're sure…' The rest of the sentence was drowned out by Clover's yells of excitement and before he knew it they'd swapped numbers and Rosy made arrangements to collect the girls the following afternoon before walking off with a wave. Jack watched her retreat, admiring her elegant, graceful walk and feeling that same jolt of recognition and attraction she seemed to provoke in him every time they met. But one thing was sure, he would be checking in with Sally Fletcher tonight. Attraction or no attraction, he wasn't sending his girls out with a stranger. Their happiness and safety came first. Always.

CHAPTER THREE

'ALICE IS REALLY nice, Daddy. Her mummy said that I can go over whenever I want. But I want her to come here and play in the treehouse. Can she, Daddy?'

Arrosa had barely had a chance to ring the doorbell before Jack had opened the door and Clover tumbled inside and onto him, babbling on excitedly about the afternoon's activities. Thank goodness she'd had such a good time; since yesterday afternoon Arrosa had asked herself several times what she'd been thinking of, volunteering to look after two complete strangers. Children at that! But once she'd collected them in Clem's small car her doubts had lessened then disappeared completely when they'd reached the cinema, where Clover and Alice had fastened onto each other like lifelong friends separated at birth, insisting on sharing their popcorn and sitting next to each other throughout the film and at the café they'd visited afterwards. However, Arrosa had been a little bit more concerned about Tansy and, despite their short acquaintance, that concern lingered.

There was something about the girl's preternatural maturity, the wrinkle of concern on her forehead, the way she watched her sister and fussed over her that made Arrosa's heart ache in recognition. She knew the signs all too well of a child who'd needed to grow up too fast, who'd shouldered responsibility beyond their years, but at least Arrosa had had summers here in Cornwall, a break from the rigid routine of her life, and her four years at boarding school to alleviate the pressure. Right now, she didn't see any sign that Tansy ever relaxed and, judging by the shadow lurking in Jack's eyes when he looked at his oldest girl, he too was worried.

At least Jack was aware; so many parents were oblivious to their children's struggles. Recognising them was the first step to solving them. Simone had taught her that and so much else that her own parents had been too busy to teach her.

Tansy followed her sister into the house, leaving Jack and Arrosa alone. Jack leaned on the door and smiled, his eyes filled with an approving warmth that seared through her. 'I'm sorry,' he said, holding the door a little bit further open. 'Where are my manners? Would you like to come in?'

She would like to, very much, but Arrosa held back. 'I'm sure you're busy,' she said. 'I'd hate to intrude.'

His eyes crinkled. 'You've given me the afternoon to work, I'm very appreciative. Please. Come in and have a coffee, it's the least I can offer in return. Are you sure they weren't too much trouble?'

'Not at all,' Arrosa assured him as she followed him into the wide two-storey hallway. She looked around with interest. She'd been impressed by the white nineteen-twenties Art Deco cube of a house with its stunning position on top of the cliffs when she'd driven up, but now she was inside she realised that the interior more than matched its outside. The house hadn't been clumsily extended or garishly modernised. Instead, it was as the architect had intended, spacious and graceful, the furniture chosen to complement the era but comfortable and obviously meant for a family to live with and use, rather than expensive antiques.

Arrosa had been brought up in a mediaeval château and spent many days in the imposing castle in the capital city where her father spent much of his time in the state apartments, and she had visited many of the heads of state around the world. She was used to money and she was used to luxury; she was used to historic and impressive buildings. Gorgeous as Jack's home was, it wasn't a palace, although money was clearly no object. But what struck her as she noted the carefully chosen art interspersed with framed children's pictures and family photos, the half open boot cupboard filled with sandals and wellies, the wicker basket stuffed with throws and cushions, was that this particular historic house was also a home. And that, as she knew all too well, was a much rarer combination.

'Nice house,' she said as she followed him into the

kitchen. It was a huge room with views out towards the sea. The island in the middle held a jumble of paper, crayons and a half open book, the table by the French windows was already set for dinner. She swallowed. Jack Treloar was clearly a good father, embracing his children's clutter, not hiding it.

'We think so.' Jack leaned against the island and gestured for her to sit. 'I grew up here, in Polhallow, you know. I used to see this house and vowed one day it would be mine.' His mouth quirked into a self-deprecating grin. 'Some things should never be said out loud. That sounded like a line from a bad film. Apologies.'

'Not at all, it sounds impressive. How many people go on to achieve their dreams?' She didn't have dreams, didn't have anything to strive for. She just had duty. She envied him his purpose more than the achievement. Taking a seat at the island, she opted for a mint tea as Jack put the kettle on and took down two of the distinctive blue-striped Cornish mugs from the dresser. 'Thank you for loaning me your girls, they were great company. Alice and Clover definitely took to each other.'

Jack poured hot water into one of the mugs and handed it to her. 'That's good, they need friends. I didn't really think it through when I took them out of school after Easter. I just wanted to get them settled in before term started, give them a chance to have a long summer by the sea, to learn to surf and just enjoy being here. It's been a difficult couple of years since they lost their mother, I thought they could do with a break. But, of course, they are a little lonely. And, as you probably guessed, Tansy isn't keen on the school I chose. She wants to go to the local school.'

'That's where Clem went and where Simone taught,' Arrosa took a sip of the mint tea. 'I think it's a good one.'

'It is. But it's also the school I went to once upon a time.' He paused as he picked up his own mug. He didn't take a seat but resumed standing against the island, staring out to sea. 'I don't know if your cousin has mentioned me…'

'No, she hasn't. Besides, I don't like to gossip.' Although she *was* undeniably intrigued.

He laughed. 'Then you won't fit in around here. I've been the main topic of conversation in Polhallow for longer than I care to remember.'

'Either you have a very inflated sense of self-importance, or you really do have a reputation I should ask Clem about.'

'Probably both,' he said. 'The thing is, I don't really want my girls to know that side of my past. Not yet. I don't want them to overhear people talking about the theatre or raking up ancient history, gossiping about their mother. Besides, I've got the money, I can afford the best schools money can buy, so why shouldn't they attend them?'

Arrosa picked her words carefully, trying to dampen her interest. What past? She really *didn't* gossip but maybe she should check in with Clem. 'I don't think that my opinion matters here,' she said. 'You should do what's right for you, for your girls, not because of what anyone else says or thinks.'

His smile was rueful. 'A diplomatic answer. Forgive me, this is probably not what you expected when I asked you in for a drink. I seem to have forgotten how to do small talk—not that it was ever one of my skills.'

'I didn't have any expectations.' Arrosa picked up her mug again, glad of the distraction, but he was right. She'd expected a little bit of chitchat about the film, not this strange, intense conversation that felt almost as if they were jumping past the basics and getting straight to intimacy. But she couldn't let her guard down, not really. There was only so much that anyone could know about her. Not just because of her own need for anonymity but because Clem's identity was also at stake. Polite chitchat was all she could allow.

'Let's start again,' Jack said. 'So, what is it you do when you're not housesitting for your cousin?'

'I'm a special adviser,' she said. It was almost true. She *did* do a lot of advising, trying to guide the politicians towards the policies she thought necessary for the development of her country. 'I work in diplomacy.'

Jack's eyebrows rose. 'Impressive. Do you offer lessons? Diplomacy is also something that doesn't come naturally to me.'

'Not to me either,' she confessed. 'I've had to learn.'

'And you can work from here, you said?'

'It's not usual, but as it's the summer I managed to make some arrangements. And I'm mostly taking the time off. It's been a long time since I was in Polhallow. I could do with a proper holiday and really get to know it again.'

'Any plans while you're here?'

'Actually, I am enjoying being plan free. I was a bit overstretched when I arrived, hence the time off. I had some tough decisions to make, so time and space is exactly what I need.'

'Personal or work?'

'Both, they get a little intermingled.' That was the understatement of the century. But at least she'd managed to step back enough to see that and to put right her misstep with Akil. She hadn't imagined the relief in his voice when she'd spoken to him a couple of days ago and suggested they stay friends and pretend her clumsy attempt at a proposal had never happened. She'd done her best to encourage him to see Clem again but hadn't heard anything since from either of them—which was either a really good sign or she'd completely misread the vibes she'd been getting from them.

'Tricky.'

She looked out at the view, as always, her anxiety abating at the sight of the sea. 'It is amazing what having the time and space to think does. Already I've made a really important decision and I feel so much better. But I really want to put work and home out of my mind and just enjoy being here—the only thing I want to worry about is the amount of clotted cream I'm consuming.'

He laughed then, warm and deep and toe-curlingly masculine. 'Yes, I'd forgotten how good food is here. London has every cuisine you can imagine but nothing tastes as good as Polhallow pastries and scones. If this carries on, I'll have to up my exercise time, which won't be easy with no nanny for the rest of the summer and all the work piling up.' He grimaced. 'Obviously, exercise is the least of my worries. This is a crucial time for the theatre renovation…' He slanted a quick glance in her direction as if waiting for a reaction. 'And my other businesses and interests need attention. But the girls can't just sit around and wait for me all day. I could try a temp agency to find a summer nanny, but they've been through so much change I don't want to risk a mismatch.'

'I could watch them sometimes,' she offered impulsively. It wasn't just that she had the time, although she did, something about Tansy still bothered her, even though she could see what a safe and loving home the girl had. She understood what it was like to feel responsibilities at a young age in a way that not many other people did. She also knew how important it was to let those responsibilities go and to have fun. Maybe she wouldn't be able to make any difference to the girl's life, but Arrosa felt an overwhelming urge to try.

It didn't hurt that she was enjoying spending time with Jack either, that she was all too aware of his every shift and movement, how the light moved across the planes of his face, the way his eyes darkened to navy when he was moved, the shape of his mouth.

'I can't ask you to do that!' But she could see he was tempted, relief clearing some of the cloud from his expression.

'You didn't. I'm not offering to be a stand-in nanny, I'm not at all qualified and I *am* on holiday. But I would be more than happy to take them around a little bit, go to the beach, organise some play dates with Sally, go to the cinema—they'd be a great excuse for catching up on all the summer releases.'

'I am really tempted…' At the word their gazes caught and locked, and she felt again that odd sense of knowing him, feeling the attraction building between them, unlike anything she'd experienced on so short an acquaintance—or even a longer acquaintance—before. 'But I'd be totally taking advantage of your good nature.'

'We could take it on a day-by-day basis. If I have free time and you need a hand then great, but I will be absolutely comfortable saying no if I have plans, and if you decide you need something more structured I won't be offended.'

'It sounds too good to be true. Look. Before you make a decision you should see them at their over-tired worst. Stay for dinner and if at the end of it the offer is still open we'll discuss payment and other issues then.'

Arrosa would of course turn down the offer of payment, she had no need of money. But nobody had ever offered to pay her before. She had an allowance—a generous allowance—but it wasn't a salary. It was nice to be thought worth a wage.

She had no idea what Jack did but he was clearly well-off. It was obvious from the house and furnishings, in the way he dressed, even in a casual linen shirt and jeans, both top quality and fitting as if made for him, the linen almost—tantalisingly—translucent, the jeans clinging to narrow hips and strong, lean thighs. She swallowed, mouth dry.

'What's for dinner?'

'Lasagne. I've only got a few dishes in my repertoire and lasagne is near the top.'

'With salad and garlic bread?'

'Of course!"

'That sounds delicious. Thank you, I'd love to have dinner with you.'

But as she sat down and accepted the glass of white wine he handed her, Arrosa couldn't help wondering if she was completely mad. She should be heading out of the door as fast as she could go, not offering to babysit Jack's children. She might be inexperienced with relationships in the real world but even she could feel the chemistry sizzling between them. She was a princess, and he was a widower with two small girls. Neither should indulge in summer flirtations, no matter how tempting.

But, on the other hand, she had promised herself a summer off. A summer of being just Rosy. This was just dinner—and a dinner chaperoned by his daughters. What harm could one evening do?

★ ★ ★

As June continued the British summer started to live up to its flaky reputation. The long, hot early summer days had been replaced by intermittent rain and drizzle, interspersed with moments of blazing sunshine. It was the kind of weather that meant leaving the house without a bag packed with suntan cream, wellies, sunhats and raincoats was ill-advised. Jack was seriously considering investing in a mule to help with the baggage even a brief walk entailed. Worse, the weather made entertaining the girls even more tricky and he couldn't help but think his decision to give them an extra-long summer had been ill thought through: weeks filled with adventure and time to explore was idyllic on paper but, in reality, less than practical, especially now he was looking after them alone.

This was where being a single parent was so hard. There was nobody to sense check his ideas with. But, then again, Lily had always preferred to leave all responsibility to him. She would probably have enthusiastically supported the thought of a long summer, come up with a dozen impractical plans and whipped the girls up into a frenzy of expectation before disappearing off for a summer of house parties and social events, leaving the girls to their nanny. As for the autumn, she would have wanted Tansy away at boarding school, not at a private day school just a few towns over. After all, she'd first suggested sending her when their eldest had been barely eight. He could hear her now, those languid upper-class tones caressing and yet repelling him at the same time.

'But darling, girls of that age are tricky. I should know!' Tinkling laugh. 'She'd be much happier with girls of her own age, don't you think?'

No, he would have got no backup or sense checking from Lily. It had always been down to him where the girls were concerned. So why was he suddenly feeling so lonely—and second-guessing himself? Maybe it was because Tansy was entering those dangerous tween and teen years and he of all people knew how important stability was around then, especially for those whose early years had been the opposite. His childhood had, despite his mother's best endeavours, been difficult and his early teen years full of trouble and mischief; he'd come very close to getting a criminal record. But then again Lily had had everything and she had thought herself invincible, had adored the thrill of danger. That was why she had taken up with him after all—there was nothing as rebellious as dating the village bad boy. Getting pregnant and marrying him had been the ultimate rejection of all her parents' hopes for her.

Lily had loved her girls—but she'd been impulsive and heedless, and Tansy especially had been painfully aware of how mercurial her mother could be. Her death had obviously compounded Tansy's insecurity and, although she was less than enthusiastic about the move, part of his motivation for returning to Cornwall was to try and centre her somewhere less frantic and fast paced than the big city.

'Come on, girls,' he said for the twentieth time that day. The words were fast becoming his catchphrase, maybe he should get them tattooed on his forehead. As usual they had little effect as Clover dawdled behind in a world of her own, Tansy walking in the middle, looking most put upon. But, to be fair, he knew that a business meeting was not their idea of a fun afternoon out, even if it *was* in a theatre.

Of course, he could have taken Rosy up on her offer to watch them sometimes. It had clearly been genuinely meant. She seemed to like the girls and, more importantly, they clearly liked her. But he'd been reluctant to get back in touch with her after the evening they'd spent together. Not because he hadn't enjoyed it. In fact, quite the opposite. The whole evening had gone smoothly, with conversation and laughter flowing easily. She fitted in with them, almost too well, and by the end of dinner the girls were acting as if they'd known her all their lives. But they *didn't* know her. He had no real idea where she was from, what she did or how long she would stay. And the last point was crucial. Clover was predisposed to like everybody, but his eldest was a different matter and Rosy and she seemed to have connected. He hadn't heard Tansy chat so much or laugh so much or volunteer so much information in a long time. Which was why he hadn't dared ask Rosy to watch then—she was only here for the summer. He couldn't risk his girls getting too attached.

Or himself. The attraction he felt had just intensified with the time they'd spent together but he couldn't allow himself the indulgence of a fling.

'Rosy!'

Jack looked up in surprise as Clover's cry interrupted his thoughts. There, as if he'd summoned her by thought alone, was Rosy, casually dressed in jeans, a turquoise T-shirt and a long grey cardigan, but yet again something about the way she wore the simple outfit elevated it to a high fashion statement.

Rosy's face lit up. 'Hello, how are you two? I was just thinking about you.' And then, more quietly, 'Hi, Jack.'

'Hi.' For a moment they both just stood and looked at each other, Jack almost lost in her hazel eyes, a beguiling mix of green and amber, in the warmth of her smile.

'You were? Why?' Clover danced up to Rosy and tugged at her hand. 'Why were you thinking about us?'

'I had a surfing lesson this morning with Dan, and he said that you are both naturals. Unfortunately, he didn't say the same about me. Which is very lowering because once upon a time I was not bad at all. Take my advice, girls; don't stop for years or you'll lose all your balance and skill.' She mock sighed and both girls giggled. 'Where are you off to? Somewhere fun?'

'We're going to the theatre,' Clover told her. 'Daddy has a boring meeting.'

'Boring? The theatre? Surely not. There's a stage and an auditorium, lots of fun places to discover. Do either of you like plays?'

'I do,' Tansy said. 'Drama was my best subject at school. I should have had the lead in the end of term play, but we moved.' She gulped and blinked rapidly, eyes reddening as Jack stared at her in consternation. He knew that Tansy liked acting but in his haste to leave London he hadn't even considered the end of term play which was the highlight for year six leavers. But he should have—after all, Tansy had been fixated on starring in it ever since she'd started school.

'They put on plays in the theatre and local people can be in them,' Rosy said, to Jack's relief. 'That's where my cousin Clem started and now she's a professional actress. I'm sure she'd be happy to talk to you about it and give you tips.'

'Do you really think so?'

'I know so. She's always happy to chat acting and plays—and I bet she could introduce you to the community theatre group if your dad didn't mind.'

'That would be brilliant.' All trace of tears had gone as Tansy turned to him. 'Can I, Dad?'

'It sounds good, let me look into it.' He needed to bring the community theatre onside first. The last thing he wanted was for Tansy to be ostracised because of him.

'Come with us to the theatre?' Clover asked Rosy and Tansy agreed.

'Please do, it'll be a lot more fun if you're there.'

'Thanks, girls!' Jack laid a firm hand on both blonde heads. 'I'm sure Rosy has better things to do than tag along to my business meeting.'

But Rosy didn't take the get-out clause he'd handed her. 'Actually, if you don't mind, I'd like to come. I haven't looked around the theatre properly for years. My aunt—Simone Beaumont—the theatre was her pet project. The first time I came here to stay she spent the whole summer writing out grant applications and organising fundraising events. When they reopened it after the renovations the councillor who gave a speech said that she had single-handedly saved it. They were going to demolish it originally. Simone had many causes and projects, but this theatre was her main passion—sometimes I wonder if that's why Clem took up drama, so her mother could see her on this stage. Simone could be a very busy woman. It was hard to pin her down, but she never missed a single performance.'

Jack shot Rosy a sharp glance, but she was all innocence. Maybe she had no idea of his plans. If not, if he could show her his vision then maybe she would be able to convince her cousin that he was on the village's side? 'In that case of course you're welcome to come along.'

In the end he found that he was relieved to have Rosy with him as he sat down with the PR agency he was considering hiring. Investing in the theatre was so unlike anything he had ever done before. He knew he needed guidance. He was usually the man behind the scenes, the angel investor being wowed not doing the wowing, listening to PR teams not recruiting them. It was important he brief the company well. But as he expanded on his vision he could see the girls and Rosy exploring, hear laughter and chatter coming from all areas before the three ended up on the stage, clearly putting on some kind of mini play, Tansy directing the other two.

Jack paused and watched the antics on stage. It was so good to see Tansy acting her age, he needed to ensure it happened more often. Maybe he should stop worrying about what would happen when Rosy left and take her up on her offer to watch his daughters. It would be good for the girls.

As for him, he might be attracted to her but that didn't mean he needed to act on it.

Finally, the meeting came to an end and after taking some photos the agency representatives left, leaving Jack alone at the top of the auditorium answering some emails. A slight sound made him look up to see Rosy making her way across the row to join him. The girls were still on stage, volubly discussing who should be standing where.

'Exhausted by artistic endeavours?'

Dimples flashed. 'I'm not the actor, that's Clem. Tansy definitely needs to meet her. That daughter of yours has got some real understanding of staging.'

'Never been tempted to do something that way yourself?'

'Not at all.' She laughed a little self-consciously. 'Acting has never been a love of mine. I was more likely to be found painting scenery than trying out for the lead. But in some ways, I guess, I do spend a lot of time acting, channelling a more confident, assertive me. Clem taught me techniques—how to stand, to project. How to breathe—that's been very useful. Simone was great too at preparing me to speak up in intimidating circumstances. She was one of the most matter-of-fact and forthright people you'll ever meet, she passed that quality onto Clem. They both taught me to focus on what's important. I owe them both a lot.'

'Sounds like being a diplomat is hard. You must be young to have so much responsibility. I think of diplomats as older—not that I've dedicated too much time to the topic,' he added hastily, although he had been thinking about it of late, since meeting her.

'I *am* young to have some of the responsibilities I do, but politics is the family business. I was raised to it. And yes, at times the focus is on me, but more what I represent, if that makes sense, rather than me as a person. That's why it can help to play a part, to take the personal out. How about you? What's today about? Planning to set up a troupe of players to stage your opus?'

'Not exactly. I'm not one for being on stage either, but I am interested in this theatre in particular.'

'In what way?'

He took a deep breath. Now was the time to make his pitch. 'I want to take out a long-term lease and carry on the restoration process to take the theatre to the next level. Make it an asset that *works* for the community, *not* take it away from the community.' He could hear his tone sharpen at the last words and her eyes widened.

'You clearly feel passionately about it,' she said.

Jack nodded grimly. 'I'm not the only one. According to the village—and your cousin—everything I want to do goes against what this theatre is for. That's what the meeting just then was about—I am going to have to hire a PR firm to untangle the web of gossip and rumours about what I am trying to do here. Because it *will* happen. The Council will lease it to me, they have to. This place is expensive to run, they're relieved to get it off their hands, for someone else to be responsible for the upkeep, but I'd rather go ahead with the backing of the village. I'm not interested in cementing my role as the bad boy outsider.'

Rosy sat back, eyebrows raised. 'Is that who you are? That's not how I would describe you. A hard-working father maybe, a mean maker of a lasagne, a man who obviously cares about his community, but not a bad boy outsider. And I'm usually a good judge of character.'

Her words warmed Jack through. Maybe he did have a chance to start again—with the incomers at least. 'People in Polhallow have long memories and the Treloars a certain reputation. I wouldn't care if it wasn't for the girls.' He stopped and thought about his words. 'That's not true. I do mind, I always have,' he admitted, surprised at his honesty, to her and to himself. 'But back then, instead of trying to prove people wrong, I went the other way, became the boy they expected me to be for a short while. But even when things changed, when *I* changed, all the local community could see was who they expected to see. And that is who many people in the village see now, no matter where I live or how I act. They hear I have plans for the theatre and assume the worst because of my name and the actions of a messed-up teen. That's not what I want for the girls. I want people to hear their name and respect them, respect their origins.'

'That seems like a laudable ambition to me,' she said softly and with her words he felt some of the brittleness within him break as if she had given him a benediction, a blessing on his plans.

'You want to hear what I have in mind?'

Rosy reached out and touched his arm, the warmth of her touch searing him. 'I'd love to.'

'Come on then.' This was a great opportunity to start to change things. Clem was influential and if her own cousin could advocate for him then his battle might be half won before it started. But as Jack began to expand on his ideas, he knew that it wasn't the village he was trying to impress—it was this one woman.

CHAPTER FOUR

ARROSA WASN'T JUST being polite when she said she wanted to hear more, although it was Jack's allusions to his youthful reputation and motivations that piqued her interest rather than the actual means of achieving his aims. But as the tour progressed she got swept away. There was something about Jack's vision that made things come alive. She could see the theatre as he did, filled with chattering, excited people, smell the greasepaint, feel the heat of the lights. She could see the entrance opened up and welcoming, imagine the glass-fronted café overlooking the bay, picture the currently unused boxes turned into sought-after seats for special occasions. He didn't just want to restore the front of the theatre, he also had plans to refurbish the dressing rooms, currently more reminiscent of a school locker room, and create VIP areas backstage.

'I want to attract the best,' he told her as he sketched out his ideas. 'The best dance companies, opera, repertory theatre, touring musicals, even bands. When

I was a kid we had to travel for any kind of culture, which for people like me meant it was completely inaccessible. When Lily and I moved to London I was intimidated by theatres and museums, I didn't think they were for the likes of me. I don't want any child within twenty miles of here to ever think that. I want this to be a destination theatre that attracts tourists all year round, but it's important that anyone and everyone who lives here has full access too—and at an affordable price. What do you think?'

Arrosa circled round, seeing the currently drab bar area through his eyes, bright and busy. 'Honestly? I love it! Your plans are completely inspiring.' She meant every word although she knew Clem was opposed to any changes to the current set-up. But surely her sister wasn't fully informed about what Jack had planned? Loyalty to Simone might make Clem stubborn but her own ambitions for the theatre weren't dissimilar to everything Jack wanted to do. 'But I can see your comms problem; I've not heard anything about any of this, just that the theatre needs saving.'

'I think I went about it all wrong, dived straight in without laying the groundwork first.' Jack was clearly frustrated. 'I'm not used to being the upfront spokesperson, I'm usually behind the scenes. I thought the plans would speak for themselves, but as soon as it became known I wanted a long lease and changes were involved rumours started. You can see why I need a PR agency to help turn things around.'

'Changing public perceptions can be a long process

and it's important to remember that even if opposition feels personal it usually isn't,' she assured him. She should know. After all, it had been over eight years since realising his hoped-for son was never going to come, her father had turned his attention to amending Asturia's laws in order to make Arrosa Crown Princess and eventual Queen. They'd had to work tirelessly over those eight years to get to the point where public opinion was in favour and for all the opposition parties to agree to change the age-old laws. Eight years of Arrosa not putting a foot wrong, of treading the delicate line of not looking too eager to become Queen whilst displaying leadership and diplomacy. Eight years of only being photographed looking calm, friendly and professional.

Eight years of knowing that this was just the beginning. That her entire life had to live up to the promise of her eight year-long audition for the role.

'Daddy, I'm hungry!' Clover clambered up the stairs towards them. 'Can Rosy have dinner with us again?'

Arrosa could see Jack hesitate and tried to think of an excuse she could use to help him out as after an uncomfortable pause he nodded. 'Of course. She's very welcome if she doesn't have other plans.'

'I did defrost a chicken.' It was a rubbish excuse, and she knew it from the disappointment in Clover's face. 'But you could come to me,' Arrosa offered before she could remember all the reasons getting further entangled with the small family was a bad idea.

Jack didn't reply at once. Instead, he met her gaze

as if seeking confirmation that the offer was genuine and not mere politeness. Not for the first time, Arrosa noted the wariness behind what often looked like arrogance and confidence, giving her a sense of the lonely and potentially misunderstood boy he had once been. 'If you're sure. There's a lot of us to feed.'

'I can't promise anything as magnificent as your lasagne,' she said. 'But I could cook you chicken the Asturian way with lemon and garlic, fresh salad and these little cubed potatoes covered with a special secret spicy sauce. Does that sound any good?'

Clover agreed volubly that it did and before Arrosa knew it she was being whisked back home in Jack's oversized car, despite protesting it was only a short walk away. He parked outside and she opened the little picket gate, the family following her down the path which wound through the flower-filled garden to the white cottage's front door.

'Is this your home?' Clover asked as Arrosa unlocked the front door and ushered them inside.

'No, it belongs to my cousin Clem, but it *feels* like my home. I spent lots of very happy times here.'

The cottage was very old, parts of it dating back to Elizabethan times, with a large hallway which held a cupboard for coats and shoes, a hatstand and a table flanked by small chairs. Doors on either side led into low-ceilinged square rooms, on the left the sitting room, on the other a combined library, study and dining space. This was the room where Simone had often held court, plotting out her many campaigns, the dining table more often used to paint placards than to hold food.

The kitchen ran across the whole back of the cottage, holding at one end a battered leather sofa and an ancient pine kitchen table, with wooden cabinets painted a pretty eggshell blue and worktops on the other side. Stairs led up from the kitchen to the three bedrooms and one bathroom. It was simple but, thanks to Polhallow's popularity as a holiday destination and desirability as a second home location, Rosy knew the house would sell for a small fortune—but nowhere near the amount of money Jack's stylish white cube would command.

There were colourful paintings and framed posters on every available wall space and photos on every table and shelf. Jack wandered over to examine a collection of photos on the kitchen dresser, mostly Clem in various roles. Some were of Simone, often with a placard in her hand, off to save whatever cause she was spearheading that month, but there were also photos of her as a young woman, of the chic student who had attracted a future king, of the backpacker on the deck of a boat, of the young mother with her arms around a tiny Clem. There were no pictures of Arrosa on public display, it was too dangerous in case anyone recognised her, but she knew that upstairs on Simone's bedside table a photo of Arrosa and Clem side by side had pride of place.

'Your aunt taught me at school,' Jack said after a

while. 'She was always kind. Bracing, said what she thought, but kind.'

Arrosa laughed. 'Those traits run in the family; Clem is just the same.'

'In your family too?'

Arrosa thought about her father, always King first and second, father a poor third. Of her mother, whose feelings were always hidden behind a regal smile. 'They are diplomats, as you know,' she said. 'It's an innate characteristic, even at home.'

'Sounds chilly.'

Chilly. Was that the right word? Formal, yes. But not cold exactly. 'Their expectations of me are high, that's true. That's why I liked being here, where the only expectations were that Clem and I help out making placards, or working bake sales, or one unforgettable summer trying to knit squares for a peace blanket, although it turned out knitting wasn't something either of us were good at! Simone was a second mother to me.'

'You were lucky to have her,' Jack said, and she nodded.

'Lots of people felt the same way—that Simone was like an aunt or a sister. She had a gift of drawing people in. That's part of your problem with the theatre. I think people feel that your plans might expunge what she did. It wouldn't even still be here without her, they were going to knock it down, as you know, and she spearheaded the campaign to keep it and raised the money to restore it. But, actually, I can't help thinking that she would be excited by your ideas.'

'You think?' His rather grim expression relaxed and Arrosa felt her stomach flip.

'The problem is your timing is off. Simone is so recently gone; Clem is still grieving. I think that's why she and the rest of the community group jumped straight into organising a campaign against you. Simone loved a campaign. It's a way of keeping her close, especially as they feel your plans are a threat to her legacy. You need to listen to their concerns and show them that you need their expertise and passion, want them involved, that this is an evolution not a takeover. It might help to acknowledge the original restoration campaign in all your literature and plans, name some part of it after Simone.'

Jack didn't reply at first, his face thoughtful. 'You're right of course. Thank you,' he said after a while.

'An outsider's perspective is always useful.'

'No, it's more than that. I can tell you're used to brokering deals. Treaties must fall into your hands.'

'I wouldn't quite say that.'

'You've given me a lot to think about. Thank you.' He picked up a photo of Simone standing outside the theatre, grinning widely. 'If you wouldn't mind, I'd love your input when the PR agency send me their campaign ideas. You have a real insight; your thoughts would be invaluable.'

'You're welcome.' Arrosa could feel her face flush at the unaccustomed thanks. In her job nobody ever said *well done*, there were no performance reviews, apart from tabloid headlines, newspaper articles or social media posts as likely to be sharply critical as they were to be fawning. It might be silly to feel quite so touched by a few words of praise, but she was.

It didn't take her long to rustle up dinner, setting the kitchen table with the pretty floral dinner set that Simone had bought from a car boot sale many years before and the antique pearl-handled cutlery Arrosa had given her one birthday.

'I love this house, it's like a fairy tale cottage,' Clover said as they sat round the table after dinner, an old edition of Snakes and Ladders in front of them.

'It is, isn't it? I felt very lucky to spend my summers here,' Arrosa agreed.

'What's your own home like? Did you live somewhere like this when you were little?' Tansy asked.

Arrosa paused and thought. How could she convey the difference between the small, comfortable, chic yet homey cottage and the vast palace filled with antiques and portraits of ancestors where she'd been raised without giving away anything about who she was? Of course she'd had acres of land to run and ride on, a lake to swim in, woods to build dens in, but it had all been rather lonely. Her ancestral estate might have been a more fun place to grow up if she'd had a sibling who lived with her rather than one a thousand miles away.

'Not really. I'm an only child, you see.' Every time she said that it felt like a betrayal of Clem. 'My parents are diplomats, so we always lived in houses that weren't exactly ours.'

That wasn't a lie. The family estate and the castle, where her father resided most of the time in state apartments, belonged to the country, not to Arrosa or her family. They were owned by the crown, her family were custodians not owners.

'A lot of the furniture was antique, so we had to look after it,' she continued. 'I can't complain, I've been very lucky. I've travelled a lot and I've met some important people, and I've seen many, many things that I wouldn't have if I'd lived a different life, but the truth is when I think of home this cottage is the place I see. I'm just glad I get to spend the summer here. That this is where I spent many happy childhood summers.'

Tansy shook the dice and gleefully moved her counter up a long ladder to Clover's voluble dismay. 'Polhallow is so small though. Didn't you get bored spending every summer here?'

'*Bored?* Never.' Arrosa got up to collect the cake she'd bought from Sally's family's café earlier, cutting generous slices and placing them on the table. 'Sometimes, Tansy, you have to find your own adventures. I suppose I was a little bit older than you when Clem and I started to go out by ourselves, but there was always something to do. Surfing, of course, swimming, going for ice creams, learning to sail. But simpler things too. For instance, we built our own adventure trail once in the woods outside the house and we used to camp out in the garden sometimes; one summer it was so hot I don't think we slept indoors for a month. We even tried to persuade Simone to let us build an outdoor loo and shower, but she resisted. Although I think that was more Clem than me. I was actually quite relieved to be able to go in and use a proper bath.'

'Camping! I've never been camping.' Tansy turned to her father. 'Daddy, can we get a tent? Can we sleep in the garden like Clem and Rosy did? I've always wanted to try.'

Jack reached out for his cake with a nod of thanks. 'Tansy Treloar, you have been on some incredible holidays. How many theme parks have you been to? And that amazing resort in Sardinia with five swimming pools where you got to do activities all the time. Would you really rather sleep in a tent?'

'It would be fantastic,' she said, eyes shining, and Clover joined in.

'Please, Daddy! I've always wanted to sleep in a tent too, always!'

Arrosa couldn't help but laugh. 'It's a long time since I've camped,' she said. 'And it can be amazing, but don't get carried away. It can be hard to get the balance of blankets right. One moment you're boiling hot, the next you're freezing cold, and then, of course, if you need the loo in the middle of the night you have to walk across the dew-filled field to get to it and if you forget wellies that means soggy feet. Sometimes spiders and other creepy-crawlies can find their way into the tent, but on the other hand, there is something special about sitting around a campfire and looking up at the stars and telling each other stories. Toasting marshmallows, of course.'

Oh, dear. Both girls' eyes had grown bigger and their expressions more excited, but Jack's lips were compressed. She probably shouldn't have said anything. 'But five swimming pools in Sardinia sounds pretty amazing too. And you guys have a swimming pool at your house too. If Clem and I had had a pool of our own I'm sure that would have kept us busy.'

Her attempt to backtrack obviously hadn't helped. Tansy turned to Jack, her face full of hope, her voice pleading. 'Daddy, *please* can we go camping?'

'Sorry, Tansy, but absolutely not.' He sounded adamant.

'But...'

'I said no. The subject is closed.'

Arrosa stared at Jack in surprise. He seemed like a very capable man to her. He was physically fit, and the lean muscles she was all too aware of didn't seem like gym-built bulk but rather the muscles of a man who was prepared to put his hand to anything that needed to get done. He'd been raised around here, a local boy, which meant he was likely to be outdoorsy. Surely a couple of nights in a tent wouldn't be that big a deal?

He caught her eye and she sensed that he knew what she was thinking.

'It's after six,' she said. 'Do you want a beer? You can walk back from here. And girls? How about I make you hot chocolate with marshmallows and we can take it outside and sit around the fire pit?'

The suggestion was met with approval and Arrosa got herself and Jack a beer, sending the girls out to gather some firewood from the log pile with strict instructions not to go anywhere near the matches until she was there, and showed them how to lay and light a fire properly.

'Simone got a fire pit long before it was fashionable, thanks to Clem and my obsession with being outside in all weathers,' she said as she spooned hot chocolate into mugs. She reached into the cupboard for the marshmallows. 'I'm sorry, I didn't mean to get the girls so excited.'

She dropped a handful of marshmallows into each cup and added hot water before carrying the tall mugs over to the table. 'Parenting must be hard enough without well-meaning outsiders stirring things up.'

Jack reached up and took one of the mugs from her and put it down, knowing he owed Rosy an explanation at the very least. 'Look, I'm the one who should apologise. That was a bit of an overreaction.' He winced. 'I seem to have fallen into a pattern of promising to be a better father and then messing up at the first opportunity.'

Rosy set the mug she was holding down and pulled at a chair. 'Don't be silly. I completely understand. Now I'm an adult, I'm all about the thread count and a good mattress too.'

Jack exhaled slowly. He could, he should, leave it there. Let her believe he just didn't want to rough it, that money had turned him into the kind of man who needed five-star service and all the trimmings. But he wanted her to think better of him. Needed her understanding in a way he couldn't articulate.

'It's not that. I wish it were that simple.'

She pushed a curl behind her ear. 'Jack, you don't owe me any kind of explanation. Whatever your reasons, I'm sure they're valid, but it's really none of my business.'

'As I mentioned earlier, the Treloar name isn't particularly respected around here. My father, my grandfather, even my great-great-grandfather, were petty thieves, petty criminals, lazy vagabonds all. Go through the village's history and you'll find our name over and over, mentioned for public drunkenness, begging, theft. My mother was the complete opposite. She was—is—hardworking and no-nonsense, but she came down here on holiday and fell for my father's charms, such as they were, and stayed. I don't think it was long before she realised what a bad bargain she had made when she was left alone with me, working three jobs to try and keep food on the table and a roof over our heads.'

'She sounds like quite a woman.'

He nodded. 'She is. Not an easy woman. Life made sure of that, knocked the warmth and trust out of her early, but she is everything my father wasn't. And she did her best by me.'

'That's all any of us can ask.'

He nodded. 'She was always determined that, no matter how bad things were, we would have a holiday. Now I'm an adult I can see she needed to get away herself, leave her life behind for a few days, go somewhere where she wasn't pitied or looked down upon.'

'That's understandable.'

'Of course all we could afford was to camp. She didn't have a car so we would take the bus and carry everything. We couldn't go too far because it would be expensive, so usually we made it just over the border into Devon. And then we would find the most basic, cheapest campsite we could, set up our tent and live on baked beans and sausages, cooked over the fire, marshmallows as a treat.'

He could almost smell the sausages, hear the crackle of the fire and, despite himself, his mouth curled into a reminiscent smile. 'Looking back, those were some of the happiest times we shared. She was usually too busy to spend much time with me, but those camping weeks we were together all the time. But with such limited resources we couldn't do much other than walk, swim or hang out reading at the campsite. Probably exactly what she needed, but the older I got, the more I realised how different my holiday experience was to other kids'. One year she was getting the tent out and I told her not to bother. That I hated holidays with her. Why couldn't we go on a proper holiday like normal people?' He inhaled, the old shame filling him. 'I'll never forget the stricken expression in her eyes. She didn't say anything, just put the tent away and we never went camping again. I'd give anything to go back and change that day, give anything to help her get the tent ready.'

'Jack, I'm sure she knew you didn't mean it, not really.'

'But that's just it. I *did* mean it and she knew it. Oh, I have apologised since, many times. But I hurt her dreadfully that day, not just with words but with my contempt and carelessness, like my father before me.'

His behaviour still shamed him. The memory shamed him. As it should.

'Does she still live around here?'

'She moved to Spain a few years ago.' He'd offered her an allowance but she'd turned it down, so instead he'd funded the purchase of a beach bar and bought her a comfortable villa. 'We have a good relationship now when we see each other, but I caused her a lot of anxiety when I was younger, and I'd give anything to take it back. Sometimes it feels as if those camping holidays sum up my childhood—my mother working harder than anyone should have to do to try and supply me with the basics. Although she loves me, loved me then, she was always anxious. Partly because she was so busy, so tired, and partly because she was always looking out for traces of my father in me.'

He couldn't believe he'd revealed so much. It was hard to meet her eyes, to see the sympathy there. He'd never spoken of those days before, not even with Lily—especially not with Lily. She'd never tried to understand him, never really wanted to understand him, found the poverty of his childhood picturesque, the reality would have disgusted her. No wonder he'd preferred not to discuss his past with her. Their marriage had been based on his reliability and dependability. Lily was the one who got to be flaky, Jack the lynchpin who held them together. It was lonely, unfulfilling, but he had wanted to give the girls everything he had never had—stability, both parents in their lives—and if that meant putting his own barely articulated needs away, that was a price he had been, he was, willing to pay.

But not only did he feel that he could be honest with Rosy, he wanted to be. 'Just the thought of setting up a tent, the smell of one, it brings it all back. Not just that day, but also the helplessness of poverty.'

He could see her pause, search for the right thing to say. 'Look, tell me to butt out if you want and I promise not to be offended, but I do get where the girls are coming from. I can't pretend to understand your life. Money was never an issue in my childhood, the opposite in fact, my life has been pretty luxurious. Materially, I had more than I needed or wanted. But, on the other hand, my parents were distant, not really ones for cuddles and displays of affection. I went on plenty of holidays, mostly to exclusive villas where I had no one to play with and nothing to do. I didn't want the pool or the luxury, I wanted companionship and fun. I wanted my parents to want to spend time with me. Which is why this cottage was so special, my summers here so important. I had freedom and companionship and adventure and that meant more to me than a private jet and the fanciest hotel suite.'

'My girls get both. The luxury holidays and my attention.' He wasn't over-compensating for his lack of time with money, was he? No, he made time for them, he always had.

'I know they do. But they're still of an age where camping seems like an adventure not a budget option. So why not banish some of those demons and take the girls camping? It might be cathartic. Besides, things have moved on since you were a child.' She reached over for her tablet and opened it, typing quickly. 'What about glamping? All you need to do is turn up and everything is ready, you even get to sleep on a proper bed. Why not surprise the girls?' She passed the tablet to him. 'Look, this place is just a few miles away and you can choose between shepherd huts, yurts, bell tents and even treehouses.'

Jack took a moment to scan the website. Rosy was right, the campsite was a million miles away from the field of his youth, with promises of home-cooked meals delivered to your fully furnished accommodation, underfloor heating in the showers and private baths—to say nothing of the luxury interiors showcased. 'You might be right. Look, there's some last-minute availability this weekend. Why don't you come along too?'

The words hung in the air as Rosy stared at him motionless, her pupils dilated. Part of Jack wanted to recall the words. Hadn't he told himself to keep his distance from her? The girls were clearly getting attached and she would be gone soon. But on the other hand…

On the other hand, he liked her, and it had been so long since he had opened up to anyone the way he had opened up to her. And she liked him, he knew it with every nerve and sinew. He knew by the way her skin flushed the colour of her name when their eyes met, by the way her breathing quickened when he was near, by the way she said his name. Maybe it was foolhardy to invite her along, but he wanted her there—and he so seldom wanted anything other than to keep his girls safe.

And who was to say that if something flared up between them that it could go nowhere? There were still several weeks of summer left. This attraction might peter out as suddenly as it had appeared, and if not? Well, Asturia wasn't that far away. If things progressed maybe they could find a way to work things out.

He grinned, deliberately lightening the atmosphere. 'Honestly, even the thought of luxury camping makes me a little nervous. It would be good to have another adult along who actually wanted to be there.'

Rosy looked down at her beer and then back up. 'I'd love to,' she said eventually, her voice bright and impersonal. 'And shall we invite Sally and her daughter along? As you know, Alice and Clover get along really well, it might be fun to have a group of us. The real camping experience.'

So she didn't want to be alone with him. Maybe he'd misread the signals, or maybe a widower with two daughters was too complicated a package for her. Either way, it was fine.

'Why not,' he said, getting to his feet and picking up the two mugs. 'I'd better deliver these before they get cold.'

She opened her mouth then closed it again. 'Yes, good idea. I promised to show them how to light a fire.'

The intimacy sparked by his confidences was gone as if it had never been and that was probably a good thing. It was certainly safer. His life was complicated enough without adding in a long-distance relationship or the fallout of a failed short-term fling.

But as he followed Rosy out to the patio where the girls awaited them, a pile of logs at their feet, Jack couldn't help wishing that this connection between them was exactly what it felt like, the start of something, and not just a glimpse of what might have been. The kind of partnership he had never dared dream of.

CHAPTER FIVE

JACK WASN'T EXACTLY converted to camping but even he had to admit glamping was on another level.

Usually Jack enjoyed the outdoors, cooking on fires, physical exercise, the challenge of making or putting things together. It was just something about the smell of wet tents, bedrolls and sleeping bags that took him back to those nights in their small, cheap plastic tent, shifting uncomfortably on his too-thin mat, pretending to be asleep as his mother cried after a day of trying to make the best of another soggy day. For many years he'd thrown himself into every moment, pretending enthusiasm, not wanting to give her any other reason to cry until along with adolescence came the all-consuming selfishness that often accompanied that stage of life and he'd switched from pretending too much to not pretending enough.

But his girls had none of his reservations and they were more than delighted with the luxury outdoor accommodation. The spacious round bell tents they'd booked were already set up when they arrived, furnished with actual beds, the canvas floors covered with thick luxurious rugs. He'd booked a group pitch with two large tents and one smaller one. The large tents had two bedrooms, both of which easily fitted either a double bed or two large singles, complete with small bedside cabinets and a wooden rail for clothes. The front half of the tent was a large semicircle furnished with a velvet sofa, a couple of large beanbags and a low wooden table that could double as dining or coffee table. The smaller tent Rosy would sleep in didn't have a bedroom, her double bed took up one side of the tent, a loveseat and table the other. All three tents were richly decorated in deep reds, golds and oranges.

At the back of the pitch stood a covered wooden platform that held the kitchen area complete with a sink and running hot and cold water, an oven, fridge and kettle and fully stocked cupboards holding crockery, cutlery and saucepans. Centred in front of the tents but far enough away to be safe and to ensure no smoke wafted into the sleeping areas was a sunken fire pit surrounded by sofas. Four posts sat at each corner so a cover could be pulled over to shelter the sitting area in case of rain.

'This is *not* how I remember camping,' Sally said as their host gave them a tour. The girls had run off to explore the adventure playground with Tansy in charge. Jack was relieved to see that although as usual she took the responsibility seriously, she seemed less solemn, her blue eyes sparkling with excitement and a smile lighting up her thin face. 'I've stayed in holiday cottages more spartan than this.'

'It really is quite something,' Rosy agreed as she scanned the information folder the host had left them with. 'The freezer has ready meals for emergencies, and there's a takeaway menu as well. Ooh, there's also a proper woodfired pizza oven by the kitchen and they can supply dough and all the other ingredients. I vote for pizza tonight.'

The atmosphere between the three adults was comfortable but Jack could sense Rosy hanging back, leaving Sally and him to talk. He knew Sally a little, as was natural when they'd grown up in the same village, but as she was a few years younger they'd never socialised before. Watching Rosy step aside to leave them together, he couldn't help but suspect that she might be trying to set the two of them up. He could see why she might think they would hit it off—after all, they were both single parents and lived in the same place, but although he liked what he knew of Sally, he didn't feel a single atom of the attraction he felt for Rosy.

On the other hand, he could do with friends locally. Nor could he discount the fact that not only was Sally close to Clem, she was also part of the theatre campaign. Whatever Rosy's motivations in inviting Sally along, the night away gave him a great opportunity to discuss his plans with her and see if there was any thawing in opposition. She might even be prepared to be the bridge between Jack and the theatre group.

The afternoon passed quickly and before they knew it the girls were clamouring for food. Jack was more than happy to play with the professional-looking pizza oven and after a busy day of exploring the campsite, farm and beach, Rosy, Sally and the girls made far more pizza than they could all eat while Jack experimented with cooking them until he'd perfected his technique. After dinner he built up the fire and they sat around toasting marshmallows and heating up hot chocolate using the pot provided. The adults took turns telling campfire tales, careful to keep them age appropriate whilst providing the right amount of chill for the setting. Jack couldn't remember the last time he'd had such a carefree evening, or the last time he'd laughed so much as Rosy held them all captive with a comic horror story that by turns made them gasp then giggle. She might claim not to be an actress but she knew how to speak, her voice rich and curiously intimate as if she were pitching her words at everyone individually.

By the time dusk fell all three children were drowsy, even Tansy, and the novelty of sleeping in tents meant sending them to bed was surprisingly easy. They all trooped off happily to the bathing hut with Sally to clean up and put on pyjamas. Clover had begged to sleep with Alice and so Jack kissed her before she headed into the other tent, and he settled Tansy into her bed with a torch and a book.

With the children in bed and the fire starting to die down, Jack opened a bottle of wine. After they'd dissected the day, the conversation naturally turned to the theatre and Jack tried to make his pitch as neutrally as he could, not wanting Sally to feel that she was being set up. But to his relief once he—with Rosy chiming in every now and then—explained what he wanted to achieve, understanding dawned in her intelligent green eyes.

'I think,' she said as she refilled their glasses and handed around some chocolates she'd brought with her, 'that there's been a lot of miscommunication and misunderstanding here, Jack. On both sides.'

Jack couldn't help but agree. 'I dashed in all guns blazing,' he said. 'I saw an opportunity and just wanted to get started. I didn't take account of the recent history, the sense of ownership you all feel—and rightly so. No wonder people think I'm working against you, not with you. But believe me, Sally, I am tired of being seen as a lone wolf. I want the theatre to be a partnership between me and the community. I'm doing it for Polhallow, not despite of it.'

She nodded. 'What you've told me sounds really exciting, and I really think the committee will think so too when they hear it properly. Look, why don't you set up a tour? A chance for you to show us around, just as you showed Rosy around, and then we can sit down and look at the details: what a busier, professional theatre means for the local groups who rely on it, the finances, the legalities. Be honest with us and then let's see where we are.'

It was a fair offer, maybe fairer than he had expected, and Jack gratefully accepted.

'It's exciting to hear it all coming together,' Rosy said, smothering a yawn. 'But even so I can feel myself falling asleep. I think I'll turn in, that delicious-looking bed is calling to me.'

Jack tried to push away the vision of Rosy tumbling into bed, dark curls falling around her bare shoulders. So much for respecting her boundaries, he scolded himself. It was one thing to find her attractive, quite another to allow himself to indulge in fantasies. Besides, although she'd been her usual friendly self all day, there had been a touch of reserve in her manner when she was talking to him, a clear hint that she wasn't interested. A hint he needed to heed.

Rosy's decision was echoed by Sally and Jack decided to head in also and after a quick shower in the luxurious shower block with its underfloor heating and spacious tiled cubicles he pulled on a pair of tracksuit bottoms and a T-shirt and returned to his tent. He could see the glow of Tansy's torch signifying she was still reading and, looking at his watch, realised it was far too early for him to sleep. Instead, he took his laptop to the sofa and set about trying to capture all the questions Sally had asked him around the campfire, making sure he was as prepared for the pitch to the community group as possible, but as he tried to work his mind kept drifting. All he could see was

Rosy's face lit by the glow of the fire, hear the echo of her infectious laugh as she told stories, her excitement as they toasted marshmallows, the interest she seemed to take in every small detail of the girls' day.

It was a shame he hadn't met her at a different time and a different place. Rosy was the kind of woman any man would want—beautiful, intelligent, warm, interesting. And what did Jack have to offer? Money? She didn't seem short of that. The truth was he had two goals: to raise his daughters and to redeem his family name. Anything and anyone else would have to be prepared to come in third. It was a lot to ask of anyone, especially a woman like Rosy. No, better he put all thoughts of dating aside until the girls settled and he was established, and he had the time and energy any relationship needed.

Besides, he knew very little about Rosy. In fact, he could count what he did know on one hand and have fingers to spare. She came from a small country he'd barely heard of; she was obviously well-connected, the kind of woman whose family had expectations for her, expectations she accepted, although he sensed she wasn't entirely happy; she was beautiful. But there was so much more to her, kindness and integrity were evident in every gesture. She was the kind of woman who saw a problem and stepped in to help, even helping a virtual stranger struggling with fractious children. But that was it. He didn't know her childhood dreams, her favourite colour. He didn't even know if she was in some kind of relationship right now.

He knew he wanted her.

The words blurred in front of his eyes and so he closed his laptop, and picked up his book, only to find he couldn't concentrate on that either. What he needed was some air. The fire was still glowing and so he grabbed his book and headed back out, picking up his wine glass as he went. But as he approached the fire a figure moved. He wasn't the only one who couldn't sleep. There, wrapped in a blanket, staring into the flames was Rosy. He paused, unsure whether to join her or not, when she turned and smiled, and he knew he was lost.

It was inevitable maybe that Jack would appear as if Arrosa's thoughts had conjured him. It had been far harder than she'd anticipated keeping her distance from him all day. It was as if she were connected to him by some invisible cord. She could sense when he glanced over at her, feel his sudden and unexpectedly sweet smile, couldn't look away from him as he worked to build the fire or make pizza or help the girls on the zipwire. She was constantly aware of him, of his wrists, the vee of his throat, the nape of his neck. Her own gaze lingered on all the exposed vulnerable places as if she was learning them by heart.

'I'm sorry,' he said. 'You probably want to be alone…'

He was giving her the perfect get-out clause and she should take it, but she'd been good all day and it had left her aching with frustration and loneliness. 'I don't have a monopoly on the fire. Join me, please.'

He waited just a second as if checking the offer was real and then sat on the sofa next to hers. 'Not sleepy?'

'Turns out not. How about you? Camping better than expected?'

'Do you think I was being foolish?'

She straightened at that and turned to him in surprise. 'Not at all! We all have our trigger points, Jack, our regrets, memories we don't want to relive. We all keep ourselves safe the best way we know how. Putting your daughters first makes you courageous, not foolish.'

'It's not like we're roughing it. Sometimes I worry that I have gone too far the other way from my childhood, that I sling money at my problems and hope they'll disappear.'

Arrosa wasn't sure what to say. Once again Jack was opening up to her, really opening up to her, an experience so far removed from the polite small talk that dominated her life. And she couldn't help but wonder if he would speak so candidly if he knew who she really was.

'Have you ever spoken to your mother about all of this? About your childhood?' Who was she to ask? She would never discuss her inner feelings with her parents, wouldn't know where to start.

'I've apologised.' His grin was tired. 'Several times. More than apologised. I was able to put money in trust for her, so she doesn't have to work if she doesn't want to. But she told me in no uncertain terms that she had no intention of sitting on her hands all day at barely fifty and suggested if I really wanted to help then I would buy her a business. She sent me the details of the beach bar the very next day. It's no vanity project either, it's thriving and she's already expanding.'

Arrosa laughed. 'She sounds kind of formidable.'

'Oh, she is. I don't think she quite trusts the money I give her is either legal or sustainable. If it's not been earned by her own two hands, or in this case my two hands, she doesn't see how it could be real.'

Arrosa had always been taught that discussing money was rude, but curiosity got the better of her. 'What exactly is it that you do? You can't be more than…what? Thirty? That's some meteoric rise from the childhood you described.'

'Meteoric?' He shrugged but she saw him smile and knew he liked the description. 'Maybe, but honestly it's not that exciting a story. I was interested in programming, and because we couldn't afford for me to have the kind of top-of-the-range computer I wanted I learned to build it for myself from odds and ends. Village gossip will tell you that between fifteen and eighteen I was creating chaos, but the reality was I spent a lot of time in the flat honing my tech skills. At sixteen I started building websites for other people and by seventeen I was already making more than my mother.'

'Impressive.' She meant it. 'But in that case why the reputation? It can't just be your name, can it?'

He blew out a long breath. 'Partly the name, partly me and partly the result of poverty. The fact is, Rosy, that when you're a kid and your clothes are shabbier than everyone else's, and you don't always do your homework because your mother works three jobs and doesn't necessarily have time to help you with your spellings then you are pigeonholed—as lazy or rebellious or whatever. It's not right and it's not fair, but that's how it can be. And when you're alone a lot and bored it's easy to find trouble, and I did.'

'You're right,' she said softly. 'It's not fair.' Things weren't necessarily better in Asturia, which was why she had spearheaded before and after school schemes. It was a drop in the ocean of what needed to be done, but every child provided with a hot breakfast, with a place to do homework was another child given a chance to succeed.

'The year I was fourteen I was already nearing six foot—I looked older and thought I acted it. I got into a bad crowd, the kind made up of rich summer boys. They were all older than me. You can imagine how cool I thought I was, with no idea that they saw me as a convenient scapegoat. They were loud and drunk and annoying all summer and I tagged along, grateful to be included. Then one of them took his father's car out when he wasn't supposed to and when the police got involved they all blamed me. Of course everybody believed the Treloar boy had been out joyriding. Luckily for me, I got a decent solicitor who pointed out quite clearly that it could have been any of us and got the charges dropped, but everyone immediately knew that I was on the same path as my father.'

Her heart ached for the lonely, misunderstood boy he had been—no wonder redeeming his name was so important to him.

'Only you weren't.'

'No. That scare brought me to my senses—I was lucky not to get a spell in juvenile detention, but worse was the disappointment in my mother's eyes. I swore then that I never wanted to make her look like that again. So over the next few years I kept my head down, programming and honing my skills until at eighteen I got an offer from a start-up to join them. The idea was that we would build apps for businesses and people with ideas in return for a share in the app. It was a bit of a gamble. For every ten apps we put our time and energy into, nine we effectively built for free, and they'd sink without a trace. But when an app made it, it really did. And after a couple of years I stopped just making a good living and started to get rich.'

'And that's what you do now?'

'Not any more. A few years back I took some of the money I had made and looked for ways to invest it in other start-ups, not just apps. An angel, they call it—again I provide the money in return for a share in the company. I started off backing a small local chain of Lebanese cafés who wanted to expand, an organic skincare brand, a tech concierge service. It's similar to the apps; there's a risk that many will fail, others may stay small-time, but the ones that succeed really succeed. I have a team now who scout small businesses with potential for me.'

Rosy leaned forward, fascinated by his drive, his tenacity, his integrity. 'And this is why the theatre means so much—you want to invest in the village?'

'And to show the people here who I am now. Make our name respected, not reviled. And to help create something I am invested in, not just give money to others. Show my girls who I am, make them proud.'

'Of course they're proud. And you should be too. You're an amazing father! How many eighteen-year-olds do what you did? You built yourself up from someone who had barely anything to someone who can afford almost anything, but more importantly to being the best father you could be. Your girls are very, very lucky to have you.'

He didn't answer for a long while. 'Money isn't everything. They don't have a mother; I couldn't give them that.'

There was a lot going on here, more than Arrosa could unpack right now. She knew, she sensed with every fibre of her being that Jack rarely, if ever, opened up like this. What was it about them that made confidences between them so easy? And yet she couldn't repay him with any semblance of truth. It wasn't fair. She couldn't allow the imbalance to tip any further.

'I'm sorry.' She stood up, summoning her best social voice, her best social smile. 'You came here for some time alone with your thoughts. I should leave you to them.'

'Don't go.'

The words were so low she thought for a moment she had imagined them, but then Jack spoke again, his voice almost a guttural growl, reaching out to take her hand. 'Don't go.'

His touch shivered through her, every nerve jumping to attention as her whole body responded to the feel of his fingers threaded through hers, her body hollowing out, an insistent sweet ache pulsing low in her stomach, in her breasts. She almost gasped at the sensation, her own fingers folding around his, anchoring her to him as sensation shot through her.

'I...' She had no idea what to say, what to do. She was all desire, all need, and all the reasons she needed to retreat had floated away, leaving her standing there staring at him helplessly, looking for answers. Jack rose to his feet in one graceful movement and looked down at her, tenderness and need stark in his eyes.

This is a bad idea, she tried to remind herself, but she couldn't remember why that mattered. Why anything mattered but the stars overhead, shining on them as if in approval, the glow of the dying fire, the sweet smell of applewood permeating the atmosphere and the fact that Jack Treloar was looking at her as if she were the moon and the stars.

She stared up at him, drinking in the sharply defined lines of his face, the slope of his cheekbones and the curve of his mouth. Her gaze lingered on his mouth, the sensual curl enticing, inviting her, and she stepped closer, as if of its own volition her hand reaching up to trace his cheekbone, the lines of his jaw.

'Jack,' she whispered, unsure whether it was a plea or a protest. His skin was rough under her fingers, his stubble grazing her as she continued her exploration, returning along his jaw and up until she reached his mouth. He was motionless, eyes dark and full of a desire she had never seen before, never evoked before, and it filled her with a power she couldn't resist as he finally, finally tilted her chin and lowered his mouth to hers.

This was no gentle exploratory kiss but a claiming on both sides that shook Arrosa through even as she matched him, moving so close she could feel his every bone and muscle hard against her. She luxuriated in him, in the owning of him as she explored him, her hands running over shoulders and back, neck and chest, touching and teasing and learning. His hands were wrapped in her hair and she welcomed the slight pull as he wound the curls around his fingers. He tasted of wine and salt, smelt of woodsmoke and something uniquely him that she recognised at a molecular level. She wanted no barriers between them, she wanted him naked and in her, fast and hard and sweet and slow and please God could it be now…

And then, as if the heavens had opened and dowsed her in reality, Arrosa stepped back, all the reasons this couldn't, shouldn't, mustn't happen spinning through her.

'I am so sorry, Jack, I can't. I mustn't.' She reached

towards him for one weak moment as she whispered, 'I wish I could', before whirling around and running back to her tent.

CHAPTER SIX

DESPITE THE EXCELLENT mattress and comfortable surroundings, Arrosa didn't manage to get any sleep that night, reliving the kiss over and over in glorious Technicolor until she was both exhausted and frustrated, filled with unsated desire and regret.

What had she been thinking?

The truth was she hadn't been thinking. Instead, she'd allowed herself to be swept away. Turned out a starlit sky, firelight and a handsome man were her own personal kryptonite. Thank goodness she had come to her senses before she'd lost even more control. At least it was just a kiss.

But, oh, what a kiss. The kind of kiss she would remember until her dying moment. Just the thought of it sent flames flicking through her.

It didn't help that Jack kissed in a way guaranteed to make a girl's knees quiver. It wasn't just that he had felt, had tasted, so good. No, the problem was the *way* he'd kissed her. As if kissing her was exactly what he should be doing, was born to do. And she, God help her, had kissed him in exactly the same way.

The truth was it wasn't just a kiss. It was the culmination of a promise, a moment they'd been careering towards from the very first second. A moment she should have done her best to head off, not grasping with both hands as if it was her last chance of happiness.

Only maybe it was. After all, just three weeks ago she had practically proposed to someone she had no interest at all in kissing. Had resigned herself to a loveless, lust-less future.

And now? Now she didn't know what she wanted, what to do. No, that wasn't true. She wanted to kiss Jack again. But she couldn't, not while he had no idea who or what she was. Not when her heart seemed so firmly on the line.

To her surprise—and her relief—Jack seemed to act completely normally over breakfast and if the shadows under his blue eyes were darker than usual, well, there were lots of explanations for that. Maybe she'd read him wrong, read the situation wrong. Maybe for him the kiss had been nothing more than a passing whim, he'd just been taking advantage of what was undeniably a very romantic situation. But when Sally volunteered to take the now washed and dressed girls down to see the farm animals, the look he gave Arrosa made it clear that a reckoning was due.

'Fancy a walk?' he asked so casually that if she hadn't been so attuned to him, hadn't seen the pulse beating in his throat, hadn't observed his almost preternatural stillness she might not have known the request was more of a command.

'Sure, let me just get my bag.' She took a few minutes in her tent to breathe and compose herself, before pulling on a cardigan and grabbing her bag. Neither spoke as they made their way to the clifftop path which wound steeply down to a wide pebbly cove and started to make their way across the rocky beach.

'I owe you an apology,' Jack said at last, his jaw tight. 'I misread the situation last night. I didn't mean to make you uncomfortable. Please accept my apologies. It won't happen again.'

There it was, a get-out. Arrosa could say yes, he had misread the situation and they could both pretend she hadn't touched him, hadn't explored the austere planes of his face, hadn't pulled him so tight against her she could still feel him imprinted on her.

But she wasn't a liar. 'You didn't misread the situation. I wanted to be there with you, I wanted to kiss you and I wanted you to kiss me. I was all in, Jack. You don't need to apologise.'

'Okay…' Now he looked confused. 'Was it too soon? Were we moving too fast?' His brows drew together. 'Or are you in a relationship?'

Arrosa didn't know what to say. In one way all of the reasons were true. 'Jack…' She had no idea where to go next. Her hands curled into fists as she took a deep breath. She had to be honest. He was a good man, he deserved the truth from her. 'Yes to all those reasons and no at the same time. I'm not seeing anyone romantically, but my life isn't my own, Jack. That's why I'm here in Cornwall. I'm enjoying a few weeks' freedom before I pledge myself to Asturia. I know, I have always known, that my happiness will always have to come second. And so I shouldn't have kissed you. It was selfish of me because I knew I couldn't pursue it any further, but I just wanted something that was mine, just for once.'

His expression grew even more confused. 'Do you mean you're going to become a nun?'

She laughed, although in some ways the analogy fitted. 'No, although many of my ancestors were. Convents were always a good way to deal with wayward daughters and unwanted wives. Look, Jack, my full name is Arrosa Artega…'

She waited but now he just looked blank. Her name obviously meant nothing to him.

'That's a pretty name,' he said carefully, obviously wondering where this was going.

'Thank you. But this is about more than my name. Okay.' She looked out to sea, trying to find the right words. 'What I am about to tell you can go no further, because it doesn't just affect me. It affects Clem as well. And I really want you to know that I didn't mean to mislead you, I certainly didn't mean for things to escalate between us. But they have and that means you deserve the truth. I'm not a diplomat, Jack. I'm a princess. And in a few weeks' time the laws of my country will be changed to enable me to become next in line to the throne and the next monarch.'

There, it was out, and with it a load she hadn't even known she was carrying.

Arrosa cast a quick glance in Jack's direction to try and gauge his reaction. For a moment she could have sworn she saw hurt flit over his face, only to be wiped away as if it never was as his expression became shuttered.

'I must be very slow,' he said, his voice curiously polite. 'Did you just say you're a princess?'

'I didn't mean to deceive you...' she started but he dismissed her apology with a casual wave of his hand.

'Please don't worry about it, Your Highness. Is that the right title? You'll have to forgive me; I'm not used to addressing royalty.' Each word hammered into her, and she flinched.

'Rosy is fine. Look, Jack, like I said, this isn't just my secret. It involves Clem as well and that means I can't tell you everything, but I really want to try and make you understand.'

'Honestly, there's no need. You've been slumming it with the common people, that's absolutely fine. I hope I helped you relax.' His tone was still ultra-polite, deceptively casual, but she could see by the beat of a pulse in his cheek and the tensing of his jaw that polite was the last thing Jack Treloar was feeling right now.

For a minute she toyed with the idea of turning her back on him, heading back to the campsite and gathering her things before returning to the cottage. In a few weeks' time she'd be back in Asturia and would never see him again. Besides, she didn't owe him any explanation.

But then again, that wasn't exactly true. She'd allowed herself to step into his carefully ordered life. She'd offered to look after his girls, suggested this camping trip. She'd entangled herself with him, gained his trust—and that she knew was a rarity for this proud man.

Now he thought she'd betrayed it, betrayed him, and after he'd allowed himself to be vulnerable in front of her. No wonder he was so cold. She deserved it.

They'd reached the end of the beach, only rocks ahead until the point of the headland. The nearest rock was flat and smooth and Arrosa headed to it and sat, staring out at the horizon. Jack halted a few metres away and tried to calm his tumbling thoughts, quell his instinctive anger.

How could he have been such an idiot? How could he once again have fallen for a woman who didn't have any interest in him apart from as a diversion? A momentary dabble in the real world before stepping back into her gilded life.

It hadn't taken him long after their marriage to realise that Lily had been more interested in his reputation than Jack himself. He had been supposed to be a summer rebellion, the local lord of the manor's daughter slumming it with the village bad boy. Her marriage to him, their baby, a continuation of that rebellion. She'd loved him in her own careless way, but she had never really been in love with him, he knew that now, maybe had always known it.

And now he had once again fallen for a woman who came from a different sphere, who had no long-term interest in him. He was a fool.

'Jack,' she said quietly, almost helplessly. 'Please let me explain.'

His first instinct was to refuse, to walk away, but there was something heartbreakingly vulnerable in her straight-backed posture and so instead he nodded curtly. He owed her nothing, but she could have her say.

She clasped her hands together and stared out to sea for a while, visibly searching for the words, before exhaling softly and looking up at him candidly. 'I came to Cornwall every summer as a child. It's a place that means a lot to me. It was a chance to get away from everything life in Asturia entailed. Like I said to you a few days ago, I had a very privileged but very lonely childhood. One which meant I got to stay in palaces and castles all over the world, but one where I was never allowed to be a child. I always had to be perfectly presented and perfectly behaved. Coming to Cornwall, being Rosy, not Arrosa, was the only time I was free just to be me, to even figure out who me *was*.' She blinked and he could have sworn he saw the glint of tears.

'I always knew that as a girl I couldn't inherit the throne and, apart from the innate sexism of the law, that was more than fine with me. As I got older and got to go to boarding school here in England as well as spend summers here, I could see some kind of freedom in my future. Balancing a career and royal duties is a difficult thing to do, as many minor royals have found before me, and I had no idea what that path would be for me, but I was looking forward to university and figuring it all out. It felt like I had all the time in the world. But I was wrong.' She threw him a quick anxious glance but he couldn't respond, couldn't move, frozen into place by the spell of her words.

'I spent the summer here after turning eighteen and it was golden. I don't know if that's because, when I look back, it was the last time I was truly free, or whether it really was. Clem and I were dating these guys in an intense teen kind of way and the four of us spent the summer surfing and sailing and at festivals. But then my father summoned me home and told me that the right thing to do for our family and for the country was to overturn the primogeniture law retrospectively so that I could become Crown Princess.'

He finally spoke. 'So now you're the heir to the throne?'

'Not quite yet, but soon. In Asturia, the monarch has a lot of political power. The people dislike change. I think it's partly because of where we are positioned, our history is full of war and conflict. It's taken eight years to get to the place where the overturning of the primogeniture law can be ratified. Every opposition party has agreed to support it and the country as a whole agreed in a referendum. During the eight years the change has been debated I have had to be completely perfect in appearance and word and deed. And once I become heir I will have to be even more so. It can be overwhelming at times.'

She blew out a breath. 'Clem thought I needed a break and so she persuaded me to stay here while she is in Asturia pretending to be me—and you are one of just a very small number of people who know that. Jack, if this got out not only would it destroy the public's confidence in me but for Clem the exposure would be life-changing. That I can't tell you any more about, it's not my story to tell, but I hope you see how much I trust you in revealing this much.'

'Clem is pretending to be you? Sure, you resemble each other, but you're hardly identical.' But he could feel his anger starting to thaw. She must have felt desperate to have agreed to such a risky scheme.

'That is definitely the flaw in the plan. But I'd kept my diary free this summer to help me prepare for the ratification, so Clem is being driven out every so often dressed up as me, and that's hopefully enough to keep the tabloids at bay. I've been closely followed, you see, ever since I came of age. A leave of absence would be immediately gossiped about, any kind of hint I needed a break so close to the ratification could lead to the kind of speculation I've spent the last eight years trying to avoid. It's risky, maybe too risky, but the thought of spending six weeks here, being Rosy again one last time, was irresistible. Clem had her own reasons for proposing the switch.'

She looked up at him and he could see the need for understanding, the apology in her expression and he knew her reaction was real. Lily had never cared about being understood, had never apologised to him once, no matter what. But Lily had merely been a rich man's daughter—Rosy was a princess. He had made his own money but he would never be able to create the kind of background and privilege she would need in any future partner.

'There you go, Jack. The whole story. You now know more about me than almost any other person in the world except Clem, my father and my bodyguard.'

'Your secrets are safe with me,' he said at last. 'I can promise you that.'

'Thank you. Jack, I hope you see why I had to step away last night. I couldn't allow us to continue if you didn't know who I am. I didn't want to deceive you any further. But…' She paused and her cheeks pinkened. 'I'd like us to still be friends. I have really appreciated getting to know you over the last few weeks.'

Friends? Was that even possible any more after such an incendiary kiss, after the sharing of such confidences? He'd started to fall for her, hard, and now he was grappling with the fact that she had misled him—and that there was definitely no future for them. Men like him might climb up the social ladder so far, but royalty was definitely a step too far.

Plus, he'd always sworn that if and when he started to date, the girls came first. A relationship with no hope of going anywhere failed that test spectacularly.

But, at the same time, he couldn't just walk away. There was a loneliness to Rosy that he had never really appreciated before, a loneliness that called to him.

'I need to think about it.' He saw her face fall although she tried to hide it. 'It's a lot, Rosy. It was already a lot. You started to change things for me and for the girls in ways I hadn't expected or planned for. And although I knew you weren't planning on living here full-time, that there was no future for us, I couldn't help but wonder that if things carried on the way they'd started maybe somehow there might have been. That we could figure it all out. But now? Now there can never be anything beyond this summer. I know it sounds a little crazy, talking about the future after just a few meetings as if I was still a romantic teen. But there's a connection between us. Isn't there?'

'Yes.'

'So I need time to think this all through.'

'I'm sorry, Jack,' she said, her voice breaking slightly.

Jack wanted to hold her, to promise her that it would all be okay, but that wasn't a promise he could make so instead he simply nodded then turned and walked away.

The irony was that in every other way the camping trip was a great success. The girls seemed happier and more settled, while Jack and Sally were now, if not friends exactly, then friendly, Sally willing to set up a meeting with him and the theatre committee.

But it wasn't lost on Jack that Rosy was responsible for that success—after all, she had suggested the trip and invited Sally along. But thinking of her was like touching a sore spot. He felt hollow inside when he thought about her revelations, the knowledge that it was easier and more sensible to move on with his life without involving her any further in it.

Jack did his best to throw himself into work, but for once it didn't hold his attention the way he had always relied upon it to do. It didn't help that the girls were away; Lily's parents were staying at their Polhallow house and had asked to have their granddaughters for a few days. He had a good relationship with his in-laws now; it was a long time since they'd viewed him as the teenage boy who'd seduced away their daughter.

But with the girls away the house felt too big and too empty and although there were plenty of things he could and should be doing he couldn't seem to get going and this morning was no different. He knew he had to have the promised conversation with Rosy. The problem was, he still had no idea what to say.

It was late morning and already hot as he set out on foot, popping into the café Sally's family owned for snacks and coffees before walking up the hill to Clem's clifftop cottage.

There was no answer to his initial knock on the door, but the windows were wide open and so Jack walked around the house to the back garden, where he paused, his blood rushing at the sight of a bikini-clad Rosy stretched out on a sunbed, eyes half closed and her face upturned to the sun, a book unopened in her hand.

'Are you open to visitors?'

She started and looked up, wary at first, almost scared, and with a pang of conscience he remembered what she'd said about living under scrutiny, always having to be picture perfect. He was pretty sure that description didn't include lounging in nothing but a bikini, although she did look pretty perfect to him. His mouth dried as he took in the long lines of her body; he'd rather take this relaxed Rosy than any prim and proper princess. Not, of course, that either were his to take.

'I've brought lunch,' he said and held out the paper bag.

For a moment she didn't react, just stared at him before sitting up, her full mouth curving into a wide smile. 'Oh, well, if you brought lunch…'

'It's nothing fancy…' He was barely conscious of what he was saying, just using words to try and bridge the chasm that had sprung up between them.

'Even better.' She pushed herself up to her feet with grace and Jack couldn't tear his gaze away from her long, tanned legs, her exposed midriff, the curve of her breasts showcased by the yellow bikini top. He swallowed as the desire that had never quite subsided flared up, hot and urgent. 'I was just trying to get up the energy to fix some lunch. Shall we eat here?' She gestured to the wrought iron table he was standing next to.

'Perfect.' Jack placed the coffee and bags on the table and watched her as she walked over, pulling an oversized striped T-shirt dress on as she did so.

'Hi,' she said softly.

'Hi.' They looked at each other for a charged moment before taking their seats and Jack tore open the bags to reveal the savoury pastries, olives and marinated tomatoes and peppers he'd bought, pushing a coffee towards Rosy.

She sniffed it appreciatively. 'Flat white, no sugar?'

'I've been paying attention.'

'Thanks.' Colour rose in her cheeks as she took a sip.

Jack pushed one of the bags towards her and they ate, making polite conversation about the quality of the food, the girls' plans for the rest of the week, until the bags were empty and Rosy sat back with a satisfied sigh. 'Delicious, thank you.' She looked down at her hands. 'I'm glad you stopped by. I wasn't sure you would.'

'Neither was I,' he said honestly.

She nodded. 'I get it. My situation is a lot.'

But she *didn't* get it and Jack realised how much he wanted her to understand. 'It is, but Rosy, I've been here before.'

'Here?' Her expression was confused.

'An amusing diversion for a rich, entitled girl who fancied slumming it in the real world.' He enunciated every word. 'I have no intention of ever being that gullible again.'

Understanding and hurt flared in her eyes and he saw her swallow. 'That's not who I am, Jack.' She swallowed again and with an almost defensive toss of her head reached over and took his hand, lacing her fingers through his. 'I don't think I'm entitled, and you are more than my equal in every way. I can't tell you what this thing is between us because I don't know, but I promise that's not how I see you at all. I didn't intend any of this to happen. I shouldn't have allowed myself to get so close to the girls, to allow myself to get so close to you.' Her gaze was devastatingly candid. 'Especially once I realised how attracted I was to you.'

'And I am attracted to you, but it isn't that simple. It matters. Who you are matters.'

'Right now, I am just Rosy, enjoying the sun, and I intend to be her for another two weeks.' She let his hand drop, tilting her chin, and despite her words he could see the proud Princess in every line of her.

But he could see the woman he'd got to know and care for too. 'That's the problem. Because I don't know the Princess, but I do know Rosy. And it's Rosy I want.' He hadn't meant to admit that, but the words were out and couldn't be unsaid.

Her eyes were huge, her lips slightly parted. 'So what do we do?'

'I don't know,' he admitted, 'The sensible thing would have been not to come here at all.'

Rosy sat and looked at him for a long moment. 'Why do you think I see you as a diversion, Jack? You must know how much you have to offer any woman, even a princess. You're rich and good-looking, successful, a great father, fun to be with. Any woman would be lucky to have you.'

'I shouldn't have said that,' he admitted. 'Seeing Lily's parents today brought the past crashing back; it always does, although they mean well.'

'That's understandable. You were married for a long time.'

'You think we got a happy ever after?'

'I know it ended tragically, but raising two wonderful girls together was an achievement.'

It was one way to look at his marriage. He'd always thought of it as an endurance, not an achievement. 'Lily was complicated, which meant our marriage was complicated.'

'How so?'

How could he describe Lily? 'She was wild and beautiful and talented and capricious. She could make you feel like no one else existed or freeze you out completely and you would never know which way it would be.'

'That sounds exhausting.'

'It was.' It was only now that he could look back and see how much his marriage had drained him.

'How did you meet?'

'At the Harbour pub. We set eyes on each other and it was instant fireworks, the way it can only be when you're young and naïve and think *Romeo and Juliet* is a romance not a cautionary tale. Taking up with me was the ultimate two fingers up at her parents and their expectations for her. Her parents wanted her to join the family law firm after Oxford, she wanted to study art. I was her ultimate rebellion, son of the village petty criminal with a reputation of my own. The irony is, she was a lot wilder than me. I think actually I disappointed her in many ways.' He inhaled, thinking back to the naïve young man he'd once been, who thought that love was enough.

'We didn't intend to get pregnant, and she certainly didn't intend to marry me. I was meant to be her summer fun.' He saw Rosy wince and realised she now understood parallels he'd noticed between her situation and his past. 'I think when people gossip about back then, they imagine me whisking her off to some bedsit on the outer edges of London. Instead, I was on such a good salary that we could move to a nice area and once Tansy was born Lily went to art school, just like she wanted. She was talented, but when she left college she was more interested in partying than working and I was making more than enough for her to indulge herself. It wasn't that she didn't love the girls, she just didn't know how to be a mother and didn't care to learn; the children would be brought out at parties and then sent away with the nanny. Just as her childhood had been.'

He reached out and swigged his now cold coffee, grateful for the caffeine. 'Poor Lily, rather than scandalise her parents, in the end they were actually proud of me. Instead of a husband as wild as her, she found herself married to a man with a ridiculous work ethic who made more money than her parents could ever dream of and gave her the kind of life they wanted for her.'

'Were you ever happy?'

It was a long time since he had thought of happiness where his marriage was concerned.

'Sometimes,' he said slowly. 'At least we tried to be.' After all, he'd known her as he knew himself, understood the insecurities that led to her destructive behaviour. 'She loved the girls but motherhood bored her, so I compensated. I went to every play and dance recital, created every holiday tradition. I wanted them to have a perfect childhood. Sometimes I think that somewhere between being the best father I could and my work drive I forgot to be a husband. I didn't want Lily to feel she'd made a mistake marrying me, I didn't want her to feel trapped, the way my mother did. So I never challenged her about her behaviour, never questioned her about her drinking or the drugs I was pretty sure she was taking on a night out. She took lovers and I pretended not to know. Maybe if I'd intervened she wouldn't have ended up overdosing in a hotel room at the age of twenty-eight.'

Jack couldn't believe the words that had just tumbled out of his mouth, words he had barely dared to think before, let alone say. Words that were his truth. His shame.

But there was no condemnation on Rosy's face. No horror. 'I am so, so sorry, Jack.'

He shrugged, suddenly tired. 'It's been over two years now. Clover barely remembers her. At first, I didn't want to make any big moves, all the books say to give it a year, not to make any sudden decisions in the first wave of grief. And the girls needed their routine. But we lived in a wealthy area, and I could see how young it started. The drinking, the drugs, the dangerous and entitled behaviour. I'm not saying Cornwall doesn't have its problems, I know it does, and I know every school has its own issues. But I wanted to show them a different way before it was too late.'

Rosy reached out and took his hand again and he was glad of the warmth, the firmness of her grip. 'You are not just a good father, Jack Treloar, you are an amazing one. And I am sure Lily would be glad her girls have you looking out for them.'

'You think so?'

'I know so.'

And for the first time in a long time Jack knew so too, freed from the guilt and grief that had plagued him since Lily's death. He was doing his best and that was enough.

CHAPTER SEVEN

ARROSA SAT STILL for a moment, absorbing everything Jack had told her. Every instinct she possessed told her that she now knew more about Jack Treloar than any other person alive. He'd gifted her his regrets and his hopes and his dreams. It was a precious, fragile gift and she knew how rare it was. Would he have entrusted her with so much if she were staying here? Was the intensity between them fast-tracked by the finite nature of their relationship, that knowledge the clock was ticking, and she was already over halfway through her time here?

And in return Jack knew most of her secrets, apart from Clem's identity. This was as intimate as she was ever likely to be with another human being. And that wasn't something she could just walk away from.

But what else could she do?

'How long are the girls with their grandparents?'

Surprise—and intrigue—flitted across his expression. 'Until Sunday at the earliest, possibly early next week, depending on how long their grandparents can cope. Losing Lily took a toll on them both, so I like to keep arrangements flexible in case the girls need to come back early.'

'And it's Thursday lunchtime now.' She glanced at her watch. 'If you include this afternoon then you have three days until the end of the weekend.'

Jack raised his eyebrows in bemused query. 'Three days to what?'

'To take a leaf out of my book and get away from it all,' she said. 'Responsibility and duty and shouldering everything yourself is all very well, but if you don't put down your burdens occasionally then you run the risk of breaking.'

'My girls are not a burden.' But, to her relief, he didn't sound angry.

Emboldened, she went on. 'No, of course not. But I don't know a single parent who isn't glad of a break every now and then. We all need to refill the well, Jack. And if your plans for the next few days are just work, work, work how are you going to do any refilling?'

'You think I'm in danger of running dry?' Now he sounded amused as well as curious.

'All I'm saying is that I do know a lot about burnout. I had no idea how close I was myself until the morning I woke up here. It was almost overwhelming, I almost left it too late. But I know now never to let myself get to that stage again.' Arrosa picked up her coffee and drained it. 'You know, I always thought my mother was selfish, disappearing off on retreat every summer without me and without my father. It always seemed an affectation to me, but I understand her better now. For forty-eight weeks of the year she's the perfect Queen. She puts all her own hopes and desires to one side and concentrates on supporting my father, supporting me, making small talk, being the consummate hostess. No wonder she needs four weeks a year when she's just herself.'

Truth was, Arrosa was a little ashamed of how judgemental she'd been. She, of all people, knew that her parents' marriage was no fairy tale but rather a sometimes brutal business arrangement, one broken before it had had a chance to flourish after Zorien had confessed about his love affair with Clem's mother. How could she judge her mother for taking one month a year for herself? She made a quick resolve to call her. They didn't have the sort of relationship which included cosy chats or calls to just check in, but maybe that was something that could change. She might have lost her second mother, but her own mother was still alive and well and Arrosa should not take that for granted.

'So, you think I need a break?'

'Tell me you're not tempted.'

'And you will come with me on this break.'

It was not a question. Which was a good thing because she didn't have an answer.

'That's not...'

But he didn't let her finish. 'Where do you want to go?'

'Jack, it was a suggestion, not a proposition.' But she couldn't deny she was tempted. Very tempted. She'd never been on a mini-break before. And just a few days ago she had resigned herself to not seeing Jack again and now he was offering her the opportunity to spend some real time with him.

She was inexperienced romantically, but she wasn't a fool. She knew what would happen if she agreed.

Her pulse sped up at the thought.

'And it was a good suggestion. I could do with a break, you're right. But I spend a lot of time alone without adult company. If I was going to unwind, really unwind, I might need some help.' His gaze was burning into her. 'So, any requests?'

Arrosa took a deep breath, her chest tight with anticipation. Three days away with Jack—three days and three nights. Without the girls there would be no need to worry about mixed signals and raising expectations. They were both adults and they both knew the score. Had acknowledged how they felt, knew the barriers, that there was no future for them.

Maybe it needed to happen. Maybe if she left Cornwall with this connection still simmering between them, this desire unconsummated, then she would be condemning herself to a constant *what might have been*, a refrain that might run throughout her life. And who knew? Maybe they would burn out as quickly as they'd started.

'Anywhere,' she said and saw Jack relax just a little at the tacit agreement. 'Not abroad as I can't use my passport. If I did the press would instantly be alerted.'

'How did you get here?'

'Private jet and airfield. It's an option but it would take too long to arrange.' Besides, she didn't want to involve the Court or her bodyguard, not in something as private as this.

'UK then. Probably not too far if we only have a couple of days. Besides…'

'Besides, you don't want to be too far from the girls.' She quite understood.

Anticipation buzzed through her. This was nothing Arrosa had experienced before, discussing weekend plans with a man she burned for. 'Let's just get one thing straight,' she told him. 'I know you're a man with refined tastes, but I'm a woman who is very easily impressed. Fish and chips and a decent beach are all I require. Maybe a pint in a really good pub.'

His mouth quirked into a devastating grin and the anticipation intensified. 'You don't need your own concierge service?' She shook her head. 'Chauffeured limo? Michelin stars? Personal spa?'

'None of the above. If you could manage a clear sky and some stars I'd be very grateful, and I prefer my bed to be freshly made, but otherwise anything goes.'

His gaze softened into something so tender it hurt. 'Leave it with me.'

Jack disappeared to make arrangements and Arrosa quickly tidied away the lunch things, texting Sally to see if she'd be able to feed Gus for just a couple of nights, and went upstairs to pack, singing to herself as she did, her feelings so intense she could barely concentrate. Thank goodness she could use Clem's wardrobe; her own array of tiny beach dresses, shorts and bikinis clearly wouldn't take her very far.

Clem favoured vintage cuts, bright colours, whereas Arrosa usually dressed in more subtle tones and cuts, but then again, she'd never really had a chance to figure out her own taste. Once the project to turn her into the perfect Crown Princess had commenced, a stylist had been employed to make sure that Arrosa trod the fine line between fashion and appropriateness and so although her clothes were made just for her, and although she was always completely up to the minute in terms of cut and colour, there was something depressingly interchangeable about the dresses and little jackets, tailored trousers and neat jumpers she usually wore. Looking through Clem's eclectic mix of dresses and skirts, silky little tops and jumpers was a lot of fun and, before she knew it, she had selected enough for a week away, let alone just a couple of days. But, then again, she had no idea where they were going.

Jack collected her an hour later, refusing to give her any hints, although he drove deeper into Cornwall and not away from the county until they finally reached Penzance. He continued winding his way through the town, pulling in at a car park near the docks.

'We have to leave the car here,' he said as he swung

their cases out of the boot. 'They don't allow visitors' cars where we're going.'

Arrosa looked towards the dock and the ferry sign, excitement mounting. 'The Isles of Scilly? Oh, Jack! That's perfect. Clem and Simone went one spring, and their photos were amazing!'

She'd always wanted to visit the small cluster of islands at the southern tip of Britain. Famous for their microclimate and wildlife, something about the islands had always appealed to her.

'It turns out that finding something last minute for a weekend in early July isn't that easy, but luckily I know people who know people. Sure this is okay?'

'It couldn't be more okay,' she said as he took both cases and headed towards the boarding gate for the ferry.

It was a windy couple of hours on a surprisingly rough ocean, but Arrosa drank in every second, laughing as her hair escaped the coil she'd fastened it into and whipped around her face. She, Arrosa Artega, was heading off on a romantic weekend with a man she had started to care for and right now everything was perfect.

Rosy's enthusiasm was infectious. She loved everything, from the ferry journey over to St Mary's and the transfer to the smaller boat which took them to Tresco, exclaiming at the seals and dolphins they spotted in the waves. She didn't even mind the mile-long walk to the cottage Jack had managed to borrow, despite the stiff climb and her bulky case, waving away his offer of help.

'Don't treat me like a princess,' she told him.

'It's chivalry,' he protested.

'I'm quite capable, and I'm the one who overpacked.'

Finally, they reached the whitewashed cottage which sat alone on the headland. It had been cleaned and prepared for them and Jack retrieved the key from the keysafe, opening the door and standing back, allowing Rosy to precede him.

He followed her into the small but perfectly formed cottage. The ground floor was one room, kitchen, dining space and lounge combined, with floor-to-ceiling windows framing the dramatic ocean views on one end and the cliffs on either side. It was comfortably yet stylishly decorated and Rosy turned to Jack, eyes glowing.

'I love it. I can't wait to explore!'

You would never think that Rosy was a princess, used to the best of everything, Jack reflected as she exclaimed in delight, exploring every inch of the cottage, dashing from view to view, opening cupboards, examining the bookcases.

'It's not too small?'

She shook her head, her delighted smile widening even further if that was possible. 'You know, even though I moved out of the château when I was twenty-one, I still have four bedrooms in a house where no one comes to stay, and a couple of downstairs rooms I don't even use. I don't need or want a big house; cosy suits me fine.'

And that was part of what he liked about her. She wasn't influenced by how much something cost, but by what it meant.

'That's good to hear because this place is certainly bijou,' he said. 'And of course,' he added hurriedly, not wanting there to be any misunderstandings between them, 'I'll take the pull-out bed.'

There was only one bedroom, taking up the whole of the upper floor, with a luxury shower room off it—the bath was on a raised platform by the window in the bedroom so the occupant could fill it with water and the decadent-smelling bath oil and lounge comfortably, looking out to sea.

'The pull-out?'

He nodded towards the sofa. 'It turns into a bed.'

She held his gaze levelly, but he could see a trace of uncertainty in her eyes. Not, he thought, uncertainty about what she was about to say, but more uncertainty about his reaction.

'It's a big bed,' she said deliberately. 'I would say it's big enough to share.'

Jack swallowed at the hope in her gaze. It wasn't an unexpected offer. After all, this was no platonic getaway. The prospect of consummating their connection had been there since the moment he'd suggested she join him for a getaway, the moment she'd accepted. Staying in a small, isolated cottage in the middle of nowhere, a cottage made for lovers, just set those expectations more firmly. But it was the first time either of them had alluded to it out loud.

'Okay.'

Her smile was mischievous. 'I mean, you can sleep on the sofa bed if you prefer.'

'I'm sure the bed will be fine.'

Her dimples flashed. 'Good, I'm glad that's settled.'

Jack continued to watch her as she whirled around the cottage, still discovering new things to exclaim at in surprise or approval. He needed to concentrate on the here and now and deliberately, very deliberately, not think about what he was doing. Not think about the promise that hovered over them, the evening just a very few short hours away.

This trip was impulsive, frivolous, dedicated to momentary pleasure, all things Jack rarely allowed. He liked his life planned and organised and deliberate, had done ever since the day the policeman had told his fourteen-year-old self that he could be facing a lengthy spell in youth detention. The next two hours, alone in a cell waiting for his mother, afraid of the sadness and, worse, the resignation he knew he'd see on her too-worn face had changed him. He'd realised what an impulsive fool he had been, played with by older, richer boys who saw him as little more than amusement and had no compunction in using him as their scapegoat. He'd seen his future stretched out before him, full of rooms like that, spells in and out of jail, like his father had before him, leaving a trail of broken hearts and broken potential behind him. He'd vowed then and there that that would not be his destiny and everything he'd done since had been a rebuttal of the policeman's words.

The only time he'd allowed himself to step off the path he'd set himself was when he'd met Lily. That summer his future had seemed assured, his job lined up and already enough money saved to change his life. But even that hadn't derailed him. When he'd found out Lily was pregnant he'd just adjusted his plans, used the prospect of becoming a father to motivate him even more.

Now he was stepping off the path again for a very different woman. A woman who was considered and responsible, one who accepted her responsibilities and fate, who wasn't trying to outrun her destiny but to meet it with grace and acceptance.

'You look very pensive.' Rosy came to stand next to him, close but not touching. For two people away on a romantic weekend they were very careful not to touch, but he could feel the air around them tense.

'I'm just thinking what a lucky man I am,' he said, and her face softened.

'Don't you forget it.'

'It's a little late to explore the island,' Jack said. "But we have this place until Sunday, so shall we head out and get some food? There are a couple of really good restaurants; they are probably fully booked but I'm sure I could pull some strings.'

'You know, I don't want a fancy restaurant.' Rosy put a hand on his shoulder and looked up at him almost shyly. 'I wasn't kidding earlier. What I really, really want is fish and chips, maybe a beer, sitting on the beach, watching the boats go by. Does that sound really boring?'

'No,' he said slowly. 'That sounds perfect.'

Too perfect. This was a summer idyll, nothing more, but with every passing moment he knew he was falling harder for her.

'They were the best fish and chips I ever had in my entire life,' Rosy said, leaning against him with a contented sigh, and Jack agreed. The takeaway had been perfectly cooked, slightly crispy chips melting in the middle and covered with the perfect amount of salt and vinegar, delicately flaked fish in melt-in-the-mouth batter accompanied by a tart locally brewed beer with just the right amount of hops. Add in the soft sandy beach, the stunning sunset and the sea views and Jack realised he'd never enjoyed a meal more. Nor had he ever felt anything like the anticipation for what came next. Much as he wanted to drag her back to the cottage and kiss her until neither of them could speak, he also wanted to enjoy the wait a little longer.

'Fancy trying the local pub?' he asked and she agreed, exclaiming how lucky they were to find a small table by the window as he fetched the drinks, like any normal couple out on a date, making small talk about books and films and dreams.

'Have you ever thought about who you would be

if you weren't you?' Jack asked after a while and Arrosa stared at him in confusion.

'If I wasn't me?'

'I'm trying to be discreet,' he said. 'You know, if you didn't have to do the job you have to do.'

'Oh.' Her face fell a little. 'It's not something I think about,' she said at last. 'It is what it is, and I can't change it so I try not to waste time wishing for something else. But I'm glad I don't have one overwhelming passion. If Clem was me, for instance, and couldn't act, then it would have destroyed her. I wasn't overjoyed about the closing down of other paths, but I accepted it. I think if I can keep some semblance of normality in my life, like living in my villa, that kind of thing, then I'll be okay.'

'That's a very healthy attitude.'

She shrugged. 'I could have said no to my dad, I guess, but then how could I advocate for change if I didn't want to be that change? I can't run away from who I am, from my responsibilities, at least not for ever. How about you? Any unlived dreams?'

'Obviously, I was married and a father young, so like you, I suppose, I accepted responsibility then and learned not to waste time on daydreams. But the truth is my girls give my life meaning and purpose. I wouldn't want to imagine a world where they aren't my life. I guess,' he said slowly, 'what we have in common is that even if circumstances don't work out the way we thought they might, we know how to make the best of the situation we're in. That's pretty rare in my experience.'

Rosy held up her drink. 'To the cards we're dealt'.

He clinked his glass against hers but as they made the toast couldn't help wondering if they would be so philosophical when Rosy left for good.

Her gaze was fixed on his as she finished her drink. 'You know I don't want another drink here. Let's get back.'

'You sure?' he asked, and they both knew he was asking about more than the drink.

'Yes,' she said. 'I have never been surer. Let's go.'

CHAPTER EIGHT

NEITHER SPOKE AS they walked back in the rapidly darkening dusk, anticipation colouring every step, every movement, every glance. Arrosa was attuned to Jack's every move, breath and glance. Desire swirled, hot and intense, throughout her entire body, pooling in the pit of her stomach, causing flickers of heat in every nerve, her breasts heavy and almost painful. It was like some specific kind of torture, almost painful, apprehension mingling with anticipation.

They still hadn't spoken by the time they reached the cottage and Jack once again unlocked the door and ushered her in. Arrosa swallowed nervously as she slipped off her wrap and stood slightly awkwardly in the middle of the lounge watching Jack as he closed the door behind him and moved towards her, graceful, masculine and seemingly unaffected by the nerves that now consumed her.

He reached her and paused, tilting her chin up so

that he could look in her eyes. It took everything Arrosa had to meet his dark gaze.

'We don't have to do anything you don't want to,' he told her, and she loved him for it.

'But I do want to,' she said and before she could change her mind wound her arms around his neck, bringing him closer, until once again she was kissing him the way she had wanted to since their first kiss a few days before.

Just like the kiss at the fire, there was no gentle introduction as once again the kiss ratcheted from nought to sixty without passing go. His mouth was strong and possessive, his hands sure and knowing, and even though he was only touching her back and waist, her whole body ached for more, arching towards him. She found herself tugging at his shirt, impatient to get to the skin underneath, to run her hands over the smooth muscled planes of his body, needing to know him in every way, to discover every inch, to make him hers. She dragged her mouth from his, pressing kisses along his jawline as she finally wrenched his shirt off, leaving her free to explore the skin underneath.

He hissed as her hands moved lower, now pulling at his belt. 'Rosy, we have all the time in the world.'

But they didn't! They had here and now and if they were lucky a couple more weeks and that was it. What had she been thinking of, waiting an entire month? They could have been here already; this could be one moment in a long line, not the first. She pressed even closer, holding his face between her hands as she kissed him harder, impatient for him to touch her in all the places that ached for him.

Jack didn't protest any more, kissing her back with equal intensity, finally, finally sliding his hands up her back, his clever fingers tracing every inch of skin until she was boneless with desire and only then sliding down with excruciating slowness to explore every rib before slowly, so slowly, inching back up towards her aching breasts. Arrosa moaned as his finger finally brushed against one tight nipple, arching into him as sensation engulfed her. 'Can we go upstairs?'

She felt his rumble of amusement, 'I feel like I should be sweeping you up and carrying you to the bed,' he said. 'But that spiral staircase isn't made for grand gestures. Ladies first.' She felt cold as she stepped away from him, her legs shaky as she made her way upstairs and turned to face him, all too aware of the giant bed which dominated the room.

For all her bravado, and her desperation to get past the niceties, her nerves had returned in full and her hands shook as she unzipped her dress. Jack stood near the staircase watching her, his expression unfathomable.

'What's wrong?'

'I'm a little nervous.' She tried to smile but his expression darkened.

'Rosy, I meant every word. We don't have to do anything you don't want to do. I have no expectations.'

'I know.' She bit her lip. Now it came to it, she

couldn't quite find the words. 'It's just I've not done this before.'

She flushed hot at the surprise in his eyes, followed by understanding. 'I see.'

'It's a princess thing, you see,' she said hurriedly. 'I don't really date. The only people that ask me out are those that see the Princess, not the person, and that is possibly the least sexy thing I could imagine. Plus, there's always that fear in the back of my mind, if things don't work out, what if they go to the press? I couldn't bear any *My night of passion with the Princess* headlines. So there's never been anyone I've been willing to risk it for before. Not before you.'

His eyes darkened even more as he took a step closer. 'I don't see the Princess. I see the woman. I see you, Rosy. And it's you I want. But if it makes you feel better, I am just as nervous.'

'You are?' It was her turn to be surprised.

'Of course I am. For a start, you are one hell of a woman and that would make any man nervous. Secondly, now I know it's your first time I want to make it as special as I can. And thirdly, in a way it's a first time for me. You see, I've only ever slept with Lily.' Her gaze was glued to his but all she could see was candour and honesty.

'Really?'

'Really.'

'But…'

'It's a little bit like the princess thing, I suppose. When I was younger the kind of girls who were attracted to my reputation weren't the kind of girls I wanted to be with. Then I was married to Lily for ten years and, although it was an imperfect marriage, I took my marriage vows seriously. Since she died the girls come first and I haven't even considered dating. So, it's a first for me as well.'

'Then I'm the one who's honoured.'

It was as if their confidences had broken the ice. Her shyness had gone, her trepidation disappeared; all she wanted was this man now. She laughed a little breathlessly as he backed her onto the bed, luxuriating as she felt his weight upon her, as he kissed her until she could barely think any more, the last layers of clothing expertly discarded until there was nothing between them.

'Is this okay?' Jack kissed his way down her throat, one hand expertly palming her breast, and she moaned.

'Yes.'

'And this?' He drew her nipple into his mouth and she bucked as sensation flooded through her, barely able to articulate assent.

'And this? And this?'

He continued to murmur endearments, checking in as he explored her with a languid ease that left her panting and writhing until she was begging him to just please do it *now*, crying out as he finally entered her, pulling him closer, demanding more.

'Are you sure you haven't done this before,' he said many hours later as they lay tangled together. 'I must be a very good teacher.'

She laughed, raising herself onto one elbow to look down on him and kiss him. 'I didn't say I was a total novice. I'd done stuff.'

'Stuff? What stuff?'

'Do you want me to show you?'

His smile was pure wolf. 'Yes, please.'

She stayed there for a moment, drinking him in, luxuriating in his evident desire for her, for Rosy, not the Princess, and then bent her head, flicking her tongue along his chest and enjoying his intake of breath.

'As you wish.'

What happened in the Isles of Scilly was supposed to stay in the Isles of Scilly, but although they had both agreed that it would be too difficult to carry on their relationship back in Polhallow, Jack managed to find time nearly every day to sneak over to the cottage to make love to Rosy. Despite their good intentions, one weekend together had not been nearly enough time and they couldn't bring themselves to stop, not with the time till Rosy's departure ticking away faster and faster, the nights and days flying by at unbearable speed.

They were very careful not to let anyone suspect what had happened, was happening, not to show by a single glance or touch that there was anything more between them than friendship. It was hard, fiendishly hard. Jack allowed his gaze to linger on Rosy, sitting at his kitchen table helping Tansy learn her lines for a forthcoming audition. She looked like summer personified in a lemon sundress, her curls escaping from her ponytail, and it was all he could do not to kiss the tempting back of her neck. He'd had his doubts about whether Rosy should see the girls regularly with her departure so close, but he couldn't deny that she had a knack with them, especially Tansy, and as they didn't know that there was more between their father and Rosy it seemed a shame to deny them the friendship.

As Jack had hoped, the sea air and the change of routine was working miracles with his oldest daughter and she was visibly blooming before his eyes. Thanks to her surf lessons and the theatre group, she'd started to make friends and she'd also stopped second-guessing his every decision and was acting more like a sister than a mother to Clover. Their relationship seemed far more normal now for siblings, and he was surprisingly relieved to hear them bicker over everything from which film to watch to what he should make for dinner.

'That's really good, Tansy.' Rosy closed her copy of the script and smiled at his daughter. 'You're going to be a real asset to the theatre group, I can tell.'

Tansy's face lit up. 'You think?'

'I know. Don't forget I grew up with an actress. I see the same determination in you that I saw in her.' She picked up her phone. 'I need to get back. Make sure you let me know how the audition goes. Bye, Jack.'

He raised a nonchalant hand as if he hadn't got plans to spend the evening at hers once he'd dropped Tansy off at her new friend's house, a fellow aspiring actress she'd met at the theatre.

'Dad...' Tansy was watching him '... I like Rosy. I really like her.'

'We all do, she's been a good friend to us.'

'Dad, you know, it's okay if you want to start dating someone. Clover and I wouldn't mind. Not if it was someone like Rosy. You like her, don't you? I mean, *like* her like her.'

Jack stilled. His girls had idolised their elusive, fragile mother. 'Tansy...'

'Mummy's been gone for a long time now. I just wanted you to know we'd be okay if you wanted to see someone.' Her blue eyes were filled with hope and Jack's chest tightened. This was everything he'd tried to avoid.

'Rosy is great, and you're right.' He made the decision not to lie to his daughter. 'I do like her, and if things were different, who knows? But her life isn't here, kiddo. She doesn't belong in Polhallow, she has a really important job in Asturia. So, friends is all we can be and that's great. You can never have too many friends.'

'But you don't have to stay here. Couldn't you do your job in Asturia?'

'Honey, we've only just moved here. We don't want to keep moving.'

Tansy shrugged. 'I'm just saying that if you and Rosy did like each other we could move again.'

Jack searched for the right words, not wanting to

quash her honesty nor raise her hopes. 'Thank you for saying that, but we have only known Rosy a few weeks. It would be far too early, even if we *were* dating, to be talking about moving. Sometimes, Tansy, the timing just isn't right, and you just have to accept that. It's part of life. What time are you due at Clara's?'

But she clearly wasn't going to drop the topic. 'Clover thinks you should get married, but that's because she wants to be a bridesmaid. It's too early to think of *that*, but I think it's silly not to at least try if you like each other. Rosy likes being with us. She looked all worried when we first met her and now she laughs all the time. I like it when we all laugh. It's fun to be in a big group.'

Guilt pierced him. He'd done his best to provide his daughters with everything they needed. More, a good education, the kind of exclusive experiences most children dreamt of. And the three of them were a tight bubble of love and laughter. But outside of that bubble there wasn't a great deal of humour or socialising. Lily had preferred the dramatic to the everyday and was so often absent, and there was no extended family of cousins and uncles and aunts. Nor did they have a large social circle. In some ways, their childhood was as solitary as his had been. As Rosy's had been.

'Tansy, I'm glad you and Clover like Rosy so much.' He searched for the right words. 'And it's good to know that you'd be okay if I started dating again. It's not a priority, but who knows what will happen? But darling, it can't be Rosy. She goes home next week.'

He hated to disappoint her, but he also needed to nip this in the bud. Any prevarication and they might carry on hoping.

'Like I said, her home is far from here and we are building lives here. Friendship is just as important as romance, Tansy. Don't forget that. Romances can flare and disappear as if they never were, but a good friendship lasts for ever.'

Tansy's eyes were clouded with disappointment as she nodded and ran upstairs to pack a bag for the night ahead. Jack watched her go, heart heavy. He'd done this, roused hopes in his girls he couldn't fulfil. They'd tried hard to be discreet but the connection between them was so palpable even his girls had picked up on it.

There were just a few days left. They needed to be more discreet than ever. And he needed to heed the words he'd said to Tansy because they were true. He and Rosy might not be able to have a real romance but maybe they could be friends. Hell, he had few enough of them. Maybe there would be a way of keeping her in his life, because there was no way he was ready to let her go for good.

CHAPTER NINE

It was another beautiful afternoon. In fact, every afternoon over the last week had been beautiful. There had been something restorative about the light summer rain that had punctuated the week before, something dramatic about the sheets of rain that had cleaned the beaches and outside tables the day before that. Every type of weather seemed fresh and restorative. But today was the best afternoon of all: hot but not humid, sunny but gently, glowing not glaring. And every atom in and around Arrosa was glad to be alive.

She laughed a little self-mockingly as she shook flour into the mixing bowl and reached for the cubed butter she'd cooled earlier. She knew she was being slightly ridiculous—more than slightly—but she couldn't help it. And if this was what good sex, lots and lots of sex, did to a person then she'd clearly been missing out all those years. Those long afternoons of listening to speeches, soothing the overinflated egos of local bureaucrats and top politicians, of dress fittings and hair appointments and ribbon-cutting would have been a lot easier with this sated languor playing through her body. The radio switched to another song, one she loved, and she joined in, singing loudly as she continued to rub the butter into the flour.

Jack was coming over later, and she wanted to wow him with home-made scones as if they were a real couple, as if this was just another date, not the beginning of the end. Because the truth she was denying was that Arrosa was running out of time. Next week Clem would return and they would switch back, and she would have to say goodbye to her life here, to her friends—and to the small family who had captured her heart. How had this happened? What had started out as a flirtation had developed too quickly and too intensely. She knew Jack felt it too—the other evening he had suggested that maybe there was a way they could remain friends once she returned.

In one way she wanted to, but in another she thought it would be harder to have Jack in her life but not by her side. She spent long hours imagining introducing Jack to her life in Asturia, the girls to her pretty lakeside villa. Her imagination worked when they were in the palace grounds; it was the wider world where it failed completely. Her life was one of formality and discipline; there was little fun there for two girls still learning how to smile again after tragedy had robbed them of so much.

Any consort of hers would spend their life in the spotlight. Every word, every look and expression dissected. Jack was an intensely private man; how could she ask him to give up that privacy and allow his past to be raked over after just a couple of weeks of an idyllic summer romance? She couldn't.

So she needed to push any daydreams of the future aside to enjoy the here and now. To focus on the good part, to remember that Jack had shown her that she was capable of loving and being loved. That there was a living, breathing woman in the proper Princess.

Arrosa's hands stilled. Where had that thought come from? Capable of *love*? Attraction, of course. Desire? Liking? Yes and yes. She really, really liked him and she really, really desired him. But she couldn't have fallen in *love*, not in just five weeks.

But, then again, how could she *not* have fallen in love with Jack? Her mind ran through memories like a movie montage: Jack strolling over the beach, Clover on his shoulders, explaining the tides. Jack handing over his ice cream to Clover because she'd dropped the one she'd bought. Jack hearing Tansy's lines yet again. Jack spending many anxious moments deliberating over whether the hoodie he was buying her was too babyish or too adult or just right. Jack pacing on the stage, explaining his vision, lit up with an enthusiasm that inspired her too. Jack sitting opposite her, confiding things she instinctively knew he had never confided to anyone before. Jack holding her, touching her, kissing her, making her feel like a woman reborn.

How could she *not* love him? It was impossible. As impossible as loving him.

With a herculean effort she pushed the thought away, resuming singing and rubbing the sticky mixture, focusing fiercely on the here and now until the sound of her phone made her look up and she realised she'd missed a call. She used her voice to activate the voicemail, still humming along to the music.

'Arrosa?' And, just like that, her mood evaporated.

'Papa,' she breathed as she began to brush the mixture off her fingers. Even though he couldn't see or hear her, it was as if she could sense his disapproval down the line.

'I hope you've had a good break, Arrosa. I wish you'd been a little more discreet, but indiscretion seems to run in the family at the moment.'

Shamed heat flared up instantly. Of course he'd had her followed, she'd expected it. And yet she'd also allowed herself to forget it. Had her father's spy followed her to Tresco? Had they watched her sitting with Jack on the beach? Flirting with him in the pub? Had they seen them the day after, wrapped around each other, unable to let go of each other's hands as they explored the island? Reported on the kisses and the way they touched?

Of course they had. The thought filled her with revulsion.

'Well, it doesn't matter now, because I'm going to say to you exactly what I said to your sister. Holiday time is over, Arrosa. It's time to come home.'

Her hands dropped to her sides, still sticky and covered with the flour and butter mixture. 'No,' she said to the phone, as if it weren't a recorded message she was answering. 'It's too early, I've got another week.'

'People are beginning to talk, Arrosa. Your sister's absences from the palace with no explanation are beginning to be noticed. I need you back here doing your normal day-to-day duties to allay those suspicions. And you are allowing your personal life to become public. It just needs one person to recognise you in the background of one photo or video for the whole thing to blow sky-high. You are staying in one of the most photographed spots in the UK, the chances of you being spotted with this man you're spending all your time with are too high.'

She had nothing to say. Of course, as usual, he was right.

'Look...' and suddenly he sounded kind and that was so out of character it felt worse than his usual hectoring tones '... I allowed the charade to go ahead because I understood that you needed a break. But you had your fun, and your sister's had hers, and it's time for you both to go home. Henri will be escorting your sister to Cornwall tonight and will collect you. I'll see you tomorrow.'

The message came to an abrupt end. Mechanically, Arrosa carried on making the scones, but she couldn't have said what ingredients she added. Instead, her mind repeated the inescapable facts. Her time was up. By this evening she would be back in Asturia and that would be it, her life prescribed and small and necessary. She'd known it was coming. She'd thought she was prepared.

Her phone pinged with a couple of follow-up messages from her father, arrangements for meetings over the next few days, but she ignored them, watching the scones turn the perfect shade of brown and pulling them out of the oven. They looked and smelled delicious, but she had no appetite, no sense of achievement.

The desolation overtook her as she sank onto a chair, eyes dry and sore. She wasn't ready to go home, not yet. How could she be? She'd fallen in love and before she'd even had time to come to terms with what that meant she had to walk away.

Her phone rang again and this time after a few seconds' hesitation she picked it up, noting Akil's name on the screen. She summoned up her best princess persona.

'Akil, is everything okay?' She winced at the words. She knew Clem had grown increasingly close to Akil. She was unlikely to be looking forward to coming home either.

His voice was grim. 'Not exactly. Have you spoken to your father?'

'Funny you should ask that. He's left me a voicemail and a couple of messages, telling me it's time to come home.'

'He's told Clem the same thing, that her time here is up.'

'I guess we always knew it wasn't for ever,' Arrosa said, unable to keep the unhappiness from her voice.

'You certainly couldn't keep this pretence up for ever. At some point people will want to see the Princess's face. Clem needs to be able to leave the Palais without disguises and subterfuge. But that doesn't mean that things should have to go back to the way they were. Don't you agree?'

Agree? With what? 'What do you mean?'

'We're about to begin a new era here in Asturia, spearheaded by you, Arrosa. Don't you think it's time for a new start in every way?'

'Is this about Clem?'

'I love her. And I think that she loves me, but she won't stay here with me, she won't put her happiness first, because your father has told her that if anyone finds out who she is the scandal would be too much for you and she loves you too much to be a burden to you.'

Of course he had said that. *Of course* he had. Zorien Artega, the arch manipulator. 'But that's not it at all, Akil. I would love everyone to know who she is, I am so proud of her, but how could I do that to her? Clem has never been the target of the press. She's never been followed anywhere, she's never been commented on, she's never had her outfits dissected, her love life speculated on, her every expression misinterpreted until she had to learn to show no expression at all. She has a freedom that I can never have, and that freedom is the greatest gift I can give her. If anyone knew who she was, she'd lose that.'

'I think that should be her decision, don't you? Arrosa, don't you see, you're protecting her and she's protecting you and the only people losing out are the two of you?'

'And this is all altruistic on your part?'

'I don't deny that I would like her to stay in Asturia, that I would like to carry on seeing her, but this is beyond us, whatever we are. She is all alone, Arrosa. She is going back to Cornwall with no family, no one who really cares about her apart from you and me.'

Arrosa looked around the cosy cottage filled with memories. Akil was right. Clem's future had stuttered to a halt the day her mother was diagnosed. She had friends, many of them, but her family—and the man who loved her—were hundreds of miles away. 'What do you want me to do?'

'I'm going to go and see your father to tell him that I think he should come out and acknowledge her if that's what she wants. And then I am going to see if I can persuade your stubborn sister to give us a chance. I just need to know: will you back me up or not?'

Arrosa didn't hesitate. 'If that's what Clem wants, then yes. I will.'

'Thank you, that's all I needed.'

Akil rang off and Arrosa sat and stared at her phone, her heart filled with hope and happiness for her sister even as she could see no reciprocal happy-ever-after for herself. After a long time, she pulled her phone to her and typed a message to Clem.

I just want to say that whatever you do decide I have your back, always. I'm proud of you and I'm proud to have you in my life and I am happy to shout it from the rooftops to anyone and everyone if that's what you want. I love you, big sis.

The reply came back quickly.

Right back atcha!

Arrosa smiled and sent another text, this time to Akil.

Whatever Clem wants, whatever Clem decides, I will always back her.

She had no idea what would happen next, but if Clem found happiness then at least one good thing would come out of this swap. That had to be enough.

Something was wrong and Jack couldn't put his finger on what it was. Rosy looked the same as usual, delectable in a flowery maxi dress, her hair down and cascading over her shoulders. She'd set the table with freshly baked scones, fresh fruit, jam and cream, flowers from the garden in a jug in the centre.

But even so something was definitely wrong, her

smile mechanical and her eyes dull as she kissed him. 'I made you scones.'

'They look delicious,' he said cautiously. 'Can I have one?' But his appetite had gone even as he split it in two, adding cream and jam to the still-warm scone. Rosy had retreated to the sink, washing up, her hair veiling her face. 'Hey, why don't you come sit with me?'

She stayed silent and every quiet second filled him with dread until she finally turned, her face still completely expressionless. 'I have to go home, Jack.'

'I know,' he said, searching for the right words. 'I've always known.' Although he realised, with a shock, he was by no means ready. He'd known this time together was finite, and told himself that was okay, but the truth was, like a child ignoring something unpleasant, he'd not allowed himself to look forward, hoping that maybe they would mutually decide they'd had enough, that this relationship would just peter out.

But he knew that wasn't going to happen, not yet at least. Maybe not ever.

'I have to go home tonight.'

'What? Why?' Had he heard right?

'My father has summoned me. He's sending Clem home and he wants me back.'

'You're a grown woman. You can go when you're ready.'

'It's not that simple. I have responsibilities and a

destiny I can't walk away from, no matter how much I may want to.'

'*Do* you want to?'

She didn't answer for a long moment, then her mouth curved into a sad reminiscent smile.

'In the pub in Tresco you asked me who I would be if I could be anybody I wanted. And I told you that I don't waste time on such thoughts, that it's a waste of energy imagining anything different. Remember?'

He nodded.

'I meant it, Jack. That's how I live my life. But over the last couple of weeks I've allowed myself to imagine a different life, imagine what it would be like to really live here. Imagine that I was free to know you, to love you.'

Love. The word hung in the air, almost physical, he could trace the lines of it.

'I think I've been doing the same thing.'

She looked at him then, and her lip trembled. 'It's a lovely dream. But I'm not Rosy, I can't be. And although I don't and won't ever regret the way you make me feel or the way I feel about you and your girls, my feelings don't change anything.' Her expression was anxious. 'You do understand, don't you?'

Of course he did. He was also a man with commitments and honour and responsibilities, and he knew how that could drive a person. If Rosy had been the kind of woman who put her own needs before those things then she wouldn't be the person he was falling for. It was that integrity he'd first noticed in her, and ironically it was that integrity that meant they could never be.

'How long do we have?'

'A few hours.'

'Right.' He sat for a moment, absorbing this change in events, the feelings coursing through him: disappointment, sadness, the sense that something rare and precious was about to slip through his fingers. But not yet. They still had a few hours. 'Then we'd better not waste them.'

Rosy's troubled expression turned confused, and Jack pushed his chair back, leaving the scone uneaten as he stood and strode over to her, taking her hands in his. 'Jack,' she half whispered, and he captured her mouth with his, urging himself to seize every moment, every sensation, every touch.

'This has been more than just a fling for me,' he said, breaking away to cup her face in his hands.

'Me too. If things were different. But these are the cards we were dealt.'

'We just need to make the best of them.'

She knew him, she understood him, and Jack knew how rare that was. Lily and he had shared passion and built a life together, but she had never understood him and, try as he might, she had eluded his understanding too.

'I wouldn't change a thing either,' she added. 'You're a wonderful father and a wonderful man, Jack. That's why I have come to care for you as much as I do. But...'

'You don't have to say anything else. We both knew that this was a one summer thing. I went into it with my eyes wide open and I wouldn't change a thing.'

'You wouldn't?'

'Well, maybe one thing. If I'd known you were leaving so soon I would have kissed you the first day I met you and not stopped.'

'That might have got awkward. People would have definitely noticed.'

'It would have been worth it.' And then he did kiss her, slow and sweet, as if they had all the time in the world, not just a few hours, breathing her in, memorising her, trying his best to show her what she meant to him without words. Rosy responded in kind, holding him close so he could feel her imprinted on him. Jack refused to think of the countdown until she had to leave, not deepening the kiss or rushing them, instinctively aware that whatever they did, whatever they said in the hours to come, this right here was the real goodbye.

Rosy filled his senses, her scent, sweet and warm and uniquely her, her taste, the sound of her breath and her occasional murmured endearments, the silk of her skin under his fingers until all he could think of was the here, the now and her.

She pulled back and looked up at him, lips swollen and expression hazy with desire. 'Let's go upstairs,' she said. 'I want you.'

'You have me,' he vowed and swung her into his

arms, enjoying her surprised shriek as he carried her upstairs. 'You have me.' And he meant every word. For today at least.

CHAPTER TEN

'MAMAN, ARE YOU OKAY?'

As usual Queen Iara was impossible to read. Arrosa's mother had perfected the art of the professional mask a long time ago and Arrosa had never seen it slip. But if she was ever going to falter then today would surely be the day because in less than half an hour the Asturian Royal Family would hold a press conference and announce Clem's existence to the world.

'I'm fine, dear. Clemence is a lovely young woman, and I am happy to be welcoming her into the family.'

'Maman, this is me; you don't have to repeat the press statement.' But they had never had a close relationship, never confided in one another and maybe that was why Arrosa had not told her mother about Jack and how much she missed him.

She'd hoped time would help but although she'd now been apart from Jack for longer than she'd known him, she still felt his absence keenly. She'd been too busy to pine but she couldn't shake the feeling that something was missing, a constant sense of loss. As a result, she'd welcomed her packed diary, preferring to work from the minute she poured her first coffee until she cleaned her teeth at night.

The ratification of the law had gone through unanimously the month before and Arrosa was now the Crown Princess and official heiress to the throne, tripling her workload and responsibilities overnight. She, her father and Clem had discussed making Clem's existence public before the ratification, but Clem had not been ready, nor had she wanted to overshadow Arrosa's big moment. Just knowing that their father was willing to acknowledge her had been enough for her then. But Clem had accepted Arrosa's invitation to stay at the villa and house share with her and, even though the press didn't have access to the estate, Clem's existence was being noticed and questions were being asked, especially as she and Akil were seen more and more in public together.

Once Clem had agreed that she was ready to face the spotlight they had just needed the Queen's agreement for today's announcement. An announcement that would change Clem's life for ever. Arrosa just hoped her sister was ready. And that her mother really was as comfortable with it all as she claimed.

'The past is about to be raked over, that's got to be difficult.'

'Your father's romance was over before we married.' The Queen's smile was serene.

'Barely. And you might not have been formally

engaged when he was with Simone, but you had an understanding…'

'Arrosa. Things are different for us, you know this. I didn't love your father when I married him, and I didn't expect him to love me. We married because I knew what being the Queen would entail and I was willing to make the sacrifices necessary. I respected your father and I still do. Clem and her mother didn't change that.'

Was that true? After all, Arrosa's mother hadn't found out about Clem's existence until after she was pregnant with Arrosa and there had been no more children once she was born. Her parents had separate suites of rooms, separate beds. Had they tried for more children or had the realisation that her husband loved another poisoned their marriage, despite her mother's calm words? Once again, she wished she had the kind of relationship with her parents that would enable those questions to be answered.

She laid a hand on her mother's arm, wishing she could give her the kind of easy, warm hug Simone had doled out so easily. 'Well, I just want you to know how much I appreciate it. Thank you for making Clem welcome and agreeing to let her be part of our family in every way. It can't be easy, but it means a lot to me. I hope you know how much.'

'Her mother was very good to you, and I was always grateful for that. You bloomed in Cornwall, would come back refreshed and invigorated—and you did once again this summer. I was pleased to see you looking so well. I had been worried about you but since you returned you seem more like your old self.'

'Thank you.' Arrosa had had no idea that her mother had noticed that she was run-down. Arrosa could feel her cheeks heating as memories of the summer—of Jack—flooded her senses. 'I understand why you always needed your summer retreats now. Time away from the public eye.'

'I accepted a role with certain expectations. I can't complain when those expectations get too much, but a month away every summer ensures I never get overwhelmed by the pressures of my life. And I hope you will always make sure you have time to recharge.

'Things have changed, Arrosa, your new role is testament to that. You don't have to follow the same path your father and I tread; you will be a new kind of monarch in a new Asturia.' Her mother looked over at Clem, who stood in the opposite corner, unusually smart in a blue dress and matching jacket, looking up at Akil with a trust and love that took Arrosa's breath away. 'Your sister's life is about to alter irrevocably but she has you and the Ortiz heir by her side. And after today she can be publicly in your life as you take on your new duties. I know you'll need that support in the years ahead.'

Was that why her mother was agreeing to stand by her husband's side when he announced the existence of a child who wasn't hers, for Arrosa's sake? Arrosa knew her mother loved her, but she was always so hands-off, the thought of her making such a personal sacrifice for her was almost overwhelming. Maybe they could have a warmer, more intimate relationship, maybe it wasn't too late.

'I know the next few weeks will be difficult for us all, especially Clem, but I have to admit I'm happy we won't have to hide any more—and you're right. Having her here in Asturia and openly part of my life will make everything easier.'

'I hope that you will find a different kind of support too, Arrosa. That you will meet a man who looks at you the way Akil Ortiz looks at your sister, who will support you the way he supports her. Being a monarch can be a lonely job but with the right people around you it doesn't have to be that way. Ah, your father is ready. It's time.'

Without a backward glance her mother glided over to Arrosa's father and laid a hand on his arm, her expression calm and inscrutable as ever. Arrosa took a deep breath as she joined her sister, falling in behind her parents and, with a reassuring squeeze of Clem's hand, the four of them made their way out to face the awaiting press.

As expected, the news of Clem's parentage made headline news across the globe. It had, Akil noted wryly, all the ingredients any good royal scandal needed: a secret love affair, an illegitimate child, a wronged wife standing by her husband's side and two beautiful young women, one a Crown Princess. Any hope that the scandal would be a twenty-four-hour wonder soon disappeared as the world's press descended on Asturia, desperate for a new angle on the story. Descended on Asturia *and* Polhallow, where the cottage was besieged by photographers despite nobody living there, Gus having accompanied Arrosa to Asturia, where he'd promptly taken up residence in her villa.

Arrosa should have foreseen that it was only a matter of time before someone put two and two together and realised that Clem's French cousin Rosy and her royal half-sister were one and the same. Sure enough, a few weeks later, just as the original scandal started to abate, the connection was made, creating a flurry of new headlines and speculation. Sally's family's café was surrounded by reporters wanting the inside scoop on her friendship with both the Princess and Clem, and worse, someone mentioned 'Rosy's' friendship with Jack to one reporter, who immediately splashed the story with suitably salacious headlines.

'Look at this.' Arrosa pushed her tablet over to Clem, her chest tight with anxiety.

'You shouldn't read this stuff, any of it,' Clem said staunchly, but her sister was pale and Arrosa felt a stab of guilt at the world she'd been catapulted into. Adverts Clem had starred in were all over social media, a love scene from a daytime TV show replayed endlessly, her headshots reproduced over and over.

'It's not about me or you. It's Jack.'

'Jack?' Clem's eyebrows shot up. 'Jack Treloar?'

Arrosa had always been able to tell her sister anything, but somehow she'd not found the words to talk about Jack. The memories were too raw, too recent to share, her own feelings so mixed up, especially when Clem and Akil were obviously falling deeper in love every day.

'Yes, we were…friendly.'

'Friendly?' Clem reached over for the tablet. 'How friendly?' She started to read out loud. '*Princess's Summer Fling with Local Bad Boy*—honestly, you babysat for him a couple of times and they turn it into some kind of torrid romance. Listen to this: '*Princess Arrosa enjoyed more than a secret Cornish getaway this summer. We can exclusively reveal that the twenty-six-year-old heir to the Asturian throne enjoyed a summer fling with local self-made millionaire Jack Treloar. Jack, thirty, was married to tragic socialite Lily Fforde-Browne, who overdosed two years ago, leaving two daughters. Now it seems the not-so-grieving widower has moved onwards and upwards. Treloar's teenage marriage to Fforde-Browne raised eyebrows amongst her friends at the time, thanks to his reputation as the town troublemaker, but Treloar put his past behind him, founding Treloar Capital Investments and buying a mansion in London's exclusive Primrose Hill, before moving his family back to Cornwall where they live in a stunning Art Deco house, last valued at a cool three million pounds. The Princess and the rebel are reported to have sneaked away for a romantic getaway on the Isles of Scilly. "They seemed very much in love," said fellow tourist, Lucy Christie. "They couldn't keep their hands off each other."* Honestly, the things they make up!'

Arrosa couldn't answer, her cheeks hot, and Clem

narrowed her eyes. 'Not made up? You and Jack Treloar? It's true? Why didn't you say anything?'

'I don't know,' she said miserably. 'I was going to but there's so much going on it just never seemed relevant.'

'Relevant? You're my sister. What hurts you hurts me. Was it serious?'

'How could it be? You know my life! Jack's so private, he would hate my world.'

'Well, that's unfortunate because right now he's right in the middle of it.'

Clem's words were bracing but her tone sympathetic as Arrosa took the tablet back and read through the article again, cringing at every word. 'So hateful, implying he's some kind of social climber—and mentioning Lily as well. I knew I should have stayed away from him. That there was only one way this could end.'

'In that case why didn't you?'

'I thought that nobody would find out. I thought I deserved the chance to grab some happiness before everything changed. Truth is, Clem, I couldn't help it. Jack's not the man in this article, he's kind and principled and...'

'And drop-dead gorgeous?' her sister helpfully supplied.

Arrosa groaned. 'So gorgeous. I have never in my life wanted anyone the way I wanted Jack. You know, at times I thought there might be something wrong with me. It was so easy to behave like the proper Princess I was expected to be, I was never truly tempted by any man, not enough to let my guard down. And then there was Jack, and it was like *boom*! I couldn't have resisted him if I'd tried—and I didn't try very hard.'

Clem reached over and took her hand. 'You're allowed to be normal, you know. You're allowed to fancy someone, to date, to have romantic getaways.'

'They make it sound so sordid and it wasn't. It was beautiful, Clem.'

'Are you still in touch?'

She shook her head. 'We said we'd try and stay friends but it was too difficult, I couldn't see how to do it. The girls didn't know who I was, although I guess they do now. And the way my life is, it was easier to make a clean break. It was meant to be easier anyway.'

'But you miss him?'

She nodded. 'I really do.'

'You know what I think?'

'I think you're about to tell me.'

'I think I am going to say to you what Akil said to me and to Zorien.' Clem still didn't call their father *Dad*, maybe she never would. 'Secrets only have power while they're secrets. Once things are out in the open, they can't be used against you. Look, I was thinking we need to help Sally out over the next couple of weeks. She's besieged by reporters; it's impacting on the café and it's scary for Alice. Let's invite her and Jack and all the kids here.'

'Here? To Asturia?'

'Here to the estate. There's plenty of space in the

château itself, thanks to all those unused apartments. Your parents are never here, you don't use your rooms and there's the grounds to explore and soldiers on the gates. It's the perfect place to ride out the media interest safely. And with you and Jack in close proximity, well, who knows? At least you'd get a chance to see if there is anything real here.'

Arrosa could see the sense in everything that Clem said, and she should have thought about how to help Sally negotiate the press herself. She did have plenty of room. There were several unused guest apartments in the old medieval Artega palais—and with her villa a mile away, even though it was in the estate grounds, she and Jack wouldn't be forced into proximity. 'But if Jack comes to Asturia everyone will think we're an item and we're not.'

'Well, either we keep it a secret, fly him in quietly and hope no one sees or let them think it. Legitimise the headlines and get rid of the speculation. Seize control of the narrative. Maybe there is more there than a summer fling, maybe not. Either way, you steer the story and get some more time together.'

Arrosa bit her lip. Clem was making sense except… 'He won't come. School's started and the whole thing will be too disorientating for the girls.' Plus, she suspected he was too proud to seek shelter from her. He probably blamed her for setting this circus on him.

'Want to bet?' Clem slid her phone over. It was playing a British news channel showing helicopters circling over Jack's house, photographers at his gate.

'It's October now, nearly half-term, so they wouldn't miss more than a couple of weeks, and I can't imagine they're finding it easy to concentrate with all this going on. Call him and ask him to come. I think he'll say yes.'

'Daddy, Daddy, it's like a fairy tale.' Clover circled a suit of armour a little warily, as if unsure whether it really was inanimate or not. 'This is a real castle!'

Jack had to admit that Clover had a point. It had been late afternoon when the private plane had landed in Asturia and he had glimpsed mountains and valleys, seas and flower-filled villages as the plane had circled before landing. They had been transferred directly into a limousine before being driven through a back gate and straight to the Artega family estate. Soldiers had checked their ID at the imposing gates and then they had been driven for what felt like miles through parkland, woods and formal gardens until they'd reached the old château, graceful with its turrets and spires and carved stonework. It had been a visceral reminder that, although he might now have wealth, he and Arrosa came from worlds apart.

A housekeeper had taken them through the receiving hall and up a grand staircase to an apartment as elegant and well-appointed as any top hotel, where dinner had been served to the by now weary travellers. It hadn't taken Tansy, Clover and Alice long to recover themselves, although he suspected he'd worn an identical shell-shocked expression to Sally throughout the five courses accompanied by some excellent wine, thanks to the juxtaposition of the morning spent escaping the baying photographers and their present situation with candlelight and silver service.

Since Rosy's summer adventures had hit the headlines, it had been an intense couple of days although, to his relief, both girls, even Tansy, seemed to find the whole experience a huge adventure. He'd worried she might feel betrayed by Arrosa's secret but instead she viewed it as impossibly romantic.

It wasn't his first brush with the tabloids and gossip columns, thanks to Lily's bohemian lifestyle and tragic death, but nothing had prepared him for the shock of being in the sightline of the world's media. He could understand Rosy's need for time away now, her determination to keep her stay secret—and her insistence her life wasn't for sharing. Who would willingly put themselves in this position?

'Alice and I are meeting up with Clem this morning to explore. She says she's only walked in a quarter of the grounds at most. Imagine having a place so big you can go for a walk in your own grounds. Apparently, we can swim in the lake as well. Can you believe how warm it is for mid-October?' Sally looked a lot more relaxed this morning. Jack just wished he felt the same way. 'Do you want me to take your girls so you can work—or do you and Rosy have plans?' She sipped her coffee, a demure expression on her face as she waited for his answer.

'She's not Rosy here, she's Arrosa.' Jack poured himself more coffee and surveyed the sumptuous spread of fresh fruit, pastries, cheeses, meats and bread, but despite the tempting smells he had little appetite.

'She's the same person.'

Jack looked around at the silk curtains, the antique furniture, the high ceilings with ornate mouldings, polished wooden floors and vast amounts of gilt. This was a guest apartment—a guest apartment with four bedrooms with en suite bathrooms, a dining room, morning room, formal sitting room and snug. What were the royal apartments like if this was a guest suite? What would it do to a person to be raised amongst all this?

But she didn't live here, she had moved out at twenty-one. And Sally was right. She was still the same person. A person who he was supposedly friends with. A person he had made love to the last time he had seen her.

'If you don't mind having all three?'

'Not at all. Don't feel you have to hurry; Clem and I have a lot of catching-up to do and it will be nicer for Alice if she has friends to play with.'

The girls were delighted with the plan to spend the day exploring, swimming and visiting the stables and getting to meet Clem, who had taken on mythological status in their eyes as she was a real-life actress—Tansy—and a long-lost princess—Clover. Jack let that one stand, he wasn't up to explaining illegitimacy laws and royalty to a six-year-old, leaving him free to follow the path leading to the lake, where Rosy's house was situated. He didn't allow himself to think about how she hadn't been there to meet them, nor how formal she had sounded when she'd called and asked him if he would accompany Sally and Alice to Asturia for a few days until the interest in them died down. Nor did he want to think about how much he'd missed her over the last few months, how often he'd considered picking up the phone, only to remind himself there was no point. Now here he was, in her country, in her grounds, walking to her house.

To his surprise her cottage was charming rather than grand, a one-storey whitewashed villa by the lake, surrounded by a beautiful garden. He took a deep breath and let himself in at the gate and walked down the path. It didn't feel as if he was calling on a princess, there were no visible guards, no servants, but he had no doubt that every step he was taking was being tracked. Before he could knock on the door it opened and there she was.

Jack had no idea why it was a shock that she looked exactly the same—what had he expected, that she would open the door in a ball dress and a crown? It might have been easier if she had because with her hair loose, wearing a green maxi dress cinched in at the waist, she looked like the Rosy he had fallen for, not the Princess he'd said goodbye to three months before.

'Hi,' he said, hovering a few steps away, not wanting to complicate things by touching her, kissing her, not trusting himself not to if he got within touching distance.

'Hi. Do you want some coffee?'

'Sure.'

'Come in then.'

The house was simply but beautifully furnished, wooden furniture polished until it glowed, colourful rugs on the floor, cushions on the grey sofas, pictures on the white walls. Everything was well made and no doubt expensive but also clearly chosen because it was wanted, not because of how much it cost, a landscape next to an abstract, hand-thrown vases next to a stack of books. The scent of coffee permeated the air as she led him through to a light-filled kitchen with French windows that led into the garden, the lake visible beyond.

'Your house is nice,' he said.

'Thank you. I always loved the Cornish house and wanted a similar vibe; I don't have Simone's eye or taste but I'm pretty happy with how it turned out.'

'It's very different to the palace.'

'Oh, dear. I had you put in the Mendoza Suite because it's the least formal, but the décor can be a bit much.'

'The *least* formal?'

'Can't you tell? The gold leaf is pretty pared back.' Her mouth was twitching as he nodded solemnly.

'I thought so.'

And with that the ice was broken and Jack found himself at the table, a coffee in his hands and a plate of pastries before him, his appetite returned, but she was careful to step around him, and he waited for her to take a pastry before he took his, both equally careful not to touch even by accident.

'I'm so sorry,' Rosy said, taking the seat opposite him. 'We realised that telling the world about Clem would send the press sniffing around Polhallow and her life there, but I hadn't really factored in my unmasking. I guess I thought I lived so quietly I'd slipped under the radar. I'm not usually that naïve. Regardless, I should have prewarned you and Sally. Planned for this in advance—to be fair, my father cautioned me that I might be recognised in retrospect and of course he was right.'

But Jack didn't blame her. 'You *did* warn me—you made it clear that getting entangled with you came with risks. As for Sally, her family have been taking full advantage. They've put tables all over the pavement and any member of the press trying to get a picture or a quote is forced to buy food. They've even introduced a Princess Afternoon Tea in your honour.'

'I'm glad someone's getting some benefit from this mess. But I am truly sorry, Jack. The attention must have been scary for the girls. Are they okay?'

'They are. And thank you for having them here. It's made the whole thing into a huge adventure.'

'But to be missing school when they were so looking forward to getting settled in.'

'All the headteachers agreed that taking the next couple of weeks off before half-term made sense, it was hard to settle with press at the school gates. They've been set work. It's fine.'

'And you? Are you okay?'

Okay? The whole experience had brought back memories of Lily's death, the most private, difficult moments chronicled in the headlines, but he knew Rosy was feeling guilty enough.

'I'm fine. If it wasn't for the girls, I would have ridden the whole thing out, but it was all a little intense for them.'

'We can make it up to them now they're here. There's loads of fun things for them to do here on the estate and Henri is a master at smuggling people out the gates. I've thought of loads of activities.' Her smile was hopeful.

Jack was sure the girls would want to do every one of them—but the fine line he and Rosy trod was already too blurred. 'I'm sure, but look, you don't have to worry about running after us, you must be far too busy. Just point us in the right direction and we'll be fine. We don't want to encourage more speculation about the two of us after all. Don't get me wrong, I'm grateful for the seamless way your guys extracted us, but the last thing we want to do is encourage any more rumours. No one knows we're here and I'd like to keep it that way. Being seen out with you would be the quickest way to heap fuel onto the fire.'

'Of course. I totally get that. But...' She hesitated, twisting a tendril of hair around her finger.

'But?'

'I can see that you want to just lie low and wait for

all this to pass, but there is a good chance that your stay here will leak despite our best efforts.'

That had occurred to him, but he hadn't been able to pass up the chance to give the girls a safe place—or, if he was honest with himself, the chance to see Rosy and make sure she was okay.

'If it makes it easier, we could go somewhere else.'

'Or...' She hesitated again. 'We could give them what they want.'

'What do you mean?'

'Look, the reason everything has gone so crazy is because the press think they are cracking this huge secret. But if we take control of that secret then there's no reason for them to hound you.'

'Okay,' he said cautiously, trying to figure out exactly what she meant. 'In what way?'

'Well, we could give an interview, say we met through Clem and have been dating for a few months but wanted to keep it quiet until we knew if it was going somewhere. We are seen in public a few times then you go back to the UK and after a few weeks we say it didn't work out and we called it off. It won't stop the press interest completely, I get that, but we control the story. You know, make it all open and out there until they lose interest.'

'Just for show?'

'I guess that's something we could decide. Things ended abruptly between us. We weren't ready. I wasn't ready. I regret that.'

Much as he didn't want to, Jack knew that he had to

end the conversation right now before he was tempted into doing something stupid like agreeing to her plan.

'I miss you, Rosy.'

'I miss you too.' Their gazes caught and held, and he drank her in.

'And I understand your reasoning but…' He saw her straight-backed posture sag just a little as he said *but*. 'I can't do that to the girls. They like you, Rosy. *I* like you, you know that, but I'm a grown man and I can cope with a little heartbreak. They can't.'

But how he wanted to agree. How he wanted to spend time with her as if it were still the summer, be with her openly, hold her hand and kiss her and make love to her. Because after all it was the fish and chip loving, ice cream eating, denim shorts and bikini-clad Rosy he'd fallen for. Surely spending time with the Princess in her formal world would be the cure he needed? But it was too much of a risk—and not just for his girls.

'I appreciate you giving us a place to lie low for a while and I know the girls can't wait to see you, but let's think of another way to put a stop to the rumours.'

'Of course.' Her smile was determinedly bright. 'It was just an idea. What are you thinking?'

'Well, the theatre, for example.' Inspiration hit him. 'After all, we're all connected to it. Who's to say that's not why you were in Polhallow this summer? Nobody has any proof that we *were* together, apart from a woman who thinks she saw us and a few rumours.

Let the romance talk die a death but use it to do something good for Polhallow instead.'

She stared at him for a long moment, her expression unreadable before nodding. 'Yes, that makes sense.'

'Good, well, let me make some plans. Thank you for the coffee. I'd better get back.'

'Sure.'

He sat there for a moment, wishing for one moment things were different. Jack knew that he was about to turn his back on an opportunity that would never present itself again, turn down the second chance that he had been dreaming of in his heart of hearts.

'Okay. I'll see you soon. No, don't get up, I'll see myself out. Thanks for the coffee.'

As Jack shut the front door behind him he couldn't shake the image of Rosy, straight-backed again, a serene expression on her face, only a hint of a shadow in her eyes giving any hint that she wasn't completely happy with his decision. He could tell himself with perfect truth that all his reasons for saying no were to do with the girls. After all, the last couple of days had been bewildering, terrifying and out of control. They'd had to flee their home, seek sanctuary in a strange country. If this was just what the rumour of a romance between himself and a princess could do, what would any confirmation of that rumour provoke? No, better to let all the speculation die down and return to their normal life as soon as possible.

But Jack was also aware enough to know that there was more to his decision. He'd been burned before, and he couldn't risk being burned again. Of course, he absolved Rosy from having similar motives to Lily. She wasn't looking to shock anyone, to rebel against her parents and societal position, but if they were together, for whatever reasons, it would still be a mésalliance. Nobody in her world would think him a suitable consort for their Crown Princess. He had no idea about court life, he knew nothing about Asturia—until a couple of months ago he couldn't have pointed it out on the map—he didn't speak the language, didn't know the customs. If he was with Rosy, in reality or pretence, then he would be repeating the same pattern as before, be completely out of place, a scandalous object of interest.

None of Lily's friends had believed that she was seriously considering marrying him. Boys like Jack, he'd heard one of her friends say, were perfectly acceptable for messing around with—after all, everyone knew that boys with everything to prove were the best lovers—but one simply didn't marry them. He'd done everything in his power to prove every single one of them wrong and he still got a visceral sense of satisfaction when *they* now courted him, asked him to dinner parties, solicited his advice and sought his investments. But he'd never forgotten how they'd made him feel. Vowed never to be put in that situation again.

And that was why he had to walk away. Because here she wasn't Rosy, she was the Crown Princess, and girls like her simply weren't for guys like him.

CHAPTER ELEVEN

'DID YOU SEE JACK?' Clem asked when she returned to the villa that evening. Sharing a home with her sister was something Arrosa wasn't sure she would ever take for granted. She would never not appreciate having Clem on hand to laugh with, cry with, watch meaningless television with, chat through her problems with.

It wasn't just the companionship; she was so proud of her sister it almost hurt. Clem had risen above the headlines and started to carve out her own identity here in Asturia. She was looking at university courses, still volunteering at the local hospital and was officially assisting Arrosa. She was also dipping her toes into court life and had been invited to a ball at the British Embassy in a week's time.

But, of course, the downside to having her sister so close was that she knew Arrosa better than anyone and there was no dissembling, no hiding behind her princess face.

'He turned me down.' Some of the heartbreak she didn't want to admit even to herself cracked through the armour she had donned and quickly she added, 'It's complicated. It's fine. I expected it. It's probably for the best.'

'Okay.' Clem poured them both a glass of wine and nodded towards the garden. 'It's still so warm out even if it is October. Shall we?'

With unspoken accord the sisters headed down to the lake. They shared a deep love of water, and both felt better when they were gazing into it. They sat on the comfortable chairs Arrosa kept on the jetty and Clem sniffed the wine before taking an appreciative sip.

'This is much needed; three children are a lot for a full day! But it's so nice to see Sally. I've asked her to come to the ball with me. Akil is attending, but in a work capacity, and I could do with moral support—and she could do with an evening off.'

'Sounds good. And what did you think of Tansy and Clover?' Arrosa half held her breath as she waited for her sister's reply. It really mattered that Clem liked them, she realised.

'They're nice girls, a credit to their dad. And they're both wild about you. I was a pretty poor substitute. They kept asking when they would see you.'

Arrosa stared down at her wine. 'I'm not sure that's such a good idea. Jack made it clear there's no future for us. I don't want to complicate things further.'

'I met him too, back at the château.'

Arrosa couldn't bring herself to ask what Clem thought of Jack. 'He's right, you know. If we tried to control this thing by saying we were in a relationship, by trying out being in a relationship, it would just confuse the girls, and that's the last thing they need. He wants them to have stability and I support that, I always have.'

'He's obviously a great dad. I have to admit it, I got him wrong. He's not the overbearing tycoon I expected but, from what you and Sally say and the little I've seen, he seems a surprisingly kind man. A principled man who I would guess is also clearly head over heels about you and I know you feel the same way. So what I don't understand is why you are both so sure that you have no future.'

'He doesn't want the kind of life I lead, Clem, not for him, not for his girls, and I don't blame him.'

Clem sipped her wine and sat back, her expression thoughtful. 'Rosy, is your life really so bad? I know it got a little overwhelming recently, but I would say that Asturia allows its high-profile people more privacy than many other countries, and the world's press will get bored with this story eventually. I'm not saying that if you gave it another go the first few weeks and months wouldn't be a challenge, but after that I think you could build a pretty decent life here. I should know! It's easier for me in some ways, my education included handling publicity, I know how to work the camera, speak in palatable soundbites and ensure my social media is squeaky clean and, yes, I admit I've still been overwhelmed. But there's been beauty amongst the madness and I'm seeing my way to a future, the opportunities my position gives me. That could be true for Jack as well.'

How Rosy wished her sister was right.

'But you wanted to be part of the family, Jack doesn't. He has some past experiences which make him shy away from publicity, from high profile relationships. He thinks we're better denying everything, using his investment in the theatre as a pretext for our friendship. I owe him that, Clem.'

'The theatre?'

'I haven't really had a chance to discuss it with you, but I think you will love what he has in mind, that Simone would have too. If we say that we were working together on the theatre in memory of your mother, that gives me a reason to have spent the summer in Cornwall and to have been seen with Jack. And in the end Polhallow will have the kind of theatre Simone would have been proud of. It all makes sense.'

But Arrosa knew she was trying to convince herself as well as her sister, was trying not to think about how differently she could have played the morning's conversation. Because absence really had made her heart grow fonder. The moment Jack had walked through the door her home had felt complete.

She'd known what he was thinking, could have sworn that her heart beat in time with his, and she knew that if she'd just reached out, had just touched him, that everything would be different and he would be hers, for now at least.

But she wanted him to come to her because that was where he wanted to be, not seduced into intimacy. The theatre was a worthy project. It gave them an angle. It was a memorial, and these were all good things. Just because her whole being ached with sadness and loss didn't change any of those things.

'Look,' Clem said, putting her glass down. 'Whatever you decide I will support, I hope you know that. But if having Jack in your life is what you want, and if having Jack by your side makes your difficult role an iota easier, then you should fight for that, Rosy. You have always done what's right, you always put other people first. Maybe now is the time to concentrate on you. I believe you deserve someone by your side who sees how special you are. If that person is Jack then don't let him walk away because he doesn't understand your life. Show him how he fits in. Show him that your life has magic as well as duty. I get how he feels. I didn't want to stay here as Akil's mysterious English lover. I had to figure out how I could be here as me and I found that. But I didn't find it alone—Akil helped me. You don't have to do this alone either, nor does Jack. Just promise me you'll think about it.'

Arrosa blinked, her eyes hot and heavy with tears she refused to shed. Was it simply as easy as deciding she wanted Jack in her life? How could it be?

'I'll think about it. Thank you, Clem.'

Her sister smiled affectionately. 'What are sisters for?'

Over the next ten days Arrosa did more than think. Instead of hiding away from Jack and the girls she made time in her hectic schedule to show Jack exactly what made her country so special and why she loved it so much. The girls were usually busy during her pockets of free time, once, to her amazement, with her parents, who had never been the kind to spend time with children before. She suspected Clem of making sure Jack was on his own when she was able to join him, but her sister denied the charge with an innocent look that didn't fool Arrosa one jot. But she wasn't complaining because, whatever the reason behind Tansy and Clover's busy schedule, it left her free to smuggle Jack out with her bodyguard, Henri's, help to show him the country she loved and the work that was needed to bring it properly into the twenty-first century. Just as she'd hoped, Jack was soon filled with enthusiasm and ideas for how things could be improved.

They weren't long excursions, just a few hours here and there, never a full day, although there was some time in every day, but in those moments she was the perfect blend of Arrosa and Rosy, princess and person, and she could feel herself falling harder and harder for Jack. But although he seemed to enjoy their time together, there was still a chasm between them. They didn't touch, and never alluded to any kind of future together. It was as much torture as it was joy. It was all she had.

She walked into the house late one afternoon, looking for Clem, who was getting ready for the ball at the British Embassy. She found her sister in her room, putting the last touches to her hair and make-up, a stunning red floor-length cocktail dress hanging ready.

Arrosa whistled in appreciation. 'You look amazing.'

'Thank you. It feels odd to be there as an Asturian representative.'

'You'll be brilliant.'

Clem sucked in a breath. 'I'm glad I persuaded Sally to come, she deserves some fun and I could do with the backup. How was your day?'

'Good. I spent the morning going over my speech for the day after tomorrow and in meetings then I took Jack on my favourite mountain walk. I needed the exercise. You know, even though it's still quite warm, I can feel winter in the air. Those trails will be under snow within a month.'

It had been a lovely walk but sometimes Arrosa wondered what she and Jack were doing. They seemed no further forward. If anything, they seemed to be slipping away from each other every time they spent a polite, distanced time together.

Clem swivelled round on her stool. 'It's been over a week, Rosy. Have you told Jack how you feel yet?'

'I...'

'Told him that you love him?' her sister went on remorselessly.

Arrosa stared at her and swallowed. 'Love? I…' But she'd stopped lying to herself a long time ago, she wouldn't lie to her sister. 'I've told him that I like him, Clem, he knows how much I fancy him…' *Fancy*. Such a trite word to describe the depth of longing she felt whenever he was near. 'I think we both know that it might have been love if things were different but, after all, we've not really known each other that long.'

'About as long as I've known Akil,' her sister reminded her.

There was no point quibbling or reminding Clem that she and Akil had spent far more time together because she knew it had taken just a few weeks for her sister and friend to fall firmly and irrevocably in love. To forge the kind of partnership Arrosa had only ever dreamed of.

'I can't.'

'Rosy. This last week and a half you've been lit up with happiness and I know it's not because you're finally addressing the Senate in two days' time! It's thanks to Jack, and he deserves to know the truth.'

'I've seen him every day and he's made no attempt to even touch me. He likes Asturia and he has ideas, good ones, but he hasn't offered any more than those thoughts. It's obvious he doesn't see a future here. And, even if he did, there's the girls. Who knows, maybe we can try again when they are grown up, maybe in ten years or so.' The thought was bleak indeed and her chest constricted at the thought of spending those years alone.

'In a decade? Come on, Rosy, listen to yourself.'

'Clem, you don't understand. If I told him how I feel then I am forcing him to make a choice. His marriage was hard, Lily manipulative at best, I think. It wasn't a happy marriage, Clem. She used him. I won't do that to him.'

Clem sighed. 'Rosy, have you ever thought that by not being honest with him maybe you're the one doing the manipulating? That maybe you're the one depriving him of agency. He should know how you feel. Tell him.'

Jack had enjoyed the last twelve days almost too much, and the more time he spent with Rosy, seeing Asturia through her eyes, the more he could see her hopes and dreams. More, in every project and plan he saw ways he could contribute, how he could be an integral part of her world. But still he hesitated. This was no more real life than Cornwall had been, their friendship still kept firmly under wraps.

If friendship was what this was. The air between them was still charged although there was no intimacy, but he was still more relaxed with Rosy than with anyone else, than he had ever been with another person.

There were still some intrepid photographers hanging around the Palais walls, trying to photograph every car that left the house, but Henri was an old hand at shaking off unwanted attention and some days Jack and the girls were completely free to wander around and explore with nobody giving them more than a quick half amused sideways look.

And the more he explored, the more he fell in love with the small country. He loved the crispness of the mountain air as early autumn which felt more like an English late summer softened and cooled. The actual autumn was short, with snow usually expected by December. This, of course, sent the girls into spirals of excitement and they begged to be able to stay until the snow came. Every day he had to remind himself as much as them that this was just a visit, that they were establishing their lives in Polhallow. Somehow his plans didn't feel certain as they had before, that sense of rightness that had driven the move eluding him.

And, of course, there was Rosy. His tour guide, filled with infectious excitement about her country and the plans she had to improve it. She seemed to know every hidden corner and selflessly shared them with him.

They had successfully renegotiated their relationship from lovers into friends, and that, he knew, was rare and precious. But he still felt an almost overwhelming sense of loss when he stood next to her but couldn't hold her, when he said goodbye but didn't kiss her, alone in his huge luxury bed.

'Look, Daddy!' Clover pointed at the TV. 'There's Rosy.'

He'd found a cable channel of English language children's programmes and Clover and Alice had been curled up in front of a film while he packed for an afternoon on the beach, but somehow the channel had switched to a local news one. The anchor was speaking about this historic day in the fast-paced Spanish-accented French dialect he was slowly starting to understand. This was the day Arrosa was finally presented to Parliament as the Crown Princess and heir to the throne.

Jack had learnt a lot about Asturian customs and politics over the last few days and knew that, unlike the UK, the Asturian monarch sat in the Senate, their Upper Chamber, and was very much engaged in Parliamentary procedure. When he chose, the King could deputise his heir to step in for him—and now she was officially the heir that meant Rosy, who today was taking her place as the Royal representative. Custom dictated that a new member of the Senate would need to be presented, approved and welcomed by the House before giving their first speech.

Jack knew how nervous Rosy felt. She was no stranger to politics or public speaking, but this was her first formal step into her country's political arena. It was a relief to see Akil, a prominent member of the opposition and a fellow member of the Senate, was there, looking strong and supportive, and to hear the whole chamber burst into applause as she entered.

Jack stared at the screen, his heart hammering, mouth dry. This was not Rosy, this was all Arrosa. Her hair was up in a complicated knot and she wore a calf-length blue silk dress with a short matching jacket, diamonds at her throat and in her ears, a crown perched on the top of her head. She could almost have come straight out of the fairy tales Clover adored.

'She looks beautiful,' Clover said breathlessly.

'Yes, but she looks scared too,' Tansy said.

'No, she doesn't,' Alice chimed in and Sally laid a hand on her daughter's head.

'Why do you think that, Tansy?'

Tansy studied the screen. 'Her hands are pressed together, and she bit her bottom lip just then. She does that when she's nervous, have you noticed?'

Jack *had* noticed, but he was surprised his daughter had. 'You're right,' he said. 'But she hides it well. That's very astute of you, Tansy.'

His oldest daughter tossed her hair. 'I'm an actress,' she told him. 'Studying people is what I do.'

He laughed but quickly quietened as Rosy started to speak. There was no trace of any nervousness in her voice as she spoke, her voice rich and melodious. Her father beamed proudly from behind her.

The family had plans for the day. With their time in Asturia nearing its end there was plenty they still wanted to pack in, but Jack forgot to hurry the girls up or to gather his own things together. Instead, he stood transfixed as he watched the woman he loved address the country she was born to rule.

The chasm between them had never felt bigger and yet in some ways he felt that he should and could almost step into the TV to stand beside her and support her just with his presence. Jack had been telling himself over the last twelve days that Rosy needed a man like Akil. She needed someone versed in Asturia's culture and politics, someone with a background similar to hers. But as he stood watching her speak that certainty escaped him.

Culture and nationality and birthright were all important and all things he lacked, but he did have qualities he knew she needed. He could provide her with the reassurance that she could do the immense job that lay ahead of her, he could be the person she bounced ideas off—after all, she had run every word of her speech past him, practised it on him until he could probably recite it himself in Asturian and English, could have cited her sources as she focused on education, equality and the need for a sustainable future.

But, at the same time, although they had spent a great deal of time together there was a consciousness between them that hadn't been there before. Rosy was her usual thoughtful, enthusiastic self, unfailingly courteous, great with the girls as always, funny and sweet, but he knew he wasn't imagining the distance between them, and he wasn't sure who was responsible for it. In some ways he welcomed it. After all, there was no future for them.

But the knowledge didn't feel as certain as it once had. The future he'd mapped out no longer felt so safe or so desirable. Instead it felt empty. Lonely. His girls were everything, but they would grow up and have their own lives and that was how it should be. And when they were gone what would he have? A white box on the top of a cliff, a self-made fortune and no one to share either with.

Rosy's speech was coming to an end. Her pace had quickened, her tone reaching an emotional peak before calming once again as she laid down her notes and gazed confidently into the camera, just the pink in her cheeks betraying her nervousness. There was no need as the chamber erupted into applause and a few whoops. She bowed her head respectfully to the chamber of men—and it was still all men—before retaking her seat. Jack could see her father—King Zorien—in the background, also clapping along, his face red with pride, but as he struggled to his feet the colour seemed to drain from his face and, to Jack's horror, he sank back down again, hands pressed to his chest.

Time seemed to stop as the applause stilled and all eyes focused on the clearly struggling King, the camera cutting away as Arrosa sank to her knees beside her father, fear evident on her face.

And Jack knew one thing. None of the barriers or problems or reasons to keep his distance mattered. Rosy needed him; it was as simple as that.

CHAPTER TWELVE

ARROSA HAD NEVER spent much time in hospitals before, apart from as a royal visitor, there to cut ribbons and talk to pre-selected patients, and she was more grateful than ever for the presence of Clem and Akil. Thanks to their volunteer work, they were both well-known and familiar with the city hospital and on friendly terms with many of the staff.

Her father had been rushed to the private rooms reserved for the Royal Family and other VIP patients but, even with the comforting décor and peace, it was clear that this was a medical facility not a five-star hotel. The lingering smell was one of boiled vegetables and antiseptic, there were medical instruments evident all around and she knew that, even though she was in a plushly furnished sitting room, the tight ball of dread preventing her breathing properly was the same as that in the chests of everyone waiting in the wards and family rooms across the wider hospital.

Her father had been rushed straight into emergency

surgery. Arrosa had tried to take in the words from the family liaison nurse, words like *heart* and *bypass* and *serious*, but she couldn't concentrate. Her mother had been at a prearranged event at the other side of the country. Although Arrosa knew she was sorry to have missed her speech, she hadn't wanted to let the school down, duty as important to Queen Iara as family. She had been informed about the incident straight away and was on her way back, so all Arrosa could do was pace and sit, pace and sit and let the various hot drinks cool untouched.

'Go home and rest,' Clem said, taking her hand. 'Or at least change.' Arrosa touched her hair, almost surprised to feel the cold of the platinum crown on her head. The morning's speech felt like a lifetime ago. She removed it with shaky hands, her head instantly lighter, and pulled out the hairpins keeping her hair confined in the intricate knot, pulling it back into a loose ponytail instead.

'I can't leave him.'

'Then at least try and drink something.'

And to please her sister Arrosa managed a couple of sips of coffee before her stomach tightened and she couldn't swallow any more.

She paced over to the window and stared out at the hospital grounds, the trees now turning to orange, red and yellow, seeing her sister and Akil reflected in the glass. They were sitting together on the sofa, Clem leaning into Akil, his comforting arms around her shoulders. For one brief, shameful moment she felt a pang of such pure envy it shocked her out of her stupor. Not for Clem's happiness, that was something that filled her with joy, but because she wanted something similar for herself. Because she'd been so close to having something similar, but life and obligation and cowardice had pushed it away.

At that moment the door opened and she whirled around, expecting to see a doctor. Instead, Henri walked in, followed by the one person she realised she needed more than anyone else.

'Jack?' Had she dreamed him? But no, he felt solid enough as she ran to him, and he pulled her against him. 'You came.'

'I didn't want to intrude,' he said, looking uncharacteristically diffident, and she reached up to touch his cheek.

'You're not intruding, you never could.'

He led her to the sofa opposite Clem and Akil and pulled her down to sit next to him. 'How's your father?'

'It's not good, Jack. They rushed him straight in for bypass surgery. It's his heart.'

'I see.'

'His *heart*, Jack. It's like history repeating itself. You know his father abdicated because of *his* heart and then he died anyway, just a couple of years later. What if…?' She broke off, swallowing back almost hysterical tears. 'I can't lose him yet. I'm not ready.'

Then Jack's arms were around her, pulling her in tight, holding her, allowing her the freedom to let go, to be supported. She was dimly aware of Clem and Akil muttering something about going to get coffee and food and then she and Jack were alone and for the first time in a long time she allowed herself the luxury of tears. Once she'd started, she couldn't stop, all her fears and worries and regrets mingling with the shock and worry for her father's health and what that meant for the whole family, for her.

Arrosa had no idea how long she cried. When she finally choked back a last sob she was cradled in Jack's arms, his shirt wet through, a damp tissue clasped in her hands.

'I'm sorry. Look at your shirt,' she said, pulling back a little.

'I'm used to it,' he said, and his smile was tender. 'I have a six-year-old.'

'I didn't mean...'

He shook his head. 'Never apologise to me for having emotions, Rosy. You're allowed to be scared and upset and all that entails.'

'My father has dedicated his whole life to duty. He needs more time to live, not just be. He and Clem have only just started building a relationship. It would break her heart if anything happened to him before she really got to spend time with him.'

'And what about you?'

'Me?'

'Like I said, you're allowed to have feelings too, especially around me.'

Arrosa buried her head in his shoulder, her voice

muffled when she did speak. ‘I feel so selfish to be thinking of me at a time like this.’

‘But?’

‘Oh, Jack. My father was around my age when he had to become King, and because of that he left Clem’s mother, left Clem, and married Maman, and they haven’t had a happy marriage. Instead he dedicated his life to service, as did she. I know that is my future, I’ve come to terms with it, but I’m not ready, not yet. And…’ She almost choked back the next words but she made herself keep going. ‘I don’t want to do it alone. I know I have Clem, but…’ She couldn’t quite bring herself to say the words quivering on her tongue. To say that she didn’t want to do this without Jack. To tell him that having him here by her side, in her country was more than she had ever wished for, hoped for.

To tell him that she loved him.

But this wasn’t the time and place.

‘I’m sorry. I’m being cowardly and weak.’

Jack took her hands in his. ‘Arrosa Artega, you’re the bravest person I know.’

But she wasn’t being brave now, was she? ‘I…’

Before she could say anything else Clem and Akil arrived back with fresh hot drinks and an array of food. To her surprise, Arrosa discovered that she was a little hungry and managed half a roll and some of the coffee but the time to confide in Jack had passed. The day stretched on as the minutes slowly ticked by and there was still no news of her father.

Her mother arrived soon after Clem returned and

Arrosa was both surprised and moved by the Queen's evident distress. In some ways it seemed that the events of the last few weeks had brought the royal couple closer together, which made it even more imperative that her father should make a swift and full recovery. If she had to take on more responsibility to enable that to happen then of course she would. She wanted her parents to have the time to enjoy this new understanding between them, for her father and Clem to have the time to develop a proper relationship, for her father to be able to enjoy his grandchildren when they finally came along. She was prepared to do whatever she needed to do to enable that. But she knew now that it would be easier with Jack by her side.

Clem was right. Arrosa had thought she was protecting Jack by hiding her feelings from him but, really, she was disempowering him. He deserved the chance to know how she felt and to make his own decisions.

It felt like an age before the doctor came in, removing his mask and rubbing his eyes wearily. 'I'm pleased to say that the operation went as well as could be expected,' he said. 'We're not out of the woods yet, but I'm as cautiously optimistic as I can be. His Majesty is sleeping now and although I can allow Her Majesty a few minutes at his side if she wishes, I suggest the rest of you go home, get some sleep and return to see him tomorrow.'

The Queen waved off their suggestion that they waited for her, insisting that her car and driver were waiting and she would rather be alone tonight anyway. Arrosa lingered, knowing her mother's tendency to hide behind what she thought she should do rather than what she wanted, but her mother met her gaze firmly and nodded.

'You too, Arrosa,' she said. 'You've had an exceptionally busy day. Go and get some rest.'

Her hug was warmer and more heartfelt than usual and Arrosa impulsively pressed a quick kiss to her mother's smooth cheek before allowing Henri to escort her out of the room, Jack closely behind.

Jack stayed in the car until they drew up outside Arrosa's villa, rather than asking to be dropped off at the palace. He checked in with Sally from the car, relieved when she reassured him that the girls were fine and although they were naturally worried about Arrosa and the King, who they had all met and liked, she had managed to distract them for most of the day. They were currently enjoying dinner in front of the television after an afternoon at the beach and barely mustered up the energy to shout hellos when she prompted them. Sally finished by telling him not to hurry back, and that she was happy to look after Tansy and Clover for as long as he needed her to. Jack said a few words of heartfelt gratitude before, with a nod at Henri, following Arrosa into her home. He took her bag out of her unprotesting fingers and set it on the hallway table.

'Go on,' he said. 'Go and get changed. That dress is

beautiful, and you look beautiful, but it doesn't look that comfortable.'

She laughed a little shakily. 'You know, I spent the first hour we were at the hospital still wearing a crown. Isn't that ridiculous?'

'For anybody else, maybe.'

'Par for the course for me?' She made no move away, but stood looking up at him, confusion and hope in her eyes. 'He is going to be all right, isn't he, Jack?'

'The doctor seemed optimistic. That's encouraging.'

'Yes. Thank you for coming, Jack.'

'Any time.'

'Do you want a drink?' She was nervous, he realised as she whirled into the kitchen and found him a beer, grabbing one for herself, opening the back doors and ushering him outside. The evenings were chilly now but she didn't seem to feel the cold as she stood staring out at the lake.

'Jack,' she said at last, turning to him. 'When you arrived at the hospital I realised you were exactly who I needed. That you are always who I need. I can't let you go without telling you how I feel. I love you, Jack, with all my heart. I tried not to, but I can't help it.'

Jack stood there, unable to move or speak as each word sank in, warming him through, bringing him to life like soft rain on parched earth.

'I know what the papers say, and how you feel, that my world isn't yours, but I don't believe that. To me you are the knight in shining armour I didn't believe existed. A man who is kind and dependable and who understands me. A man I can trust with every thought and emotion. A man who has proved that over and over. I know you come as part of a package, and I love that too—but I also know that's why you are wary. If this life isn't for you then I will never blame you for that, but I had to tell you how I feel. I want you in my life for ever, you and the girls. I love you.'

'Oh, Rosy. I love you too. I think I have done from the moment you bought us ice cream and saved me from a full-on meltdown.' Jack inhaled, long and deep, searching for the right words. 'I wasn't going to say anything today. I thought what with the speech as well as your father you'd probably had all the emotion you could handle but, as usual, I underestimated you.'

She laughed and took a step closer. Deliberately, Jack took her undrunk beer from her hand and set it down on the garden table next to his and entwined his fingers through hers. The simple act of holding hands after so many weeks apart was like a balm to his soul.

'I told myself I had to stay away for the girls' sake,' he told her honestly. 'And there was truth in that, but I was also hiding behind them. My experience of marrying someone from a different world to me was difficult. My marriage brought me my girls but little happiness. I had to prove myself every day, and still I knew that to the world I was an interloper. I knew if I was with you it would be a thousand times worse. A boy from my background daring to court the Crown Princess? I don't care what the papers say about me, what the Court says, but I care about you. I didn't want you put in a difficult position. I didn't want you to ever regret choosing me.'

There it was, Jack's truth, and Arrosa knew how privileged she was to hear it.

'I will never regret choosing you,' she told him, cupping his cheek and luxuriating in the rough stubble under her fingers, losing herself in the heat in his eyes. 'Never. The Court will say how clever I am to have snared a man who has made a fortune in such a short time and will wonder how we can best use your talents here, and the papers will come around, they always do. But even if they didn't, I wouldn't care. I know the truth and that's all that matters. But the girls, Jack, if we do this then you would have to be here. Would that work, would they mind?' With the headiness of the relief over her father and the knowledge that Jack loved her, the practicalities of their situation had been too easy to ignore.

'The girls love you and they love it here. There's an international school in the city with a great reputation and they have been begging to stay until the snow comes. It won't always be easy. Tansy is so nearly a teenager, there are bound to be storms ahead...'

'But if we navigate them together...'

'Then nothing is impossible.' He smiled down at her and she found herself laughing in giddy relief.

'Does that mean you'll stay?'

'It means that I will be looking for a place for me and the girls in the city...'

'But...' she interjected, and he put a finger on her lips.

'Get them settled in school and start to figure out my life here. And while I'm doing that, I want to do some old-fashioned courting. I know I could stay in the apartment where we are, and I am getting rather fond of all those ancestors of yours even if every male is brandishing a sword in a threatening manner and every woman a fan in an even scarier manner, and I am sure you would welcome us here, but Rosy, I rushed into one marriage. This time I want to take my time.'

'You do?' She completely understood—and courting did sound like fun. 'What do you have in mind?'

'The usual. Dinner, walks, theatre trips.' His voice deepened. 'Kissing, I think there should be lots of kissing.'

'Me too.'

'And touching.' Her knees weakened at the intent in his smile. 'Lots and lots of touching.'

'I could get on board with that.' They were so close now there was no space between them, her arms wound around his neck, her body pressed to his. 'What else?'

'I think I will have to show you.'

She laughed out loud as he swung her up into his arms, carrying her towards the kitchen. 'You might have to show me every day.'

'Oh, I intend to.' And then his mouth was finally on hers and Arrosa could lose herself in his kiss, his scent, the surety of his touch. With Jack by her side, she could face anything, any future, any obstacle. It was more than she had ever dared to dream of, and she couldn't have been more excited about what the future held.

EPILOGUE

'THE THEATRE looks stunning, Jack.'

Arrosa squeezed Clem's hand gratefully. Even though her sister had become close to Jack and the girls over the last year she knew Clem still struggled with the changes to her mother's restoration work, even with the lack of facilities and comfort in the original theatre. But Jack had worked miracles and the theatre had come alive in the way he had envisioned, from comfortable backstage areas to tempt the biggest stars to Cornwall, to a café open all year round, a fancy restaurant with sea views and a beautiful bar area. The seats were still the original carved stone and open to the air, but patrons could rent or buy seat pads and the theatre sold long raincoats for the times the elements didn't cooperate.

They were here for the official opening night, a Gala in Simone's honour for the local hospice, for which they had all combined their resources to lure in some big names to perform songs, musical theatre numbers, dances and scenes from Shakespeare.

The eight of them sat in the newly created Royal Box, with an actual roof and cushioned seat, its own dining room and cloakroom. Jack had created several of these VIP areas with an eye on the hospitality market and Arrosa was grateful for the shelter even as she looked nostalgically across at the seat where she had met Jack for the first time.

'Do you wish you were performing, Clem?' Queen Iara asked. Arrosa still couldn't believe her mother had asked to attend the Gala in honour of her husband's great love, but she had insisted she wanted to get to know the town where her daughter had been so happy—and to pay homage to the woman who had loved her daughter so selflessly. She and Zorien had the seats of honour at the front and Arrosa was sure she had seen them hold hands earlier—and not for the first time.

'Part of me does,' Clem admitted, her hand straying to her stomach. Akil had not been able to keep his word to wait a year before he proposed, and the pair had married in the spring with their first child expected at Christmas. Arrosa couldn't wait to be an aunt—a hands-on acknowledged aunt who would always be part of the baby's life. 'But it is fun to be in the audience too. I'm just glad the community group still gets to use this space. Thank you, Jack.'

'The theatre wouldn't exist without the community—and I wouldn't have met Rosy either. I'm just glad we had a happier outcome than Romeo and Juliet.' Jack reached for her hand and smiled and Arrosa leaned over to kiss his cheek.

'Me too.' She looked down at her engagement ring, loving the way the rubies caught the light. Jack had stayed in Asturia and they had spent the past nine months really getting to know one another over a slow, sweet courtship which had given the girls plenty of time to adjust to their new lives in Asturia. Jack had proposed a couple of weeks ago, a year to the date they had met, with Clover and Tansy's help in a play the three had written and performed for her. Arrosa couldn't have imagined a more perfect proposal—or a more perfect ring, picked out by the girls for her.

The girls sat next to the King and Queen, bickering amicably over the programme. Over the last year Tansy had lost the last of her worried look and now had a social life to rival Arrosa's and was pursuing acting in the youth theatre in Asturia, while Clover had developed a love of horse riding, never happier than when they were at the Artega estate and she could spend the day in the stables. Both girls would be bridesmaids at the wedding in early autumn, with Clem as maid of honour.

'A toast.' Akil handed around the glasses of champagne, with elderflower cordial for the girls and Clem. 'To Simone, who I wish I had been able to meet, and her legacy.'

'To Simone,' they all chorused, even Queen Iara,

while Clem held her cordial up to the sky, where the first stars were visible.

'To Mum.'

'And to Cornwall,' Arrosa added. Clem had decided to keep the cottage so her baby would get to know the village she loved so much. Jack had sold his dream home, reassuring her that his dreams had changed, but the pair could borrow the cottage whenever they wanted, with Henri always on hand to ensure their privacy was respected.

'And to the Asturians for making us so welcome,' Jack finished. 'Thank you for letting us be part of your family.'

'Thank you for letting me be part of yours,' Arrosa replied and as he leaned over to kiss her she made a mental note to never forget this feeling, surrounded by those she loved and who loved her, in a place dedicated to a woman who had helped raise her. Just a year ago Arrosa had felt completely alone, with the weight of the country on her shoulders. Now look at her, engaged, a stepmother, a soon-to-be aunt.

As the stage lights blazed to life and the show began, she sent a small prayer of thanks to the heavens. Nothing was impossible as long as she was with those she loved, and right now Arrosa Artega, Crown Princess of Asturia, knew she was the luckiest woman alive.

★★★★★

Keep reading for an excerpt of
Wedding Night Reunion In Greece
by Annie West.
Find it in the
Local All-Star Anthology 2022 anthology,
out now!

CHAPTER ONE

'CONGRATULATIONS, CHRISTO.' DAMEN grinned and gripped his friend's arm in a hard clasp. 'I didn't think I'd ever see the day.'

'You didn't think I'd invite you to my wedding?' Christo smiled. Who else would he ask to stand up as his best man but Damen, his friend since childhood?

'You know what I mean. I never expected to see you married till you'd played the field for another decade and decided it was time to breed some heirs.'

The look that passed between them revealed their shared understanding of what it meant to be the sole male heir to a family dynasty—Damen's in shipping and Christo's in property. There were expectations and responsibilities, always, even if they came with the cushion of wealth and privilege.

At the thought of his newest responsibility, Christo rolled his shoulders. The stiffness pinching the back of his neck was familiar. But now he could relax. With the wedding over, his plans fell into place. He'd had a problem and he'd fixed it, simple as that. Life could resume its even course. The glow of satisfaction he'd felt as he'd slid the ring onto Emma's small hand burned brighter.

Everything had worked out perfectly.

'I'm glad you could get here at short notice.' Despite Christo's lack of sentimentality, it felt good to have his old friend with him.

Besides, it would have looked strange if there'd been no one from the groom's side, even at such a small wedding. Damen had arrived in Melbourne just in time for the private ceremony. Now, in the gardens of the bride's home, this was their first opportunity to talk.

'She's not what I expected, your little bride.'

Christo raised an enquiring eyebrow.

'She's besotted with you for a start. What she sees in you…' Damen shook his head in mock puzzlement, as if women didn't swarm around Christo like bees around blossom. It was another thing they had in common.

'Of course Emma's besotted. She's marrying *me*.'

Christo had no false modesty about his appeal to the opposite sex. Besides, he'd wooed old Katsoyiannis's granddaughter carefully, taking his time in a way that wasn't usually necessary to win a woman. Having his proposal rejected hadn't figured in Christo's plans.

He'd done an excellent job. A spark of heat ignited at the memory of Emma's wide-eyed gaze and the eager way she'd returned his perfunctory end-of-ceremony kiss, tempting him to prolong it into something more passionate. Christo's hands had tightened on her slender waist and he'd found himself looking forward to tonight when he'd take her to his bed for the first time.

Damen huffed out a laugh. 'There speaks the mighty Christo Karides, ego as big as the Mediterranean.' He frowned and glanced back at the house, as if confirming they were alone. Everyone was at the wedding breakfast on the far side of the building. 'But, seriously, I was surprised. Emma's lovely. Very sweet.' Another pause. 'But not your usual type.' His look turned piercing. 'I'd have thought her cousin more your speed. The vivacious redhead.'

Christo nodded, picturing Maia's pin-up-perfect curves in the tight clothes she favoured. Her confidence, her sexy banter as she'd tried to hook his attention. She would have succeeded, too, if things had been different.

A twinge of pain seared from Christo's skull to his shoulders and he rubbed a hand around his neck.

'You're right, she's gorgeous. In other circumstances we'd have had fun together.' He shook his head. His situation was immutable. Regrets were useless. 'But this is marriage we're talking about, not pleasure.'

A muffled sound made Christo turn to scrutinise the back of the large house. But there was no movement at the windows, no one on the flagstone patio or sweeping lawn. No sound except the distant strains of music.

He'd have to return to the celebration soon before his bride wondered what was taking him so long.

A beat of satisfaction quickened Christo's pulse. 'Emma's not sexy and sophisticated like her cousin, or as beautiful, but her grandfather left her the Athens property I came to buy. Marriage was the price of acquiring it.'

Damen's smile faded. 'You married for *that*? I knew the deal was important but surely you didn't need to—?'

'You're right. Normally I wouldn't consider it, but circumstances changed.' Christo shrugged and adopted a nonchalant expression to camouflage the tension he still felt at the profound changes in his life. 'I find myself in the bizarre situation of inheriting responsibility for a child.' Saying it aloud didn't make it sound any more palatable, or lessen his lingering shock. 'Can you imagine *me* as a father?'

He nodded as his friend's eyes bulged. 'You see why marriage suddenly became necessary, if not appealing. It isn't a sexy siren I need. Instead I've acquired a gentle, sensible homebody who wants only to please me. She'll make the perfect caring mother.'

Emma's hands gripped the edge of the basin so tight, she couldn't feel her fingers. That was one small mercy because the rest of her felt like one huge, raw wound throbbing in acute agony.

She blinked and stared at the mirror in the downstairs rear bathroom. The one to which she and her bridesmaid had retired for a quick make-up fix as the bathroom at the front of the house was engaged. The one with an open window, obscured by ivy, that gave onto the sprawling back garden.

In the mirror, dazed hazel eyes stared back at her. Her mouth in that new lipstick she'd thought so sophisticated was a crumpled line of colour too bright for parchment-pale cheeks.

Around her white face she still wore the antique lace of her grandmother's veil.

Emma shuddered and shut her eyes, suddenly hating the weight of the lace against her cheeks and the long wedding dress around her shaky legs. The fitted gown, so perfect before, now clasped her too tightly, making her skin clammy, nipping at her waist and breasts and squeezing her lungs till she thought they might burst.

'Did you know?'

Emma's eyes popped open to meet Steph's in the mirror. Instead of turning into a wax doll like Emma, shock made Steph look vibrant. Her eyes sparked and a flush climbed her cheeks.

'Stupid question. Of course you didn't know.' Her friend's generous mouth twisted into a snarl. 'I'll kill him with my bare hands. No, killing's too good. Slow torture. That's what he deserves.' She scowled ferociously. 'How could he treat you that way? He must know how you feel about him.'

The pain in Emma's chest intensified from terrible to excruciating. It felt as though she was being torn apart. Which made sense, as she'd been foolish enough to hand her heart to Christo Karides and he'd just ripped it out.

Without warning.

Without anaesthetic.

Without apology.

'Because he doesn't care.' The words slipped through numb lips. 'He never really cared about me.'

As soon as she said the words aloud Emma felt their truth, despite the romantic spell Christo had woven around her. He'd been kind and understanding, tender and supportive, as she'd grappled with her grandfather's death. She'd taken his old-fashioned courtesy as proof of his respect for her, his willingness to wait. Now she realised his patience and restraint had been because he didn't fancy her at all.

Nausea surged as the blindfold ripped from her eyes.

Why hadn't she seen it before? Why hadn't she listened to Steph when she'd spoken of taking things slowly? Of not making important decisions while she was emotionally vulnerable?

Emma had been lost in a fairy tale this last month, a fairy tale where, as grief struck yet again, her Prince Charming was with her, not to rescue her but to be there for her, making her feel she wasn't alone.

Everyone she'd loved in this life had died. Her parents when she was eleven, abruptly wiped out of her life when the small plane they'd been in went down in a storm. Then her grandmother four years ago when Emma was eighteen. And now her opinionated, hopelessly old-fashioned yet wonderful Papou. The sense of loss had been unbearable, except when Christo had been beside her.

She drew a sharp breath that lanced tight lungs, then let it out on a bitter laugh. 'He doesn't even know who I am. He has no idea.'

Wants only to please him, indeed!

A homebody!

Obviously Christo had believed Papou, who'd insisted on thinking she studied to fill in time before she found the right man to marry!

Maybe Christo thought she lived in her grandparents' house because she was meek and obedient. The truth was that, despite his bluster, Papou had been lost when her grandmother had died and Emma had decided to stay till he recovered. But then his health had failed and there'd been no good time to leave.

The tragedy of it was that Emma had thought Christo truly understood her. She'd believed he spent time with her because he found her interesting and attractive.

But not as attractive as her *vivacious, gorgeous* cousin Maia.

Pain cramped Emma's belly and her breath sawed from constricted lungs.

Bad enough that Christo viewed her as a plain Jane compared with her *sexy siren* cousin. But the fact he hadn't noticed that Maia was warm-hearted, intelligent and funny, as well as sexy, somehow made it worse.

Christo was a clever man. According to Papou, his insightfulness had made him phenomenally successful, transforming the family business he'd inherited. Clearly Christo didn't waste time applying that insight to the women he met.

Because we're not important enough?

Because he thinks we're simply available for him to use as he sees fit?

What that said about his attitude to women made Emma's skin shrink against her bones.

He had a reputation as a playboy in Europe, always dating impossibly glamorous, gorgeous women. But in her naivety Emma had dismissed the media gossip. She'd believed him when he'd assured her his reputation was exaggerated. Then he'd stroked her cheek, his hand dropping to her collarbone, tracing the decorous neckline of her dress, and Emma had forgotten her doubts and her train of thought.

She'd been so easy to manipulate! Ready to fall for his practised charm. For his attentiveness.

Because he was the first man who'd really noticed her.

Was she really so easily conned?

Emma lurched forward over the basin as nausea rocketed up from her stomach. Bile burnt the back of her throat and she retched again and again.

When it was over, and she'd rinsed her mouth and face, she looked up at her friend. 'I *believed* in him, Steph. I actually thought the fact he didn't respond to Maia was proof he was genuinely attracted to *me*.' Her voice rose to something like a wail and Emma bit her lip.

She'd been gullible. She'd brushed aside her friend's tentative questions about the speed of Christo's courtship. At the time it had made sense to marry quickly so her Papou could be with them. And when he'd died, well, the last thing he'd said to her was how happy he was knowing she had Christo and that he didn't want her to delay the wedding.

She should have waited.

She should have known romantic fantasies were too good to be true.

'I've been a complete idiot, haven't I?' She'd always been

careful—cautious rather than adventurous, sensible rather than impulsive—yet she'd let a handsome face and a lying, cheating, silver tongue distract her from her career plans and her innate caution.

'Of course not, sweetie.' Steph put her arm around her shoulders, squeezing tight. 'You're warm and generous and honest and you always look for the good in people.'

Emma shook her head, dredging up a tight smile at her friend's loyalty. 'You mean I usually have my head in the sand.' Or in books. Papou had regularly complained that she spent too much time with her nose in a book. 'Well, not any more.' She shuddered as ice frosted her spine. 'Imagine if we hadn't heard…'

'But we did.' Steph squeezed her shoulder again. 'The question is, what are you going to do about it?'

The question jolted her out of self-pity.

Emma looked in the mirror, taking in the ashen-faced waif dressed in wedding lace. Suddenly, in a burst of glorious heat, anger swamped her. Scorching, fiery anger that ran along her veins, licking warmth back into her cold flesh and burning away the vulnerability she'd felt at Christo's casual contempt. The flush of it rose from her belly to her breasts and up to her cheeks as she swung round to face her friend.

'Walk away, of course. Christo can find another *sensible* woman to care for his child and please him.'

Silly that, of all the assumptions he'd made about her and the games he'd played, what rankled most was that he'd recognised her longing for physical pleasure. For *him*.

A shudder ran through her at the thought of how she'd looked forward to pleasing him and having him reciprocate with those big, supple hands and that hard, masculine body.

Now the idea of him touching her made her feel sick.

Especially as the reason he'd abstained from sex clearly hadn't been out of respect for her and for her dying grandfather. It had been because sex with the dowdy mouse of the family hadn't appealed to him. If Christo had been engaged to the beautiful Maia, there'd have been no holding back. They'd have been scorching the sheets well before the wedding.

A curl of flame branded deep inside Emma's feminine core. In the place where, one day, a man she loved and who loved her back would possess her. She'd thought she'd found him in Christo Karides. Now all she felt was loathing for him and disappointment at herself for believing his lies.

'I'm so relieved.' Steph's words tugged her into the present. 'I was afraid you might think of staying with him and hoping he'd eventually fall in love with you.'

Emma shook her head, the old lace swishing around her shoulders. Papou had been proud that she'd wear the same veil his bride had worn to her wedding. This marriage had meant so much to him. But it was a sham. Christo hadn't only made a fool of her but of her grandfather too. She'd never forgive him that.

'I might be the quiet one in the family but I'm not a doormat. As Christo Karides is about to find out.' She met her friend's eyes in the mirror. 'Will you help me?'

'You have to ask?' Steph rolled her eyes. 'What do you have in mind?'

Emma hesitated, realising she had nothing in mind. But only for a second.

'Can you go up to my room and grab my passport and bag? And my suitcase?' The case she'd packed for her honeymoon. The thought was a jab to her heart. She sucked in a fortifying breath. 'You'll have to come down the back stairs.'

'Then what?'

'I'll book a flight out of here. If I can borrow your car and leave it at the airport—'

'And leave Christo Karides to face the music when his bride disappears? I love it.' Steph's grin almost hid the fury glittering in her eyes. 'But I've got a better idea. Forget the airport. That's the first place he'll look. With his resources, he'll be on your trail within hours. Head to my place and wait for a call.' She reached into her purse and pulled out her key ring, pressing it into Emma's hand. 'I'll get you out of Melbourne but so he can't trace your movements. I'm not the best travel agent in the city for nothing. It's going to be a real pleasure watching him stew when he can't find you.'

For the first time since overhearing Christo's conversation,

Emma smiled. It didn't matter that her cheeks felt so taut they might crack, or that the pain in her heart was as deep as ever. What mattered was that she had a way out and a true friend.

Suddenly she didn't feel so appallingly alone and vulnerable.

'Thank you, Steph. I can't tell you what it means to have your help.' Emma blinked against the self-pitying tears prickling the back of her eyes.

She'd cried when she'd lost Papou. She refused to shed tears over a man who wasn't fit to speak her grandfather's name. A schemer who'd played upon the old man's love and fear for his granddaughter's future.

'But you'll have to be careful not to give me away.' Emma frowned at her friend. 'One look at your face and Christo will know you're hiding something. He may be a louse but he's smart.'

Silly how speaking of him like that sent a fillip of pleasure through her. It was a tiny thing compared with the wrong he'd done her, but it was a start.

Steph shook her head and put on the butter-wouldn't-melt-in-her-mouth expression that had fooled their teachers for years. 'Don't worry. He won't suspect a thing. I'll tell him you need a short rest. He'll accept that. He knows this has been a whirlwind, plus you're missing your grandfather.'

Steph's words sent a shaft of longing through Emma for the old man who'd been bossy and difficult but always loving beneath his gruff exterior. She blinked, refusing to give in to grief now.

'Great. You go upstairs while I get this veil off.' There was no time to get out of the dress, but she couldn't make her escape in trailing lace. 'I'll hide it in the cupboard here, if you can collect it later and look after it for me?'

'Of course. I know it's precious.' Steph put her hand on Emma's arm, squeezing gently. 'Just one more thing. Where are you travelling to?'

Emma turned to the mirror and started searching for the multitude of pins that secured the veil. 'The only place that's still home.' Her aunt and uncle, Maia's parents, had inherited this house and Papou's Australian assets. She'd got the commercial property in Athens that had then been signed over to her husband to manage. She'd have to do something about that, she realised. Plus, she'd inherited her grandparents' old villa in Greece. The one where she'd gone each year on holiday with her parents till they'd died. 'I'm going to Corfu.'

It was the perfect bolthole. She'd never mentioned it to Christo and, anyway, he would never look for her on his home turf of Greece.

She could take her time there, deciding what she planned to do. And how she'd end this farce of a marriage.